Stor

MW01659832

Adam Seward

Cover art by Howard David Johnson

Sarmiento Epigraph

Tupaq Inka was a man of lofty and ambitious ideas, and was not satisfied with the regions he had already conquered. So he determined to challenge a happy fortune, and see if it would favour him by sea. Yet he did not lightly believe the navigating merchants, for such men, being great talkers, ought not to be credited too readily. In order to obtain fuller information, and as it was not a business of which news could easily be got, he called a man, who accompanied him in his conquests, named Antarqui who, they all declare, was a great necromancer and could even fly through the air. Tupaq Inka asked him whether what the merchant mariners said was true. Antarqui answered, after having thought the matter well out, that what they said was true, and that he would go there first. They say that he accomplished this by his arts, traversed the route, saw the islands, their people and riches, and, returning, gave certain information of all to Tupaq Inka.

Pedro Sarmiento de Gamboa
The History of the Inkas
1572

CHAPTER ONE then

The Chanka Scout
Hunchback Hill, Kingdom of Qosqo
15th Century CE

Ramram smelled something, something animal, but didn't think much of it. The trail was steep and rough, and he hoped it was almost at its end. He sensed something up there, some strong *Kamay,* living spirit.

The Rumipuqyu, Stone Spring Village, volunteers, seven boys and men, climbed the faint trail over a rocky spine and continued up a steep hump of hill, passing down one arroyo and climbing again, edged anticipation beating in their hearts. None of them were warriors but they were going to war. Chonta, Ramram's dad, pointed out ghosts of smoke over a crest ahead, that might be the Inka army. Or the Chanka enemy. Or charcoal burners. They must be almost there.

They had come at the call of Prince Kusi Inka Yupanqui, the outcast son of the Sapa Inka Viracocha, King of the Inka people. Unique Ruler Viracocha had abandoned Qosqo, the sacred city, and run with his court, army, the mummies of his ancestors, and his people, to his eyrie high in the hills over the Valley of Yucay. He hoped that the invading Chanka would not bother to follow him there. The prince had not run. He had sent an officer to Rumipuqyu. He made this offer:

"The Sapa Inka commands you to follow his Royal Person to safety. This is your duty to your Lord. Do it.

"Prince Kusi Inka Yupanqui offers you death by the spears of the Chanka warriors, who have never known defeat. Those who choose to die Inka, be in Qosqo in ten days. Weapons for fifty are stored in the town qolqa warehouses for your use."

Strangely, seven had taken up weapons and set out for Qosqo. Who knew why? Ramram had because he was pretty sure the warrior Chankas would have no use for a sixteen year old boy who wandered the hills looking for stones with souls.

Ramram was a lean boy, hard-stomached, strong-thighed from ranging the mountains. Unafraid of heights, blade-nosed, with thick, glossy black hair, large deep eyes and sharp-carved lips. He laughed easily, loved the feel of the ground under his feet, the way it pulled him to it. His neighbors and kin looked at him sidelong because of his strange power and compulsion; he would not inherit his father's work; but they valued what he brought to them, and he held them close in return. Now they were gone for safety, except for these few on this trail.

Ramram saw that they were scared. They trod dry-mouthed, shifty-eyed, light-footed, shallow-breathed, twitching, yawning, licking their lips, with pinpoint pupils, their sweat stinking of fear. They pissed too often and farted too much. They walked weak-kneed in a fog of dread, afraid to die.

Ramram wasn't afraid to die, most of the time; he had always known that Pachamama, Mother Earth and Time, moved through everything coming, here, and gone. That was nature. He was afraid to kill. Afraid that in doing that he would lose Pachamama's hand on his head and heart, lose his ability to sense Kamay in *waka*; stones, river eddies, twisted trees, caves, wherever spirit lived. To lose the gift of his communion with Eff Ram, his companion from another time and place, one that had not happened yet, to see through each other's eyes and limbs and minds and hearts into their different *pachas*, their times and places.

So they walked in fear. But on they shuffled, hoping to find an army organized and confident, knowing better.

"What do you think your sexy new wife is doing right now?" Achuqalla laughed. Uchuchukuy laughed with him, unworried, as the path threaded into some low thorn bushes by a short cliff, where a bladed club took off the top of the newlywed's head, disintegrating it in a red spray from east to west. Achuqalla, smile melting, staggered backward into Chonta, whose macana mace had reflexively lifted, so both stumbled backward another step, clearing the way in front of Ramram, who froze, gawking at his first Chanka warrior. Whose scent was animal strong.

The Chanka scout was sharply defined, vibrating with energy. He was small, thin, many stiff braids exploding from beneath his black-and-yellow feathered helmet, eyes hot and quick. In a blur, his spear sped underhand from behind his wide round shield, sending the bronze point unerringly into Achuqalla's throat. The words "I'm dead," spoke distinctly in Ramram's mind as his eyes shot to his father and Chukuri teetering on the steep edge. He threw himself at their tangled bodies, propelling all three of them into space.

The Chanka spun, quick as a cat, following the impetus of his heavy club, coming back to a solid fighting stance on the lip of the drop. He looked down at Ramram. "*Kunan wañuki, maqta*," he growled in accented Quechua, "now you die, boy," and he leapt.

Ramram scrambled backward, feeling rough rock slam into his spine, asking himself in a honeyed suspension of time if he was hurt and if he could still move. He saw the Chanka's club rise in the sky above.

In that timeless instant a rich, surging energy sucked into his nerves, emanating from the rock at his back. The five-bladed weapon above slowed, and the grimacing grin of the Chanka writhed like a snail on salt, while he himself moved in accelerated time, rolling onto his chest and over the crest of the stone upon which he had landed. He could see it clearly now, the stone, long, knobbled, plated with textured medallions and crusts of lichen, orange, black, pale green. It seemed a living thing, a breathing reptile, a dark spot above its nose like an eye.

He got his feet under him as the murdering enemy stepped forward, the club descending a blink too late, missing Ramram, swinging away to subvert his balance, making him stagger a step.

Ramram heard his father and the potato farmer recovering themselves, risked a quick glance to see one-eyed Waywash coming up behind. "Run," yelled the old farmer, grabbing Chonta and Chukuri by their unku tunics, turning them around, "up the hill! *Run!*"

Ramram turned, strangely at ease, to see the Chanka soldier reset his feet, teeth clenched, puzzled by his own weakness. He wrenched the jagged-edged javelin from Achuqalla's corpse, and thrust it at Ramram.

Ramram had never been in a violent argument, much less a physical fight. He was not that kind of boy or man. But then, what was he here for? Crackling energy made his club light as a wand, his hands fast, he felt all-powerful. The spear jabbed at his face, he deflected it with his shield, bringing his stone club down hard on the man's temple below the helmet.

For an instant Ramram was sure it would glance harmlessly off, only making the deadly warrior madder. But the skull imploded, an eye popping out of the shattered socket, the face collapsing. Ramram's heart filled with a shy hope. His cudgel swung across his shoulder. He brought it back through, taking the Chanka in the cheekbone, tearing his jaw loose, filling the crisp mountain air with teeth and red spray. The Chanka flopped onto the rock, bounced off, and died.

Looking Uphill

The Inka Ramram stood panting, star-shaped stone mace in his left hand, painted wooden shield in his right, looking down at the twisted corpse of the Chanka scout he has improbably killed, smelling the evacuation of the man's bowels. Blood dripped thickly from a dull point of his mace.

The immense Kamay of the *siq'i rumi* stone of power rising to his heart and head, the universal energy of Pachamama present in every being but intensely concentrated in this rock, overwhelmed him. He was alive. He killed a man infinitely more skilled at war than he. It was the stone, its emanations, that saved him, slowing and hindering his enemy. The siq'i favored the Inka. Why?

A familiar rush of charged warmth surged through him up from his entrails, to pulse above and between his eyes, expanding, and another consciousness rushed into his nerves and his mind, that opened to accept the visitor who had come to him from time to time since he was a boy.

It was Eff Ram, staring down at the killed Chanka through Ramram's eyes, shocked. He recoiled from the sight, and Ramram snapped into Eff Ram's pacha, his place and time.

There it was again. Some world sick and dark. He recognized a looming stone door, the massive wall it penetrated, as Inka. But everything around and above it was hideously alien, ugly and unknown. It was his own world, but something bad had happened to it. The other boy, Eff Ram, collapsed, knees weak, backsliding down that defiled wall, carrying Ramram with him.

His vision whirled, and he was back, standing over the slain man, breath ragged. His father and Waywash stood silent, staring at him.

This was not something he talked about.

"Let's go," Chonta said. They all looked up the hill. Their old life was over. This was their new one.

The Uninvited Visitor

There had been a double rainbow over the crest of Rumipukyu ridge the first time Eff Ram came to him. Below, hundreds of his father's workers built *qolqas*, stone storehouses, on the terraced slope. Ramram was ten then, when he climbed the hill, pulled by call of some powerful Kamay, the spirit that lived in all things. He was born with the ability to sense that force. With it, he identified *wakas*, sacred things—mostly stones, water, caves—that the people would honor with offerings. It made him strange, he would not follow in his father's work, but the village valued what he found for them.

This one was strong. It was in a boulder bulging from the side of the hill, twenty *rikras*, a long pace and a half, above. He approached, cautiously. It seemed to hum and pulse at him. He found the courage to lay hands on the rough stone. Heat surged up from his gut, chills ran along his spine, a light burst in his skull, he seemed to cartwheel in space and land on his feet again. Then the boy Eff Ram, the stranger from another time, came to him, sharing his self; his eyes, body, breath, even his emotions.

Something took him over from inside. It was another world. It was where he was, and it wasn't. It was the buildings his dad was raising, but in ruins, overgrown. The air smelled different, the eyes he looked through were not his own.

It was another self, other senses, desires, questions, sucked into his nerves and his mind. He seemed to expand within to accommodate the visitor. From the energy, he recognized that it was a youth, like him. Strange, different, but a boy too.

That lasted for three breaths, then it changed. He was no longer looking through the other boy, the other boy was looking through him. He was back in his own world. He felt the surprise, fear, and confusion of his uninvited visitor.

When he was in the boy Eff Ram he had no control; he could only watch and feel, as if from a window, as if a guest in the other's body. When the Eff Ram was in him, Eff Ram was the guest and could only experience, not act.

So Ramram would speak, trying to make Eff Ram understand, or Eff Ram would speak. They could exchange names and very little else.

This happened seven times in three seasons and then Eff Ram went away. Ramram came to understand that Eff Ram was from that different, pacha, time and place. He showed Eff Ram his little village, Rumipuqyu, below the hill where his father supervised the construction of a storehouse complex. He showed him his family, his friend Tuya, whom he assumed he would grow up to marry. Only Tuya knew Eff Ram was there.

"Is Other Boy in there?" she asked once, laughing. "Haw Other Boy, I see you!"

But when Eff Ram showed him that other world, Ramram drew back in disgust. It was Ramram's world, he recognized the broken bones of Inka things beneath the conquering crust of this other time, but in ruins, overgrown and broken, or buried under the alien construction of some incomprehensible corruption. They were humans, they were people, those who made these things, who wore these things, but barely. And they walked on the rotted corpse of what had once been Inka.

Before they could teach each other enough words to begin to understand, Eff Ram vanished.

Now, on the verge of Ramram's death, Eff Ram had returned.

The Unguarded Rear

"I'm going home." Chukuri shook his head. "Sorry, guys, but I'm not built for this." They watched as he retreated down the trail.

The remaining four loped up the hill, scarcely believing they were alive. Not a word was spoken. When Ramram looked over his shoulder at the dip where the stone lay humped he saw their assailant sprawled in a wrenched swastika, a broken thing. Above, the other way, was a ragged frieze of figures, semi-silhouetted, feathered and speared.

"I hope those are our guys," grunted Waywash, "I never want to see another Chanka."

"Ari," nodded Chonta, "and he was only a little one."

The amazing power drained from Ramram. He saw the others had lost it too. He looked back. He had to be sure. "I'll catch up," he said. "Don't go too far." His father looked at him sideways but didn't argue.

Ramram scrambled back down the hill, regretting every step he would have to take back up. But he had to verify the Kamay of that rock, and that he had really killed the enemy warrior.

It was as he thought. As he stood over the stone looking down on its gnarly surface, seeming to crawl with some alien mind, he breathed in deep again the heady vitality and the sense that he could do anything and live forever. This advantage was for *Inkas*, not for the others. He nodded to himself. It had worked for him, against the Chanka fighter. He hadn't misperceived that. There were smaller rocks and shards of rock in the tufts of ichu grass and round-eared cactus surrounding the main stone, and these fragments too emitted the same uncanny force.

He shook his head, climbed out of the hole, nudged the dead scout with his sandaled toe, vaulted the bluff, hauled the corpses of his companions to the lip of the hollow.

He eyed their limp remains, thought of Uchuchukuy's young wife. Uchu had seemed unaware that she thought herself too pretty for him. He was spared that. *Achachaw* for everyone. *Too bad, but there it is*. He gathered their ch'uspa pouches, shields, spears, and clubs, and loped back up the ridge toward his friends.

The rock's force made the climb easy. As the hilltop rounded off, he came upon the unguarded rear of the fear-ridden little army.

Ramram Cannot Get Across

Ramram passed through loose crowds of more or less military volunteers, with their various degrees of armament. He was looking for his father, and he was looking for someone important who would listen to him.

There was no visible organization and everybody looked frightened. Some were gathered around small llama dung fires. Others just stood in desultory clots showing matching insignia of place of origin or *ayllu* extended family. The closer he got to the top of the hill, the more rank and military bearing increased, judging by the quality of their unkus, sleeveless tunics, and the elaboration of their head gear.

He surmised that the men with the black-and-white checkerboard unkus were professionals. Some had gold disks on their chest, gold ear plugs, and helmets with an ear-to-ear crest of shiny feathers. He took a deep breath and approached a cluster of them, but was intercepted by a crusty-looking middle-aged man in a three-feathered helmet.

"I've seen that mark on your headgear," he said with a menacing amiability, "green and brown. Where's your company?"

"It doesn't matter, there are only three of us and none of us can fight. But I have important information. I need to tell the Prince or someone who he will listen to."

The soldier affected bemusement. "You got five thousand fresh fighters from your town? No? You want to tell him that we're outnumbered twenty to one?"

"*Mana*." No.

"You want to tell the Auqui Inka Kusi Yupanqui that you changed your mind and you don't want to die?"

"Ari. That's it. I want to tell him that we don't *need* to die. This is important. I can show him a powerful waka. It gives strength to Inkas and takes it from Chankas. A rock."

Two more men with the same helmet insignia sidled over to allay their boredom and their fear. "What's this, *Pichqa Chunka Curaca*?" a younger one asked. A Pichqa Chunka Curaca commanded fifty men. Call him a platoon sergeant. He seemed to expand a little at having an audience.

"The whelp says he has a magic rock." He looked at Ramram. "Are you another *umu* from back in the hills? Look, I can't stand here all day. I've got balls to scratch. Where's your unit?"

"There were seven of us and a Chanka killed two. Then I killed the Chanka. Because the waka I'm talking about made me strong and fast, and the Chanka weak and slow. That's what I want to tell somebody."

The noncom lost his smirk, squared off. "A Chanka? Where is this Chanka now?"

"Down there. There's a hollow place with a rock in it. He's dead. Listen, I think he was a scout. That rock, it can make these," Ramram swung an open palm at the muddled clusters of volunteers, "scared farmers into warriors."

The platoon sergeant snorted. His face got hard.

"You killed a Chanka. By yourself."

"No. The siq'i killed the Chanka. Any Inka could."

"Your magic rock." He turned to his two privates. "Get an officer here."

"They're at the briefing with the colonel," said the older of the two. "You want to break in on them for this?"

"Well, who have we got?"

"There's the *Tocapucamayoq*, right over there."

"Good thinking. We'll offload this shit onto him. Get him."

The private came back with a thin man wearing more and longer feathers and silver ear plugs. Ramram's heart lifted a little. Here was someone with authority.

"Sir, this puppy says he knows a big waka that can make Chankas fall over dead. He wants to tell the Prince. Do we take him seriously?"

The skinny officer eyed Ramram, looking his outfit up and down.

"I don't know. I'm a Sign Decryption Technician. I just identify where people are from and what they do. This is a kid who doesn't do anything, and his outfit's over there by that yellow standard on the other side of the Chinchero bunch. You two, see that he gets there. I'll ask the *Tarpuntay* Sacrifice Priest if we need any more wakas. Anyway, Prince Yupanqui is off somewhere talking to the gods again."

"The whole Chanka army could come up this hill and take you in the rear," Ramram needled the noncom in a parting shot. "There's no guard."

"Shut up," quipped the sergeant.

Ramram shut up and walked between the spearmen, head down. As they passed below a large crowd of listless-looking men with long javelins and square hats, he heard a shout. "Ramram! Son!"

He looked up. It was his father, with Waywash, Papa Chakra, and a dozen men from his district. One of his guards lifted a hand, and they both picked up their step approaching the cluster, as if glad to have this duty done with. Ramram saw an opportunity and took it. He dropped his armful of scavenged weapons in a clattering heap.

"I got the runs," he yelled, more or less audibly, and took off bowlegged back down the hill. He heard them yell "Haw!" at him, waited for the thump of following footsteps and a hand clawing his shoulder, but it never came.

CHAPTER TWO then

The Inka Scout
Hunchback Hill, Qosqo

Ramram fled the Inka militia without a plan, scorned by the army. He found himself on a rise looking down at where his rock and his dead friends lay, maybe sixty rikras away. It was broken ground, no good for growing. There were rocks, cactus, agave, thorny underbrush, a rough drop to the left. He heard running water and was suddenly thirsty. He fought his way between two bramble bushes that clawed at his cloak, dotted blood on his bare arm; stumbled out into a small humpy clearing. He stopped, frozen.

A man hunkered there. His eyes bored into Ramram's. Ramram pissed himself.

What turned his guts to water? The man was as helpless as it gets, squatting to defecate, and there was nothing intense in his expression. His macana was out of reach. But it was as if he, Ramram, were being weighed by Death himself. The man had the eyes of a predator.

The air juddered with an insectile hostility. The black stare, both freezing and burning, paralyzed Ramram. He forgot to breathe. The squatting man was nothing but muscle and bone but looked like he weighed a mountain. He generated his own gravity. Ramram could not move or close his eyes, though he felt he would die if he didn't. A small rill rushed between them. Ramram wished it were a canyon.

The eyelock went on for a lifetime, a death, another life.

Just as his knees began to tremble, at the most inopportune moment, he felt a throbbing between his temples and his strange friend rushed into his head. He felt the boy recoil, shocked, then be taken by a wondering curiosity. And the same revolution came to Ramram, and with it, a detached calm, as if he were in that other world with his guest, far away, safe.

Together they inspected the hunkering man. Ramram wondered if this was another Chanka. There were no wild braids and the unku looked Inka, rough-spun, dung-colored, grubby, probably llama wool, like a poor worker on a dirty job. A worn greasy sling around his head of short-cut, spiky hair. Wear-darkened grass sandals unravelling in loose ends. Hands thick with callous. Eyes still fixed on his, he saw the man wipe his anus with a smooth stone. What was he going to do? When would this end? He saw the man's lips move, not much, just enough to be speaking.

"Well?" The voice was reasonable. "What?" Without breaking eye contact, the man reached forward, dropping the beshat stone in the rivulet. "Do you think you can stare me down?"

Ramram thought he could get out the word 'mana,' No, when there was another shift within him. He was pulled from this place and taken to that other place, the boy's.

He was looking down on Inka walls built over and defiled by some graceless construction. A woman and two children passed in the street, absurdly dressed. An old man bent, pulling some indefinable awkward entity flanked by circular objects that blinded Ramram's mind. Their eyes lifted to a chaos of things moving and static, it was a town, and the smell was not good.

For the first time in all these visits Ramram knew what he was seeing. It was the *hamuq pacha*. The future. A far future. The dark future.

He felt a shared understanding come to both him and the boy. There was a reason they were brought together and it was in what he was seeing. In this time and in that.

Then the boy's presence pulled away and he found himself staring at the squatting man again. The man was piercing him, mouth half open, with a demanding enquiry.

"You there. Lump. Speak."

"What do you want?" he croaked.

The man barked a laugh. His face seemed to grow longer and younger. “The lump talks.” The eye lock broke. Ramram’s breath came back. “About time. You see what I’m up to. What do *you* want?”

“Are you a Chanka?”

“Well. Lump-boy. No. If you see one, you will know. I don’t look like much, yet you are afraid of me. Why?” He seemed to consider. “But you should be afraid. How did you know that?” He reached under his unku to re-fix his loincloth.

Speaking slowly, trying to be accurate, Ramram explained, “It is your Kamay. It is strong. Kamay speaks to me.” Every word was like walking a cliff in the dark.

“Yes? How?” The man unfolded himself and stood, twisting the small of his back to stretch. The whiff of his dropping crossed the distance on a zephyr. He seemed to be taking Ramram seriously.

“I don’t know. I find Kamay in wakas. Not men. Until you. You and your Kamay are one.”

“I stay with my Kamay. Always.” His eyes on Ramram. “If everyone did that, everyone would be strong.” The man looked at him, not with the death stare, but from within himself, weighing. “Now. When you see me, what do you see?”

Ramram stood too, slowly, carefully, as you would before a mother puma guarding her young. The man’s brows knitted slightly but he was otherwise like a standing stone.

“Maybe a scout.”

The man’s stare didn’t seem so black now. More river brown, the light entering like sunbeams. What was to fear?

But he had said, ‘You *should* be afraid.’

The face was square with two deep grooves running from nose to chin, guarding his hard-set mouth. Ramram saw that he was younger than he looked. The weight of his character aged him. And the weight he carried. Ramram opened his mouth to flatter, to appease, then closed it.

‘Think,’ said Ramram’s inner voice. ‘Don’t lie.’

Then the fear began to retreat. Ramram saw that they had something in common. This man too saw the Kamay in the earth. But differently. Where Ramram's job was to find, to identify, this man's work was to act.

"You are Inka," he answered slowly, word by word. "You are here for the war." The man might have nodded a little, it was hard to tell. The eyes stayed on him.

"You are not afraid because you know what you are going to do." Ramram's words came a little faster. He was excited by his own insight. "You are sure. And if you are sure there is no need to choose whether to stand or to run."

Ramram realized that he had just taken a small step closer to the hard man the better to see him. The man seemed to tower over him, yet he and Ramram were the same height.

"You are full of love." He couldn't believe he had just said that. The man's lips parted a hair. Ramram found the guts to go on. "Love of the Inka, of this land." Now the man's hands lifted from his thighs, fisted at his hips, and he leaned forward. 'He wants to scare me again,' thought Ramram. Some of this man's certainty had passed to him. He was going to say his say, die or not.

"You would kill me for that and feel nothing." That seemed to satisfy the hard man a little. Unless he was imagining that. "You would kill your mother for that. Or your woman. Or your brother." Now the head tilted a finger to the left, and the eyes widened.

"You are very alone." The man actually shifted his weight and bared his teeth a glint. "But you are never lonely." The man seemed to relax a hair, to exhale. Ramram, who rarely lost his temper, felt a shaft of anger.

"No, I'm wrong. You are lonely. But you can't feel it. There is your weakness."

The man grinned. Ramram's terror returned a half measure. "Q'urpa," he said — Lump — "You cross a line."

"You are not lied to."

The man's face returned to its stony rest. "Not much. What are you doing here?"

"I am here for the war." The man's eyelids raised. "Like you, I think. I came here to fight and to die."

"Not to win?"

"Not at first."

"'Not at first'?'"

"I am willing to die but I would rather win and live."

"Not. At. First?"

"No. But now I think we can win. There is a chance. If I can get the ear of the Prince Yupanqui, if someone will listen, I think we can beat the Chanka. I think you are a scout for the army?"

The man stared at him, waiting.

"I have seen a Chanka, and you are right. I knew. Right over there." Ramram indicated the place with his head. "He killed two of us, fast as a viper. He would have killed the rest of us."

Now Ramram couldn't stop talking, it was those river eyes, attentive. "We tried to run, we fell on a rock. I told you that I sense Kamay." Now the memory came back, no, it had not been illusion. "The rock is a waka. A siq'i. Much Kamay. It touched us. It made us strong, fast, alive. It made the Chanka slow, weak, it took his Kamay from him. I killed him. I am not a killer."

"A siq'i."

Ramram spoke slowly again, stressing every word. "It helped us Inkas. It hurt the Chanka." He stopped, trying to assess the worth of telling this man anything. "With this, we don't all have to die. Qosqo will stay Inka."

"How?"

"*Wawqis*. Brother stones. You know wawqis?"

The hard man deigned to nod.

"I think the Kamay will flow from the great stone to many other ones, if they touch. From them, the brother stones, the power will flow into us. It might require a villaq, an umu, I don't know. But I've done it with waka before. I have transferred the Kamay from one to another." Silence from the man. "It didn't always work."

The scout, if that's what he was, without moving his right foot, stretched to lift a heavy, star-headed bronze club, handle worn shiny with use. "Up there?" He indicated the hill above with a look.

"Over that crest."

"Show me." Moving like water, as if he had never been still, the man was striding uphill.

Ramram follows the scout, full of relief, everything has changed. He has this dirty ragged man on his side, more or less. This man has killer Kamay. He will not be easy to stop. If they get to the prince, or anyone important, they will listen to this man. He might even be a military scout on mission.

On the way, the ragged man picks up a sizable chunk of stone, lichened like all of them, and forces it into his ch'uspa pouch.

Ramram sees the man's head come up and club lift. He follows the arrow of the eyes, and there are five big men clambering over a stone outcrop. Faces painted black and yellow, teeth clenched, long spiky braids, condor feather headdresses splayed wide, moving fast. They growl and howl, grinning at their prey.

The scout turns to face the Chanka warriors, macana raised.

"No!" Ramram said, "The siq'i!" Ramram grabs the mangy unku, turns to run.

The scout stands solid, gives him a sharp glance, then swivels to lope up the slope with astounding fluidity and velocity. He passes Ramram, grabbing his unku at the shoulder to pull him along.

Ramram puts everything he has into this, maybe his last, run. The Chanka are gaining, one brawny fire-eyed fighter almost on them, round black and red shield trying to hook Ramram's shoulder, his club bladed with keen obsidian.

The scout steps onto the lip of the hollow and turns to face the enemy. Ramram passes, sees the siq'i below, seizes the Inka by the arm and pulls him backward, almost toppling him. The man gives him a look of imperious annoyance but follows as the volcanic glass blade, sharper than the most refined scalpel, parts the air by his ear.

They step over the long reptilian rock and turn to face the oncoming enemy.

Breathing the Kamay of the siq'i, he is infused with that sudden vigor expanding from the crotch on up. Ramram hears a growl deep in the chest of the scout. His own stone-headed macana again seems flower light in his hand. The world slows, his hands accelerate.

And the pursuing Chanka, now all within striking distance, powerful men bristling with deadly weapons, are suddenly slow, confounded as if they've run into a thick spider web. Brows furrowed in bafflement. They are fuddled and spastic.

The scout's club swings horizontally into the leading Chanka's jaw, tearing the mandible away in a red cloud of teeth and tongue. The club swings backward, catching the next assailant in the cranium, the coppery star-point spraying blood and bone as the skull discorporates.

Ramram steps forward, every muscle in harmony and sure of itself, twisting to evade a lethal bronze spearhead, to bring his club down on a forearm, snapping through radius and ulnar, then up again into the face, now almost in his own, it's great grimace exhaling hot breath, and he sees the hooked nose collapse up between the hating eyes.

The scout and Ramram exchange a fierce, triumphant glance and together slaughtered the third man up against them. The following attacker, his red and black unku already spattered with his companions' gore, hesitates, steps backward, as the Inka scout swings his shield top forward, the spear gripped in his fist slicing through skin and muscle, glancing off rib, destroying the heart of his foe, and the Chanka folds into himself and goes down dying.

The last Chanka invader tries to run, but his knees are weak and his stamina gone.

With oiled coordination Ramram strips his sling from around his head. The scout lays an egg-shaped stone in his hand. He fits it into the cup of the leather strip, whipping the sling twice around his head, freeing one end of the strap, sending the stone perfectly into the back of the fleeing man's skull, dropping him dead on the ground.

They stand now silent, not even panting, looking at what they have done.

Ramram feels Eff-Ram come to him for a breath or two and depart, shocked.

"We are enhanced," the scout says. "They are impaired."

"Ari. Yes. You see." He looks at the scout. "Now. Can you get the ear of the Son of Viracocha Inka?"

The scout grunts, eyes down at the knobbled stone.

"*Inti*! Maybe I feel something from this pebble," he says. "Now we test." He holds up his found rock. "This has no power." He lays it on the waka. Looks back at Ramram, still above, eyebrows raised. Lifts the rock. "Now walk away until you can't feel the Kamay."

Ramram walks uphill, toward the Inka's army, sixty rikra. Still he feels something. A hundred. Still, a trace. A hundred ten. Nothing. "Here."

The scout approaches, striding effortlessly. Fifty paces away, Ramram knows it has worked. A lesser force, but there. He looks back at the sprawled enemy dead.

"Maybe a trick of the mind," the man says. "But I will take this to the war."

CHAPTER THREE no time

The Condor
Timeless

A brown-feathered adult female condor banks between the peaks. Below, a hollow note rises and bends in minor key, a young man plays a wooden flute high on a cliff; beneath, three young women bathe naked in the river, touched by the first sun of the Andean day. One looks up at the boy and then to her friends; they laugh.

The condor's shadow dips and folds over a jewel-like village cupped in a nest of peaks; silvery stone, golden thatch, touches of color on painted walls; a web of water in rivulets weaves through the town; ribbons of smoke rise from the courtyards, with scraps of voice.

Badges of orange lichen pulse brightly, scattered across the rocks; the blades of grass in their billions crawl with scintillation into the ultraviolet range; the small hard leaves of the thorn bushes reflect colors invisible to the human eye. What the great bird sees is not the surfaces but the microscopic life seething on those surfaces.

The condor catches a rising breeze, circles high, returns. Now the village is dark, buried in brambles and brush, a ruin forgotten. Still, the stones glisten with luminous growths, and all the living beings phosphoresce in her eyes.

On the crest across the deep ravine a young man with a wrench leans back over the sheer drop, fearless, making final repairs to a steel signal relay tower. The floating bird's shadow passes across his dark eyes, high bronze cheekbones. Far below, light glints on the river where no one walks.

At the north end of the valley, the condor turns again, rises, and falls again; on the west side of the canyon a boy stands silent, his carved flute at his side, a woven sling wound around his brow, rough wool tunic rustling in the wind at his knees. He is looking across the void at the worker on the mysterious silvery latticed tower, who looks silently back, knee hooked over a steel strut. They see each other, and they don't.

The condor's shadow passes again over the village. It is there, and it is not there. Now it is another, a third, living, village, glinting and shimmering with exotic materials, and there is a halo of aerosol luminescence surrounding the enigmatic town; not now, not then, but a time yet to be, or that never will. The condor is not surprised. It has always been this way. She rises, soars over the jagged ridge at the bend in the river, and is gone.

CHAPTER FOUR now

On Our Planet
Port Angeles, Washington

"Okay. Dark upon dark, I speak to you. As you stare at the invisible wall of your 'self' standing between your heart and knowing that the world is alive, I send you this."

Here is Nick Nieman, in his murky basement studio, smiling thinly into the webcam, commencing the seventh post of his video blog, "We Live In You." Few are watching and none of them get it. Yet.

"On this planet called Dirt from numberless single-cell organisms too simple even to grow a nucleus, messages are sent. Proteins seeking receptors, ion channelling, potassium signalling, by light and sound, by other means still unknown to man. These are bacteria, the kingdom of Prokaryotes communicating within itself. And when enough messengers find enough receptors, a change occurs, and the isolated microorganisms unite to become a single being. Then they begin to send out more messengers, more complex and more sophisticated in intent than those before, seeking enough receptors to transform again into a larger organism — a superorganism — that is more aware."

Outside in the wind and rain, in the thin shelter of a madrone tree, a tiny animal, wet and dirty with black and orange fur, shivers. One eye is blue and one is green. It opens its mouth but no sound comes out.

He takes a breath, centers himself in the camera. He swipes his trackpad and the screen turns to a video showing bacteria, the primordial ocean. Meteors strike the earth, cells swarm, there is a great die-off, then oxygen dominates.

"This superorganism is old, billions of years, always changing, always evolving. It is one, and it is many. It is very aware, on a level humanity can never hope to decrypt. It is aware that the world it lives in and upon has settled on a future that will result in the destruction of themselves and every planetary life form lesser and greater than themselves except for maybe a few anaerobic cells in the Challenger Deep."

Lightning strikes a few blocks away. The kitten shrinks into herself.

"This global superorganism can be called a holobiome. Science might label it a macrobiota, a eusocial collective intelligence. You could call it a co-evolutionary non-mutualistic extracellular endosymbiotic commensalism.

"The Greeks called it Gaia, the Romans Anima Mundi. Teilhard de Chardin called it the Noosphere. P.K. Dick called it VALIS. You could call it the Overmind. The wise men of the Inka called it Pachayachachiq, the common people Pachamama, Mother Spacetime. None of them understood it. I call it the Presence. Neither do I."

"This planetary holobiome foresees biosphere extinction. The Presence exists outside of the medium of time, and it sees this as a certainty. Everything on earth dies. That is death on the crust of the planet. Some say that we, people, are a disease; and it's functionally true. We will kill Earth."

Nick pauses.

Lightning explodes in the old madrone, rattling Nick's windows and frying his modem. The little cat streaks toward a tiny point of light leaking through the foundation of the house. Nick ducks, peers out the basement window, resumes.

"The Holobiome is one thing, infinitely simple, and it is all things, finitely complex. We do not and cannot know what the Presence perceives, but in its multiplicity there are elements of it that do know. One of them — I call it The Question— searches for a crack in this doomsday certainty."

"A crack is found. It is a connection across time between an Inka and an American, both young. I don't know who they are, or were, but I am informed they were, and are."

An Inka boy chases birds in a field; a boy on a bus thumbs his cell phone like all the kids around him.

"Distant points in spacetime have touched."

The webcam rocks as Nick surges to his feet, bumping the monitor. He elbows the computer. The camera rocks. He is frantically slapping something hairy off his plaid shirt.

"Cats! I fucking hate 'em! I'm allergic! And this little son of a bitch is ugly. How the hell did you get in here? Ah fuck. Sorry. Okay."

"Francisco Pizarro stands on the ship's deck as it rolls. He rolls with it, doesn't reach for a line, never let your men see you off-balance. He is the illiterate bastard son of a pig farmer, a hard-horse conquistador licensed by the king. He is as hard as his armored fist.

"It is as hot as the inside of a pig's belly on the deck of that caravel off the jungle shore but he is in full armor — never let your soldiers know you feel heat or cold, need anything, fear anything, doubt or do not know. The only thing he has with which to conquer empires is to be absolute.

"But we know he will win. It has already happened, one hundred and eighty men against an empire. He will look into the eyes of an Inka emperor and kill him. We know this from the hallucination we call History.

"The musk and sight of land are before him. Gulls craze the air.

"So many men against so few, but the future is fixed. The Inkas will die, by sickness and by sword, and then sink to squalor and shame — their world stolen. The Four Parts of Spacetime will become 'Peru.'"

"On the wooden curves of this ship, in the stinking hold, on the masts and frayed sails, are life forms; algae, mosses, lichen, germs. In the eye of a soaring albatross, they swarm with light.

"The ship approaches the doomed Inka town of Tumbez. On that shore, the future is there, complete. But there is a shift. A minuscule rift, too small to sense. The rift is doubt. Then it is gone. Francisco Pizarro slips on the wet deck, reaches for a bowline; frowns."

An NSA scan misses a connection between bacteria and Inkas because neither word is quite there.

A Tweet from Little Alaska:
-30° Room, USAMRIID HQ, Detrick Maryland
Six years after first contact

#An alien intelligence dominates this planet. It is a prokaryote superorganism. It is not our enemy, it is us #True, it wants to give LA back to the red man. When you learn that it is real you will try to kill it #In doing so, you will kill organized life on Earth #Don't

Security found Irvin Hatman, MD, icy dead in the cold room, known as 'Little Alaska,' of the United States Army Medical Research Institute of Infectious Diseases headquarters a little after three in the morning. His final tweet went out to under a hundred people, but could be searched by keyword.

The area was cordoned off, the hermetic doors were sealed, men entered in biohazard suits, determined that what he held in his hand was not an open container of some deadly biological warfare agent but a photograph of his daughter at the age of six. He was naked. He had taken a lethal dose of Paracetamol but was killed by hypothermia. He was sitting on his cell phone.

At home, his den was littered with notes, formulas, and annotated data sheets. His hard drive was missing and never found. The source of the documentation could not be identified. His estranged wife, also a microbiologist, said his obsession with a microbic "entity" drove her away. His colleagues said that he seemed normal except for this mildly annoying knowing look.

Shortly thereafter a small budget was allocated within the United States Army Medical Research and Materiel Command to fund a task force dedicated to investigating the plausibility of Doctor Hatman's assertions. It was named the NTT.

The Egg

Two Months after the Tweet from Little Alaska

The General called his germ expert — given what the NTT was all about he had to have one of those — over to check out this YouTube video.

"Doc, watch this crap. Tell me if it has anything to do with us." The old fentanyl addict leaned over the screen, exhaling cigar. He had lost his license for malpractice. He came cheap.

"Yeah. He's talking about the same thing. Basically, he is repackaging your guy's suicide note."

"Our guy's. You work here."

"Our guy."

The General had a staff of four in a crappy little suite of offices near Quantico, Virginia. The computers were third hand and the wiring was Vietnam era. The NTT was his baby and it was still in the egg. He had to do something with this turkey he had been handed but he had no idea where to start.

He started starting by getting an old military buddy in the NSA to track everybody who had picked up on Hatman's goddam twitter thing. There were a few weak leads.

One of them was a crackpot in the Olympic Peninsula, Washington, who was video blogging about a bacteria overmind with some connection to a bunch of dead indians who wanted to invade California.

It was a place to start. He had one of his other losers watch the videos and sift them for keywords.

Turned out it was called "*We Live In You*" and the guy was the assistant manager of a Safeway in Washington. The state, not the district. His name was Nick Nieman. No military or medical background. His loser got back to him.

"He claims he's channelling some Inka wizard in Peru. Name sounds like a sneeze.The only substantive hook I can get out of this is that there was a kid, maybe American, who was doing the same thing with another Inka kid. They make a connection through some kind of infected rock in a town in Peru. They might be somekind of threat to US territory. The place is called like O'Yannity Tomboy."

Well, thinks the General, I gotta do something and it's a place to start. When in doubt, charge.

He knows a retired colonel who has a little private-army outfit in California. Ex LRRPs, Rangers, and jarheads, working cheap. ‘Briarpatch.’ He'll get one of those down there to look at that.

CHAPTER FIVE then

The Seventh Son
Seven years before the Chanka war, Qosqo, Reign of Viracocha Inka

With cold eyes, the old Sapa Inka Viracocha, Unique Ruler of the Inka Kingdom of Qosqo, looked upon his seventh son, Prince Kusi Inka Yupanqui, who stood with a Chanka warrior bound and bloody at his feet. The King deigned to speak.

"There are four kings and five sinchi warlords between the Chanka and Qosqo."

"Ari," Yes, replied the Prince, respectful, "the Chanka armies will be here in eight years. Less."

"This one told you that?"

"Not in words, Apu Inka."

The Lord Inka lifted his chin, laid eyes on the captive. "What were you doing in Inka lands?"

The prisoner grinned through broken teeth, his left eyeball hanging on his cheek. "Was I on Inka land? I don't know. I was lost. The sun seems to rise in the wrong place around here. Too far west." His remaining eye, under an explosion of black braids, mocked.

With a flick of his eyes the king ordered the Chanka scout taken away. Viracocha Inka looked into the face of his son, frowning.

Two days earlier a great brown-winged condor landed on the tall thatched roof of the palace. The High Umu – Umu meant Necromancer, Wizard, Seer – reported to the Inka. "It is an omen, Apu. I don't know what it portends, but something significant. Now it has landed on our sacred white llama."

The Inka and his courtiers paced out to see. The llama stood as if paralyzed, the bird on its back ruffling her feathers. Her eye on the king's was like the eye, however masked with humility, of his seventh son, now in the great hall.

The day after the condor came, that son was spied returning from four years banishment to explore the wild and foreign lands to the northwest. Reports were that the kings and queens of those lands, both rivals and allies, had not much liked Prince Kusi Inka Yupanqui. Their sons had. And their daughters. He returned with a captive.

Now the King instructed,

"You will lead a herd of one thousand llamas into the upper reaches of Mount Ausangate, now that the way is clear. You will look for the uppermost grazing lands. When a llama starves, you will seek another pasture until you know every pampa on which a beast can feed. You will remain until called for." He watched the Prince's face. It looked, if anything, pleased.

"En route, you will inspect the work underway on my new retreat, Shaqishawana, on the heights above Calca.You will do the same at the construction of the great temple of Tunupa Viracocha at Racchi. That is all."

The Sapa Inka thought, if the Chanka do come, they will not follow me to Shaqishawana.

In the courtyard, Prince Urcon, heir to the King, stood in Kusi Yupanqui's path.

"Had general Waman not been killed, our army would have taken Chinchero and the Ayarmaka would have submitted to us without your interference. Had I not been down with fever I would have led them myself."

"True. Winning through negotiation cost the Inka, sadly, many dead heroes. Men now alive. Yet it leaves us with more treasure and more new subjects to work our projects in the annexed lands. And fewer dreams of rebellion. How is the work going on the Qolqa construction at our new settlement at Rumipuqyu?"

Prince Urcon did not feel moved to reply. Kusi Yupanqui's eyes shifted to Chaski Yuyu, a Khipucamayoq record keeper, newly returned from the site.

"Well underway, Prince," said Chaski Yuyu, "and the population of the new town is well integrated. Your suggestion, if I may say, of placing such an extensive construction there, to the benefit of our Ayarmaka subjects and allies, rather than some oppressive military pukara, has settled the people very effectively. May I wish you a pleasant journey to Ausangate?"

The young prince cast an eye at the condor, still perched on the stoic camelid, and smiled. "Any journey is a pleasure, friend. But I go there to work. And to learn."

Chaski Yuyu, the keeper of the knotted strings watched the man amble away southeast, comfortable on his feet, at ease on the land, as if going home from a long day's work, rather than to exile in a high icy range where men die.

The Prince Urcon stood stiffly, glaring at his younger brother's back.

In the morning, the Uma Umu reported to Viracocha Inka. "The condor has flown, Apu. To the southeast."

The boy Ramram is nine years old.

CHAPTER SIX now

The First Flip

"This is the first time you have made me feel badly," Lily Tran said at the station, "And you think that you are hiding something from me."

"No," "Ephraim Arrowsmith said back, stock still, "I am just not telling you."

"I don't know how I'm going to be about this."

"Wait. Wait 'til I come back. I'll know more."

Now he wanted to get off the train at the San Francisco Civic Center station and run back to her. Wanted to badly. But the scales tilted to Peru and he was going. He was sixteen and it was time.

That first flip. His dad took him to Peru when he was ten, they looked at a lot of ruins but they were mere curiosities to Ephraim until Machu Qolqa.

It was a complex of ruined stone storehouses high above the Maras plain an hour out of Cusco. His dad was far below, taking notes, catching his breath. Ephraim always had more energy than he could handle. The old stone walls were all around him, floating in ghostly cloud, spooky, terrace after terrace like battlements above, crusted in cryptic growths he knew now were lichen, and there something in the boy changed, even before he felt the pull of that high place.

Behind, the landscape fell away, level after level, down through the drifting clouds, to aerial views of tiny towns along the road and the river.

The ruins filled Ephraim with a strange dark beauty. They were a revelation. He was shot through with delight that he was really there, where hands and minds once made these things. At that instant he fell in love with the Inkas.

Then something else happened. Something alive, electrical, bloomed in his gut and above the bridge of his nose, tugging him uphill. He was being by some unknown influence wafted up without exerting his own energy.

Cloaked in the rags of fog above was a crumbling stone cluster like a decayed molar, and in that - it came back to him now, the memory of his hand on the broken fieldstone wall with its traces of ancient clay - and there in that he saw what was pulling on him. The back wall of this ancient shrine was a bulging, textured boulder, crusted with rusty growths. A smooth shelf was cut into the rock with laser-edged precision. An altar. It was from this that the energy pulsed.

He hesitated, afraid, then pressed his palms on the lichen and moss, and beneath, the stone.

A light erupted in his head, shock slithered down his thin body, and he was pulled dizzy from where he stood, from who he was, into another world.

That was the world of Ramram the Inka. A kid like him, but dead for hundreds of years. Ephraim saw through Ramram's eyes, felt the air on his skin, the stretch of his muscles, his heart and his thought, he himself put back into a corner helpless except to watch as through a window as hundreds of men in rough tunics wrestled stone water and wood up the hills, building those ruined things he had just climbed through.

Once, briefly, they had changed places, and Ramram had seen through Ephraim's eyes what would become of his father's work. The inka absorbed the shock thoughtfully.

Ephraim was with the Inka boy for maybe an hour. They managed to trade names. When he came back to himself his father was still below, looking upward for his son.

Ephraim had always been a careful, rather methodical, character. He took a breath and knew he would not tell his dad, or anyone, until he fully understood what had happened to him. But he knew.

The Inka Ramram had taken a piss off the mountain. He took his time, enjoying, in no hurry. Ephraim had always resented the time spent to urinate, spasmodically contracting his urethra to force the flow faster.

There, in Ramram, he finally knew how it felt to be calm. To be at peace. Not to fidget. And he felt a soul in the mountains, he who did not believe in souls. Overhead, together, they watched a condor ride the wind. Ramram felt reverence. Ephraim, riding the train to catch a plane, wondered if that sensation would come again.

Ephraim hoped that someday he would be able to tell Lily. That would depend on what happened when he got back to Ollantaytambo.

What did Lily mean, you *think* you are hiding something?

Twenty Minutes to Touchdown
Final approach to Lima, Peru

Ephraim Arrowsmith had never told anyone, not his dad, not Lily. Not in six years. Not about the time-travel thing. He wasn't that crazy.

He already had super-nerd status at school, though no one bothered him about that.

It was in the wind that he had skydived at thirteen years old. Just once, but it happened to be the same flight in which two jumpers had tangled up with one another and gotten themselves killed on YouTube. He had tried hang gliding. He also had gotten his black belt in Wado Kai karate at eleven years old. He was a National Merit Scholarship finalist. So the fact that he ignored competitive sports, current pop tunes, all the subtribes, couldn't sit still in class, walked alone, and seemed to have no interests beyond pre-contact Andean culture and a few other geeky topics, didn't earn him any wedgies. It didn't hurt that word was out that he was doing Lily Tran. Or rather, she him.

Now he was flying back to Peru to do it again. If he could.

Twenty minutes to touchdown. That was too long. The meaty dude in the middle seat was going to go off.

High Taper Fade
Sixteen-Year-Old Ephraim□ Landing in Lima, Peru

The Inkas loved two things: water and stone. Ephraim tried to turn quietly the page of the paper he was reading, but he could see that the big guy in the center seat was about to blow.

Ephraim Arrowsmith bobbed his Adam's apple, rattled his knee, wrung his hands, drummed on the table, wiggled his toes, and he had this thing where by pushing his lower lip upward, he double-folded his upper lip, so he appeared to be smiling when he was not. In the world at large he typically sat cross-legged, rocking side to side. Now, in seat 29A of the Airbus, the window seat over the wing, he just rocked a little forward and back. His mother, like the school, wanted to medicate him. H□is father fought them off.

Ephraim tried to localize his life force in the cramped tube of the plane, but still surmised that the hulking male in the center seat, 29B, was annoyed and about to act out. He had the shaved-side haircut the kids called a "high taper fade," with glass-blond hair-spikes writhing on top glistening with product, as if lusting to stab into the world and make it bleed. He looked to Ephraim like a drug-enhanced gym rat.

He was already man-spreading his legs wide into Ephraim's space, as his elbow shot well over the armrest. Likewise, he was invading 29C, the aisle seat. The seedy looking little guy there had to lean into the aisle to avoid the man's tattooed right arm.

In that seat slouched a round-faced, bespectacled character with a close cut auburn beard in a faded, patched,□ tweed sports coat and worn jeans, tapping at the keyboard of a laptop that appeared to be seven or eight years old. He looked like born bully bait.

The 29B guy's elbow kept nudging at the computer, making him miss keys.

The steroid guy didn't hide his exasperation; he kept tilting his head and frowning at Ephraim, revving his engines in anticipation of conflict.

Ephraim sighed through his nose and focused on the academic paper spread out on his closed laptop.

"*The first thing to know about the Inkas is, nobody knows anything about the Inkas.*"

Ephraim smiled again, reading his dogeared printout of the paper. The flight into Lima was banking to land, and the first sun shot in on his left, splattering across the container ships on the harbor of Callao. He was coming back to Peru.

The paper's title:

"Rumimuqu: A Speculative Investigation into Archaeological Theory and Exegesis of a Persistent Autochthonous Topological Anomaly in Late Horizon Ashlar, Wanka, Cyclopean, Cellular, Coursed, Cushioned, Convex, Pitted, and Polygonal Masonry Construction in Ollantaytambo and the Lower Yucay Valley: The Stone Gnomons — What Are Those Bumps For?"

Ephraim spread the binder-clipped sheaf with his palms. He liked this guy, the author. He understood him. This man loved the Inka the way Ephraim loved the Inka, for their strange and subtle beauty and their humor. Invisible to most people, an acquired taste. He was sure the guy shared his suspicion that the world would be better off under an updated Inka regime. There was just something about the way the old Andeans had handled themselves. For all the Sun-King despotism, for all the warring, something deeply intelligent. Plus, like he himself, they were distinct. Nothing in his life came close to what he felt about the Inkas. Nothing except Lily Tran.

The author — a B.B. Bonnaterre, Ph.D — had crammed every sesquipedalian syllable of academia into that title, except maybe 'hermeneutics,' but ended with a simple question, then gone on to tell the simple truth in simple words. No one knows.

True. Not even he, who had actually experienced fifteenth century Peru through the lens of a long-dead living Inka boy, a form of non-physical time travel, knew what those protuberances on the Inka masonry were for. Knew what the Inkas were thinking when they did anything that they did.

The mental time-travel thing had happened seven times. First with his father on their brief stop at the Machu Qolqa archaeological site, then in Ollantaytambo.The author of that unlikely paper, so raw in its honesty, was dead on right. Nobody knew anything about the Inka. Not really.

It came from touching a stone. He speculated now, from the lichen growing on the stone. Maybe from the bacteria in the lichen growing on the stone? As the vlogger at *We Live In You* lectured? Unless, of course, he, Ephraim, was delusional?

He called that bifurcated boulder, half sunk in the earth of Ollantaytambo, Peru, Split Rock. It was there that he had first divided the world into the Now and Then. He had seen Then. The Inka. He hoped urgently to see them again. He missed their presence in his life, and in history. He missed the wonder of it. He missed Ramram, his Inka host boy.

It was there, in Ollantaytambo, that Ephraim had for the first time in his life, calmed. The fidgeting stopped. From the first moment he was pulled into the Inka kid's perspective, into his life and soul, peace had come to Ephraim, and stayed, until the flight back to...what was it that Nick Nieman called the US? The Untied Snakes. Then the writhing and jerking and pacing had begun again. It only let him be when he was alone with Lily.

Now he was going back to Peru. What if Split Rock was gone? Built on, buried, hauled away? What if it didn't work anymore, what if the peace would not come back to him? Ephraim's knee bounced at the thought.

"Shit! Are you ADHD, you spastic little freak? How am I supposed to focus on my MMA with you jerking around?"

The seat mate turned to him, leaning far into his face so that Ephraim had to recoil. “Briarpatch” was embroidered on the polo shirt over his sculpted pectorals, above what looked like a ninja with rabbit ears.

He jabbed Ephraim with his finger, hard on the words 'freak,' 'MMA,' and 'around.' "Stop that, okay? Can you do that?"

Ephraim released a slow breath, shook his head minutely, looked the man in his testosterone-swollen face and said, "No?"

The man's lips pulled away from his big capped teeth, his mouth opened to blast something possibly interesting at Ephraim when the hobo-dude in the aisle seat leaned far across the bully's chest, took the man's nose between his left thumb and forefinger, and twisted hard. His right hand held a cell phone, recording the event.

The gym-rat corkscrewed around in disbelief, working to repurpose whatever he had been about to say to Ephraim toward this outrage. Seeing who it was that had violated him, he broke into a wolfish grin and cocked his right fist.

"You want to wake up on the No-Fly list?" asked the balding bearded man, almost gently, "and on YouTube?"

‘Briarpatch’ looked into the bearish little man's hard brown eyes, and his fist hovered, vibrating.

"This is a fifteen-year-old kid you just assaulted on video, and I am an invited guest of the Peruvian government. How is your Spanish? Mine is perfect. What do you think will happen if I raise my voice?"

'Well, I read him wrong,' thought Ephraim.

The man in the polo shirt thought so too. He hesitated, and when the scruffy man's eyes shifted toward a tall flight attendant, whose gaze suddenly zoomed in on them, 29B subsided back into his seat. As an afterthought, he hastily drew in his knees and elbows. He held up a meaty, palliative palm, shook his head, said "Okay, don't lose your shit, bro," He struggled for some move to regain his dignity. "Don't be a dick. It was just a question."

He turned his pale blue eyes to the little screen upon which men hit other men in Mixed Martial Arts, sliding earphones delicately over his aggressive haircut.

'The essential American,' thought Ephraim, 'territorial, adversarial, empty of empathy, self-consumed, self-deluded, and afraid of authority.'

"Look," said the nose-twister mildly, "What about this? What if we switched seats? You could, like, expand out into the aisle instead of all over us." He said it in such a reasonable, friendly sort of way that the big guy responded doglike to the tone.

They maneuvered around one another, touching as little as possible. The slightly tubby bearded guy settled next to Ephraim, smelling much less like a derelict than he looked. They exchanged a subtle glance, and each returned to their own business. Ephraim re-opened his academic publication. His hands and knees were shaking. 'It's different in Peru than in the US. It has got to be different,' he told himself, breathing deep.

After a moment, his revised seat mate spoke.

"I wrote that," the man said. Ephraim's eyes glanced reflexively at the binder-clipped paper, then back at the speaker.

"My function is not to intrude, friend, but I wrote the paper you are reading."

Ephraim felt the world had changed, and for the good. "You are B.B. Bonnaterre?"

"Bingham." He held out a hand that proved surprisingly calloused.

"Ephraim Arrowsmith." There was a pause. "I really like it." .

"You take an interest in the Inka?"

"Very much. I spent a summer in Ollantaytambo a few years ago, and was ensorcelled by what I saw. Now I'm going back for the school break." 'I should be more hysterical about meeting B.B. Bonnaterre,' he thought, 'but it feels more like...obvious.'

"Ensorcelled were you? I'll be there in a few weeks, my annual trip. Maybe we'll see each other. Ah, your name, Ephraim — you weren't named after E. George Squier were you?"

Ephraim laughed. "No, after a great grandfather. But I cut my teeth on *Incidents and Explorations in the Land of the Incas*. And you, the "B" stands for Bingham? Did your name influence your choice of professions?"

"Yep. My namesake. My dad was an historian, pre-contact cultures. He left all Hiram's works when he died." Hiram Bingham was credited with finding Machu Picchu.

Ephraim was briefly tempted to tell Bingham Bonnaterre about his time-travel experience — who would appreciate it more? But his long standing conservatism — he didn't talk much about anything to anyone — and the fact that the flight was touching down, prevailed.

Bingham Bonnaterre was being flown into Lima to speak to an archaeological conference on the university's dime. "I can stake myself one trip a year," he said, "and that'll be later."

He invited Ephraim to attend as a guest. Ephraim was booked straight through, and was inclined to decline, but took a breath and told himself 'Learn to flex, Arrowsmith. It's not the last flight out of Dien Bien Phu.'

He watched the author of his paper wave backward over his shoulder as he ambled away from the luggage carousel, shouldering a faded backpack, his only luggage.

The 'Briarpatch' man looked at them over his shoulder as he swaggered out the exit.

Make Your Own Web of Light
The day after landing in Lima

Ephraim followed the crowd into the auditorium to hear Bingham Bonnaterre's disquisition at the National University of San Marcos, Lima, Peru. There were a couple hundred people there, not many empty seats.

Bingham didn't test the mic, sip water, or shuffle papers. He just stood there quiet in his beat up tweed and waited for sufficient silence. Then he spoke, clearly and without emphasis, in Spanish.

"The ancient South Americans were, like feral children raised by wolves, alone in the world.

"All the empires of the old world: Sumer, Egypt, China, Scythia, Harappan of the Indus Valley, Babylon, Persia, Rome, Khmer, Mongolia, Vijayanagara, hundreds forgotten and not taught in school, were knit together by the silk route and the sea. They traded knowledge and technology, cross-pollinated, and, as allies or enemies, guided each other through the dark.

"But the peoples of the Americas, just as ancient, walked alone through the wilderness of creation, uninformed by cultural gossip, and so created their own web of light.

"Their ideas are not those of the rest of the world. Their roots are in different soil, they are not a branch of the same tree, not for the last fifteen to fifty thousand years, long before the planting of seeds, the building of walls, or the birth of writing."

Bingham paused to scan his audience. Ephraim thought that the University had done well.There were young students, old professors, motley non-academics, Peruvians and foreigners, an eclectic salmagundi invited to an open event. They were there because they wanted to be. Bingham's gaze found Ephraim, in the back. He met Ephraim's eyes and smiled, looked down at his notes, and went on.

"The Andeans were separated even from the other isolates to the north — the pyramid builders of Mexico and Central America — by deep jungle and the Darien Gap, the choke point between the continents. If there was contact it doesn't show.

"They could have been a laboratory experiment in how a culture would evolve in isolation, in a clean-room beyond contamination by any other human influence."

"*Pas des Egyptiens? Pas des Grecs?*" Not Egyptians, not Greeks?" A bald man heckled, weirdly, in French, finger in the air.

“Contain yourself, buckaroo," replied Bingham conversationally, in English, "Your big moment is coming right up.” He smiled affably. Quiet laughter rippled through the audience.

“Maybe, just maybe, lost sailors from some old world port did wash up on that unknown shore before the voyages of Erikson and Columbus. Maybe Phoenicians from Carthage, maybe Egyptians, or Chinese from the armada of Zheng He, Vikings, or the lost fleet of Mansa Musa. Maybe Portuguese blown off course found themselves at the feet of Moche fishermen, of Lambayeque, Chincha, Wari.

"But if the ancient Andeans were touched by any such wayward wayfarers, they were not given to know of writing, the wheel, iron, furniture, paper. And most of all, about money. Not of stringed instruments, brass, gunpowder, long pants, the phalanx, the hinge, horses, corsets, the vanishing point, the nail, boots, the octave, swords, the keystone arch, the pulley, stockings, bellows, the saw, domes, the adze, the oven, the screw, the frying pan, pockets. Not of beds, chairs or tables. No one came with wheat or horses. When Europe was building cathedrals and cannon, entering the Renaissance, the Inka lived in the early Bronze Age."

He paused, took a sip of water from the podium. Ephraim wondered how many in the audience followed that list of things the Inka lacked. Almost everything was in it, yet it touched the truth of life so lightly.

“Having no one to ask for advice but themselves, they filled the vacuum of time and place with their own vision of human invention, one of stone and water and knots and system and subtle beauty. They carved great chunks of hard rock into gem-like interlocking geometries and fused them to one another so cannily that the explosive mountain earthquakes just settled them stronger. Their buildings grew seamlessly from the living rock of the earth. Their towns, temples, and fields were woven together by a circulatory system of fountains, aqueducts, fresh water channels, cascades, and reflecting pools that nourished the crops on the tiers of terraces that made the barren hillsides fertile and fed the towns with clean water. They did not dominate the earth, they walked with it.

"They had a sense of beauty still not understood nor recognized, now forgotten. Who sees the playful humor in their stone walls? They created one continuous living rock garden of unified harmony with earth, river, mountain, and sky, four thousand kilometers long."

"So it was Zen monks, then?" a stunning woman in the front row mocked, uncrossing her legs. Bingham met her flirtatious smile with his own. A couple of people applauded softly. More laughed.

"They created what was arguably the strongest economy on earth without money. Without any form of commerce, without middle-men. What would that do to the infection of greed in human affairs?

"If a house was left empty, a stick was laid diagonally across the open door, in confidence that no one would enter, even if the occupants were gone for years. You can still see that practiced in the mountains of Peru.

"There was order, peace and safety, it was clean. There were no beggars, no prostitutes, everyone worked, no one however unable was abandoned.

"They were also alone in this: they were the only civilized culture or polity to maintain a wholly sustainable relationship with the earth and its resources. This was intrinsic to their soul, deeply felt, and consistently executed.

"There were conquerors and God-kings and bloodshed, as in any hungry empire, but they lived in a balanced harmony with their natural world and with their own people. As long as the people didn't mind getting up at dawn and coming home at sundown. Everyone worked. And everyone got a hundred days of the year off, at the expense of the Sapa Inka.

"By the primordial bond of *Ayni*, reciprocation, they limited the power of kings and barons. Nearly every offense was capital, so they had no jails. They were tyrants whose agreement with their subjects was more reasonable, kind, generous, and just, than any other government whose story has survived. They did this alone. Then the Old World came and killed them."

"*Antes de que pudieran matarnos*," before they could kill us. This from a Quixote-esque gentleman propping a gold-headed cane between his knees.

"*Dejalo hablar, caballero*," a dark woman with intense eyes spoke in chilling contempt. "Let him speak, sir." She was the rogue archeologist Katari Kuntur, though Ephraim would not recall her when they met later. Again, quiet approval.

Bingham continued. "There are a few of us who mourn the Inka and the long sequence of earlier kingdoms, astounding in their variety, mutating through fifty thousand seasons of isolated artistry, alone on the nameless land mass that was all the world they knew, improvising their own universe unguided, pure.

"The binary view of the Western world is black and white, with gradients of gray between. In the East, it is male and female, the sixty-nine of Yin and Yang. But to the Inka polarity it was the spectrum of visible light, from ultraviolet to infrared. It is written that the standard, the *wiphala*, of the Tawantinsuya, was the rainbow. The Inka were an 'enlightened' people.

"We Andeanists regret their disappearance, the loner swarmed by the sneering clique. What would the Inka be like now, left to themselves?

"They were not inoculated against the germs, steel, and guns. Most lethally, against the lust for gold. Had they been prepared for those infected and armored men, had they taken them and wrung them for their knowledge, had they used their gold as leverage against the Old World, had the Tawantinsuyu survived unto this day, our world may have had an example to emulate, an advocate to turn to. They were beautiful. Do not let that die."

Bingham shook hands, gave thanks for praise, but broke loose to catch Ephraim slipping out the back. "I try to be kind to the finger food," he said, "It's all I'll eat until I get back to Berkeley. I have cab fare to the airport and then, stoney broke." He grinned. "Don't offer money, I been through worse for less. Thanks for showing up. When I saw you there I knew at least someone got my drift."

Ollantaytambo (Ol yan tie TAM bo) Peru
Three days after landing in Lima

Ephraim steps down from the fifteen-seat *colectivo* and inhales a first breath of Ollantaytambo air. It takes him three minutes to get into trouble.

He looks over the heads of the walking-stick vendors and mountain women in their red wool skirts and bowl hats, to Temple Hill, the ruins cascading down Bandolista hill. He scans the high range to the west and south, seeming to cup the town in gentle hands, peaks still flagged in morning cloud. He breathes deep, feeling the calm return to his chest and gut, relaxing, smiling. There is an ATM on the corner. Close behind, looming above the roofline to the east, is his mentor spirit, Pinkuylluna Mountain.

This craggy trapezoidal eruption of gouged, rugged, volcanic hydroclastic breccia and hard igneous rhyolite thrusts up between Ollantaytambo and the rising sun. Reddish rock outcrops stud the sides like petrified monsters. Stone ruins cluster on the lower slopes imitating palaces, forts, tenements, levels of row houses.

The angry profile of Tunupa Viracocha, his rocky nose hooked over a toothless mouth, scowls westward. He is a geological trompe l'oeil carved by wind and water into the mountainside. Atop his head is a square watchtower, *rikachakuna* in Quechua; it is called the Crown of Tunupa.

Legend has it that from there Virgins of the Sun who broke their vows of chastity were thrown to their death. Some locals still call it *horca del Inka,* gallows of the Inka.

He sees early climbers going up the trails. The color red stands out. It's like life, he thinks, a lot of people go a little way up, then the paths thin out.

On its slopes the boy Ephraim systematically learned to defeat his fear of heights. There, on a ledge not far above where he stands, is Split Rock, his connection to the long dead Inka boy. Here he learned that reality is tricky stuff. It breaks its own rules.

He feels his fidgeting recede a little more. Peru and Lily, his soul tranquilizers.

He steps to the cash machine, slides his debit card into the slot, enters his password, gets the maximum, four hundred fifty Peruvian sols, about a hundred twenty US.

As the bills drop into the tray, he senses a presence behind him, too close for ATM etiquette in any culture. The shadow, the breath, the scent of cologne and carnivore sweat. He looks over his shoulder.

"You little shit."

The beefy face of the Briarpatch-shirt guy from the flight, jaw thrust out, hair sticking up, fills Ephraim's view. He backs up, braces against the edges of the machine. The man leans , a wet smile growing below his lit-up eyes. Ephraim folds the bills into his jacket pocket.

"Do I have your attention?" The man cocks his head, eyebrows raised.

Ephraim notes the callouses on the man's knuckles. Fist push ups on a wood floor. Martial arts.

"You and your asshole buddy put shame on me. Now it's payback time. Step away from the wall." He takes a step back himself, drops his weight to his hips, takes a basic fighting stance. Ephraim notes that the stairs down to the street are about three paces too far. He takes one tentative step forward, stands awkwardly, off-balance.

"What do you want?" he asks. The guy grins.

“I'm not gonna jack your funny money, little boy. I'm just going to get what's mine. A nose. Twist. For a nose. Twist.” He thrusts a hand at Ephraim's face, index and middle finger clawed. Ephraim wrenches away, ducking his head, lifting his hands ineffectually, weight on his left foot, right knee lifting to cover his crotch.

The big man's left foot comes forward, Ephraim's right foot slams down edge-first into the man's ankle. He feels it give. The guy's mouth opens and a sound like a boiled kitten squeaks forth. He doubles over, grabbing his leg above his suede and mesh hiking shoe. Ephraim circles carefully around, steps to the street, still watching. His assailant appears to be out of action. 'Eleven years in dojo,' he thinks. 'For one snap kick. Awesome.'

He turns on his heel, shoulders his Quechua daypack, peculiarly a French brand, and pulling his carryon heads past the plaza toward the bridge separating the center of town from the main ruins and the long road northwest through the Vilcabamba mountains. From behind, he hears the man call, strangely cheery, “Remember the attention?”

He lifts his eyes to the horizon, to the hills. Feels their serenity. Exhales. So he has an enemy. He has never had one of those before. He breathes the trouble out of himself and walks on. Downhill, the ancient fields; then the Urubamba River runs far through the Machu Picchu ravine down to the Amazon.

He looks up at the massive artistry of the Inka stonework, dark blocks merged as if melted together. Jean Pierre Protzen's ‘fancy terraces,’ looking down on everyone. “*We are INKA*!” he laughs to himself. Water braids itself in the acequia along the foot of the cliff, then jets silvery over an antique stone terrace.

He recalls what he read in Bingham Bonnaterre's paper. “The Inka loved two things: stone and water.”

His trainers scuff in the deep dust. Beyond are the purple terraces — *andenes* — holding up the fields still farmed by families to whom a sol, thirty cents US, is good money.

He turns down along a wall of great boulders crusted in orange lichen, past a diagonal flying staircase of protruding man-sized stones climbing to a plaza above, now a lot for municipal vehicles. A stairway for giants. Not a pragmatic access for farmers. Something important was up there once, unrecorded in books, unexcavated. There are so many questions.

The glaciers still gleam on Mount Veronica, *Wayka Willki,* on the west end of the valley, although higher on the slopes, shrinking. All around are mountains. He feels their protection conferred upon him.

Weathered wooden doorways crack open onto cryptic courtyards. He is wondering if his room in the mud brick house will still be there. He called in February saying he was coming. The owner said that he could rent the whole place. The family had mobilized upward to a new one.

He wonders what the rent will be. He has just over four hundred sols on him now. He can always get more from the…

"Oh lord." He left his ATM card in the machine. What he has on him is all he has.

Is that what the man meant by "Remember the attention?" He has been played.

The fight was real, but he underestimated his opponent, who probably has his plastic now.

He has what is in his pockets and that is all until he can get a replacement card. US banks do not send cards offshore, and couriers do not deliver except to a postal address and they do not exist where he is going. "Oh lord. I've got ten days maybe, barring imponderables, from being penniless."

Random Consumer Larva

Ephraim was broke, he would have to look out for his nemesis guy every time he went to town, he had antagonized Lily, and he had no idea what would happen at the Split Rock. But he was fine. This was where he belonged. Something big was going to happen here, one way or the other.

He rented the second floor of a mud brick house by an ancient acequia outside of tourist territory. He knew the owners of old. He dropped his carry-on and daypack onto the musty rat-shat mattress he could not now afford to replace, shrugged off his rucksack, swung open the wood-framed windows, peered up the hard-packed trail, past the black bulls, the patchwork *chakras* — fields — to Pinkuylluna, where his rock would be waiting. If change hadn't taken it. He steps out the door. Across the near quinoa field, an unrestored Inka terrace, built of heavy boulders, stood ten feet tall; the range of size, situation, color, and texture, spoke to Ephraim in deep voice, making him feel good. He was young, free, back in the land of the Inkas.

A hundred meters away, the man in the Briarpatch polo shirt spied on Ephraim through small, military grade binoculars. The big man frowned, poised gingerly on his sprained ankle. Did this kid have anything to do with anything, or was he just one more random consumer larva? He looked like a US kid and the target was a US kid.

The Ballad of Lily Tran

When Ephraim stepped out of the mud brick house the next morning, he had three fears. One, that the rock would be inert, or that if it wouldn't be he would, and would feel nothing.

Two, that he had been wrong all along, deluded, and all that inner peace was placebo effect.

Three, that he had lost Lily.

Actually, Lily was Fear One. She had wanted to come with him on this trip, almost begged. "I'll pay my way, I have plenty of money. From the acupuncture job." Her voice, raspy from a nagging strep throat, had a hard edge under the pleading. Supplication didn't suit her.

He had always given Lily whatever she asked, and she never asked for anything that didn't give him some form of pleasure. Mostly the greatest pleasures he had ever known.

The closest rival, and distant, was a mango he had eaten on a psilocybin 'shroom trip she'd urged him into. At the first bite, he'd thought, "A little green. I'll just take one more bite for Lily." The second bite he found himself taking led to another and then another. Then he was smashing the orange fruit meat into his mouth, müshing it into his face, he normally so fastidious, like a wolf wolfing down a faun, eyes closed, head filled with a wide blue sky full of fat white clouds spinning majestically overhead, bright sun swelling with each bite, filling the world with shining ecstasy from the tongue on out — he was laughing out loud, his head thrown back, ecstatic with mango.

That's as close as the world had come to the feeling of her arms going around him as he pushed into her infinite animal vortex, soon unable to distinguish between himself and her. Her breath in his brain.

This he stood to lose. She had told him of a new lover she had taken from her work as a student practitioner at an acupuncture clinic in Emeryville, a professor of some kind. That in itself wasn't much, she had always been open about her other boys and he had never minded, in fact it was fine. All he wanted was his share. But this was a man.

Lily dressed down on the street. Bulky clothes, knit hats and plain-glass specs. She knew what she did to men. When she walked in shorts and a lace top, you could hear hearts shatter like champagne flutes all down the block, men would moan out loud. In school she wore crisp plaid shirts and loose light trousers. She didn't need more. She liked sex and made no bones about it.

He was fourteen, she fifteen, when she came up to him one day as he sat on the school steps taking notes from a book about the Inkas and stone. "May I sit here?" she asked.

"Sure?" he said.

“I’ve been watching you. Did you notice?” No? He said. “You are going to be my smartest boyfriend. Sam is a jock. Bod like a rock. Eddie Farmer’s a charmer, a smile to melt your heart. But I think you’re different. You are the river that runs deep. I’ll tell you a secret.”

“What?” he said.

“I’m smart too.”

They took BART into Berkeley, walked together appreciating the architecture, guessing who lived inside the interesting houses, stopping for smoothies, letting their conversation wander. She made him feel comfortable, to forget about the problem of sex — he didn’t expect to have a girlfriend until his junior year, or to have sex until university. When he got home, he couldn’t remember what they’d talked about. The next day when they passed in the hall she gave him a sidelong glance and a subtle smile.

That day, too, he heard her name in gym. He tuned in as some of the basketball clique talked about her and her football boyfriend. “Sam’s balls deep into Lily Tran. He was on about it last night, hammered on Jack and ketamine.”

“Word. Gloria heard about it, and she is busting his balls.”

Later, he saw Sam exiting a classroom, rolling and swaggering, a complacent smirk on his ruddy face.

The next school day he saw Sam again, head low, looking like he was going to cry, Gloria pulling him along by the arm. He suspected that it wasn’t Gloria he was down about.

That night Lily called Ephraim’s cell as he practiced kata on the back deck.

“Hi,” she said.

“Hi?”

“I liked our walk. Can we do it again?”

"Of course?"

They chatted some, and she brought up the Sam thing. “You heard about him and me?”

"In gym."

“Exactly,” she growled. “It’s not a secret, but he was boasting about it. That’s not kosher.” Then she sort of laughed. “But it’s okay, there are eleven boys with ripped bods around. There wasn’t much he could show me.”

"Okay," he said.

“But maybe there’s something you can show me.”

"Okay," he said, "what?"

“Your turgid raging beast of desire!”

This is where E. Arrowsmith’s subliminal joker came through for him. It disinterred something he had overheard his mom whispering to his father, they not realizing he was on the other side of the tree.

“You mean, my purple throbbing engine of love?”

“You got it boy. Next time, after we walk, let’s screw.”

Now, after two years of being the luckiest nerd-boy on the Orion Spur of the galaxy, Ephraim was afraid he had blown it. He remembered Sam Thornton’s miserable face when he had crossed Lily. Maybe he should have gone, “Yeah! Fantastic! Me and you in Peru! Start packing!”

But he had this secret. This he had to do out of view and alone.

Disparate Times
Pinkuylluna Mountain, Ollantaytambo

Ephraim knew the Split Rock was there and alive when he scrambled down the outcrop to the cactus-studded meadow. It was pulling at his third eye, a throbbing behind the bridge of the nose. The force field was intense and when he approached. he didn’t bother to mount the larger part, just leaned his palms against it and was taken into Ramram.

He found him eye-locked with a hunkering man whose stare made Ramram’s bladder let loose. Ephraim smelled the piss, felt the loincloth and the legs go warm and wet.

He had always counted on Ramram's composure. The Inka had always seemed so rooted in the earth.

Ephraim looked into those cobra eyes, that granite face, and knew that it was his turn to provide and not to take.

He offered Ramram a refuge within himself, his calmness. Ramram took it. When it was over, and Ramram had also seen through Ephraim's eyes — Ephraim took the Inka's sick shock into himself — he sat dazed, absorbing.

Who was that scary guy? Where were they? What was going on? What was this gut sense that there was something he needed to *do*?

Panting a little from the psychological exertion, he climbed onto the rock and closed his eyes for a rest he felt he deserved. Instead, Ramram came back, and Ephraim was sucked into a world of fear and confusion.

A face-painted figure with exploding dreadlocks leapt at him, grinning horribly. Three or four others crowded behind. The squatting man was there too. Ephraim felt Ramram's panic as he reached for the man's filthy tunic. The wild attacker raised an evil looking mace less than an arm's length away. It filled the sky. Then Ephraim was yanked out of Ramram.

Less than ten seconds had passed, Ephraim was back in his own time. He had tumbled off the rock. He got control of his buckling legs, stood panting, heart slamming at his ribs. What the sam hill had just happened? Was Ramram killed?

For all that, the first question was answered: he was back and the memories were more than real. Still, less vivid than at Machu Qolqa, where he and Ramram had been in the same place in different centuries. Now both place and time were different so there was a loss of sensual production value.

"Get it together, boy," he told himself in Lily's voice. "These are disparate times." He laughed feebly.

Ramram might be dead. Had Ramram's killer taken over the Split Rock?

CHAPTER SEVEN then

The Recruit

Ramram decided to go to war the day the Prince Urcon, heir to the Kingdom, retreated through Stone Spring village, deserting Qosqo for the safety of his father's mountain refuge.

He stood with his family and townspeople in the small village square, watching the Prince's jeweled palanquin rush through, the eight bearers breathless beneath the weight, their burden in his gold and finery leaning forward intently, eyes on the track ahead, not on the village he left behind. Hundreds of soldiers went before, a long ragged line of refugees behind, bent under the few possessions they carried.

A squad of spearmen split off, entered the plaza, pushing the crowd back with their javelins. "Silence," a scarred sergeant ordered, "Hear your instructions."

An officer stepped forward and addressed them thus:

"The Chanka armies will be in Qosqo within one moon. Sapa Inka Viracocha will lead his people and the mummies of his ancestors to safety in Shaqishawana above the Yucay Valley. When the mighty Inka people, beloved of Inti the Sun and Viracocha the Creator, are told by the omens that the Gods are ready, he will return with his armies and the Sacred City will be once again Inka. The Sapa Inka will pass here within three days. Be ready. Bring only what you can carry."

His friend Tuya took his hand. "Where will we live?" she whispered. "Now I will never see the Sacred City."

When they were gone, a lanky man wearing a white helmet edged with red and black and wearing a checkered unku, stepped from the shadows between the small local shrine of Inti and the house of the Pichqa Pachaca Curaca, the village head-of-five-hundred, with five other soldiers. He rapped the butt of his spear against the cobblestone road and the crowd fell silent.

"Sapa Inka Viracocha will not return to Qosqo," he said, and the villagers inhaled sharply at this blasphemy. "He abandoned the Sacred City to the invaders. So have six of his seven sons, including the Prince Heir, as you have seen. One son of the Sun does not run.

"Prince Kusi Inka Yupanqui will stand between the Chanka and Qosqo.

"You know of him. The last and least of the Sapa Inka's legitimate sons, he is not loved by his father. He was sent to the highlands to herd llama and alpaca, and to learn humility. He learned to endure. He was exiled to alien lands to learn that he is less than Inka. He learned the world. He was ordered into the mountain peaks in expectation that he would starve, freeze, or be meat for the big cats. He learned to talk to the Apus, the spirits of this land." The soldier offered them the opportunity not to run and to die.

Ramram had never struck anyone with anything. Anger was foreign to him. But he saw anger in the eyes of his father, and his mother, and Tuya, whom he loved. He saw the last of his king's entourage fleeing his kingdom. He saw the cool eyes of the officer rest on him, on them all, advising him to follow the Inka Viracocha, challenging.

His hand curled on empty air as if on the shaft of a macana mace. His heart thudded behind the bones of his chest. Some ground you just do not give.

CHAPTER EIGHT now

Where Is This Coming From?
Berkeley, California

Doctor Noe Zoe Kroeber leans into her computer in her culture tube-cluttered Berkeley apartment/laboratory. It is a hot night and she is in plain white underpants and a Pastafarian-themed t-shirt. Bingham Bonnaterre sent her the YouTube link. "This is right up your alley, Noe," he had texted, 'I followed a link about Inkas and this turned up.' She rarely gave time to anything outside her academic specialty, microbiotics, but Bingham was her only real friend at Beard College, maybe in the world, and knew her, so she gave the thing a try.

On screen, the gaunt haunted face of Nick Nieman speaks into the webcam:

> "This is We Live In You, reporting from the fringes of science, where speculation unsupported by empirical data takes you thirty-five years into the future of accepted scientific theory and a hundred years into the future of common sense."

Rain machine guns on a basement window to his left; thunder rolls.

> "All these stories will come together, fellow trekkers, they will mean something, the germs, the Sons of the Sun, the Twist, time and space, lichen, the One and the many, your gut, your heart, light and dark, this little jewel of vocabulary.
>
> "The Inka had a word, Pacha, that meant both time and place; you could not express one without the other. It also meant the earth on which you walked, the instant you were in, this planet, and the cosmos entire. It grasped perfectly spacetime, that elusive concept that made Albert Einstein the paradigm of genius. Every Inka farmer, every woman

weaving as she walked understood intuitively that location is duration.

"For the rest of us, place is easy to understand. It is where you are. Time? That's a little harder to close your fist around. What is time? Is it made of anything?"

That scrawny kitten is back, trying to climb up his knee. The wet fur is an exploding mess of dull black with one orange eyepatch. It looks filthy. The animal's mouth is open but no sound comes out. Maybe the green eye is blind.

He scoops the persistent varmint into his lap. For the first time, he inspects it in detail. The feline looks back, mouth wide. Finally, out comes a minuscule audio signal. It sounds like "Kwee." He shakes his head.

"Okay. I'm a crank, a conspiracy theorist, a pseudoscientist. You don't want to believe me. It could cost you your marriage, your job, your last friend. But most of all, you don't want to believe me because you don't want it to be true. But believe me or not, your great grandchildren will be brought up in the truth that: (echo effect) We! Live! In! You!

"'We" is the global holobiome, the prokaryote overmind that is the dominant living entity of the planet earth. In pure carbon biomass, around five hundred petagrams. That's a gigaton, Two point two trillion pounds. Nevermind. It's a lot of trucks."

"Wait a minute. What is this?" Noe is sits up straight, fists on her knees, alert.

"It is a being of immense awareness and it lives inside of you, all over you. It is your contribution to the larger system enlivening the planet and it is called your microbiota. It is the bacteria and archaea in and on your body.

"While mankind looks outward, deep into the galaxies, in the hope of, and in the fear of, not being alone in the cold dark emptiness, wondering how an intelligence not our own would present, we live in utmost intimacy with a sentience so immeasurably more profound than our own that we cannot recognize it though it lives within our own bodies, within our own brain, and everywhere around us."

"It lives on your skin, on the surface of your eyes, in the crack of your butt. It concentrates in your mouth, people; in your vagina, sister. It is thick on the surface of your eyes. Alphaproteobacteria are found in the human brain. We do not know what they are doing there.

"But its headquarters are in your lower intestine. Did you ever get a 'gut feeling' about something? That was the Presence sending you a dispatch from beneath your wood-burning little brain. Letting you know what's up."

"What?" she breathes. "Who is he? Where is this coming from? This frightens me," she whispers. She is a microbiologist and mycologist, esteemed in her field. She is a full professor at the University of California, Berkeley, a research scientist at Beard College, has three PhDs, publishes at least twice annually in the best journals, but only the mildest, the least disturbing, of her material. No one else knows how deep her research has taken her, the implications. "I was hoping I could publish posthumously, but this man is going to force my hand."

This is a post, not live. Noe pauses, switches screens, does a web search on the title, then gets a name and tracks his academic record.

Now she swipes back to Nick Nieman. His hollow-cheeked, hollow-eyed, stubble-chinned face stares back at her from beneath the brim of a pink and orange camo hunter's cap: lonely, stoic, determined, oak-hard, humor crow-footing his eyes, quivering at the corners of his mouth.

The weird-eyed kitten has climbed the monitor. It's one good eye eclipses the camera.

"This asymmetric little intruder is contraindicated by my medical professionals and has got to go." He picks it up by the nape, goes off camera.

"Dear lord," she marvels, "he has not even a masters. Where is he getting his theoretical insight? Is anyone taking him seriously?" She wonders. "Is there someone else whose work is more advanced than mine feeding him results? Could we collaborate? But no, there is no one, I would know. Just as everyone in the field knows that I am out in front. They just don't know how far."

She clicks the start arrow.

There is nothing on screen but a dark corner with shelves of jars full of things no one will ever use. A door slams. Nick is back.

"Wet out there. Feline-free in here.

"That's it, my bored, lonely, spiritually hungry, emotionally isolated, intellectually wired colleagues. That's all you can take for tonight. No need to remember, there will be no quiz. I'll be back with much more. Because I have not merely been digging around on the web for grisly gobbets on which to feed. I have been there.

"This won't mean anything to you unless you live in or around the Olympic National Park, in say, Port Angeles, Washington, from whence this comes tripping from tower to tower, but I am the only one known to have gone into The Twist more than twice, and to have come back out. I will tell you what I found there. What found me."

The tiny cat is back, trembling. He domes his two hands over it, giving body heat, looking down, expressionless. There is a scaly redness under the hair on his wrist.

"This aminal is crawling with bacteria and no doubt archaea. Who knows which side they're on? Not mine. Do cats carry scabies? Okay, I'm done. Class dismissed."

He leans toward the keyboard, hesitates, stands again. He knocks his fists together, bows his head.

"It is more than allergy. I am afraid of cats. I have ailurophobia. Not entirely irrational, a cat killed my sister. I saw it. I was four. She tried to pick it up, it scratched and bit her. In the night, a red line ran from her wrist to her heart. Blood poisoning. She died on the way to hospital."

He goes off-stage, comes back with a ratty old bathrobe and an oval plastic wash tub, stuffs one into the other, drops the cat into that.

Nick stares at the camera, deadpan. There are a few long seconds of dead air time.

"I don't care if no one out there is watching. Even if that's a lie, it is almost true. But I am going to tell this tale. Peace out."

Noe sits in her room alone staring at the screen saver. This freakish dispatch from a self-professed crackpot has shot her life in the face. His promise to his followers, whoever they are, is a threat to her. He has stripped her naked. His screwball theories are her scientific truth, and that truth is her professional secret, one she has no intention of revealing now, and possibly not in her lifetime. To do so would destroy her career, and if taken seriously, bring dangerous people to her door. Her hands begin to tremble.

"Ah, just relax," she mutters aloud, "No one will believe him, and none of my colleagues will watch him. It is beneath their dignity." But something whispers in her mind, saying what if someone does hear him, and takes his cue, and publishes first? "They would be Darwin, I would become Alfred Russel Wallace."

The NSA search subroutine coded for the NTT notes a new IP address viewing the WLIY site for a second time. The owner is tagged but triggers no red flags.

CHAPTER NINE now

The Moon Hung

The moon hung over the smokey crag like...oh who gives a damn how the moon hung? Everyone skips description anyway. Who did you think was writing this? God? No. A writer. But not some chain smoker in New York City making crap up. I was there then. As far as 'there' or 'then' go in this history. I saw it. I still see it. Without me, you would never know. So:

Flashback
Ephraim's Dad

It was the end of summer in Ollantaytambo and they were about to go back to the states. Ephraim was ten years old and had linked up with his Inka familiar Ramram seven times. He had not told his father and didn't intend to, but he had questions and his dad was likely to have something useful to say. Ephraim collared him in the garden behind the mud brick house they rented, next to a massive unrestored Inka wall.

"Hey Dad. What is this stuff growing on this rock? I see it all over. Is it moss? Fungus?"

"Partly. It's lichen. An interesting life form, but peculiar. This orange pinwheel is *Xanthoria elegans*, Elegant sunburst. Why?"

Ephraim's father was foursquare against time travel. He said the universe would implode if you added or subtracted one charmed quark. He also said there is no such thing as natural law, that physics is a local phenomenon, entropy does not drive the cosmos, knowledge is a state of mind, and truth is a series of fads.

But Ephraim (who had not mentioned his outré experience to his dad and didn't plan to) hadn't gone anywhere physically anyway. Still, being crazy made more sense than being right.

Nevertheless the sunburst circles of flaky stuff found on all the rocks, living on and in the graceful, enigmatic, Inka walls still seemed to light up and pop out at Ephraim ever since his first flip into the Inka boy. And the Andean world around remained animate and was watching him. In a kindly way, but watchful.

He decided to call his dad in on the question, carefully. You never knew what the sarcastic old crank would turn up.

His father was just an economic consultant, brought to Ollantaytambo to help the town get more money, but his mother said he was also what he used to hear as a "Polly M'Ass." This turned out to mean polymath, a guy who knew a lot of things about a lot of things. He would have been a Triple Nine had he paid the ten dollar annual dues.

"It seems...strange."

"Well...'son'...it is strange. For a life form. Not animal, not mineral, not vegetable. They aren't of the kingdoms eukaryote or prokaryote. They are a *composite* organism. Fungus and algae. And/or cyanobacteria." His father removed his glasses and cleaned them with his shirt, pretending to consider. "They do some plant things, like feed by photosynthesis, but this guy here on this stone — these three guys, from the look of it — aren't plants. Are you following this?"

"Not a plant, 'Dad.' Give me the short story first, please."

"Alright. Lichen is old. And strong. And ubiquitous. You phlorp 'ubiquitous?'" 'Phlorp' was his dad's baby talk for 'to totally sort of get it.'

"It's all around everywhere." Ephraim scored high in vocabulary. You had to if you wanted to survive and thrive around Dad.

"Yep. Desert, tundra, jungle, mountain, forest, field. Blowing in the wind, attached to nothing; those airborne lichen are called epiphytes. Lichen lives inside solid rock, in the Arctic and Antarctic, in alkali deserts, in toxic slag, in clouds, in outer space. In fact, your sunburst here is a space traveller and one of the most all around everywhereiest of them all. Lichen is tough and curious stuff. Science doesn't really know how to classify it. Can I do the long story now?"

"Okay. But don't expect me to pass any pop quiz."

"Deal. All Right. Symbiosis! Fungus can't photosynthesize nutrients, but algae can. Alone in the world, algae face many dangers. Under the shelter of a fungus, they are protected; and fungi also bring water. But lichen is greater than either and both. It emerges, like consciousness emerges from meat. Bear in mind some fungi are hallucinogens. Mind-enhancing.

“A lichen is — snap to, Ephraim my son, this is the heart of it — an emergent of a symbiosis between a fungus, and either an algae or cyanobacteria. Or both.

"Fungus alone is a self-contained microcosmic ecosystem. Algae are undefinable. Cyanobacteria are the only photosynthetic bacteria able to produce oxygen. So. We have these anomalous life forms working together to create an organism having properties transcending any property of its component organisms, sometimes reproducing sexually, sometimes not. Some types can fix nitrogen, some not."

"Cyanobacteria? That's the stuff that killed off everything a long time ago and made air?"

"Right. The Great Oxygenation Event."

The two of them leaned toward the heavy, faintly convex wad of pink rhyolite, with its fields and badges of flake. His father turned his square, porous face to him. His breath smelled of Tic-Tacs.

“Lichens are a holobiont, collaborating with yet another level of participant, the vast and mysterious microbial world. Bacteria, archaea, sometimes viruses. All working together in a synergistic dance of mutual support toward an end that science does not yet fathom. It may generate advanced intelligence. Am I going too fast? Too far?"

"I'm just letting it wash over me, Dad. Like music?"

"Got you. Okay. Remind me to ask you what you think of when you think of music. So I'll wrap it up. Lichen may be superior to you and I, son. So be careful where you sit, you may be butt-schmooshing your future boss."

Ephraim just rolled his eyes. But he wondered. On that rock, was he *working for lichen*? Is that why it sent him to visit the Inkas?

Shortly after, his father's six-month contract completed and they returned to their current home in the District of Columbia. Before, they had lived in Kyoto, Qatar, Burkina Faso, Port Moresby, Baton Rouge; after the return they relocated to Pleasant Hill, California.

Ephraim went back to the USA obsessed with the Inka and other pre-contact Peruvian civilizations. America was boring but it had libraries. Lichen, superorganisms, and the nature of time also interested him. He knew he would go back to Peru.

His father slapped him on the back. "I don't know what happened to you down there, but go get 'em, sport. When the revelations stop, so does life."

Flashback
Lily and the Assistant Professor
Ten days before the landing in Lima

Lily Tran liked to audit adult classes. She had been finding avenues of entry since she was twelve, often based on social engineering. Despite his minuscule web presence, she tracked the author of *Rumimuqu* to Beard College, got his class schedule, found that the school accommodated young visitors, got on the class list as an asterisk.

After her first class session welcomed as a high school invitee, she stuffed her bulky gray hoodie into her book bag. Now in a low-cut lace-trimmed jade green tank top, she leaned over his desk as he stuffed papers into the burnt orange llama wool carryall he used as a briefcase. She laid the stained and dog-eared copy of his paper down flat, then, smiling shyly but brightly through her meshed eyelashes, snapped her fake California 18-year-old ID on one side, and a business card with her name and the logo of the Emeryville Happy Heart Acupuncture Clinic at which she practiced, on the other, facing him.

"You are not unappreciated in the world of amateur Inka aficionados," she told him. "Your opening line, *The first thing to know about the Inkas, is that nobody knows anything about the Inkas*, hangs on the bedroom wall." She didn't say whose bedroom. She indicated the business card. "The first puncture session will be on me." Now *there* was a demi-entendre or two. "Please come," she piled on top. "I hope it won't be too hard for me to fit you in."

He admitted later, in his cramped North Oakland studio apartment, that he had been worried. He was shy with a new woman, so often panicked on the first try. "Well, that's over now," she said. "When I flipped you on the table and saw the topology of your trousers I knew we were going to catalyze well. I said to meself, 'we'll be screwing by the weekend.'"

A few orientation sessions later and she was wing-manning his annual jaunt to Peru.

Nick in The Twist

"My first time in the Twist, I walked out with a naked woman of gold and a classic mystical experience. The second time I met the priest of thunder, lightning, and storm. I knew I was being called to a mission, I just didn't know what it was."

Nick Nieman leans back in his swivel chair wearing a plaid hunter's hat, backwards. There is a clot of spiky fur stuck to his shirt below his chin. It seems to be breathing. *Also Sprach Zarathustra* is hamming it up in the background. You may know it as the prelude to *2001: A Space Odyssey.* Nick speaks to the camera.

"My dad was a logger, a topper, at the pinnacle of his trade, but the logging economy collapsed in the seventies, and he was working as a choker setter when a steel cable lashed back at him, another man's fuckup, and sliced off the top of his head.

"Carlos — 'Chuck' — Nieman, born Nadie, was Atticus Finch to me, the best of dads, the best of men. Once, when I was ten, he took me hiking back in the Olympic Mountains behind Port Angeles. At a fork in the trail, he pointed out a jagged boulder, frosted in lichen and moss, and said, 'That's the gateway to the Twist, Nicolas. Back in there, nothing is the same. Men go in and don't come out.'

"I asked him, 'Did you ever go in?'

"He goes, 'Once. With Hank and Stan Wilson. The mountains change as you walk, and the river runs wrong. You were walking west in the morning and suddenly you were facing the sun. Compass worked, but that didn't help. And sometimes your partner didn't see the same land you saw.'

"'Did you see anything in there?"

"'I saw a great stone fort built by some far gone people, no one knows who they were. They say it is never in the same place, and some people never see it.'

"'How did you get out?'

"'That's hard to say, *Niño.* I think the place just let us go.'

"'Will you take me there someday?'

"'I might. But never go in alone, always go with someone who has been there. And never go in three times.'

"So when I was fourteen and Dad was dead, I got summer work tree thinning down by Forks. In the crummy on the way home, I heard the word pass between two boys from Sequim, and I talked them into taking me up there in trade for a hammer-lock double-barrel sixteen-gauge shotgun my mom's dad left us.

“So we go in. We passed the landmark rock and hiked in up a trail. Sure enough, after half an hour, the path that we had seen going way up a rocky grade, was suddenly and without apology going downhill. But the real proof that we were in the Twist was, the river was still flowing the other way. Up.

“On a rocky drop overlooking a meadow we stumbled into this looming sawtooth wall of great black boulders fitted without mortar, standing sixteen feet high, the corner pieces standing on end, overgrown with doug fir, cedar, madrone, and scrub. The roots try to pull the stones apart, but they can't.

"Jack and Wilmer stayed back, they were, like, cowed. I climbed right up a jumbled stone staircase behind this hulking gateway, risers made for giants, onto the brush-choked first level, and I could see two more levels above. So I go up top. It's overgrown up there, by burdock, purple thistle, goldenrod, Queen Anne’s lace, rust weed, yellow bushes I don’t know, maybe scotch broom. Devil’s club. There were disintegrating foundations of buildings. I go nosing around, kind of stunned. Then I see something shiny.

“In a crack between two stone blocks there’s this metallic glint. I pry it loose. It’s a two-inch tall naked woman, hands folded between her breasts, vulva cloven, hair combed straight, very simply made. It looks like gold. I do not tell Jack or Wilmer. It throbs in my fist with a pulse that warms my sinews and nerves down into my gut. She’s in my pocket now. I don’t show her around.

“Back to the story. It was then that my innards seemed to melt, and the top of my head to rise and spin away from a point above the bridge of my nose, and the whole landscape of forest and mountain to be limned in shimmering points of color. The world was like filled with light, and with a presence that resonated to me directly. Like I was sung to. It wasn’t celestial, it wasn’t from on high, I wasn’t Saul on his ass to Damascus, it was from the earth itself.

"And a hard fist inside my, Nick Nieman's, being, one I had never known was there, opened up wide, and light came into me and filled my skull and veins and synapses.

"I looked down at my two hiking partners and understood that I had never liked or trusted them, that I had thought them dull and angry men. I saw that they were just afraid, and alone, and crying inside.

"Well, I recoiled from that insight, lest their misery enter and infect me, and then a key turned and my heart opened. For an endless instant there was no me, no Nick Nieman, no borders or boundaries, no fear, only everything just as it was, perfectly placed. I saw ants on the leaves, I saw beetles and millipedes down in the boulders of forest loam at my feet, I saw plants and insects and birds intermeshed in intricate harmonies, helping one another to flourish in flawless equilibrium. There were tears, all warm on my face. I go, 'Dad. Dad. I get it.'

"Don't ask me what I got. That was then.

"Jack and Wilmer called from below, they sounded...uneasy.

"Now I call it The Presence. It departed quietly, no fuss, like it was just going to the kitchen for a glass of water. I came down from the fort, every footfall perfectly placed, and the two white faces looking up at me were just me in a different form and were full of secret ecstasy.

"They were trying to hide a rising panic. They couldn't find the way out, nothing was familiar. I kept my mouth shut, I was sure that they'd be fine. I felt that I could have slept all night in a cold rain in total comfort and peace.

"Twenty minutes or so — it was hard to tell — later, just when panic was becoming irresistible, the Twist let us go. It's like that.

"That overgrown ruin had entered into my psyche and filled me with a sense of mystery, of twilight beauty, of a desire to know. I couldn't bring the transcendent aspect of the experience back with me, that's the very nature of the mystical. It evaporated with every downward step to town. It would not fit into word or concept. But it changed the heck out of me.

“So I major in history, Western Washington U, Bellingham, and there I blunder onto a photograph of Sacsaywaman, the archaeological park above Cusco, Peru, and I dig that what I crawled around on in the Olympic National Park was indisputably Inka. So I study Inkas.

“I get my batch, work my way up to assistant manager in...a job...to support myself and my disintegrating mother, now with the angels. She always wanted to ride a Harley. I go back in. Second time. I found the fort on the second day, set up camp on the top. I would squat for a long time, fingering that lost-wax cast gold Inka princess, consensually. Waiting for something to happen. Then, chilled and cramped in the joints, I'd get up and pace for a while.

“Psychological blindness is pretty common if you know how to look for it. I lose things, search for them obsessively, give up, then, months later, find them in the first place I looked, exactly where they should have been.

“There was at one of the zig-zag corners in the top terrace, deep in a bed of bracken, a jagged stone column, lichen-thick. I walked by it six-seven times before lit up for me, glowing through the ferns, thirty paces off. I mean, it was suddenly obvious, and I felt a need to lay hands on it. I did.

“A crazed crowd of wild, hand-waving, feather-headed men, masked and dancing and chanting dithyrambically materialized around me. The present world was dim and far away, this one was in my face.

"I was pulled into the point of view, the living body, of someone there. Someone who was stoned out of his mind on some psychotropic substance that I would later recall as like the mescaline I had once taken in high school.

"From my studies I knew something of what I was seeing. I recognized the fan-feathered skull caps from the drawings of the embittered Inka artist Guaman Poma de Ayala. I recognized the architecture of the room as classic Inka. They danced around a child-sized golden figure, one hand raised, fingers splayed, the other waving a golden staff. I isolated one word chanted many times in the ceremony: Ilyapa. Later I found it in the books as the Inka lord of lightning, thunder, and rain.

"One of the priests, they're called villaqs, would sometimes come and stare straight into my face, intently, distorting in the weirdness of the drugs. When my point-of-view guy looked down at his own body, I saw that I was skinny with painted arms sitting in a circle of guys more or less like me, but bulkier, watching the madman ceremony. This went on for maybe forty-five minutes subjective time. It was overcast so I couldn't estimate it in Universal Coordinated Time. The skinny guy that was me is Kachoo, my Inka liaison and instructor. He began to talk to me, to himself, and something changed, like an anesthetic hitting.

"I could understand him, not in words, in some other medium. And he me. I began to answer though we had no common language, no common world. Something was interpreting for us in a form of comprehension I will get to another night.

"I went back that forbidden third time. Despite the warnings. The same thing happened, and this time that one thin, intense, dude, stoned again but alone in a stone-walled chamber, switched to looking through my eyes, and began to question me. He wanted to control my arm and head, I let him. He pointed to the camp stove, the LED lantern, my cell phone, the cargo pants I wore, the mosquito netting of the tent, my boots.

"I would name them for him. I said we communicated, but more of what we said to one another was like gibberish than not. Then he left me alone.

"I thought of the men who were rumored to have been trapped here, and I could see now how it might have happened. How many skeletons lay under the thick moss in these woods? Down in the root system of that conifer forest? I was afraid I would, as I was warned, not be able to get out.

"But it turned me loose. Then I knew we had a deal, this place and I, the Presence, and I had to do my part.

“Over the years, working with clues and books and web links, I have put together a working theory.

“Now I am the MC of *We Live In You*, pimping the theory that a bacterial superbeing, an ancient Inka and a modern American boy are plotting to reboot history to make the Inkas a global superpower, while Certainty, my guys, want to flow with, not against, the arrow of time.

"As for Kachoo, it turns out his name is 'Qachu' in Quechua. It means ‘skinny.’ He calls me Umu Nikniman. They think I’m a wizard.

“I’m a partisan on the side of science, and of sanity.

"This last ditty is called Anthem. ‘There is a crack in everything, that's how the light gets in.’ Naked gnosticism.

“I have a few followers. Most of you just like the weirdness, but I think a few people are beginning to take my riff seriously. Mostly on the east coast. I think some agencies are lifting their snaky heads. Bub, if there is a super-intelligence in their world, much less in their very bellies, they need to know about it.

“But some of you are standing in that thin shaft of light. For you, I go on.

“And maybe there are those out there who have been where I am and past and know more. Who have taken this further. When the time is right, will I hear from you?"

He hooks his finger into the tab ring of a can of high-end filet of tuna. It makes a distinct pop. A piebald blur streaks between his feet then climbs his leg.

CHAPTER TEN then

The Appreciation of the Scout
The eve of the Chanka War

The ghosts of smoke were closer. Ramram and the scout, if that's what he was, labored up the grade, the power from that rock slipping away.

"Name?" the ragged man demanded.

Ramram told him. "And yours?"

The man considered. "Alder tree. You don't look like a tree. I'll stick with Q'urpa." Ignoring Ramram's question.

"I go to another Pacha," Ramram ventured. "A hamuq Pacha, a time that hasn't happened but will. Pachamama takes me there."

The scout eyed him sidelong, unreadable. "And?"

"And it is full of Inka things, once great, now built over by some other people. Strange people I have no words for. Inka walls covered by their ugly buildings. The air smells bad."

"Chanka things?"

"No. Not like anything in this Pacha."

"So. There is a world in which the Inka, not the Chanka, once ruled."

They strode on, Ramram waiting for some argument or scorn, getting silence.

They came up through the first scattered defenders, men digging a latrine with bent-blade *lampa* shovels, and women looking for fuel for cooking.

Above, a line of helmeted men spread like wings along the crest, flanking a cluster of luminaries gleaming with gold, precious fabrics, and rare feathers.

A check-tunicked officer broke off and strode toward them, shoulders rolling.

Ramram glanced toward the scout to see how he would react. He didn't.

A few paces off the soldier hesitated, almost tripping over himself, then stood, mouth working. The scout walked on, and the guard backtracked, stumbling. Heads turned their way as they neared the line. A tremor passed through the crowd, like the onset of an earthquake. Ramram saw it ripple through, heads bobbing, feathers and shields shaking as if the earth was uncoiling under them. Voices clucked in hushed alarm.

The scout led Ramram straight at the line of armed men. It parted as if the two of them carried some hideous plague.

'*Achachaw*,' he thought, 'I'm with the wrong guy to be with with.'

Frantic murmuring rolled through the crowd ahead of them. Men in opulent robes threw themselves to the dirt, cringing.

An assembly of even more gaudy functionaries sprinted toward them, waving vivid standards on long poles, and a careering palanquin canopied in shiny scales. Pikes of gold, still lethal, flashed. They stampeded directly to where Ramram crouched, turning to run. The scout gripped him by the shoulder and stood stoic, waiting. The on-comers swung out left and right, and fell to their knees, eyes down.

'These people really know how to appreciate a scout," observed Ramram numbly.

Majestic men bowed before them, plucking at their eyebrows and blowing kisses. As far as he could see, men abased themselves in a vast field of lowered heads. Servants, eyes averted, took the worn club from the stocky, silent scout's hand, took his stained cloak, pulled his grubby tunic over his head, removed his loincloth. A silken breechclout was threaded onto him by a woman of breathtaking nubility, a sumptuous unku anointed with cryptic tocapu from neck to hem pulled over his head. A cloak of tiny golden feathers was tied around his shoulders. A circlet of gold with three black-and-white feathers in a triad was set on his forehead. A golden battle-ax topped by a spray of feathers placed in his left hand. The scout was transformed. The spectacular litter was lowered for him, but he waved it off. He turned to Ramram, who stood mesmerized.

"You wanted to inform the *Inkap sapay churin* of something?" There might have been the ethereal hint of a grin on the transmogrified scout's lips.

"Um. The Prince? Does he know you?" Ramram had a feeling that he had understated the case.

"Q'urpa, meet Awqaqkunap Apo Mayta," the scout said, introducing a towering lord wearing armor of small golden rectangles over an unku of red and white squares, and a skull cap with an ear-to-ear fan of scarlet feathers. "General of the Armies of the Left. Apo Mayta, tell Q'urpa, whom I now pronounce *Wakacuraqa*, who he has been prattling on to."

The general tilted his long bronzed face, cheekbones like sling stones, narrow eyes, and whispered confidentially, "He is Apu Kusi Inka Yupanqui, Son of the Sun, soon to be Sapa Inka of all the peoples of the world, or, with the rest of us, dead."

Ramram took a knee, bowed his head, tearing at his eyebrows and making the kissing motion he had seen from the others, hoping it was appropriate for whatever he was supposed to be. "Apu Yupanqui," he said.

"I have *willay,* instructions to impart," Kusi Inka Yupanqui said to his general. "Bring the Apus to my tent." Then, to another ranking officer, "Get this man dressed and armed according to the rank of Pachacacamayoq, with tocapu indicating that he will locate, identify, assess, and index waka according to their respective degree and nature of Kamay. Situate him within fifty rikras of me until otherwise notified. Arrange a body of men capable of finding and moving rocks of up to *pisihatun rumi* magnitude. Report."

An official, wearing a white unku with tocapu'd waistband and gold diadem from which sprung a gleaming stem tipped with a flashing sunburst, escorted Ramram to the top of the hill. "Please wait here," he said, and called a bevy of subordinates to his side, giving instructions. The youth Ramram now had the equivalent of power over a hundred men and their households. But no men or households, so no power.

All around him were people of varying status, peering out across a deep shadowed valley toward another hill, on which Ramram could make out a ragged black mass of men crested by spears reflecting the lowering sun. Ramram gaped.

"Where is this?" Ramram asked a soldier standing silent.

"Here? This is Puka Muqu, Red Hunchback ridge. But everybody just calls it Hunchback Hill."

"And that?" Ramram queried, eyes on the other hill, pretty sure that he knew.

“That is the Chanka army,” the soldier whispered, “just waiting and watching. And more coming all the time.” The man had a lined, hawkish face. He tried not to show the fear in his eyes. “One of them. Just one of their pickets. Wiped out one of our patrols. Right over there.” He pointed to a grove of alders below, between the lines.

Ramram looked down upon the sacred city of Qosqo for the first time . He saw a low huddle of silver-gray thatch over fieldstone and adobe walls, a few painted, a few more impressive than the rest. It wasn’t much, even to a country boy. It looked deserted.

“It won’t happen again,” Ramram said. The soldier looked at him curiously.

Virgins to Save

At the top of the hill, twenty girls, not yet nubile, clearly drugged, stood in a line before a shallow trench. Behind them stood twenty soldiers with clubs. In front, priests, led by an emaciated, glint-eyed little villaq with an elaborate headdress and a gilded staff.

Ramram turned to the man beside him. Tears flooded the man's face. "What is this?" Ramram asked.

"It is a *Qapacocha* sacrifice," the man answered, "to Inti. For the war." He choked back a sob. "That one is mine." He lifted his dripping chin. "I am honored."

"Who is that?"

"That is Qachu, the Tarpuntay sacrifice priest. He officiates. He picks the girls."

Ramram stepped toward the Tarpuntay, a boney, bug-eyed little man, with an Adam's apple like a sling stone, wondering what the Kamay of a man with such power would feel like.

It felt like nothing. The Tarpuntay Qachu looked at Ramram looking at him and a shock of dislike passed between them.

The Prince Kusi Inka Yupanqui, Ramram's former piss-pulling scout, stood in a clutch of generals, gesturing at the Chanka army. Ramram strode across the distance, wondering what he thought he was doing. Eyes turned to him. A young officer stepped out, palms signaling him to stop. Ramram recognized him from somewhere. The Prince lifted a hand slightly. The soldier stepped back.

"Q'urpa?" the Prince said flatly.

"Apu Kusi Inka Yupanqui," Ramram said hesitantly.

"Ari, ari, ima?" Yes, yes, what?

"Have I proved myself as your Wakacuraqa at all, Apu?"

"Let's say that you have."

"That Tarpuntay, that priest. He has no Kamay. None at all. Inti does not want this sacrifice. He does not need it. You are his sacrifice."

"Me?" The Royal scout stifled a laugh, turned to the orderly. "Take the Tarpuntay's staff. Give him a spear. Cancel the Qapacocha." He walked into the disconsolate crowd on the crest.

Otoronqo Kuy

Prince Kusi Inka Yupanqui generated order wherever he went. The world organized in his wake. One chaotic cluster configured behind the prince to center on the tall young staff officer who led them directly to Ramram, who stood shifting his weight from foot to foot, still trying to absorb the situation.

"Lieutenant Otoronqo Kuy," said the officer, sharp eyes checking Ramram out head to foot, "I am assigned to you. This is Uma Camayoq Runku Runtu, director of the brother stone project. You will instruct him. Be efficient, time is short."

Ramram recalled where he'd seen the rangy officer before. He was the one who had given the terse little recruitment speech at Stone Spring village.

"That strong bunch will lift the rock onto the litter," the director said. "Those with the litter will carry it up to the HQ. Those following will spell them when they tire. That section will gather any surrounding rocks that may hold the original Kamay. You will check for presence and intensity as they pass. That man is a *Rumicamayoq* Stone Master. He will study the original rock, instruct the leaders of those four units, who will spread out across the hill looking for similar stones that might take the Kamay into themselves as wawqi brother stones. Any further instructions, Wakacuraqa?"

"Look for those green and orange growing things." It came to Ramram suddenly, more an intuition than a conclusion. The Rumicamayoq waved over another professional type whom he asked about the lichen.

The Rumicamayoq turned back to Ramram and pointed. "That's *kusma,* subgroup *Rumi Qara.* Rock skin. There are three kinds here. The black foundation growth is called *yana wisu*. But of course you know that." The director then called the rock-hunter *Uma Runa,* boss, instructed him to add kusma to his list of criteria.

Lieutenant Otoronqo Kuy returned his attention to Ramram. "The Prince orders me to tell you that he is not convinced that your rock has any power beyond that people tend to feel what they are told they will feel. He feels the same in its presence as he always does. Strong." Otoronqo Kuy, expressionless, looked into Ramram's eyes.

Brother Stones

Still dark. A soldier stuck his head into the opening of Ramram's shelter, "Prince wants you, Chief. Move it." He noted the tocapu on Ramram's unku. "Sire."

There stood Kusi Inka Yupanqui in all his dominion, backed by a host of servants and officials, some of them visibly trembling.

"Your stone is called Wanakawri," he said. "Replacing the waka by that name in Qosqo. My father took it with him. I am telling the army that it was *pisi kallpa*, weak, compared to this monster. If it is not true they will know to act as if it is. Good work, Wakacuraqa Q'urpa. Now get these brother stone placed where they'll do the most good. Otoronqo Kuy will provide tactical guidance."

Men were situating the stones, large and small, all around the perimeter of the slope leading to the weedy plain between the heights. Some were set upstanding, draped in military unkus that had been infused, to Ramram's certification, with the Wanakawri's Kamay, some fitted with spear, shield, and helmet. Ramram paced from stone to stone, testing their potency — he had learned to hold his hands out palms forward, as if feeling a fire. It helped a little and encouraged the others. He had the second-strongest placed at the mouth of the battleground-to-be, at the military crest of the hill he now knew was called Hunchback. Bodies lay on the low ground where the enemy leader Uscovilca's Chankas had killed Inka pickets in the night. The weakest brother stone were set at the other end, closest to Qosqo, where any last stand would be. The Wanakawri itself was to the rear of the crest by fifty rikras, on a gilded litter, surrounded by staff officers and villaq priests.

Otoronqo Kuy stayed attentively by his side. When Ramram hesitated in placing a group of mid-range rocks, the lieutenant pointed at a subtle dip in the hillside. “Low ground. They’ll be tired, they’ll channel there. Run stones up top on both sides.”

CHAPTER ELEVEN now

The Hour of the Wolf

"It is four in the morning, the hour when weak men die. The sick, the old, the injured, the heartbroken, the cornered, those too tired of themselves. Courage fails."

Nick Nieman stares out his one-by-two basement window at the lightning-blasted trunk of the madrone in his backyard, bark peeling from the trunk like the skin of a burn victim, in his left hand, a sandwich. He takes a bite, chews, swallows. Stares at the camera long enough to make you nervous.

Nick tips the monitor so that the webcam picks up the spiky-haired beast from between his hiking boots. It looks up, mouth wide, no sound. Nick's feet shift, he puts a plate down, peels a half-eaten slice of multigrain bread off a sandwich. "Tuna. It's fish. You...things...eat fish, right?"

The kitten's wide mouth finally emits a tiny pulse of sound. 'Kwee.'

"Kwee. Very informative. Now let me finish, okay? How the hell *do* you get in here?

"All right.

"So sometimes I don't have the guts to tell you everything. But. But what came to me tonight is this. From the Inka sneeze monk. There is a US nerd kid and a fledgling Inka communicating by means of the social media platform I call The Question. Those two kids in their different eras, struggling to understand one another? Might they end up sending a fleet of Inka marines up to Ohlone indian territory to colonize what is now California? Long before Fremont or Columbus?

"There it is. Thing is, I got clear picture through the eyes of my sneeze monk Kachoo that let me identify a specific location on earth. A mountain. I found it online. Pinkuylluna, Flute Mountain. It is in what is now a tourist town in Peru. Ollantaytambo. The 'Living

Inca City.' Where time and space run together, under the auspices of We Live In You."

He looks himself in his own isolated, eyes as he extends his left hand to switch off the camera. From somewhere off camera you hear a minuscule 'kwee."

"Damn. A rash. You gave me a rash."

Ambush at the Telegraph Bistro
Oakland, California
Back from Lima

Bingham Bonnaterre addressed the table in the near-empty bistro on Telegraph Avenue in Oakland, California:

"Byron Shrubby claims that the Inkas did not build the great stone walls, because they did build the fieldstone walls. Some more advanced civilization must have done the fine masonry.

"Using the same reasoning, we have proof positive that the agency that constructed Byron Shrubby's head could not have built his butt. Compare the quality of work, the necessary technology. Not until the most advanced contemporary genome-sequencing techniques has modern society been capable of synthesizing butt cheeks so perfectly symmetrical, so tightly fused that not even a diseased mule dick can be inserted into the crack. Note the albedo!

"Compare the head. Crude construction, substandard materials, fabricated of confirmation bias, bungling non sequiturs, blatant misdirection, lies, and reliance on the ignorance, laziness, and the predisposition to self-delusion of his followers."

Bingham knew he was foolishly drunk. He knew he couldn't trust any of the faculty in his department, these four least of all. He knew they didn't like him, he knew they held his faltering career in their hands, he saw the tight smiles, the sniper glint in their eyes as they watched him posturing like a gargoyle over his third Old

Smuggler scotch. He was pretty sure Mac was getting a cell video of this.

But he couldn't stop himself. He was lightheaded from being informed that afternoon that he was being promoted to Assistant Professor, and invited out for drinks in celebration. He leaned forward, eyes narrowed, spiking each of them in turn with eye contact. 'I'll just finish this rant,' he told himself, 'then I'll get a grip. But this is *funny*. Isn't it?'

"Clearly, the butt was designed and executed by an *advanced civilization* at least *ten thousand years* before the Inka, with *superior technology*. From Lemuria? Intergalactic engineers? Who can prove not? Conventional Science will deny, afraid of the truth. But the head is *undeniably* superimposed on the butt by a primitive and debased culture, the knowledge of their forebears long lost. I paraphrase a mystic poet and artist also ahead of his time:

"'Byron Byron spamming blight in the YouTube of the night, did the hand that made thy butt make thee?'"

He paused, looking around the table. Agnes Bodkin, his department director at Beard College, sipped her sauv blanc. Mac McFarland golf clapped in Bingham's peripheral vision. Forrest Coffin smoothed his mustache. Iris Lubbock, leaning far enough forward to flash a nipple ring, faked a smile.

"Very cute, Bing Bing. I must quote you to Byron the next time we meet. He will be attending the Rebirth Ceremony of my niece as her godfather. He won't mind, the mockery of the Establishment just makes him stronger. Ah, Agnes, wasn't there something you wanted to tell Doctor Bonnaterre?"

"Ah, yes," rumbled Agnes in her throat. "Bingham, we would like to make a small amendment to your curriculum. Your lectures on Joseph Campbell have been so popular among your students…"

Bingham's heart sank. His faculty, Postmodernist to his Historicist approach, had imposed Joseph Campbell's Monomythic perspective onto his lectures. Campbell saw all cultures as coming from the same primordial vision. Bingham saw each as evolving individually despite interaction, especially the Americans, and he saw the Andeans as *sui generis*.

"What there are of them, his students," muttered Mac McFarland from behind his stein.

'What there are of them ignore that part of the lecture,' Bingham thought.

"...that we would like you to replace your Inka Architecture slot with some material on your Andean cultures in light of the insights of Graham Hancock and Robert Bauval. If that goes well, you might work in some Frank Joseph, Michael Cremo, Immanuel Velikovsky, and maybe David Hatcher Childress." He looked her in the eye. Yes, that was a smirk. His eyes slid away from her thinly masked schadenfreude.

All 'alternative,' or pseudo-scientific, archaeologists, he snarked to himself, depending on with which bathroom you identify. He raised his shot glass to his lips, then lowered it unsipped. The alcohol rose acidly into his throat. He suspected that he had visibly paled.

It came to him now. He got it. As an assistant professor, he would be on tenure track. If he was refused tenure, he would be expected to resign. They were trying to drive him out, and if that didn't work, to kill his career. He wasn't sure why they didn't just fire him...maybe fear of civil suit? He also didn't know why they were afraid of him, but they were. Maybe his Doctorate from Berkeley. He was respected there, despite his failure to publish well. Both his papers that did go into ink were weak, and mocked when read at all.

He recalled the kid on the flight, and smiled within. He composed his expression.

"Professor Bodkin, you honor me. When you ushered me through the gateway of Joseph Campbell, I doubted that I would have the courage to descend through the circles to Childress and ultimately, inevitably, to the Web celebrity that I just roasted for you all, the world-renounced, wholly effable Mister Shrubby. But you have shown the confidence that I can dare this anabasis and survive to cry ‘Thalatta!’ Thank you for your belief in me. I will endeavor to make it so.”

Silence.

“Isn’t it ‘thalassa?’” asked McFarland, puzzled, looking to Agnes. She chewed her lower lip.

“Not in the Attic,” answered Forrest for his department head. He had some classical education.

“And not in the basement, where I’m going,” added Bingham, standing, now steady and strangely clear. He looked at Agnes. “I live in a basement, you know.” He laid a hundred on the table. He would be skipping lunches. “But I guess there is lower to go.” He walked into the night.

On Sunday his only true friend at Beard, Noe Zoe Kroeber, sent him a link. His Byron Shrubby rant was on YouTube, and getting hits.

Ruby Woo

Noe Zoe Kroeber slouched at her monitor in her darkened room, applying lipstick in the light of her web-camera image on FaceTime. She rarely wore the stuff. She was preparing for an informal meeting of Beard College colleagues to discuss Bingham “Bing Bing” Bonnaterre’s promotion to associate professor, so that they can deny tenure and wedge him out without losing their grant from the Betanzos Foundation for Andean Research.

"I'm a good girl, daddy," she said to the digital mirror, pouting out her lower lip. "I don't make waves. I go along to get along. I watch the way the wind blows. I am lucky they let girls like me be a really and truly scientist at all. Why do I even have a fwend like stupid bad-boy Bing Bing Bonnaterre? He's not even in biology!" She was included as an obligatory extra-departmental member of his tenure committee. One who would sit down, shut up, and go with the flow. But something inside her was hardening.

She aimed the crimson-tipped bullet at her mouth just as the screensaver came on, cycling her favorite bacteria samples, many-formed populations from the prokaryote universe. Her attention vanished into those images as she finished her lips, thinking, thinking. Her research was stalled. She was going in circles. How could a failing archaeologist help her with that? Let him burn at the stake.

She got up, padded to her closet, ruffled past the lab coats to the knee-length black dresses she wore off-lab, always with some small silver pin. She slid her feet into black mules, shouldered her canvas purse, lifted her khaki trench coat from the doorknob, walked down the steps and onto the street with a mouth of Ruby Woo red painted halfway across her cheek.

They met, as usual, at the Telegraph Bistro.

"Did you actually literally read *The Aesthetic Surface of the Tawantinsuyu: The Look and Feel of Inka Society*?" Agnes Bodkin, Department Head, asked, waving her shot glass. "Like, talk about non-substantive."

"I think the accepted term is 'content-free,' Forrest Coffin said with a donnish moue, downing his lager.

"I audited his lecture on Friday. It was hilarious." Professor of Archaeo-linguistics□ Iris Lubbock pressed two black-polished fingertips against her lips. "He announced that the topic would be David Childress. He looked like he was in front of a firing squad. His students started to heckle him. One of the girls — a very tasty ginger — started to cry. 'What happened to you Doctor Boney-Terror?'" Alice's voice going up two octaves, 'You used to be all smart and everything!'"

"And?" Mac McFarland leaned forward, fingers laced.

"And he asked the class what they wanted. Some guy in an Indiana Jones hat said he signed up for an education in Pre-Columbian Andean Architecture, and Bing Bing caved."

"He dropped the curriculum he agreed to teach?"

"Threw Cremo and Hancock to the wolves, went back to his boring old stones and bones."

"Then we have him." Agnes soft-clapped her palms together. "Insubordination, breach of contract, something. And he hasn't published anything worth lining a bird cage."

Noe took a breath. They had been looking at her strangely since she walked in, smirking even.

"Bingham just doesn't push past his data," she said. Now they were grinning at her for some reason. She pushed on. "He doesn't propound much, it's true, but everything he does propose is substantiated. He is out of step with your alternative archaeology approach, but he is respected in his field."

"Among the stodgy, convention-bound old guard," Agnes retorted, eyes narrowed. "I don't see them offering him a position though. And you don't think we see the contempt he has for our methods and conclusions?"

"We like you, Noe." Iris spoke slowly as if to a child. "Some of your ideas are a little — well, way — off the map, but your research is impeccable and you drip prestige, and you are kinda cute, but aren't you out of your territory here?"

"This is not my field. Perhaps it is not my place to intrude. But I do know funding and the Betanzos Foundation brings more than half of your departmental budget, and the anonymous philanthropist who is their founder requires an Andeanist — a real one — on your staff. He accepted Bingham Bonnaterre."

Forrest Coffin stirred upright, made a pursed-lip snigger, brushed his fingers along his cheek. "Are those extra lips for him? We know you have a 'soft spot' for him, even if you try to hide it. You tend to telegraph your inner self."

Noe Zoe Kroeber walked home alone, fighting off humiliation. They had been mocking her all evening. All those in-joke glances. Lipstick smeared on her face. But they couldn't dismiss Bingham outright, they didn't have the leverage. Noe would tell him so when they got together to watch Nick Nieman's next post.

She felt for him. His part-time salary forced him to choose between basic amenities and his annual trip to Peru. He always picked Peru.

Drat. Publicly pilloried for Ruby Woo, her chosen shade of lipstick. She would never live it down. In a petty world.

Extraordinary Evidence Requires Extraordinary Claims

Two nights later, Sunday, Noe gets a notification chime on her computer. Bingham sends a link. The Niemann character is back. She is deep in research and doesn't want to be distracted.

"But poof. This study isn't going anywhere tonight and you know it, Kroeber," she tells herself, "and just feel the *fear* bubble up at the thought of this Nieman demon. I hate fear. I haven't heard a word about him since the last post. Let's see what he has to say."

Nieman is sporting horn rim glasses and cupping a briar pipe in his left hand, unlit. Later Noe will detect from reflections that the lenses of the spectacles are plain glass.

> *"I call it The Presence. It is a set containing many sets.*
>
> *"Two of these collide. I call them Certainty and The Question. Yes, I will tell you. But first.*
>
> *"Somewhere around the year twenty-ten a short paragraph was injected into the ideosphere all over the world wide web, just to see what we would do with it. Who would scoff, who would shrug, who would take it and run. I took it and ran with it, all the way. The line was this. Did you catch it?*
>
> *"'The human body contains ten times more bacterial cells than human cells. Non-nucleated prokaryote cells in the human body outnumber eukaryotic — human — cells by 10 to 1.' Ten trillion cells of us, one hundred trillion cells of it.*

"That is, our bodies contain ten times as many cells that are not Us than that are Us.

"What does this mean? What are the implications? Well, one of them is, if our cellular composition is capable of generating the emergent quality of 'intelligence' — if our ten trillion cells can make us smart, might not, say, ten times as many cells be ten times as smart?"

'Good,' thinks Noe Zoe, 'Luckey's data has been exploded. This man's vaporing is harmless.'

"Well, that number has been busted. The authors just pulled it out of their ass. We have no way to know yet, too many variables, we are flailing in the dark. But kilo per kilo there are gazillions more of them than of us.

"Oops," Noe sighs, "He's off that hook."

"'Nah,' you say, 'our cells are organized, they're not.' But check it out. It is well known that bacterial cells do something called 'quorum sensing.' Less well known but more critical, they communicate through electrical impulses, ion channelling, potassium signals, far faster and farther than we knew a few years back.

"They do organize. They do unite. To become superorganisms that can act on levels far above what they are capable of as individual organisms. This is known. It is science.

"Every simple no-nucleus cell alone in its own dark mystery has a synthesizer on its outer wall that sends a signal into the world looking for a receptor protein on another cell. This signal molecule is called an autoinducer. You probably know them as pheromones, they remind you

of sex. But they are more like words. Which work like autoinducers and may lead to sex.

"Cells reproduce, and if enough of them crowd into a limited space, increasing population density, the autoinducers begin to strike, to bind to many receptors, and their own receptors are hit by many incoming signals. Then a thing happens.

"When they hit a threshold level, the lone cells recognize each other, unify, synthesize into a community."

"They agree to be a single organism. They agree to up-regulate their level of communication. They emit enhanced signal molecules that activate gene transcriptions designed to change behavior, to create new communal traits and actions. To become phosphorescent, for instance. They agree to make light. They become aware.

"Thus they permeate the world, then, and live in you. They speak to you personally, affecting your mood, your thoughts, what you want to eat, what you think you need, where you want to go, whom you love. They become you. They connect you with the rest of the world."

"And when this process reaches the planetary level, integrating every superorganism, there comes the fundamental urge of life, of being. That is, to do everything that can possibly be done; to fill all the nothing with something. This is the ultimate imperative. Is it the driving urge of the universe. It is the point of existence."

That kitten is back. She has imperceptibly infiltrated onto Nick's shirt, nuzzling his neck. He peels her free, lets her flow to the ground through cupped hands.

"The very point of existence."

"The very point of existence? A little too woo-woo mystical. Good." Noe tries to smile.

“And we begin to see it, some of us. This is the beginning of our wake-up. We begin to realize that the world is smarter than we think. The components of the meta-ecology speak to one another in tongues we just begin to hear.

"Yes, and so big S science, cautiously, coyly, like a virgin in a biker bar, gravitates toward the hypothesis that our microbiota might be a superorganism with unexplored potentials."

"Our microbiota is not only in us, we are in it. Because it is part of the global holobiome. Which is, in case you forget, the Roman Anima Mundi, the Greek Gaia, de Chardin’s Noosphere, P.K. Dick’s VALIS. It’s not like I’m alone in this.

“In 2016 the White House announced the National Microbiome Initiative to foster the integrated study of our stomach bugs across different ecosystems, funded at a hundred and twenty one million US through 2107. The Microbiome Interagency Working Group picked up the torch."

“Oh dear me! He knows the NMI!” Right now Noe feels as lonely as Nick looks. She rarely faces that in herself. She wonders if Bingham is awake. Should she call him? Would that test their friendship? Why have they never had sex? She knows he wants to but is afraid. Of what? Of her? Why?

“There is resistance, and there should be. You need to know that you can believe yourself. Extraordinary claims require extraordinary evidence.

“But then, extraordinary evidence requires extraordinary claims. Turns out, the biggest living things on earth are superorganisms. The Argentine Fire Ant Very Large Colony and the Oregon Honey Mushroom Fungus colony. The Brazil Leafcutter Megapolis. And they are finding out,

reluctantly, some scary things about coral reefs. We are discovering how smart "lower animals" can be. African Grey parrots know what they are saying, can count, make rasty jokes at our expense.

"Prokaryotes are the electricity of the planetary grid. They synergize and energize all other organisms. They swarm the ocean and land, congregate in the clouds, my people, drift through cold airless space, all at home in the airless freeze. And they all get together with the trillions of interlinked cells in your body to make the planetary hive mind. The other vast superorganisms, insects, fungi, coral are in synergy with them.

"I call the whole thing The Presence. It subdivides infinitely into others.

"Two of these star in the story I am going to tell you, if anyone out there is listening."

"I am listening, you inconvenient son of a pup." For a second Noe considers letting him know who she is, but lets that thought go. "That would get out of hand toot sweet."

"One I call Certainty. It is he who calls to you when you stand on that hilltop and gaze in wonder at the stars. Certainty wants off this isolated rock chained to its boring orbit, to find its counterparts, his sisters, lovers, compadres, out in the vast starscape.

The other, The Question. That is who sings to you when you stand on a hill and feel the earth breathing. The Question loves the planetary carbon cycle and wants to Save the Planet from the oncoming extinction event.

"Let's say that they can't both be right. There lurks a fight. An ancient Inka youth and a modern American are pulled into it, whether they like it or not.

"All in all, The Presence is a vast chorus of voices, a choir singing a lullaby. Listen: We Live in You in you in you in you...

"And with that, buenas noches, beautiful dreamers."

"'All right. Just amateur speculation, but taken to another level. My level, drat him."

Noe Zoe Kroeber sits on her duct-taped swivel chair, resigned now. The man somehow knows what he is talking about. She can only hope nobody else does. She opens a text app she shares with Bingham, clicks on the microphone icon to send a voice message.

"You were right to send this. The concept of the superorganism is growing on us, he is correct. The word was coined in seventeen eighty-nine. It's that old. It was used by an entomologist, Wheeler, in my grandfather's time, to describe the eusocial behavior...um...to explain why an anthill is so much smarter than an ant. But it has only been in the last ten years that serious science has opened its eyes to the idea of the superorganism as an intelligence. We have started looking outside our vertebrate-centric egoism for thinking beings. I mean, this isn't even science-fiction fodder yet."

She sends, thinks, starts another.

"The Gaia reference is invalid. This theory doesn't lead to a conscious geological planet, just to its unified microbial biofilm. 'Noosphere' was probably coined by Édouard Le Roy. VALIS is fiction. The rest is dangerously accurate. But what was that about the Inkas?"

Bingham comes online, the upper screen reads *typing*. Noe's heart soars.

"That's what got me here," he texts. "The inka thread. It's his primary theme." She smiles. "You know," he texts, "this guy could bring us together on a deeper level. The Inkas and the prokaryote noosphere connect. How likely is that?"

She takes a deep breath, exhales, speaks into the mic. “This man — this Nieman — has no real science. But he makes me, strangely, rather awkwardly if I may introspect, warm inside. He seems to actually get it. So if he makes you feel the same,” she smiles shyly in the dark, “we may revisit this with another post.” She feels herself blush. “He is — how did you once put it, so poignantly — crazy as a shit house rat. But then, if those in my own field could see my notes, so am I. He is the canary in the coal mine. If they don’t come for him, maybe they won’t come for me. But now I think: if he wakes them up, we are both dead. Or at the very least social and academic pariahs.”

She is faintly ashamed of herself. She gets up, pulls on a darkly printed kimono, sits again, sends a text.

“Why haven’t we had sex?”

She highlights the message and hovers over the ‘delete’ command, then leaves it there, breath in her throat.

No response. She sighs, stands, peers out the window at the bloody hue of the streetlights in the Berkeley night. ‘What is happening tonight?’ she asks herself. ‘This maniacal thing Bing sent me. This thing I said to him. The universe is losing friction.’

Her computer chimes a notification.

“Sorry. Piss,” he answers in audio. “We will.” His voice is rich with humor, honesty, and gladness. “What about now?”

“Tomorrow,” she says back. “This thing you sent has affected my equilibrium. Tomorrow.”

“Tomorrow,” he replies.” There’s a long pause. “You never know where a day will take you, do you, Kroeber? I kiss your brow. For now. Sleep deep.” She sees him go offline.

She smiles after him, then the implications of that video hit her. She frowns, rubs her temples.

The only other actual scientist who might have followed her reasoning killed himself in the USAMRIID cold room after filching a sheaf of critical research results from her Geo Metro. She was beginning to hope that their single conversation would not be tracked back to her.

‘What am I afraid of?’ she asks herself. ‘It is just scientific research. I could receive the Nobel prize. It is not terrorism.’

She stands, scans her data again. 'Why do I feel that they will kill me?'

In the NSA's S35, a subroutine picks up dozens of data points, recognizes the post as dealing with prokaryotic superorganisms and Inkas, links to the NTT, sends them everything associated with Nicolas Nieman, including the IP addresses of his viewers. Noe is flagged for the NTT, USAMRIID, and Homeland Security, but low priority.

CHAPTER TWELVE then

The Rainbow Sign
War Day

It rained hard on both hills. Ramram saw Cusi Inka Yupanqui, hands on his hips, gazing at the Chanka side. Ramram turned to look. There was a double rainbow there, backed by storm black. The sun came out.

Later, Prince Yupanqui stood with his generals, staff officers, and priests under a new standard, a square *wiphala* of stiffened textile on a tall pole: it featured, backed by dark blue, a brilliant rainbow.

The Forlorn Hope

The sun was in the west. The stones were placed. Ramram's father, Papa Chakra, and Waywash, were sent down into Qosqo with a widow named Chañan Curi-Coca who had refused to abandon her house, strategically placed atop the road into the city. A contingent went with them, carrying four brother stones on stretchers.

Ramram wondered whether he would see his father, or any of them, again. He wondered how many men shared that question about their people now.

There were shadows moving in the underbrush down the hill. Ramram spied the soldier who he had spoken to the day before. "Are those ours?" he asked.

The soldier looked at him bleakly. "Chanka. There's a ravine down there, just out of sight. And cliffs over there." He jerked his head to the left. "So the approaches up here are limited. The Chankas know them all. If we send people down to hold them, the Chanka kill them at night. Now their recon guys are massing at every point where they can get men up in force. We don't dare fight them, we can't afford the losses. They'll come through those points in columns, spread out left and right, form a line, and come for us."

"When?"

"Just about now. Look, our guys are going into formation."

Lines of Inkas cut across Hunchback Hill, all down to the slope. The Chanka army had gone quiet.

"Can we stop them?" A wave of stink came up from under the soldier's unku.

"That answer your question?" said the man.

Someone put a hand on Ramram's shoulder. He turned his head slowly. It was the lieutenant.

"Come with me, please," Otoronqo Kuy ordered. "You'll see something about men."

The lieutenant stood in front of the troops, a grizzled noncom at his side. "Listen up," he said. He had some trick for making his voice carry. "The prince wants volunteers for a *Wañuy Kawsay*, a Forlorn Hope. That's a suicide mission. If you survive, you and your family will gain rank, honor, and land. It will pass to your children. If you don't, and you probably won't, you will leave a good looking corpse, and your family will still receive those benefits.

"The mission is this: when the invaders come up this hill, you go forth to meet them. You slow them down just enough for us to get a contingent of brother stone bearers to the front. They are slow. Who stands with Sergeant Yana Puma?"

Ramram found himself stepping forward. "Not you," hissed Otoronqo through his teeth.

Around a hundred and fifty men stepped out, one by one. As the sergeant herded them away, in the corner of his eye, Ramram thought he saw Qachu the Sacrifice Priest flit into the little clot of men. With a spear.

On the Chanka ridge, drums slammed into voice. The scattered Inka forces double-timed to their assignments, shifting from one battle order into another. The brother stone carriers, about five hundred of them, picked up their litters, sagging with the weight of their stony burdens, and formed up behind Otoronqo Kuy. 'So he's leading,' observed Ramram.

Soldiers began to hustle Ramram back toward Kusi Inka's palanquin, a thickening of color in the ranks of men above. His heart tore at his ribs. "Ñakasqa," he cursed. He broke away from his escort and stepped in behind the formation. The lieutenant spied him, pushed through the ranks.

"*Not you.*"

"Lieutenant, I outrank you."

Otoronqo's grim face took on a suppressed smile, something like the Scout Prince's, Ramram noted. He was carrying a captured Chanka's five-bladed club. He handed it to Ramram. "As you say. Sir."

A fifth of a million voices rose from the enemy's hill. The land seemed to come alive and to avalanche down upon itself. Battalion after battalion, horizon to horizon, descended to the deafening drums.

This was it. War.

There were two weak points in the defense of Hunchback Hill, d□ips in the ridgeline that could ease the grueling two-hundred rikra ascent of the enemy. A low point to the west and a lesser depression in the center of the Inka line.

Kusi Inka Yupanqui, and doubtless Uscovilcas, the Chanka general, saw that the strategic advantage would come from the western approach, to take the smaller Inka force in the flank. Kusi Yupanqui had brother stone strong points at both, but he guessed that the Chanka arrogance would lead them to attack the hard way, straight up the middle along the central depression, splitting the Inka army. There he positioned his lead counter-assault battalion, and to the fore of that, the few volunteers of the Forlorn Hope, whose hope was to delay the Chanka assault just past the halfway point, where a rock upthrust would wedge the lead elements of the attack to give the Inka a minuscule and temporary advantage.

On they came, the enemy, crying battle despite the breath-stealing angle of the slope. Thirty-three thousand men end to end, six lines deep, howling triumphantly, conch horns blaring, spearmen in the van. The sky was dark with sling stones flying both ways. Men fell.

Ramram watched the Forlorn Hope trotting down the hill, then, as the enemy line broke around the pointed hump of rock, hurtle headlong into the mass. That was the signal for their own advance, two thousand warriors formed around the five hundred brother stone bearers and their guards, led by Otoronqo Kuy.

The Chanka line was meant to flow around all obstacles and form a spearhead impacting the Inka defense. Instead, the Chanka center scattered, the kamikaze band injecting just enough chaos into the equation to allow Otoronqo's company to hit the enemy vanguard before it could recover the lead.

The Forlorn Hope was cut down in a spray of their own blood, but they stuttered the chanka attack.

The waka stones were heavy. One of the litter bearers had stumbled, breathless, and Ramram took his rear pole. Ramram felt the elixir of the Kamay rush into him, and realized none of the bearers would have endured this far without that tonic.

The squad leader ordered "Now!" and they laid the stone down facing the Chanka line of advance.

Ramram saw the ferocious enemy, grinning with the lust for slaughter, hit an invisible wall. The stones were placed so that there was no gap in the force field, and he could almost see the air ripple as the Chanka ran into it and foundered. The stimulated Inka infantry struck. The Chanka corpses collapsed on top of the massacred Forlorns.

Ramram tried to force his way through the Inka battle line to get at the invading fighters but by the time any of the prince's soldiers tired of killing enough to give up their place, the Chanka line had passed on both sides. Ramram admitted feeling relief. For all their malicious intent those were just men, like him, being butchered in front.

From under the rainbow standard on the crest of the hill, the Seventh Prince watched the Chanka battle plan disintegrate, and his own unfold perfectly. The two wings of the enemy line separated, with the far ends in the lead and the ragged center trailing. The assailants on the far left and right ran into the heaviest concentration of brother stone rocks with their defenders, and, just as Kusi Yupanqui and his generals had dared to foresee, were slaughtered.

For a few breaths, Ramram thought the battle was won.

Hunchback Hill

The Chanka army has fallen into Prince Kusi Inka Yupanqui's trap. The main thrust is crippled, the wings isolated. But those two wings still each outnumber the Inka forces.

The broken center of the Chanka assault passes beyond the field of the brother stone stones, depleted of stamina, cohesion, leadership, and morale. Dogged from behind by the brother stone assault force and the meager survivors of the Forlorn Hope, they stagger over heaps of their own dead and wounded.

Then, beyond the reach of the accursed stones, their energy and coordination revive, their chins lift. They look on the weary Inka infantry with teeth bared and fire in their hearts.

To a condor's eye, the Chanka army curves like a scorpion's claws around the disorganized and exhausted Inca center. As the Chanka swarm up the hillside they pass new lines of brother stone stones defended by companies of Inca spearmen and slingers, but the attacking numbers are great enough to absorb the casualties inside the lines of stones and to send full divisions up around the outside of the cowardly Inka sorcerer stones. The Inka counter-assault is being enveloped.

The Chanka leader Uscovilca is lost somewhere in the blood-soaked center, but the generals of the left and right, Asto-huaraca and Tomay-huaraca, lead their wings howling toward Kusi Yupanqui's meager cluster of guards and officers marked by the bright canopy of his palanquin above.

Ramram kills his third man, clubbing the baffled warrior as he crawls over an enervating power stone.

The act sickens him. The killed man would never do anything again. He vomits until the coughing and spitting finally tapers off. He lifts his eyes. He is being left behind, his army and its enemies are a hundred rikras up the slope. He pushes himself to his feet, takes a step onto a tangle of bodies, one of which cries out in rage and agony. He stumbles to his knees, pukes again, crawls upward between the mangled men.

The stench and the sounds of pain and hate make a wall between Ramram and his ability to act, but he forces himself to stagger on. He is insanely thirsty.

He can see the Chanka fighters working through the imploding lines of Inkas on his front right. He lifts his macana, finds a spear that is not stuck into some body part, and follows the fight.

He sees the Inka line break, summons his guts and runs toward the breach just as a mass of Chankas come boiling through, mouths, nostrils and eyes wide.

He is alone and the enemy are charging. The leader, burly and fierce, swings a mace over his head, grinning. Ramram braces, lifts his shield, takes his last breath, as a platoon of Inca shock troops in quilted armor slams in from the right, spearing the mace man and sweeping the rest away.

Otoronqo Kuy grabs Ramram by his unku, yanking him up the hill.

"There were only ten of them," he grinds into Ramram's ear. "Don't be trivial."

Otoronqo and the battered remnant of his company follow the narrowing Inka center as it falls back toward the command post. Ramram gasps for breath, knees watery, but keeps up.

Ramram hears Asto-huaraca's Chanka left flank swarm up the slope where Ramram met his Royal Scout, over the drop where his Stone Spring buddies' bodies lie unburied, to come upon the Inka rear.

On the right, Tomay-huaraca's division thunders toward victory, seeing the depression in the hill that Uscovilcas' scouts had reported. This shallow gulch will shelter his troops from the Inca slingers and javelins, take him to the gaudy standards marking the Inka's last stand.

Prince Kusi Inka Yupanqui turns to face them, bronze-headed macana dangling along his leg.

Otoronqo Kuy's depleted company swings up below Kusi Yupanqui's stand, hooking around the mouth of the hollow as Tomay-huaraca's massive assault enters the other end.

"Haw," wheezes Ramram, "That's the low ground where you had me put all those brother stones!" Otoronqo gives him a savage grin.

The Chanka spearhead, so very close to the Inka and his few guards, have run between two lines of charged power stones. They are halted like ants in honey.

Rawboned Apo Mayta, Inka General of the Left, leads his reserve division from their ambush beyond the crest.

The remains of the Inka center run leaping over the Wanakawri siq'i rumi and the sister brother stone laid in line on either side, reforming into an arc of battle line before the Inka. The Chanka pincers run into the force field and are stymied. A few Chanka warriors get through to the Sapa Inka's position. Kusi Yupanqui dispatches them almost absent-mindedly.

Asto-huaraca's division finds itself channeled between rows of potent brother stones, met in the front and from both sides by the Inka rear guard, still fresh, armed with distance weapons. The Chankas are murdered by red-hot sling stones, javelins, the arrows of jungle archers invited to the party by Kusi Inka, once their guest in exile.

This is as Kusi Inka Yupanqui, who knows how to count heads, had foreseen.

Blood in the Eye

Ramram watched in a welter of conflicting emotions as the Chanka fought, with blood in their eye, until there was nothing left in them, including for sixty thousand of them, life. That many of their men lay dead.

Kusi Inka strode calmly downhill, through the clots of men still fighting, snagging Ramram by the shoulder as he passed. "He will be down...around...there. He will be dead or near dead, I know him. He will have been where his men were falling."

They came upon Major General Uscovilcas lying on his back clutching his spear. When Kusi Inka's shadow fell on him, he opened his eyes, pushed himself onto his elbows, looked disdainfully into the prince's eyes, snorted, then turned to Ramram. "You are the god damned wizard, aren't you?" The Chanka general used the word 'Umu.' He fell back, regretting what little life remained in his ravaged carcass.

"Umu?" said Ramram. "Wizard?"

"You'll see," said the Inka. "There aren't that many words for things."

The last spasm of the battle took place below, where the widow Chañan Curi-Coca's roadblock crew listened to the cheers of the victors on the hill above, just as the Chanka battalion assigned to curl around the headland and follow the supposedly unguarded road into Qosqo came into view.

Chonta, Waywash, and Papa Chakra's names were on the khipu, the book of colored knots, recording the slaughter that showed them what war is. Honor and privilege came to every veteran of The Widow's Stand.

On the hill above, as the clamor of the victors finally subsided, Ramram heard triumphant voices rise from below, signaling the final humiliation of the proud and invincible Chanka nation.

That day, the outcast Prince Kusi Inka Yupanqui took upon himself the title Pachacutiq, World Changer.

CHAPTER THIRTEEN now

Now Then

Ephraim's cell chimed — Colonel Bogey March — kicking him out of his reveries about food. He hadn't eaten in three days. The ATM card was still lost. His few remaining sols were saved for transportation and emergencies. He scrambled to remember where the cheap local mobile phone was and how to accept a call. The incoming number was Peruvian and unknown.

"Si?" he answered.

"See what?" He knew the voice.

"Lily! Are you okay?"

"Better than that. I'm here."

"'Here' is kind of a relative concept." His diaphragm tightened.

"I'm in Ollantaytambo. By the town square. And guess who's with me?"

Ephraim took a breath, restraining himself from making some hysterical noise. The next few seconds would be critical. But for all his having refused her petition to travel with him, for all his certainty that she must not be here, his heart went nova with happiness.

"I don't care. I'm just delighted?"

"Even though you barred me from coming."

"Or because? Do you really think I'm like, rational? Okay. Who?"

"Come see." She was laughing.

Seven minutes later, walking alternately fast to see her, slowly to process and prepare, he arrived at a working man's restaurant near the market. He paused at the door, then entered, scanning the room.

There she was, gorgeous in midnight blue with a macrame beret, beaming and radiant. His heart went off like a drum riff.

Kittycorner to her at the table was a bearded man with a Ministerio de Cultura bush hat on his head.

"Ephraim No Middle Name Arrowsmith, meet Bingham Beauchamp Bonnaterre. Bonnaterre of the Bumps?"

"Bingham?"

"Affirmative. You thought I wouldn't track him down? He's all right, Eph."

The archaeologist grinned. "Hey Ephraim." He cocked his head at Lily. "She paid half my airfare."

"Hey Bingham." Ephraim's smile was real. "Glad I caught your talk in Lima. It was prime."

Lily frowned. "You already know each other?" Bingham gestured to Ephraim palm up.

"Met on the plane," explained Ephraim, "He deflated a man-spreader. Then noticed I was reading the bump paper?" He had a heady feeling of undefined danger, but was perversely thrilled at catching Lily out. The food on their plates was distracting.

"You didn't tell me, boy."

"You didn't tell me, Lily Hoa." Hoa was her middle name. She was understandably sensitive about that in school. Her lips compressed and eyes narrowed. She lifted a warning finger at Ephraim. Before she could speak, Bingham interjected.

"Good people." He laughed. "Nobody told anybody anything. That's how Shakespearean comedies are born." His brown eyes were clear, watchful, smile-crinkled. His bristly eyebrows lifted. He was ceding the initiative to Ephraim.

Lily paused, looked intently into Ephraim's eyes, then slid a delicate hand across the table, touching his fingertips.

"Wait," Ephraim said. "He is your professor?" Her eyebrows went up and she smiled at the ceiling. He pulled out a chair and sat. "Good to see you again, Doctor Bonnaterre. But wow?" For the first time, Ephraim tasted jealousy.

Lily watched them bending toward each other in obvious rapport. Something bothered her. Was this jealousy? “Did you know?” she accused Bingham.

“Lily darlin’, you always referred to him as “My boy. My bonny boy. My ramblin’ boy. My Best BF. Making sure I know I’m not competition. Never a name.”

Lily shook her head. “Yoiks,” she said. “Now I’ll have to dress in drag and turn out to be the missing Marquess.”

“So you are the professor?” Ephraim's eyes met Bingham’s. Bingham looked back, unreadable. 'So this is the green-eyed monster, Ephraim thought, ‘don’t let us die this way.’ He hid it. Their look held until Bingham lowered his eyelids, not in surrender, but out of courtesy.

“Assistant Professor,” he answered dryly, “about to be promoted, I think, to Associate, so they can deny me tenure and fire me.”

“In the destructive element immerse,’” said Ephraim, quoting Conrad, “Jump right in. Why would ‘they’ want to do that?” Ephraim eyed Bingham’s plate of rice and chicken.

“Because I like the Inkas, and Peruvian cultural traditions, exactly as they are, as far as I can discern them. My department wants to crumple them up and stuff them into that global paradigm where all cultures share the same primordial mythology.” Bingham, who knew hunger, noted Ephraim sneaking glances.

“Like, New Agey? Ancient Masters of Lemuria?”

“What I like, really empathize with, from this continent, is that it is sui generis. It invented itself without influence from along the silk road, from any other source. It’s original.”

With two fingers he shoved his plate into Ephraim’s table-turf.

“Brought up by wolves. I heard. And I read the English transcript of your speech that you emailed me. Thanks for that.” He raised eyebrows at Bingham, who nodded. Ephraim began to eat with controlled moderation.

“Or guinea pigs. Yes.”

"And your school wants you to toe the whole Power of Myth line?"

Bingham thought, 'This is a kid?' His heart sank. Lily would never be his alone.

"That, and worse. Fingerprints of the Gods."

"Ork. So how do you like the 'Chakana' crosses everywhere?"

"Yah. Makes me want to cry. I mean, even these guys at that table over there have convinced themselves it is their ancient patrimony, and it's a tradition invented by two jerkoffs in year two-thousand-three." Bingham rolled his eyes. "A Bolivian tour guide and some woman from like Ohio with a degree in psychology. Con artists."

Two Peruvian men looked up from their bottles of Cusqueña beer at Bingham's gesture. A skinny white man with a t-shirt wrapped around his head, sleeves tied in back, observed the exchange, eyes narrowed.

"Total tonteria, but now it's cultural canon. We just have to live with it." Ephraim leaned across the table. "You can call me Eph. Everyone else does."

"Oh, that's why I didn't recognize your name. Lily, you did name him to me," Bingham said. "I didn't make the connection. I thought you were calling Ephraim the letter 'F.'"

"So, Letter F," she said with a mocking edge in her voice, so unLilylike, "are you going to show us how to time-travel?"

That stopped Ephraim. "What?" He stared at her, stunned. What???"

"You don't remember, do you? That you told me?"

"I told you? When? How? I would never!"

"You disgorged the legumes, boy. You spilled the beans. On 'shrooms that time. You crawled up in my lap sniffling into my armpit saying "Promise you won't remember this?"

Silence between them, aji de gallina cooling on Lily's plate. Bingham watched them, puzzled.

"How much did I tell you? How much did you tell him?" Ephraim's voice was low and flat. Lily had never felt threatened before, not by Ephraim. Maybe she had gone too far.

"No. No one else. You told me...can I say this now? Here?" She slid her plate of food toward him. He hesitated, took it.

"Legumes out of bag. What did I say?"

"That you felt yourself go into some dead Inka's mind and see through his eyes."

Now Ephraim was light-headed, tremulous, there was a vertigo that left him insecure in his seat, as if gravity might fail. "And you never mentioned it to me after."

"It seemed...tabu. Sort of."

"And you blindside me with it now. In public."

"I'm not public," Bingham broke in quietly. "I'm the least public man on the planet. Listen. If you think you have channeled some pre-Hispanic Peruvian, you are probably at best deluded. But I live for, my whole career and inner world is directed at, knowing what an Inka street, what this town we're in right now, would have looked like in Anno Domini fourteen fifty-five. And you don't conduct yourself like a lightweight. So I'll listen to anything you have to say, any insight you've got."

Ephraim decided then not so much to trust Bingham as to recognize that Bingham was the one Andeanist on the planet who deserved to know what he had seen.

"Jeez," said Ephraim, "this conversation. This whole day. Has sure as shit gone off the fucking rails."

"Now I'm scared," Lily said. "We're like twins in the womb and I've never once heard you curse."

Suddenly none of them could look at the other. They sat in silence.

"Lily," Ephraim said finally, raising his eyes, "I'm so happy to be with you I will forgive you anything, and you have done nothing wrong. Bingham, I am glad it is you. I'll show you how I do it, and you can judge for us all whether I am insane."

They lifted their eyes to him, then Lily and Bingham shared a glance. Ephraim scraped the last of the food off the plate. “But I can no longer sit still. Can we absquatulate?”

“Blowing pop stand, mon Capitaine!” reported Lily.

Back on the street in the morning shadow of Apu Pinkuylluna they walked in silence. Ephraim felt strength rise in him from the food upon which he had fed.

“Now then,” said Lily at last.

“Now then,” Eph concurred. A few more steps.

“Whooeee,” went Lily Hoa Tran.

“Whooeee,” hooted Bingham and Ephraim together, and they laughed.

Like a Starving Dog

“So why are you scarfing our leftovers like a starving dog?” They dropped Bingham in a ten-bed dormitory at his hostel.

“Left my debit card in the ATM.”

“Why? Where?”

“Distracted? There?” Ephraim pointed to the upcoming corner opposite the plaza. There was a tourist restaurant behind the ATM. Lily beelined across the street toward it.

“Lily, it is long gone. Forget it.” The Briarpatch man-spreader probably had it.

Lily inspected the cash machine, then the restaurant, then strode through the door. Ephraim followed. Lily gave the proprietor a big smile, nodded at her husband, was about to speak, then turned to Ephraim, pointing at the glass sheet covering the counter.

“One of these yours?” Under the glass was an array of six ATM cards.

“Ah. Yah. Yes, this is mine! Didn’t think of that?”

“Why didn’t you just travel back in time and not leave it there?”

“Doesn’t work that way. The Inka didn’t have ATM machines. They didn’t have money.” Lily had been here less than an hour and had already saved him from himself.

A Sharp Turn into Murder

Morning. They headed for Split Rock. Ephraim was shaking inside. His Inka might be dead now. There was carnage in the Inka time, where they intended to go. He fumbled in his mind for a way to stop this excursion, found none.

They rounded □up Bingham at the hostel where he shared a ten-bed dormitory, and started up the street to the hill. Ephraim tried to keep his worry out of his voice.

“Lily. You knew about this paranormal thing of mine, but you’re here anyway. Don’t you find this condition of mine a little disconcerting? Me believing that I go back in time?”

“I don’t know, what is time, anyway? Half the people I read, including, like, Buddhism and quantum physics, say it doesn’t even exist.”

“Be serious, Lil’. Science does not accept time travel. Nor does Buddhism nor physics. Doesn’t my story make you nervous about me?”

“Eph, if it did" — she laid two fingers on his bicep — "have I treated you differently since ‘shroom day?”

“A little maybe.” He shot her a grin, “But, better.”

“Let’s say that you aren’t insane. You don’t seem that way to me. So.”

Both, man and boy, looked at her, waiting for her judgement. She shrugged.

“Thing is, you don’t, you know, bodily go anywhere, right? So there’s no problem with conservation of energy? Or the integrity of the system? So as long as you don’t interfere with their time, no problem. None of that sci-fi paradox brouhaha. Ha.”

“But if it’s real, that means my contact with the past is affecting the Now, and then the future. Doesn’t paradox kick in?”

Bingham picked that up. “I don’t think so, going forward. That time is affecting This time,” he analyzed. “It always does. Is there any reciprocity in this?”

“Do you mean, does the guy I’m inhabiting know I’m there? Yes he does. And he sees this time through me. He doesn’t like it at all." He looked away and back. 'And I might have watched him get killed,' he thought but didn't say.

“Then we *are* dealing with some serious breaches of scientific theory. And potential paradox. The Now then affects Then now; the past is the mouth from which the word ‘Now’ is uttered.”

“And the Future is the halitosis breathed onto the dinner party of the eleven-dimensional universe,” concluded Lily. “But where, exactly, then, is this dinner party? In time, or in somewhere else?”

“I’ve been chewing on these questions since I was a kid? Of course. The role of time in the universe, is it just a biological convenience, all that mess?”

“I don’t think we’re going to sort this out today,” Lily said. “Maybe it doesn’t matter.”

“Exactly. Except that if I’m not a madman, Ramram will be acting in his time on information he got from our time."

“Then,” Bingham’s eyes took on a wolfish light, “maybe we can go back and stop the conquest.” He grinned, teeth clenched. “I’ve always wanted to do that. Even if I do kill off my granddad. There is always plenty of granddad material around.”

"That's what I am here to do?" Ephraim said. "I didn't really think of that until I heard you say it."

They were almost at the wooden gate to the ruined stone staircase when Ramram’s vision slammed into Ephraim, knocking him back against an Inka wall, a massive adrenaline attack. First was terror, then a savage, homicidal glee. He, Ramram, was killing people. Blood was everywhere. His body was full of calm power, in his eyes a hurricane of violence. Ephraim knew that he was with

Ramram and that Ramram was too occupied with murder to realize that he was occupied by Ephraim. He turned to face a man of calm ferocity who handed him a stone that Ramram then slung at another man who tried to run but whose head snapped back and radiated blood. There was a horror in them both, Then boy and the Now boy, and a glory.

The world spun in a checkerboard whirlpool and he was back in his own time. His knees gave out. He felt his back slide down against the stones as he collapsed. He heard voices.

"Eph? What the hey? You all right?" Bingham asked.

"Arrowsmith, boy, get a grip!" That was Lily. Her voice injected him with pleasure, which turned to cold misery. He should not have brought them into this. Everything was moving too fast.

He recovered, panting, waved off his concerned friends. "Yes. Food faint."

Ramram was alive. The dreadlocks dude was dead. It couldn't have taken three full breaths. Ramram's confederate was the same man they had faced together by the stream. Ephraim was shocked and bewildered. This time travel thing had taken a sharp turn into bloody murder.

"I'm good." He lifted his gaze toward the gateway to the Split Rock, took a step.

Half a block ahead in the Inca-wall lined street stood the man-spreader. Ephraim froze, elbows in the air. Bingham reached out and clutched his arm. They exchanged a look. The two of them walked deliberately, toward the big man. Lily kept up.

"What the heck was that, Arrowsmith?" Lily looked at him sidelong.

"Hypoglycemic syncope, low blood sugar?" Ephraim offered. Bingham raised an eyebrow at Ephraim.

"Okay. That guy up there? He's the one from the plane."

"Old Twisty Nose?" Lily's eyes narrowed, and she shouldered between them to get in front.

The man stood with his hands on his hips, then, seeing Lily, made a whistle-mouth, raising his eyebrows in surprised admiration. The two men flanked Lily. With a grin, the man turned, sauntered away.

Lily gave Ephraim a look. It said, 'And you didn't warn me?'

"Well," he said, "there's a lot to catch up on?"

"Right," said Lily, "And you need to be a little more sharey with us. We're in this together now."

Flip Fail

They climbed the old Inka stairway toward the split rock. Ephraim mounted the stone.

Instantly, Ramram's vision supplanted his own. He was looking at a dead body, twisted, grimacing, bloody, wicker helmet rolled to the side, woolen unku wrenched up across the muscular, hairless shins. The wrecked head was thick with stiff out-thrust braids. A spear lay across his punctured chest. He noted the Inka youth's coppery feet in straw sandals almost toeing the corpse.

He was drawn by the magnetic pull of the stone those feet stood on, its power, stronger even than Split Rock. The character of this stone was very different. It was warlike. Ramram lifted his eyes to look at the man in the frayed and soiled cloak, who inspected the fiercely painted, wild-haired, dead warrior with a considering gaze. The man's mouth opened to speak when a dizzying darkness came and Ephraim was back on the rock. For just a moment, he felt Ramram with him, then he was gone.

This was no way to introduce his girlfriend and his more-or-less hero to tripping back in time.

The two of them watched him, waiting.

He stayed on the rock, eyes closed, until he had full control of himself. Then he looked at them and shook his head, smiling. They looked back, wary.

"Whew!" he said, "I'll get back to you on that. Maybe this isn't the best day flip into Ramram."

“Flip?” Lily asked.

“Ramram?” asked Bingham.

“‘Flip’ is what I call the experience. Ramram is the name of the Inka boy. He’s about my age now.”

"And why not today?” Lily demanded.

“Well.” Ephraim frowned. “He seemed kind of busy.”

He could see from their faces, especially Bingham’s in its avidity, that it was no use.

"Brace yourself," he said, "Ramram seems to be in rough company right now."

Each of them tried the rock. To Ephraim’s relief, nothing much happened.

“Yes,” Bingham said, “there is a frisson. A sense of the magnetic. But no Inka! Dammit, no Inka!”

“No,”Lily said. “Something is there, but no, I didn’t get off. No Inka for me.”

“So it’s all delusion.” Ephraim sighed, recognizing his dishonesty. “And I am crazy. That scares me.” And suddenly it did.

“Wait.” Lily lifted a palm, “Remember that post of We Live In You? Where Nick Nieman ‘flips’ the sneeze-wizard?”

“Qachu. Yes.” Bingham’s eyes widened, he straightened. “They were high.”

“They were all on drugs.”

“Ayawaska probably, or San Pedro cactus. That’s right. We need to at least try a catalyst or two.” Bingham shoved Ephraim’s shoulder a little. “We can’t all be the Chosen One.”

Ephraim looked at them, baffled. “Sneeze wizard?”

“You don’t follow that Inka/bacteria vlog? Nick Nieman?”

“A little. No sneeze wizard.”

“Eph, boy.” Lily punches him lightly in the gut. “You need to do your homework. We’ll link the latest for you.”

“Does he always make people shove and punch other people?”

“And,” says Bingham, “I’ll rustle up some *medicina*. What they call wachuma cactus around here. Mescaline.”

Cactus Juice Contact
The next day

Awed and excited Ephraim stood in the swarm of an actual Inka army. He was really there. There were smells; sweaty wool, wood smoke, the stink of latrines. Colorful and fun, until the attack.

Across some kind of valley, maybe a quarter mile away, in a roar of voices and drums, a black mass of men launched down a slope toward them.

A shock of fear hit Ramram, and passed into Ephraim. Many men were coming to kill them. How would it feel to be in his Inka friend if he was killed? Would he, Ephraim, die? It would hurt, that was for sure. Could he flip out at will? Focus on himself and escape to his own Pacha? It didn't seem likely. Anyway, he wouldn't. Ramram had needed him before.

Fighters yelled nearby. The crowd of soldiers he was in shuffled forward. The fear expanded, Ramram's knees jellied. Ephraim picked up the idea, ‘well, I can always run away. But they’ll catch me.’ They approached a field of rocks, of different sizes, shapes, and colors, lain on cloth litters. Men were straining to lift them, knuckles bulging around wood poles, six to each stretcher.

As Ramram pulled up next to a carried stone, long and dark, medaled with orange lichen, the fear lifted away and a rich, electric sensuality replaced it. The muscles of Ramram's arm contracted deliciously as he lifted a club into view, its metal head leafed and dark bronze, transferred it to his right, shield arm, dropping the spear, taking the litter pole with his free'd left.

The enemy ahead roared like the sea.

Ramram's rock-bearing squad double-timed forward and down. Ramram was making low animal sounds in his throat.

'Holy shit,' Ephraim thought, 'this is real. This is amazing. We might be going to die. I can't let this happen to Lily.'

'No?' Lily's voice raised in his imagination. 'Try and stop me.'

The backs of a hundred heads rose and fell ahead of him, then he was back on Split Rock.

When he caught his breath, he said, "It's bad where he is. There's violence. You don't want to do this. Once you're in, it's out of control." He wondered if he had abandoned Ramram to die alone.

Bingham went next. He and Lily had drunk the thick green liquid an hour earlier and were showing the effects of mescaline intoxication. He lay across the surface of the stone, relaxed. "Just phosphenes and shades of dark rolling behind my eyelids," he sighed, and went quiet.

His eyes snapped open and he began jerk and spasm, his legs moving like a dreaming dog. He grunted and made little attempts to yell, spraying spittle. He began to gasp and wheeze, then crawled to the edge of the stone and dropped into the rocky split, vomiting violently. Ephraim and Lily laid hands on his back and shoulders, but he shook them off with a snarl.

"It was a battle," he said when he came to himself, spitting. "Thousands of men hitting each other with impact weapons. We, he, I — the Inka I was in — was trying to crawl back up a big hill in the middle of it, puking his guts out, just wave after wave of nausea. At the killing. I mean, I never saw a man die before. Now I have seen hundreds. Killed." He lifted his head, looked at Ephraim.

"It was beautiful, Eph, a full-scale Inka battlefield. I saw the fighting gear, the standards, the formations, the techniques. I don't know who the enemy were, they looked tough as all fuck but they were, like, drunk. They were trying to fight but couldn't. The Inka were all over them. Every once in a while my guy would get a shot of some kind of stimulant, an energy infusion. Then it would fade as he stumbled up the grade. Once he crawled to this big rock dressed up like a warrior and hugged it, and zam, he was wired again. He went to club a staggering, wheezing enemy and couldn't bring himself to do it. He just kicked him over and went dragging himself uphill behind the fight.

“It was hideous. I felt shitty about the whole human race and especially about the part of me that liked it. A big part. Maybe that was your Ramram I was with? Where is my hat?”

“It fell off the cliff when you were writhing around,” Ephraim said. “Lil', you don’t have to go.”

“I’m going.” As she turned toward the hump of rock, it’s aura buzzing the air, there was a smell like burning brakes. Her face lost all trace of the smile that was her native resting point. The muscles in her cheeks and jaw went slack with desolation and for the first time Ephraim saw how hard it was to be Lily Tran.

“She’s too tough,” Bingham whispered.

She set herself grimly into the lotus position, hands folded in her lap and began to breathe slow and stoic.

Then she smiled. Smiles of marvelous variety and subtlety passed across her face for the next twenty minutes. Once she spoke her own name, a kind of cooing, four times.

“Her name is Tuya,” she told them. “She has the most beautiful soul in the world. And she *is* beautiful, you can tell by how people, men, women, children, look at her. No one has ever looked at me like that. But you, Ephraim, but you.

"I met her resting with her...I don’t know, family? Village? At a clearing along a grassy track, by a big boulder. A power stone. They were moving all their things, women, children, old people, a few adult men, and dozens of soldier guys carrying household goods. Maybe three hundred in all. They were moving their lives, but not as refugees. Happy. Excited. She felt me come to her, sensed my fear and she comforted me. She sang to me. We got up and walked. She is strong, a strong walker. She was pulling thread from a wool tuft. She carried an old granny on her back in a kind of shawl. She told me her name. I told her mine. A face kept coming into her mind. A young man. It hurt her, and made her happy. So happy.”

Ephraim's relief was palpable. His whole being relaxed. They were getting out of this okay. He stretched, looked out over the town, busy now with tourists, it was high season.

He decided to keep this to himself for a while. "Are you guys hungry?" The corner of his mouth spasmed and he started picking at a cuticle. He was going spastic again.

"There goes the 'My Boyfriend's Insane' Theory," murmured Lily. Bingham cut his eyes at her and nodded.

Ephraim led up over the rock spur toward the exit. Standing on the stone-walled terrace, making no effort to hide, was the Briarpatch shirt guy, binoculars focused on the three time-travelers. Ephraim gazed at him blankly.

The man lowered his field glasses and grinned. He stood in their path. Ephraim was about to warn his friends when his antagonist turned casually and ambled back down the old stepping stones.

FOURTEEN now

Katari Kuntur
21st Century CE
Lima Peru

Katari Kuntur, dust-coated, two weeks unbathed, grit under her nails, on her eyelashes, in her nostrils, and between her front teeth, climbs the three flights of warped wooden stairs to unlock the door of her small apartment in a poor district of Lima, Peru. She unshoulders her pack onto the sagging sofa, shrugs out of her hooded parka, snags her laptop off the old wooden bureau-desk, goes into the bathroom, turns on the water of her electric shower, pulls her military cargo pants down around her knees, sits on the toilet, and turns on the portable computer.

She is returning from her lone work at an archaeological site high in the Andes, on a barren wind-ravaged pass above Huarochiri. She has been working the ruin for fifteen years, unfunded, during the summer season, her work supported by teaching and by small rents on her family properties north of Huancayo. Katari is of Chanka blood, ancient enemies of the Inka, but her loyalties are to all indigenous Andeans.

The alpaca herders who work those highlands call the place Ñawpa Ñawpa, the Ancient Ancient.

She is lucky today. The wifi works. The last time she was back it didn't. She scans the sender and titles of over two hundred incoming emails on her university account, another eighty or so on Gmail. She doesn't open any of them yet.

She is not smiling. She rarely does. In 1983 twenty members of her family were murdered in one night by the *Sendero Luminoso*, Shining Path guerrillas. She alone, almost a baby, survived. She pulls the rubber band from her ponytail, shakes her coarse black hair. Several classifications of dirt drift to the cracked, faded tiles.

Katari has spotted an email from UC Irvine but is afraid to open it.

She logs into her blog, *Apu Manqo*, an ongoing fantasy in which the rebel Inka Manco annihilates the Spanish in the siege of Cusco, reviving the Inka empire and changing the course of history. It is popular among her students and pre-Colonial jingoists. Among the comments, she sees that one of her most promising former pupils and disciples, now a newscaster in Mexico City, has sent her a link, without text.

She finishes, wipes, tosses the tissue into the wicker basket by the toilet, re-pants, turns off the water, carries the laptop to her desk, clicks the link.

Tawantinsuyu Redux, reads the post title. But the site is in English. Katari refuses to speak English, she despises America and Americans, but she is fluent. She has a graduate degree in Latin American Studies from Georgetown.

'*We Live In You*,' is the name of the site, a video blog. "*Ima?*" she mutters in Quechua, "What? What is this? But Raoul wouldn't waste my time. There must be something here." So she clicks on the arrow.

It seems to be about preventing the European conquest of the Inkas by the combined efforts of modern and 15th-century agents though a form of mental time-travel, at the behest of a consortium of sentient microbes. It purports not to be fiction. She watches it twice. Then she looks at the other post titles and isolates a few that seem promising. Most of an hour later, at the kitchen table now scattered with the detritus of food, she remembers that shower and closes her computer.

"The man is insane," she assures herself. "But is there a chance? Is there the *ghost* of a *chance?*"

After showering, she goes back to her professional email, opens the one from the University of California, Irvine, radiocarbon dating laboratory. She has been saving it, eager and afraid.

"Hah!"

The results are in on the textile analysis of the *shikra* cording and woven sacking, as well as carbon dating of seeds, charcoal, and two wooden staffs. All confirmed to six thousand years Before Present, give or take two hundred years. Her proto-Chavin ceremonial center is now the oldest verified monumental site in the Americas. She is vindicated. She will be funded and will not again need — nor be able — to work alone.

The Knowers
Port Angeles, Washington

Nick postures with a samurai sword, swinging it two-handed across his chest. He lays it down, turns to the webcam.

“When Gautama the Buddha’s head blew into white light under the Bo tree, when the desert prophets were gob-struck by wild visions of flaming sky wheels, when stereophonic voices spoke to the medieval mystics, they were not communing as they believed with the Godhead, the metaphysical, with the Cosmos. They were only in touch with a local, biological, phenomenon. The holobiological Presence. All mystical experience is just us talking with the We Live In You. Microbes. We do its work, it brings us Oneness."

"Our tiny human task in this mission is to turn raw data into complex systems. Whatever you are thinking and feeling is an example of that. Maybe we do it too well. We, who are unknowingly in and of it, who have been guided and formed by it in the billions of years of coevolution, been given intelligence, thumbs, mobility, invention, have gained so much power that we can kill ourselves and with ourselves, all of organized life on this earth, including that which gave us the power.

"It is no joke. We may be about to kill life on earth back to a few anaerobic microbes at the bottom of the ocean. We are indeed a disease, maybe incurable. And more, those nuclear bombs won't stay on the shelf forever. One drunk driver is all it takes. It is two minutes to midnight.

"We are all One. Yet there are countless beings within the one, the Presence. Two of them have involved mankind in the struggle to live here or to abandon the planet.

"This is the heart of our story. Certainty and The Question. Both components of the Presence."

A sloe-eyed furball appears on the splintery wooden computer table, tries to leap four-legged high in the air, belly flops, spins, chasing her tail. Nick picks her up, rubs her head, puts her down.

"The The Question knows only life on this rock trapped in its track around a star. Its thin film on the crust. It sees that one of its experiments, mankind, has gone out of control. It tells itself, and the One, that there must be some way to stop this speeding truck from hitting that wall."

Nick scratches the back of his hand.

"Allergy rash. Of course. What did I decide to call you? Kwee. That's right." He pulls the ring-tab to peel open a can of cheap cat food, lowers it to the floor.

"Certainty only wants off this planet and into the arms of whoever is out there. There must be more of what we are, find them and join them. Every year there are more space programs, NASA, Russia, China, Japan, India, billionaire dilettantes. Israel."

"This urge of Certainty motivated the evolution of man, of the mind and the thumb, of our ability to think and do, and it seeded us with the desire to leave this backwater and travel to the Cities of Light.

"The Gnostics — the Knowers - once told us that this world, this universe, is not our home. Our home is far from here, beyond the scope or understanding of this provincial cosmos. They called it the Total Other. Now our Knowers are called 'Scientists.' They make rockets to get there.

"The rockets get longer, go deeper."

He gnaws a bite out of a cold chicken leg, drops the rest to a plastic tray on the floor where Kwee is worrying the can. She attacks the drumstick, growling. "Maybe I shouldn't feed you so much. You're getting too big too fast."

"Right. Mankind got too big too fast. Man can take us to the stars or destroy us all. Or, maybe, with a little sci fi trick, save us all. Put your money down, one or the other.

"The war is on, in the mountains of Peru, between the cult of Ilyapa, God of the Storm, agents of Certainty, and the bitch Pachamama, Mother Earth, The Question. Because there, in the high rugged Andes, in stone and water, where space is time, is the War against Certainty.

"Tune in here for the news every Now and Then at two minutes to midnight□."

Nick's expression is non-committal. You wonder, maybe, if he does not smile because in that you would see too much. When a smile fails it tells everyone everything.

"And so, my esteemed colleagues, my fellow savants, illuminated metagnostics, you polymaths and magisters, bodhisattvas, cosmologists and cosmetologists, good night. Brush your teeth, put on your PJs, go to bed. Have a deep and dreamless sleep. They do not come often in this epoch. Did they ever?"

Nick clicks to turn off the cam. He massages his temples with his thumbs. He lifts the stained list of synonyms for people of knowledge and lets it fall into the plastic trash bag by his desk. He looks into his heart. Still closed. Still clamped tight as a clam in the cold dark sea. There was this one time, though, up in the Twist...

From the shadows comes that treble 'Kwee.'

Observer Observed

In Berkeley, Noe Zoe lifted her head from the microscope, glancing at the LCD monitor over her shoulder.

'Oh,' she thought, 'that's not so bad. He's being flippant. And tedious. Gnosticism. Sheesh. No one will care'. But just in case, she formatted a secure remote drive, uploaded some of her most recent data into the cloud for a few seconds, then transferred it to the new drive and erased it from her main storage drive and the cloud.

And, she wondered, was he right about the agape, universal love, being a consequence of the human microbiota? She hadn't considered that aspect of the holobiome. Could it be identified and measured?

An upstream data scanner caught the transfer in the cloud. High alert. The NTT assigned agents to zoom in on the germ woman. And to drill down on this Nieman psycho.

CHAPTER FOURTEEN then

The Covenant of the Storm
The Qoricancha Pantheon, Qosqo

K'anchay, High Priest of Ilyapa, God of the Storm, stood in a simple unku, eyes scanning the eight subordinates chosen for this commission. Men and women who had the need to know. "The war is over. What has always been is gone. A new war has begun.The despised Prince has won. He calls himself World Changer. He is just a man."

Among them were the head of the militant monks in purple and black, the Matron of the Acclawasi of Qosqo, overseeing the Chosen Women; powerful priests, necromancers, and seers, and directly before him, Simi Apaq, the Lower High Priest of Ilyapa, dressed in his best.

Qachu was not present. He waited with another two hundred minor priests and acolytes in the pristine courtyard of the house of Ilyapa in the southeast corner of the Qoricancha, principal temple of the Tawantinsuyu.

"From this day forth all of you, and of the resources of the Temple of Ilyapa, will be dedicated to preserving the new future foreseen by the Oracle of Pachacamac. This is as prophesied but with the Inka, not the Chanka, in control of our world.

"Pachayachachiq the Creator, Master of Ilyapa the Storm God whose will we serve, sees that there will come in less than two lifetimes, a pachacuti. An overturning of the world. Men, will come across the Mother of Lakes to tear down our world. Ilyapa will choose to use this. Pachamama will try to stop this.

"There is our battlefield and our covenant.

"I will brief each of you separately as to your roles. Please return to your daily devotions and await a call. Simi Apaq, wait here."

The divines trailed out through the veiled doorway. Simi Apaq stood with his hands folded at his navel, scheming within.

"Lower High Divine Simi Apaq, you are to control your wizard priest Qachu. We need his connection to the sorcerer Nikniman in the future Pacha. This Stranger is the dividing point between the Taripay Pacha, journey to the stars, and the Kay Pacha, this world, as it is now. Ilyapa is dedicated to the Taripay Pacha.

"Qachu's powers are not yet fully known. We believe they could also work on men and women in this Pacha, to observe or affect their actions.

"Qachu is complicated. He may have plans of his own. He is also the son of the Son of the Sun, and must be treated with care. Tell him everything necessary but no more."

The Lower High Divine Umu of Ilyapa left the presence of the Higher and entered the courtyard. He encountered Qachu in a corner counting on a khipu. He waved him over.

"I didn't know you could do that. Read khipu."

"I am only learning, Apu." Yes, and learning that would give him great power.

"Well. It could be useful to Ilyapa. Come with me. I have work for you."

The Morning After

Pachacutiq Inka Yupanqui saw Otoronqo Kuy walking among the dead and dying, saw Ramram slumped exhausted on the turf a few rikra away. He signaled his coterie to stay back, approached the lieutenant. Otoronqo looked up at the oncoming emperor and snapped to attention.

“So. You thought you could get killed down there and not have to answer for taking my secret weapon to where he could die like any dog of war.”

“Apu.”

“You take responsibility for that?”

“Apu.”

“You have it. You are now responsible for that q’urpa over there on the dirt. You and your children and your children’s children. You watch over him upon my orders.”

“Apu.”

“That is including all your other duties.”

“Apu.”

Pachacutiq handed Otoronqo a khipu shot through with gold filaments, an *Imperial Warrant of Indisputable Dominion*. "Give him this."

"Apu."

“Well.”

Otoronqo plucked an eyebrow at Pachacutiq Inka Yupanqui, left-faced, marched toward Ramram.

The Sapa Inka gazed out across the battlefield, down onto his capital, the sacred city of Qosqo. ‘I’ll have to do something about that,’ he thought. Then looked toward Ramram. ‘Yes,’ he further thought, ‘And you are a place to start.’

He smiled within. As planned, Ramram had volunteered. Now he knew he would have a full man at his command, not a mere freak. So the Brother Stone attack force had gained a symbol of victory, a much needed font of morale, and a source of powerful Kamay. And Otoronqo Kuy had let him come; his aide could think for himself. ‘I am going to change the world, Lump. And you are going to make certain that the world is on my side.'

Ramram, chin on his chest, breath still labored, felt the coming of his distant partner Eff Ram, looking through him with nothing to see but his lap, draped in filthy and bloodstained unku. With effort he lifted his eyes. There was the Prince, Otoronqo standing before him.

Ramram focused his gaze on the victorious Inka Pachacutiq, took a deep breath and said aloud in a raspy catarrh, “Kusi Inka Yupanqui. Auqui Kusi Inka Yupanqui. Understand? Kusi Inka Yupanqui.”

CHAPTER FIFTEEN now

You Have to Ask?

The next morning, Ephraim in half-lotus on Split Rock looked through Ramram's dulled eyes, first at a piece of stained cloth, then as Ramram recognized Ephraim's presence and lifted his gaze, at man in lordly array chewing out a soldier in bloodstained disarray. They stood on a slope strewn with corpses, among whom men searched for the living.

It hit him who the high mucky-muck was. He recognized the face. It was the squatting character who had scared Ramram so badly. Then Ramram spoke. Ephraim felt the effort it required. What was he saying? The voice was weak, slurred.

"Kusi Inka Yupanqui."

Ephraim's heart picked up. Kusi Inka Yupanqui. Pachacutiq's birth name. Incredible.

The fighting appeared to be over for now. Lily and Bingham were maybe fairly safe. That was a blessing. He was back on Split Rock.

"Bingham. Holy Moly. What was Pachacutiq Inka's original name?"

"Kusi Inka. You have to ask? Kusi Inka Yupanqui."

"Bing, I have just looked in the face of the creator of the Inka Empire."

The Pact

"Okay. I'm going to tell you everything." Ephraim was bobbing his Adam's apple like an elevator amok and knocking his knuckles together. "We have an enemy here, and I think another one in Ramram's pacha. We now know where we are in time."

Lily and Bingham looked on in concern. They were standing on the dirt path by a grassy Inka terrace.

“The Chanka war,” verified Bingham. “I saw the fight. You saw Pachacutiq Inka.

"Yes," Ephraim said, "and it happened. It was not myth or metaphor. The Structuralists are wrong. We were there."

“Tell us about the bad guys. Here and now.” Lily looked sidelong at Ephraim, not in a friendly way.

“Okay. Pick a rock to sit on," Ephraim said. "I don’t want to be inside, I feel claustrophobic even under the open sky.” He told them everything, watching their reactions.

Then he stood and he said, “Look. Three things. Me here now. Ramram there then. Interesting but so what. But. Me here now knows Ramram there then who knows Pachacutiq Inka Yupanqui. Who rules the Inka Empire. That is awesome. That is leverage. A direct line."

Bingham and Lily watched him narrowly.

"I know what I am going to do. I am going to try to tell Ramram about Pizarro, so that Ramram can tell Pachacutiq, and Pachacutiq can stop the conquest of the Inkas.

"That is why the holobiome or Pachamama or whatever it is sends me back there and he comes here.

"I am an atheist and I don’t believe in fate. I don’t know if Nick Nieman is right about the bacteria hive mind, or if something else is giving me this job, or it's just me, but I am going to try to do it. For myself at least.” He faced them, suddenly calm again. "The Inkas. Winning. Still around today. I want it."

“Bro,” said Bingham, taking a deep breath, “what can I say. I am with you. Foursquare. Let's do it.”

“I don’t have any idea if this is possible, but I am going to try. At least until the school year in September.”

“I don’t know, kids,” Lily said. “Is that stalker guy working alone? I can’t promise I won’t wuss out. I don’t know if I want to die on the barricades for ancient history. It’s not my fight."

"Oh it's not a fight, Lil'. It's just a little science project. I tell Ramram, he tells the Inka, the Inka nabs the ships. Home free."

"That's right, " Bingham agreed, "Nothing to it."
Lily rolled her eyes to the skies.

CHAPTER SIXTEEN now

The Bacteria in Space Theory

You get a drone's-eye view of a northwestern harbor town, late sun on a fat ferry rounding the end of a wide hooked breakwater. The camera descends on Nick Nieman in a black-and-red plaid lumberjack coat that looks generations old.

There is a furry black and orange head sticking out of the breast pocket, ears up, paws hooked over, sniffing the wind. Nick's thumbs palp the buttons on a clamshell controller, his eyes flick to the little screen and back to drone in the sky. Wind tugs at his thin hair. His eyes narrow against it. He speaks into a lapel mic.

"I got a day job, folks. I'm not going to tell you what it is because I'd kinda like to keep it, but they pay me, so I got me this quadcopter. This thing goes high, it has a real smooth stabilizer." It pulls in on his lean face, then backs off into the sky as if jerked on a line, leaving Nick tiny below.

"But it doesn't go to outer space. Unlike bacteria. Unlike prokaryotes."

The aerial shots zoom over the town, climbing the bluffs over Highway 101 as it passes the curio shops and bookstore, the shutdown movie theater.

"You see, kids, we act as human drones for Certainty, as a self-directed mobile all-purpose tool — we feed it, shelter it, carry it, create elaborate environments to its specifications. We have taken bacteria the moon. We have transported it into deep space, to Jupiter and beyond, some past Neptune, headed for Aldebaran, Aquila. Pioneer Two will pass by stars in Sagittarius in four million years. To our microbic mentors, just a Sunday road trip.

"Certainty is, if nothing else, curious. It wants to know if we are a one-off, or an outlier to a larger community. It wants to make contact, especially if we are on a global death trip."

Crows and gulls whirl in a dogfight over the Tumwater Creek woodlands.

"Whoo! Darwin is out today.

"Now. If we are killing off our planet, we want to get as much of our seed off world as fast as we can, to transport our genome to the capitals of the cosmos. Maybe they will send a rescue mission. Will they welcome us to the greater mind? Treat us like hicks? Mine us for fuel? Skin the planet for its pelt? We need to know. And we are on our way. But if a bunch of clueless saboteurs — the hillbilly Question — turns the clock back to the early Bronze Age, how we gonna get there?

"But The Question thinks it is already too late to save life on Terra, so somebody in Inka time is plotting with somebody in our time to fix history so that a more eco-friendly political system, the Inka, can shift this train onto another track. In the past."

Nick frees a hand to scratch his nose, the drone flips us to the left, picking up pale cirrus-striped sky. Nick catches it before it goes rogue.

"Two young guys, Then and now. I don't know who they are yet, but they hope to roll back the death of the oceans, stop that there global warming. Avoid the eschatological pachacuti, overturning of the world. Defuse that tardy nuclear war. They think the sky is falling and we need to act fast.

"Maybe they are a touch overstimulated. After all, there have already been six major 'extinction events' on the planet that we know of, some killing off all life forms well into the ninety percentiles. The Lake Toba eruption may have killed humanity back to ten thousand breeding pairs a scant seventy-five thousand years ago. Look at us now. Going on eight billion consumers, nearly tripled since they killed JFK. So BFD, greenies, Big Fucking Deal."

The lens strafes formations of high school kids. The boys make air-shotguns at it, while the girls in their squads flip their tartan skirts, imputing prurient motive to the cruising eye in the sky.

“Where am I getting this stuff? Making it up raw? Picking it out of thin air? Kind of yes. My holobiome-enhanced mind is abstracting it from all the levels of input I’m being fed by Certainty from its communication center in the Twist, from my connection with the Inka monk Qachu in his drug-induced trances, and from everything else in the world."

The murder of crows falls back inland. The victorious gulls come at the camera. Nick flies it down toward himself.

"People tell me I look like a scarecrow. Let's see if it works on gulls.

"So. This perceptual edge. It comes from a mind state just this side of intuition, where you are coordinating a thousand different sources of information and speculation, dipping in and out of conscious cerebration, making connections too fast and deep to quite nail down but not quite as remote and intangible as, say, the religious experience that is beyond words, concepts, or communication."

“This trance state, this whirlwind of divination, when I return to normal life, some of it anyway, sticks. It coalesces into rational thought. The code generates text."

The gulls have gone off. The quadcopter lifts high again, over the harbor.

“Such as: Qachu has become aware of an Inka youth who travels into this future to meet another young man, as Qachu does to meet me. The young man on this end is pale, like me, and wears clothes more or less like mine. He likewise visits the Inka past through his host. He has a henchman and a henchgirl. No henchdoggie so far. They do not yet understand what their role is in the game The Question — Qachu's nemesis Pachamama — is playing, but they are getting there.

“So there is a drama building up. Qachu has it in for that Inka boy.

“And that, my people fierce and free, is all I got today.”

The flying point-of-view swoops toward the breakwater, where it looks down on a stocky figure in an orange slicker pointing the black eye of a 12-gauge pump gun at our face. The stock sinks into the shoulder. The screen goes blank.

Switch to Nick Nieman's basement studio, a feral grin on his gaunt face.

"That's it for my eye-in-the-sky, folks. I don't blame the old warrior a bit. Blew the shit out of my airborne intruder with that pheasant gun. May his line increase and his aim never falter. I was wrong ever to buy the bastard thing.

"I find myself filled with a pathetic hopefulness. The weirder I get, the bigger is my following, but that's not why. It is that someone who knows something will hear me and tell me how wrong I am. Is anyone out there? Anything? I know how Certainty must feel."

A paw drops over the lens. The camera goes dark.

But some other eye has opened on him. He has gotten the attention of entities whose credulity a conspiracy theorist really doesn't want focused upon them. Deep Government. As deep as it goes anyway, that would be.

That's Us

"That's us," said Lily, staring at Ephraim's Mac Air. "you are the young man, Bing is the henchguy, and I am the henchgirl. We are now famous among insane bacteria conspiracy theory groupies."

"So his contact, his sneeze monk, are real." Ephraim rubbed his temples. "And they know we are here. So I'm going to ramp it up before someone comes for us. I have an idea. I'm going to show Ramram pictures. Of the conquest and the conquistadors."

"Good idea. I thought of that too." Bingham punched a fist into his palm. "I have some stuff on my laptop. Ever see the movie "Royal Hunt of the Sun?"

"No? Never heard of it?"

"About Atawallpa and Pizarro. It didn't get around much. I found one blurry screener on Pirate Bay. I'll put it on a thumb drive with a couple illustrations of Spaniards and Inkas fighting, you put it on your laptop."

"That's going to blow his Inka mind," smiled Lily, "system overload."

"I don't know if he'll even recognize it as pictures," Ephraim replied. "The Inka weren't really into graphics."

CHAPTER SEVENTEEN then

Working for the World-Changer

"When you are done, it will look from here like a khipu, spread into a circle. To you. To everyone else it will be invisible." Pachacutiq stood, head sunk into the frayed leopard skin cloak, calloused hand circling over the sacred city of Qosqo, now crawling with tens of thousands of workers, deconstructing the place like insects chewing a carrion corpse down to the bone. Ramram swayed on his feet, a little stunned.

"What will?" he rasped. Was he supposed to already know? Did the stranger standing still, hands folded over his belly, face composed, know?

"The sayqay lines," the World Changer said. "Forty-two lines of sacred objects, wakas, extending from the Coricancha Sun Temple to the perimeter of the Qosqo district. Ramram, meet Chaski Yuyu. He matriculated from the Yachay Wasi university knowing everything about wakas, wankas, Apus, ushnus, and apachitas. Except how to find them. That's your job."

Chaski Yuyu nodded politely to Ramram. Ramram nodded back, aware that compared to this man in his top-quality tocapu'd unku, the gold crescent-moon of an amauta, horns down, on his headdress, he knew nothing. He felt a snake of defiance slither through his guts and lungs.

"Chaski Yuyu," the Sapa Inka Pachacutiq said to the professor in a gravely rumble, "Ramram has a rare gift for locating and identifying beings of Kamay. You could live and die in your studies and not find one true waka; he has found dozens. Maybe hundreds.

Ramram looked for a shadow of annoyance passing across Chaski Yuyu's face. There was none.

"Someone recognized whatever it is you carry in your chuspa," Ramram said, nodding at the amauta's shoulder bag.

"It is a brother stone of our family waka," Chaski Yuyu replied. "My great grandfather found it. He was a powerful umu. I am afraid his wizardry did not pass to me."

Pachacutiq answered. "It did. Without you I would not attempt this project. You are your ancestors gift to the Tawantinsuyu, the Four Parts of the Inka realm. It will encompass all lands walked upon by man. As for you, Lump, you had better have the powers you say you have, or an equivalent ability to lie to me."

The emperor's staff, guards, servants, and a clutch of nobles stood fifty paces off, waiting, forcing themselves not to fidget. They were there at his pleasure; there was nothing they wanted from him; the hustle for posts and favors would come later. Now they just watched the man who had impossibly become the most powerful in the world.

"You are standing on the head of the puma," Pachacutiq said."Here I will build the greatest construction ever made by man. A temple, a palace, a ceremonial center, a fortress, all in one. To the people, it will be called Inti Wasi, to the amautas, Sacsaywaman, the Hawk's Nest. It will be made of mighty stones. The body will lie below, between the sacred rivers. You will see. At its haunches, the Golden Enclosure of the Gods. From there will radiate the sayqays."

Already huge blocks of stone, the bones of the earth, could be seen crawling along the new-cut roads, pushing the sea of heads and hands tearing down the old city.

"In this land," he went on "no one will go hungry, no one will sleep in the cold, or wear rags, or beg, or whore. All will be safe, fed, clothed, cared for, all of their lives. The sick, the old, the insane, the crippled, man and woman. There will be no tyranny, no corruption, no man will be made to work beyond his ability." The black holes of his eyes studied Ramram and Chaski Yuyu, looking for doubt. The ghost of a smile hovered at the corners of his mouth. "In return, all will work. From first light to last, all will work hard at their assignment. All will run, not walk. Most of that will be in the *chakras*, growing food. A third will go to the Gods, a third to the common good - that is, to me - and a third to their families. No more than they can comfortably bear. Your old man, Lump, will oversee the building of enough storehouses to assure that famine will never touch the people.

"You will wake in the dark and come home in the dark. You will find you are capable of more than you imagined. And men will bow before you. A wonder will grow across the land at your doing. And you will not fail."

Without transition he strode down the hill, among the crews digging the road bed leading to town. Ramram and Chaski Yuyu hustled to keep up. Behind, the Sapa Inka's retinue ran to follow, the soldiers called cadence.

At the main plaza, now being filled with a layer of broken stone, drainage over the dark bedrock foundation, World Changer stopped. Behind, his attendants halted, bumping into one another. At some imperceptible signal, one man left the crowd and came toward them. Ramram, who had been surprised at his own calm throughout the lecture, now felt the tang of oncoming piss to see the man striding at an almost casual pace. Did he want to die? A soldier, an officer, came into focus. It was lieutenant Otoronqo Kuy.

"He is my man," Pachacutiq informed the two of them. "So he is a man. He maintains his dignity. He will run to battle, not to me."

With that, Pachakutiq Inka was gone. Otoronqo approached. Chaski Yuyu stood still, hands folded in front. Ramram had a moment to feel himself feeling. What he felt was hunger for the work ahead, glad desire for the deep, consuming pleasure that filled him when he sensed a waka ahead, the overwhelming lust of seeing it there, the explosive gratification of laying hands on it. Everyone he knew knew that he was called to anything full of Kamay. No one knew what it did to him to find one, and need that drove him to search for the next. Opening a new waka, the sea of peace he felt walking with the mountain spirits, with Pachamama, expanded exponentially until he disappeared into ecstasy. That was how he had his first orgasm, and some since. Only Tuya knew. He had run to tell her, she had laughed and kissed him.

Otoronqo Kuy, tall and lean, tipped his head toward them and said, “I am instructed to inform you that the Prince wonders if all you bring to us, all your sorcery, is the ability to draw men into blind belief. If what defeated the Chanka army weren’t stones of power, but the power of belief, and pure luck.”

“Even now?”

“The World Changer is a complicated man.”

What did that mean? Complicated in his mind, or in his words? But Ramram left that unsaid.

Chaski smiled at the soldier. “I hear that Ramram is not on the official list of combatants in the Brother Stone Assault Force, all of whom were showered with promotions and perquisites. And that the story of the discovery and placement of the Wanakawri stones has metamorphosed to a legend that the stones of the mountains themselves had turned to soldiers to fight for Pachacutiq. That they are called *Paruawki*, brother warriors.” Otoronqo nodded, keen eyes on Ramram’s face.

“Not entirely false,” Ramram said, aware that if the Lieutenant passed that on to the Sapa Inka he could pay with his head.

“Your role is not mentioned. I am to tell you that, lest you be taken by surprise. Furthermore, henceforth the battle will have been fought not on the hill but on a flat elsewhere, to be named Yawarpampa, Blood Plain. ‘Because,’ says the Son of the Sun, ‘more glory for us, and the hill already has a name.’”

“And he wants you to tell me these things?”

“And to know that he knows that you know.”

The man was complicated in word and being.

“Well,” said Ramram, “I hope World Changer won't someday decide I have been told too much.”

“And you trust that he will not be told too much by his adjutant.” He smiled. “Who is now a captain.”

“Congratulations, sir,” said Chaski Yuyu. “Do you have any further instructions for us? We wouldn’t want to wander off in the wrong direction, given how little we know of our task.”

Captain Otoronqo raised a finger; a corporal materialized behind him with a large sack of khipus. “Instruct Q’urpa in khipu, if you please.”

Kancha

“*Inti!* look at this place. It’s built for a king.” Ramram ran his hand over the massive masonry of the kancha wall,cut stones as big as boulders and as smooth as water, sealed seamlessly together. “We are going to live here?”

Otoronqo, standing behind Ramram and Chaski Yuyu, nodded. “This is one of the first to be finished in this district. World Changer wants you to get started forthwith. And he wants everybody to know that your work outranks theirs.”

It was a walled enclosure like the one he grew up in, with three dwellings and an open-front kitchen house, except of polished imperial masonry, and much bigger houses, workers still plastering and painting the upper storeys.

“That is our staff?” Chaski Yuyu asked, looking over the six people lined up in front of the main house, hands folded before them.

“Yup,” said Otoronqo, “cook, cleaner, doorman, and three servants, all waiting for instructions Ramram would never give.” He laughed. “But you come from good family so you’ll know how to act.”

“What do those two suspiciously good-looking young women do?” Chaski enquired.

“Keep everything clean and you comfortable,” Otoronqo said innocently. Chaski and Ramram exchanged a glance. Chaski Yuyu was courting a beauty of acerbic tongue, and Ramram had, however distant, Tuya.

Chaski Yuyu turned out to be a considerate and congenial housemate, never intrusive and with a quietly subtle wit. Ramram had a spacious loft to himself, which left him feeling vaguely uncomfortable until returning one night in animated conversation, he and Chaski Yuyu carried their talk in, having their meal hoisted up to them; this became a habit and then custom, Ramram sleeping at one end of the room, Chaski at the other. They had the two girls reassigned to a clutch of young engineers in an old ramshackle kancha across the street.

A Dangerous Friend

Soaked in a chill rain, Ramram and Chaski Yuyu hiked uphill toward a grove of old alders, at least a tupu from the Qoricancha, two hours moving slow, sniffing the air and taking notes.

"I got something. Water, I think." Ramram laughed. "Besides what we're squishing through." Chaski squinted at a khipu.

"Good. There should be a double pond up here, separated by a rock sitting on a spring. The home waka of the Wismichuq allyu."

As they labored over the crest, a beam of sunlight came through a rip in the clouds to pinpoint the rock and its twin pools.

"Cheap trick," said Chaski Yuyu, "Gaudy. What do you get?"

"Oh, it's real," Ramram replied, "it sings, not loud, but a loving tune. Who are the Wismichuq?"

"A half brother of a half brother of a cousin of the wife of Inka Roca. Small family. Only one of them with earstuds, a mummifier. You are seventeen now?"

"So they say."

"You look like a man and you act like a man. That may be unfortunate."

"I don't see how it matters at all?"

"Because a man can scare people where a boy would not." Chaski looked up from their reflection in the pond.

“You have dangerous enemies. And maybe more dangerous friends. I have heard that you prevented a capacocha sacrifice during the war? Do you recall the villaq priest presiding?”

“Qachu. Skinny guy.” Ramram laughed. “The Prince took away his feather hat and gave him a spear.”

“Yes. And he joined the suicide squad and came back alive bathed in glory. Now he re-frocked as a villaq of Ilyapa. That order is steeped in assassination and sorcery, and word is he has it in for you. So does his cult; the rumor is that you are plotting with a s’uqa, an evil spirit from another pacha, to distort the past and future.”

A cold wind blew through Ramram. “It’s not like that. I will tell you later. But where did this come from? I have told only one friend, and she does not tell secrets.”

“It appears that they have their own contact in the spirit world. And it is just a rumor. But he clearly resents you and he is not without weapons.”

“And the dangerous friend?”

“Do I have to speak his name?”

“Right. He seems to like me? At least, have a use for me?”

“Maybe you are too hard to understand. And know too much.”

Ramram smiled slyly. “And some of the glory of Hunchback hill spilled over onto me?”

“He erased you from the official history, true, but not from the stories told around the campfires.”

“Well, there’s nothing I can do about that except do my work well and keep my head down. What’s next along this line?”

How to Make a World

“This will be Inti Wasi.” Otoronqo Kuy woke them before dawn and took them to the hill once crowded with the Chanka army. “Head of the puma.You see down there, the Qoricancha pantheon. That will be its tail. Let’s go down."

Tens of thousands of workers and their bosses, engineers, masons, thatchers, artisans, all the ants of a giant hill swarmed over the remaking of Qosqo. Otoronqo took them down through the chaos of construction toward the gold-strapped Qoricancha pantheon. They backed against a new-raised stone wall as a huge rectangular monolith, edges cut sharp, was hauled uphill to rhythmic chanting.

"You may be a High Lord with gold plugs pulling down your earlobes and a hundred thousand households under your command, but you have responsibility for those people and you get up with the sun just like any farmer, and go down with the sun, and that job better be done right. That is the heart of Pachacuti's new world. You work. Every *hatun runa*, every man at his maturity, once only in his life, gives himself to *mita*, public service. Maybe only one year if the work is hard and far from home; maybe six years if it is easy and close. This is the world Sapa Inka Pachacuti creates."

All right, Ramram thought, this is Ayni, sharing, at the state level. The Inka was making a big promise.

"The mita may be construction of roads, buildings, andenes, irrigation systems, bridges, tambos, or other works of civil engineering; or maintenance of the same. It may be military, mining, or portage. People with specialized skills may be called upon for performance of those."

Chaski Yuyu looked up from his khipu. "No man can be made to leave his home to work more than once? Not by a Curaca or Tocricoc governor?"

"No. And this is not in my given message, but hear: no man can be sentenced to death by any official or noble except at the level of regional governor. Then, only in the presence of a committee of *amauta* sages of advanced education, relevant officials, and experts. And — I'm skipping ahead here — the Inka will appoint a Tocoyricoc, He Who Sees All, an agent of tested character and intensive training, for each Suyu, to travel throughout the territory assuring that every official complies with the law incorrupt. He has absolute power to punish or remove from office." He paused, shook his head. "Look, the rock is past. Shall we stretch our legs?"

Ramram was surprised to hear the punctilious Otoronqo speaking so casually. They turned a corner into a narrow street that seemed to vanish into infinity ahead. The walls were windowless and high, the stonework even and flawless. Otoronqo cleared his throat.

"The Acclawasi," he said. "The House of the Chosen Women. The womenfolk just moved in. Few will ever move out, but if they do, a farmer's daughter may find herself more powerful than a queen. The Sapa Inka has always sent out scouts to recruit the most beautiful and talented girls as his secondary wives or concubines. This will be institutionalized. An agent called an Apu Panaca will visit each town every year to select the best from among the eight-to-ten year old girls to become *Acclas*. They will be taken to the Acclawas*i*, a sequestered communal house, and trained in fine weaving, cuisine, aqha beer production, conversation, deportment, to become priestesses, wives to those favored by the Inka, to remain in the Acclawasi making what is beautiful, useful, or necessary. Some will be honored as sacrifices to the Apus, some reserved for the Inka alone. Some of these will rise from the fields to positions of power and finery."

Ramram thought of the beautiful Qantuta in Rumipuqyu, who had barely escaped being inducted into old Inka Viracocha's harem through being fevered when the woman-finder came. And her little sister Misk'i, also destined for beauty. They would not evade Pachacutiq's Apu Panaca. Would they want to go? And Tuya, his intended, saved by a birthmark on her face.

Otoronqo looked intently at Ramram, then at Chaski. "I am instructed to tell you these things," he said, "in case you are wondering. He doesn't know how to use you yet, so you must be primed for any sudden move."

Including death, thought Ramram, and exchanged a glance with Chaski.

“Now let’s look at your work,” Otoronqo said, “I have kept you from it long enough.

They climbed two thousand stairs up and out of town to the right of sunrise, along a wide cobble-stoned road, fresh built, until they came to the layers of deep construction and the builders, then left it behind on the old track to Chinchero. Ramram had walked this on his way to the war.

“That’s the Capaq Ñan back there, the Royal Highway. Wherever the Inka go, goes that road. Another of the Emperor’s promises to himself and the Tawantinsuyu.”

“Tawantinsuyu? Four parts?” Ramram had heard that before but never had it explained to him.

“Four *suyus*, sections,” interjected Chaski Yuyu, “Colla, under the cross of stars, where the Inka originated, so they say; the sacred lake Titicaca is there. So are Pachacuti’s armies now. Antisuyu; that’s the rain forest where the sun rises. We haven’t been there yet.”

“I was,” said Otoronqo, “With the Prince. I followed him into exile. Too hot, too many bugs, and the locals laugh at us mountain folk. Go on.”

“Yes. Condesuyu, where the sun sets; that’s where Mamacocha, the Mother Lake, lives; and the great kingdom of the Chimu. They make us look like hick farmers, so the tales tell. To the left, along the spine of the mountain Apus, Chinchaysuyu. Many kingdoms, much to conquer.”

“And we will,” vowed Otoronqo Cuy, “Soon. So, Ramram, your town is a couple days walk ahead, right?”

Ramram was suddenly a little dizzy. He shook his head.

“Rumipuqyu. As you know, Captain. It was your little speech that put me on the road to Qosqo

Otoronqo grinned. “Can’t say I noticed you. Down past your ville is the Yucay Valley. Been there?”

"No. Dad went there once on a project. Warm and pretty, he said, good growing land. Most of it isn't our turf, though." Yes. He was light-headed, far away. Where had he felt this before?

"It will be. There's fighting now, but not much. We're rolling over them. So up there, to the left? I have a feeling that's your future."

"Tell me more?"

"You'll see. Why are we stopping?"

Chaski Yuyu answered. "This is the third waka on this ceque line. We passed two to let the construction go by. This one is a cave under a rock. Ramram, the knots are ambiguous. Left or right?"

But Ramram was standing as if stunned, wavering slightly back and forth like a weed in the wind. Otoronqo reached out to him; Chaski put a restraining hand on the soldier's shoulder.

"It's all right," he whispered, "He is just gone to his spirit friend. He'll come back whole, and if we're lucky, we may learn something."

Meaningless Sweeps of Color

At first it was meaningless sweeps of color, held between Eff Ram's hands. Ramram blinked, twisted his head from angle to angle; he trusted that Eff Ram had something real to show him. Eff Ram tapped one complex blob of browns, greens, and gold with a fingertip, Ramram squinted, and suddenly it coalesced into magic. The Apus were showing him a man, an Inka man, portrayed like painting of a llama on a kancha wall, but much more vivid, as if whole and real. How did they do that?

Yes, it was an Inka, with gold earplugs and a feather headdress. No it wasn't, it had long hair and the headdress was wrong. But it was trying to be an Inka. And all around other Inkas, being killed by silver men or men in silver clothing with silver spears. They were slaughtering the almost-Inkas.

Eff Ram showed him another and another, held in some thin silver box, like the reflections in water. Then came one that moved and yelled. Whatever was in Eff Ram's sick world was much more powerful than anything in Ramram's, except for the Apus themselves.

There were flashes of light and thunder, there were impossible animals and the killing of brown men by pale silver men in a chaos of motion and noise.

Then there were ruins of Inka buildings, stone foundations on empty páramos.

Then Eff Ram lifted his head from the wizard box and looked around himself at a cityscape of incomprehensible artifacts on and around the stumps of what had been Inka structures. Not a place Ramram knew. It was just a glance, a glimpse, and then Ramram was back on the hillside, still on his feet, Otoronqo and Chaski looking at him with concern.

Anticipation or Fear?

The cave was a place of power, containing the mummies of local dignitaries, preceding Inka control. It was duly recorded. Then Otoronqo Kuy and Chaski Yuyu stood looking at Ramram, their patience growing thin.

"All right," Ramram admitted, "I cannot explain what my spirit friend from the Dark Future showed to me, but I can tell you what it meant. It meant the end of World Changer's Tawantinsuyu. The end of the Inka. We will be defeated and destroyed by men or demons with sorcery, or just weapons more powerful than ours. But the Eff Ram is showing it to me for a reason, not just to make me feel bad. It is a warning. That is all I want to say about that now."

"Clear your mind," commanded Otoronqo, "shake the chaff from the seed, and prepare to report to the Sapa Inka. Meanwhile, I must report to you on his behalf."

Silence. Otoronqo Kuy seemed to be thinking, gazing to the *antisuyu*, the east.

"Chaski Yuyu, in six months you will turn over the finalization of the saykay system to High Khipu Master Yachay Atoc, and accompany Waka Finder Ramram to his next placement."

"Understood."

"Ramram, at that time, you will relocate to the north end of the Yucay valley, where a newly won settlement is being built. It will be named Pachamamatambo and will be Pachacutiq's personal retreat, as well as a religious and social center. It is his belief that the place has great Kamay, and that there is potential for many waka to be established. You will exercise your talents there. Your father will be Qolcacamayoq — Inka influence is expanding too fast and too far for him to manage all of Qosqo region by himself — and your village, Rumipuqyu, will be decommissioned and its people moved to Pachamamatambo."

Suddenly Ramram vibrated awake, nerves pricking. He was sure that he had never before heard the name 'Pachamamatambo,' yet he was certain that it would wrench him from this life onto another and alien plane. He wondered if what he was feeling was anticipation or fear.

CHAPTER EIGHTEEN now

Superluminary

The muzzle of a Remington 760 pump-action pheasant gun is pressed against Nick Nieman's left temple. He is in an armless wooden chair, hands behind his back, feet tied. You see a bare-legged female in a t-shirt aiming the shotgun. She is wearing a crow-beaked Tlingit spirit mask. On her feet, gumboots. Long black hair floods over her shoulders.

He grimaces, twists his head away from the muzzle. She jabs the barrel against his skull. "Talk," she says. "To your peeps."

He takes a breath.

"It is all my fault. I've got schadenfreude against myself. Some local shot down my quadcopter. I took a closer look at the vid and now I think it was a woman walking her dog in gumboots. With a 12-gauge shotgun."

Nick's abductor is about half his size, slender, small bulges in the front of her shirt, which lifts in back as she leans so you get a little *panchira*, a show of underthings. Pink and blue floral. Great legs.

She makes a "go on," gesture.

"I know what you're thinking: 'Ha! Good for her! Already damn little privacy in this country.' Yeah, I take rueful pleasure in my own lesson learned. The lady provided me with good information. You may also be asking why her dog was in gumboots with a shotgun?"

They are in his basement studio, a place of deep shadows.

His eyes roll toward her, as if for approval. She ruffles his lank brown hair. The motion causes the gun to shift, contracting her finger on the trigger. He winces.

"Here's what I have had to deal with since I first jacked into that Inka priest Qachu and his ambient world. Here's what you have to deal with in asking yourself, 'Is he crazy? Or is he having us on?'

“Can information really be passed back and forth through time? According to freshman physics, it can’t. Bear in mind, quantum physics is very slippery stuff and tends to disappear out from under you.

"The wise ones tell you that you can’t communicate with the past using quantum entanglement because of the No-Cloning Problem."

Gun girl pokes him. "And why do they think that?" Her inflection is millennial, with maybe a touch of Native American nasality.

"They had to think that up because some French physicist hanging out with the Berkeley Fundamental Fysiks Group came up with a theory on how, since particles can affect each other instantly across theoretically infinite distances regardless of the speed of light, we should be able to send messages across infinite space. They called this Superluminary Telegraphy. Faster-than-light messaging. And space is time.”

She racks a round into the chamber. "How would that work? Do the Bob and Alice thing, Uncle Nicky. Like you did for me."

“Okay. I'm not your goddamn uncle." She snorts, he bares his teeth. "In fact, it's been done. In Jerusalem, 2013, they entangled photons that never coexisted in time. But yeah, B Bob, here and now, sends A Alice, then and there, a message by tweaking an entangled particle at this end, which causes an instantaneous symmetrical change to its partner across space, and therefore time."

She gestures toward the camera, making her finger slip on the trigger again. "Symmetrical? How?"

"'However Bob spins, entangled Alice spins the opposite. Right? Isn’t that just like her? Boink, coded information passing through time. So."

The masked one fades back into the dark. Nick's eyes close, he exhales. He lifts his haggard face, looks into the lens.

“So. This was an uncomfortable idea to many physicists, so they came up with the argument that Alice would first have to know the settings of Bob's transmitter, which she cannot unless he sends them to her, which he can't, because of the No-Cloning Problem, so all she'd get is noise. You can't clone a qubit of information, so you can't zap messages to your deceased granddad because all he'd get is raw static. There's your No-Cloning problem."

Kwee climbs onto his lap, half up his chest, eyes fixed off camera to where gun girl has gone. Nick writhes, trying to dislodge her. No luck.

She is back, the mask is gone. Her face is hidden between the wings of her long black hair, like The Ring girl. She shoulders the 16-gauge, aiming at his left eye.

"Blast 'um with the grownup stuff, Knee Man." Nick's face screws up.

"That is, to hose you with jargon," his voice creaks, "you got your Alice system and your Bob system using the controlled inverter gate and the Walsh–Hadamard gate to entangle two qubits. But this is not cloning. For one thing, any observation irreversibly collapses the system into some eigenstate of the observable, corrupting the information contained in the qubits. And sending a receiver signal, wouldn't that be observation? A single universal U cannot clone a general quantum state. This proves the no-cloning theorem."

"Obviously," she says sarcastically. "So?"

"So Alice can't read Bob's message to get the hell out, PoPo is about to land on your cook lab."

She frowns in disapproval.

"Well, okay, turns out they're wrong. For one thing, physics is on it, that's why they call it a 'problem.' I can't tell you what the next string of cryptic equations is going to be, but particle physics is edging toward scribbling it on the green board, and someone out there is right now closing in on No-Cloning. A re-observation of the Observer in Uncertainty, could be. Quantum physics is going to keep dogging the nightmares of classical science for a long time. For another, ‘cause I’m doing it."

The barrel comes down to caress his cheek. His eyes try to follow that trigger finger. "Not convinced, Uncle Nicky. Where's the logic?"

“I am not your uncle, dammit. And simple. Single-cell organisms are made of particles, and particles entangle, and for the holobiome, time does not exist. Quantum non-locality does."

"Okay maybe. And there's no word for what we are to each other, so 'uncle' will have to do. Bring it on home. Your life hangs by a thread."

"So. The global holobiome operates on a subcellular level to entangle its way to superluminary telegraphy and, through that, to carry my consciousness across this spacetime to mingle with another that has theoretically deconstructed five hundred years ago. And it does the same for my counterparts in the Question, whose names I now know."

"Oooo. No names. Your peeps are not ready. So?"

"So some Inka wakes up in the fourteen hundreds and says, ‘What? The Spanish are coming? We better hunker down and gear up.’ That's what Pachamama, The Question, desires. That's what we have to counter. I and my sneeze-monk."

She snorts a laugh. "Sneeze monk. Cute. And?"

"And that's how we do it."

She steps back, flings the firearm spinning across the linoleum floor, swipes the hair out of her face, lifts Nick to his feet. His hands were not tied. He un-loops the clothesline from his ankles, brushes himself off, twists a crink out of his neck. She is pulling on jeans in a peristaltic shimmy. The cat watches, fascinated.

Nick Nieman smiles at her. "Thanks, cousin," he says. "You did great. They might not have learned anything, but I bet we got their attention."

She smiles back at him, exeunt stage left. Kwee scampers after.

"And that," Nick repeats to the camera, "Is how we do it."

Good Luck With That

Bingham and Lily took a smaller dose of cactus juice and were ready to ride, but when Ephraim came back to them, he shook his head. “Not today. He is tired and hurting. Seeing this place as it is now was hard on him. But he is getting that the future is bad for the Tawantinsuyu. That is a good first step. Bingham, you have to see it. This town then. It will be worth everything you have ever suffered.”

Lily asked him about time sequences. He said, “We are not in synch. Twice I saw him seconds apart in his time, a day apart in ours. Now he is moving faster than we are. He is a man now, maybe twenty. That happened in one day for us. He is here now, in this town. It wasn’t even built the last time we saw him.”

Bingham ran his hand over his balding head. His hat stayed lost. “That makes sense. You saw Ollantaytambo under construction. Sarmiento says Pachacutiq built it. So that supports our operating theory that you saw Pachacutiq and we saw the Chanka war. You heard Ramram right. Anyway, whenever this is, it is before the conquest. If we can get our boy to see what they are facing, and tell whoever is in charge, we can very possibly…”

“Change history,” Lily concluded. “Good luck with that.” They turned to stare at her. “I mean it. Good luck. With that.”

The Core is Born

Climbing Flute Mountain, Pinkuylluna, Lily insisted on leading because she was afraid of heights. Ephraim and Bingham stayed back on the rocky spine, watching her look for a way around a steep fissure between two impossible outcrops.

"Cliff!" called Lily from above, turning around.

"She's gonna have to go straight up that split," Ephraim said.

"Thanks for putting me up in the mud brick house," Bingham had moved into the third room. "It'll save me a lot."

'The Prof' would get one night out of three with Lily, they agreed. Ephraim thought he took that pretty well, if he did say so (to) himself.

They watched her spider up the near vertical cleft, stone by stone.

"Okay, Bingham admitted, "What had happened to us could have been just suggestion you laid on us two drug-bent innocents in your madness. But I'm not buying it. Neither is she."

There was a scraping sound above, loose rock falling. Bingham stood "She's slipping. She's going to fall."

"She'll figure it out," said Ephraim. Bingham stayed standing, watching.

“So we are into something big,” he said. “Nieman may be the first to come out with this seeing-through-dead-eyes deal, but he's just talking. We are going to act on it. We are going to take this all the way. Agreed?”

"We talk to miss fly-on-the-wall there? I want to know what she thinks?"

For the next hour they followed her up the untracked rocky spines.

"Yay!" she yelled from the top. "I'm up! You coming?"

They sat on the summit, Lily hugging her knees, a little back from the edge but her eyes were alight and her face was flushed.

"Every direction is down," she said, "I will never be that afraid of heights again." She stood, started taking videos with her cell. The town was far below, the mountains all around.

"So what do you think, Lil', are we onto anything?" Ephraim waited for her answer.

“Oh yeah. We are the core group of something important. Others will come in. Groupies. Schools. Governments. But we will always be the core."

Bingham wanted to put his arms around her, but knew that would be out of order there and then.

"I have got to get my microbiologist friend onto this. Noe Kroeber. She will connect this to empirical science. We were boosted by some environmental interaction with our metabolism. Something took us back there. I think she can tell us what it is."

"Yep," Ephraim agreed, "I have always felt it. First with Ramram, then here in these mountains. It is a real factor."

"I feel it too," Lily said. "On the green wachuma goo. I have done lysergic acid, psilocybin, ecstasy. They may have been more mind-blowing than this San Pedro stuff, but they didn't connect to this Pachamama deal, because: it wasn't there."

"But we can't assume your friend's specialty applies here," Ephraim warned.

Bingham's eyes narrowed. "No. It could be anything. But we can rely on her scientific integrity. And erudition."

Ephraim looked down at his fists rapping on a fallen stone wall. "Okay," he said. "If you trust her."

"We are the edge of the universe," Lily marveled softly, "spinning into virgin space. We are the point of the spear. You and I, Eph. Bingham too. All of us. This is too interesting," she said. "We are the Core. Here's to us."

Ephraim saw Lily smile intimately at Bingham, suffered another jet of jealousy. 'Do not take me there,' he prayed again. 'Do not let us drown in that.'

Lily noticed. 'Men,' she concluded. 'But Ephraim is tough. My boy will stand.'

Ephraim saw her seeing him and the insecurity fled, as if he had matured a year.

"Bing, you bring your rum?"

Bingham dug his plastic flask out of his rucksack, handed it to her. She took a swig, held it aloft. "Boys, to the Core." She passed it on to Ephraim, who smiled.

“Christ,” he said. “I’m already nostalgic for this and it hasn’t happened yet.”

Maybe I’ll teach

Noe Zoe Kroeber Stood on the corner where Shakespeare & Co. bookstore of Berkeley used to be, and thought, ‘Change is good. There needs to be more of it.’ The place had been there when her mother was an undergrad, had stayed the same until it wasn’t there. In its place was a black sign with dark red kissy-lips. Nothing more. Trés chic.

The lips reminding her of her own imbroglio, blasting into the faculty meeting late, with her face smeared Ruby Woo red. No one mentioned it again, not to her.

And no one was mentioning that Noe’s research had sunk into the mud. She had found some promising cultures in the wild, but nothing that would survive transportation to a laboratory, much less grow there under acceptable conditions. And they weren’t enough anyway. And no one was publishing anything that took her interests forward, and no colleague was sending her any private communications of use either.

Studies went just so far into superorganisms — biofilms, stigmergy, symbiotic collaborations and co-evolution, but she needed an order-of-magnitude leap — that term ‘paradigm shift’ that kept falling out of people’s mouths. ‘Oh get a grip, Noe,’ she admonished herself, ‘Don’t be petty.’

She needed a miracle to move forward. “Change is good,” she said aloud, since her end of the block was clear now, “We need more of it.” As she walked away she empathized with the old Shakespeare’s. It had held for a long time, as long as it could. Then it was gone. “I guess maybe I’ll teach,” she muttered, and walked on down the street.

At home she threw herself into her one armchair. Her landline was blinking. It was from Bonnaterre.

"Noe," the message went, "Bingham. Start packing. I've got something for you. Seriously."

CHAPTER NINETEEN then

Qantuta's Song
Pachamamatambo
Now Called Ollantaytambo

"Close it up, people." Otoronqo Kuy's orderly Choque Anka looked fifteen but he had the command voice down. "Look sharp. We're there." The people, mostly civilians, ignored him, eyes eating up the landscape. This was going to be their life for the rest of their life. Pachamamatambo.

Their cortege was a column of more than six hundred assorted travelers, six days on the road, and the final checkpoint was in view.

"I can live here?" Ramram had never seen a place more beautiful. The valley was billowing with Kamay. He felt it rolling down the hillsides like a cloud at dawn. Chaski Yuyu was speeding through the pertinent khipus, while Otoronqo Kuy kept the procession in order.

"Captain," Chaski Yuyu lifted a khipu at Otoronqo Kuy, "that strange and imposing peak, that would be Pinkuylluna, Flute Mountain?"

Otoronqo nodded confirmation.

"All right. Then that would be...yes, the Qoripata is there — on Pututu, Trumpet Mountain. So the kanchas, the lodgings, will locate between the two. And here comes Tiyu Punku, the main gate. What a fine transformation of an already majestic site."

Ramram silently agreed. If this was World Changer's mitmac duty, it might have its good side.

The young orderly reported to the captain of the guard, who was expecting them. The head of the column passed through an imposing trapezoidal portal, one of two, south in, north out, in a stone wall, armed guards posted above. Behind them, road-weary officials, households in relocation, artisans, specialists, porters, and stoic soldiers trailed through, not too tired to marvel, and to become hopeful that this place was as good as it looked, and that their lives were to be wondrously transformed in its care.

Ramram revelled in the mesmerizing tranquility of the land. His work here might never end, nor would he wish it to.

They passed through the portal.

He directed his porter in placing his few personal items around the spacious chamber assigned to him in a kancha of the finest imperial masonry. He was being bestowed honor owed to a regional governor or high priest of the Sun, not to a mid-level technician such as he. Of course, Pachacutiq, if no one else, knew that he, Ramram of Rumipuqyu, had saved the Inka people. That little thing. Ramram smiled.

He began to sing. Soon he would see Tuya, his childhood playmate, bride-to-be, and the love of his life. His whole community and ayllu of Rumipuqyu, a hundred and fifty-two people, some of them pregnant, had been settled here in the chakras above the confluence of the narrow Qalikantu and great Urubamba rivers. It was good land, rich land, the blood in its veins sweet water from the high springs, carried by arterial acequias, newly cut and stone-lined by the Sapa Inka's engineers and a myriad of laborers.

He walked around the cobbled street curving below the great temple sector on Pututu hill, guided by Chaski Yuyu, filtering through clusters of Rumipuqyu folk coming their way. They were curiously grim for people newly relocated to paradise.

He recognized Tuya with other young women of his village. The sweet-potato-shaped birthmark by her left temple was the last thing he noticed, though it had kept her out of the House of the Chosen Women. His heart soared, he broke into a happy grin, then stopped. Their eyes met, hers holding back tears. Her face was pale, lips drawn tight.

"Tuya."

She stepped to him, laying her cheek gently against his chest, her hands placed light as butterflies on his upper arms.

“What is it?" he asked.

"It's Qantuta. They are going to kill her today." Qantuta, Tuya's friend, lovely far beyond the expectations of such a tiny town, desired by men for days' walk in every direction. "She broke her virginity."

Qantuta's nine year old sister Misk'i, already assigned to the Acclawasi in Qosqo, threw herself around Tuya's waist, sobbing convulsively.

"Achachaw. Oh no, she didn't, not with Sinchi Poma?" Strong Puma, the toughest fighter, fastest runner, son of the village Curaca, Qantuta's love.

"Yes. You've been gone so long, Ramsie. They came for her. The Apu Panaca. You remember, she was really sick the first time they came? Then the war, and we thought everybody had forgotten her? But she was on Inka Viracocha's old census khipu. She seduced Sinchi Poma."

"Oh ñakasqa. So so sorry." An aclla had to be virginal. To use depucelation to avoid the Acllawasi was a capital crime. "Sinchi Poma too?"

Misk'i slid down Tuya's legs, clinging to her ankles in another spasm of weeping. Tuya stroked her head.

"No, World Changer's justice system actually works a little bit. They took them to the Governor's place in Calca. The Governor and his council looked at Qantuta and decided that no man could resist her. That Sinchi Poma tried. He knew he would die if he did it, but he couldn't help it. He and his ayllu are exiled to a new settlement in the Vilcabamba jungles."

The Matron of the Acllawasi — the acllas, Virgins of the Sun were brought from Qosqo for an object lesson — came to peel Misk'i away from Tuya.

"So now," Tuya's eyes were desolate, "the whole town has to watch her be thrown off the watchtower." She lifted her eyes to the small square watchtower on top of the Tunupa Viracocha's angry stone face. "All of us Rumipuqyus in front, behind the acclas. Women and men separate. I am so comforted that you are here."

Military officers aligned them across the plaza, facing the harsh stone profile that the hands of the Apus had carved from the cliff of Pinkuylluna, the thatched watchtower his crown. The drop to the rocks below seemed at least a hundred rikras. Drums were throbbing. Talking ceased, eyes were pulled upward.

Two men appeared far in the wide tower door, escorting a smaller figure, wrists crossed at her waist. The drums stopped. Silence. Nothing was announced, the sentence had already been delivered to her ayllu. The silhouette writhed, tried to retreat, was turned back to face the void. The flanking figures moved in and she soared into empty air.

Her shriek carried starkly across the town. Her legs pumped, searching for stepping stones on the wind, long dress lifting. Her scream was a full-throated screech of rage, rejection, disbelief, horror. Of absolute refusal. No animal could make that cry because no animal could know so much about death. She was not going quiet, or unremembered. She did it in one long breath. She had always had a good voice. Her figure disappeared behind a copse of alder trees and her howl quit.

The crowd was dismissed. Again Tuya came to Ramram' arms, tenderly, softly, again light as a zephyr, no clinging or clutching. She pulled away, looked into his face. The strength returned to her features. Their eyes held. Her warmth, her selfness, her body heat and scent rose to him. She turned, and they walked toward her new home, forearms touching by their sides.

“How long do you have?” she asked, eyes on his profile.

“Today. But my work will bring me down your way often. Not often enough.”

“Two years and more. Look at you!” Now she smiled through her grief. “Look at you in your tocapu, dressed like a Head of a Hundred Households!”

He made a grin.

"We heard. Your father, your friends, back from the battle like heroes. Everyone who was there promoted, given beautiful unkus, larger land grants — Waywash and Papa Chakra are both Heads of Fifty. Your dad is in charge of the whole qolqa project here, thousands of men."

She turned her incredible eyes, deep and filled with dark light, upon him. She whispered. "They told me, in secret, that you were the one who gave the Sapa Inka the Puruawkas that won the war. That you and Sapa Inka Pachacutiq came back from speaking to the Gods together, just you and he. And that you are his special friend."

Ramram laughed. "I am his special whatever he tells me to be. Usually through a messenger. But yes, the Son of the Sun and I slew Chanka warriors together, side by side. You can tell our children that when they are old enough to keep their mouths shut." He slid his arm around her waist. "May I?"

"You may. Discreetly. Oh, you feel good."

"I surely do. And you feel so fine to me."

Escorted away under guard were the Qosqo virgins. The Mamacona looked into Misk'i's eyes, no longer tearful, and shuddered.

Pachamamatambo
Reign of Pachacutiq Inka

Ramram watched the villaq Qachu, once Tarpuntay, march through the Tiyu Punku gate in a golden and befeathered procession, stiffened standards of the Ilyapa cult waving aloft in purple and black. In the lead, walking with rhythmic, measured step was K'anchay, the Hatun — Chief — villaq, Priest of Ilyapa, the Lord of Thunder, Lightning and Rain. An alright character by Ramram, he had been in Pachacutiq's presence after the battle, was sincere, had real Kamay and a sense of humor. But his second in command, Simi Apaq, the Hurin – lower – Villaq Umu, Ramram did not trust. Behind, next in lead of the entourage, Ramram was the priest Qachu. Their eyes met with a poisonous shock.

Ramram was proud to be Inka, news coming in every day of the expansion of Inka power to the west and south. He was proud of the building projects — men moving huge ashlars of hard stone down the steep slopes from the Kachiqhata quarries, across the muscular Urubamba River, and up the ramps to create new temples and palaces at the Qoripata on Pututu mountain. Of the roads shooting up and down the valleys, chaski runners bringing messages all day and night, of the barren hillsides transformed to farmland. He took pride in the power and wealth of what had been a provincial little fiefdom exploding across the land. When some once-struggling little people were annexed by the spear, or threat of spear, or by free choice, into the Tawantinsuyu, they were at least relieved of fear, hunger, poverty, and hardship. And the freedom to laze the day away.

But there was a price. Qantuta's long death cry stayed with Ramram. And there was Qapacocha, the sacrifice of children, sometimes buried alive, each year and whenever some significant event affected the Tawantinsuyu. Did Inti really require this? He would be alert when Qapacocha came to Pachamamatambo. And now it came, in the form of Qachu.

He had last seen Qachu demoted to private soldier on Puka Muqu Hill before the battle. Ramram had been responsible for that humiliating reduction in power. Strangely, Ramram had thought he had caught a glimpse of Qachu flitting into the company of the Forlorn Hope just before it launched into its suicidal assault. That was not what he would have expected of the ambitious little monk.

And here Qachu was, in Pachamamatambo, back in holy finery, still a little man within, wielding power over others. The Tawantinsuyu had its darker side

Ramram awoke before dawn, a torch in his face and a spearpoint prodding his neck.

A squat soldier rousted him into the yard, where his cook, yanacona servants, and Chaski Yuyu were being herded by armed guards in combat uniform. “You are being reassigned quarters,” the broad faced officer informed him. “Come with us.”

In the open yard, in the midst of his ornamented coterie, Qachu the Tarpuntay smirked.

“The Servants of Ilyapa require this location, close to the House of Ilyapa, in keeping with His dominion. You will be as useful in one place as another.” A train of retainers carried Qachu’s possessions in through the finely assembled great stone portal.

The head guard looked at Ramram and then at his wasi with limited patience. Ramram looked to Chaski Yuyu, who nodded, holding aloft a khipu showing an ecclesiastical identifier. Ramram signaled his people to evacuate their belongings.

It was the second day of Inti Raymi, the Festival of the Sun. Down the already bustling street, still filled with bleary revelers from the night before, around a couple of corners, snaked their little train, out of the high-status quadrant of Qosqo Ayllu, burdened by their few goods, the bulk being alpaca wool sacks of khipu.

"You don't look angry?" Chaski Yuyu noted.

"Let's see where this takes us. Villaq Qachu is a pain in the ass and could yet mean trouble for us. But the truth is, I never really felt at ease in that fancy place."

The guard detail took them through the narrow, immaculate streets of Qosqo Ayllu, passing the fine houses of the Gold Earplug men to the fieldstone dwellings of the servants and artisans, neat and pleasantly painted, into a cluster of buildings nestled at the foot of Pinkuylluna mountain. The kancha rested in an alder grove, by a stone-lined acequia where fresh water splashed down a series of fountains.

They entered a roughly constructed but spacious kancha of unworked fieldstone, mud plaster still drying on two of the houses, two still bare. Old growth alders swayed around the walls, splintering the morning sun. The windows in the peaked gables gazed out across the river and the valley.

Ramram felt right away at home. It was his kind of place, plain but rich in sun and greenery. He moved to put his blankets and bag of practice khipus in a smaller house by the door, but his yanacona redirected him to the larger, newly plastered building to the west, where the sun would come soonest and most.

"I suppose the workers and painters are off for the Raymi," Chaski observed, as their servants discontentedly inspected their lodgings. They had been proud of their Imperial compound.

"I don't care if they never come," Ramram replied. "I like the feel of this place. And let's see if we can cut our staff in half. They don't have anything to do most days. Somebody can use them."

He inspected the foliage of the tall alders and spreading molyays on three sides of the kancha, and thought of how beautiful the leaf shadows would be with the sun in the west. "Well, release our people, let's go see the show. We can eat there."

Meanwhile, Qachu directed his acolytes to dedicate the largest building in the appropriated compound to ceremonies. His dormitory was smaller. He pulled down the rope ladder to the loft, went up, unrolled his blanket onto the wicker mat covering the log floor, lay back with his hands behind his head and closed his eyes. Here his work began. He relished the prospect.

Where most men struggled for the attention of their wives, children, and immediate superiors, he had the ear of the gods. His objective was control of the Inka Pachacutiq Yupanqui himself. From whose seed he grew.

Ayni Karpay
Ramram
Direct contact between auras

“I want to check something on the lower south side of Pinkuylluna,” Ramram said to Chaski Yuyu coming into his new lodging. The cook was whipping up a mid-day meal. Ramram passed his morning’s findings on to the Khipucamayoq, who recorded them.

“These figures look thorough." The khipu master looked up from his knotted strings. "Why go up there again?”

“I’m overlooking something in that sector. I know I am. Something important is trying to get through to me. Any ideas?”

“No, Wakacuraqa Ramram, all I know is how the knots line up.”

“Well, it’s like something is pushing me away and calling me at the same time.”

“Reminds me of the woman I’m trying to court.”

Ramram stepped out into the street, squinted up at Pinkuylluna mountain looming overhead. Something about that lower slope of the mountain annoyed and repelled him.

The place resisted him. As he urged himself to approach, he was assaulted by disgust, boredom, guilt, and ultimately, fear. It fought him with distraction, forgetfulness, an intense wrongness. At last, light-headed and shaky, he came to the rocky overlook. There he froze in panic. He had never feared heights, but now he was terrified.

Against all instinct, he forced himself to crawl to the edge. He drew back, shut his eyes, clenched his teeth, and commanded himself again to peer over.

As soon as he did so, the world transformed. The meadow filled with light, with sweet air, rushing up to welcome him. It lifted him to his feet. He had broken through. He wafted down the escarpment, carried by the spirit of the place. He was home, this is what he had been searching for since he got to Pachamamatambo, since he first knew Kamay, since he was born.

A broken stone on the edge of the plateau seemed to be the epicenter of the Kamay. A siq'i rumi of great power.

The rock was split unevenly, the right-hand part thin, coming to a sharp upper edge. The left part with a rounded top upon which you could sit. Ramram walked into its thrumming forcefield.

As he stepped carefully forward, it came to him that he recognized the view, the Qosqo Ayllu district below west, the open green and garden to his left. They were the site of that glimpse of a fouled and broken place that he had seen through Eff Ram's eyes.That vision could not be denied or ignored. In his own time, the town was pristine, elegant, this patch wild and beautiful. He took another forward step, weighing the sensations. He suspected that his strange friend from another pacha would be here, waiting.

One more step and he pulled himself onto the larger hump of the stone, and was taken into Pachamama's timeless sphere.

Ayni Karpay

Ephraim

Direct contact between auras

Ephraim mounted Split Rock. The Inka was there, waiting. This time Ramram's universe snapped into high resolution, billions of pixels: they were in the same place now, each in their own time but together on the stone.

Ephraim devoured the Inka settlement with all Ramram's senses and his own.

The town had transformed from a chaotic, dirty, undisciplined junkyard to a finely composed and executed work of art. The temple sector flowed down the slope across the valley in soft gold stone and subtle jewel tones. The tall thatched roofs of the residential district gleamed as if enameled. The narrow streets were walled with stone cut to resonate in deep eternal voice.

Across the Royal road to the south in a broad park, a girl in a blue and purple aksu, a simple cloth wrapped around her body and pinned by a metal tupu, danced along hand in hand with her little sister, murderously graceful, sneaking glances at the boys in weapons practice on the other side. The little sister broke free, somersaulted into a field of mixed flowers. Her sister ran after, shouting, then tumbled along with her, laughing, showing lithe leg for the young men, one of whom lost his grip on his macana, which clattered onto the flagstones, spinning.

Ramram sat patiently as Ephraim gazed at the scene until the sun of Ramram's time turned the facades dark blue and the Inka windows amber. Ephraim tried to weave the sights and sounds into himself, to make them his own.

But they both knew that the hard part had to come. He focused his energy on himself and Ramram relinquished himself to Ephraim's world.

The Work

The landscape, blurred at first, shot into terrible clarity, and Ramram was looking down upon a different Pachamamatambo. One mutilated, a world alien and vile; and yet his own.

When Ramram ceded control, bringing Eff Ram to the front, they stood together, hands against the rough skin of the stone, looking down on the town. The time was mid-afternoon.

"Ohl Yan Tay Tambo," spoke Eff Ram, "Kunan, Ollantaytambo."

'Kunan' meant 'now.' Ollantaytambo. What was that name? Ramram wondered. Ollantay had been a Sinchi, a warlord, in this valley, whom Pachacutiq had brushed effortlessly aside and given a rustic hilltop settlement, Pumamarka, to rule as a local curaca. So 'Ollantaytambo' was what Pachamamatambo became, lifetimes ahead? This grotesque corpse?

The walls of the Qosqo Ayllu district were broken, almost buried under structures Ramram recognized as forms of houses, poorly built but full of baffling detail. Nothing that he saw had names.

Glossy beetles as big as boulders moved by some magic along black snakes of streets where the green gardens of Inti had once thrived. People could be seen dimly inside the smoke-spewing, crawling shells that had eaten or captured them. Men, women, children walked, wearing tubes on their legs and arms. Black ropes ran from pole to pole above the walkers, vibrating with some poisonous energy.

This was his world, but in it Pachamama was sick and dying. The boy Eff Ram was showing Ramram his future Pacha. Ramram had glimpsed it before but never so sharply. it was *saqra* — ugly, obscene, and wrong.

Now Eff Ram was speaking again, with slow emphasis.

"*Noqa humuni manta siriq Hamuq Pacha,*" he said. "*Siriq Pacha, Hamuq Pacha.*"

After a puzzling moment, Ramram realized that the boy was attempting Runasimi. Ramram began to interpret the sounds. Noqa, I, humini, come, manta, from, siriq, future, hamaq, to come.

"I come from far future time. Time to come."

Ramram looked out over the crawling hell, morbidly fascinated. "*Hayk'aman*?" he asked, 'since when?' He felt the boy's bewildered frustration, in his chest. "*Imay*?" When?' Toxic smoke rose from below.

There was a long pause. Eff Ram's eyes moved to a small black stone with a rectangle of smooth ice on it, held in his hands. He moved his thumbs below the ice window, and symbols, like simplistic tocapu appeared. Eff Ram looked back at the town.

"*Pichqa pachak wata*," Eff Ram answered. "*Pichqa pachak watakuna*." 'Five hundred years.'

Ramram struggled to take this is in. Eff Ram had found words to convey a terrible message, but a critical one. He was witnessing a Pachamamatambo five hundred years yet to come. He forced himself to survey this reality.

Sadness drowned him. It was the soul of the place itself that had been drained of beauty. His heart sickened in his chest, Pachamama turned sour in his gut.

Eff Ram seemed to understand. He slid off the rock, and carefully turned his head up to the mountain behind them, to its refuge of the spirit.

Ramram thanked him inwardly. They could not have destroyed the mountain. Not entirely. It was there — the qolqas were in ruins, and the force of the mountain was lessened, but it was there and brought him peace. Eff Ram closed their eyes for a moment. Then they opened, looked out across the river to the far ridge of Waywayna Orco, to Yanantin, the twin peaks of harmony. Although when you were there, you found a chasm between the two.

Eff Ram turned his eyes again to the shiny rectangular black stone in his hand, thumbs drumming, the insectile tocapu writhing across its surface.

"*Tukuchiy*," Ephraim spoke. 'You change.'

Did he mean that Ramram needed to change himself? What?

"*Chikanyay*!" 'Change it!' It was a command and a plea.

No. He was telling Ramram to change this horrific future.To change what he was now staring at to something else. This thing that the Four Parts of the World was to become.

How was he supposed to do that? How had it happened at all? And if it had, if it was what the Apus decreed, how could he, a rock-finding Lump, heal that wound?

"Ñichun Sapa Inka!"

What? Say Sapa Inka? Say his name?

Eff Ram shook his head in frustration, seeming to struggle to find the words.

"*Yachachiy*! Teach you Pachacutiq Inka! To teach Sapa Inka! Teach!" Eff Ram gave the world back to Ramram. Ramram accepted, gratefully. His own Pachamamatambo was back, falling on them like moonlight.

Teach Sapa Inka Pachacutiq. That was the message. "Ari," he replied. "I understand," he answered in Runasimi. The boy would understand "yes" at least. "Ari."

Was it possible? He was wakacuraqa, and the Lump. He had the Sapa Inka's ear. If he could warn him, move him, did he, Pachacutiq, have the power to change the world? His very name declared that he did. But how could he? How had this happened? Ramram didn't know what to tell him. And World Changer thought he was a lump. The emperor was more skeptical every day.

"How?" he asked. "In what way? How would you have me do it?"

He spread his arms, palms up, across the world. He needed to ask the question simply, so that Eff Ram would remember, find someone to tell him the meaning of his words.

Eff Ram's Ollantaytambo was changed, but it was still Inka somewhere in its heart.

Eff Ram was tugging at Ramram, trying to come forward. Ramram was tired, ready to end this, to go back home. But apparently Eff Ram had one more task for him.

Ramram gathered up his guts, closed his eyes, invited Eff Ram back.

Eff Ram opened his eyes and turned. Two more strangers crouched near. They stood.

One was a man with hair on his face, as if his head were upside down. Looking into their shared eyes, he said, "Allillanchu," how are you? to let Ramram know he spoke a little bad Runasimi. Ramram recognized something about him, about his Kamay. He remembered now from the craze of the retreat from the massacre of the Forlorn Hope. They had both been there.

"Been Um," the man said, thumb to his chest. "Been Um."

Eff Ram shifted their eyes toward a striking girl with skin almost like a real woman. “Li Li,” she said of herself. "Li-Li." That name

Ramram knew. Tuya had met her on the road to Pachamamatambo.

Inside Eff Ram, inside themselves, Ramram felt a sudden overwhelming weariness.

"*Tupananchis kama*," Eff Ram said. So long, we will meet again.

Eff Ram's world faded away. Pachamama was done with them for now. Ramram leaned his palms against the stone, breathing slowly, deeply.

Teach the damn scout-emperor. That was the message. About this. He lifted his eyes.

He looked out over his land, full of gratitude that it was still as it was, of sorrow for what was coming.

Pachamama hid this rock, this plateau, people did not see it. But on the street below, Ramram spied one man who was not deflected, who stared up at him with intense, pinpoint eyes. It was Qachu.

“I see you Tarpuntay,” Ramram spoke flatly, knowing he was beyond hearing. “Know this: whatever it is that you want, I am going to stop what is coming, to change what is coming, to make the Inka Pachacutiq’s Tawantinsuyu last two thousand years. Whether he knows it or not.”

The Silver Demons

The next day near sundown Ramram climbed to the siq’i rumi, strangely restless and hungry to know more. Eff Ram was not there.

Instead, he found himself in the person of an Inka child hiding behind the rock looking down at a train of grotesque silver men, or demons, some of whose legs were draped over the backs of giant deformed llamas that carried them like burdens, along the unkempt street. Other silver asnaq-demons walked beside. They herded a hundred or more ragged, staggering Inka people, whipping them, prodding them with long, sharpened silver sticks. He saw young women being roughly separated from the crowd and taken aside, their breasts and buttocks poked at and palped. The town itself was being taken apart, built over. Further on, lines of Inka workers were being forced to carry stones from the Qoripata hill to be used in the construction of some sort of towered structure near the bridge. A stench rose from it all, feces, filth, sweat, infected wounds. The girl he was occupying was filled with grief and fear. Her mother and father were down there.

When it let him go, he crouched, head in his hands. He would have to find a way to question Eff Ram about this. These, he suspected, were men. The men who had brought the Tawantinsuyu down. These were what Eff Ram had shown him in his magic tapestries of light, but worse. Dirtier and more cruel. This was how it happened. This was something to sway the Sapa Inka. He needed more, much more.

But he had waited long enough to inform the Sapa Inka. Waiting until he had enough to convince him was a bad idea.

He asked Otoronqo to request an audience with Pachacutiq.

Two Pachacutiqs

The Sapa Inka, masked in gold, caped in scarlet and golden feathers, stood on high in vast dignity while hosts of pipes, drums, flutes, and human voices harmonized on the andenes above and below. Ramram was ready for the Qapac Raymi to be over and to return to work. Getting stupid on chicha corn beer didn't much interest him.

Pachacutiq's executive secretary had taken Ramram's request for an audience. That is all he knew. He had waited too long to inform the august Sapa Inca of the danger, and of the existence of his partners in the future pacha. One could die for that. The Son of the Sun needed to know of the silver asnaqs, and the destruction of the Tawantinsuyu. Ramram had seen them and they were vile and deadly.

This was his mind as he stood by Chaski Yuyu on the fifth and last day of Inti Raymi, in a crowd of Gold Earplug Men waiting their turn to cross the swinging bridge to Manyaraki plaza to witness the extravagant closing ceremonies on Qoripata Hill. Across and above, beneath the foundations of what would become the temple of Inti, the Sapa Inka himself stood in splendor, caped and masked, overseeing a sacrifice of a white llama. A thousand llamas would be slaughtered in solemn ritual, and then, less formally, eaten in savory stews afforded the Intip Churin attending the festival.

Something poked him in the back. He turned, affably, drunks were everywhere, and found himself looking into the hard, implacable face of Pachacutiq Inka Yupanqui, his Emperor. In the same worn dirt-colored worker's unku as on Puka Muqu hill.

"Q'urpa. You are not in the fine house I gave you."

"Ah, Ilyapa needed it."

"Your empty Tarpuntay wanted it. He threw away the spear I gave him and put on his fine cumbi cloth again."

"As you say, Apu Sapa Inka. I am content."

"I will give him his spear again. Up his *siki*. And you your house."

"Forgive me, Apu Sapa Inka, but can we stay where we are? I like where I'm living. There's music on Chaupi street all through the evening. It feels more like home. Let Tarpuntay Qachu have the fancy house. But please, don't let him stage more Qapacochas."

"Are you arguing with me, Q'urpa?"

"I surely hope not, Apu Sapa Inka. Isn't that you up there?" He pointed to golden figure on the hill."

"Yes, that is me. Apu Sapa Inka. This is also me, wondering if you are arguing with me."

"I wonder that too. In your wisdom, you will know how to correct me."

The royal scout looked at his feet in their tattered sandals, looked Ramram in the face with those cold-hot eyes.

"Now we stop playing. I have work for you. Several works. Come with me. You too, Khipucamayoq. I would be out of character with my own clerical staff at my heels."

Pachacutiq led them to the stone steps ascending Mount Pinkuylluna, to the first level supporting the newly constructed qolqas, now in the finishing stages of decoration. Unused building materials lay by the side. Below, Ramram could see the crest over which the split rock waited. The Sapa Inka never glanced that way. He stopped, turned to look over the town toward the flowing Urubamba.

"I want built a quiet place, down there by the river. A place to think, to be alone, to commune with Apus, to plan. Most of all to plan. To listen to the wind and the river and the *sara* growing. It will require good Kamay, a careful blend of wakas, both placed there as brother stones and native to the place. I will want to have a full view around, and facilities for small ceremonies and rituals now and then. A bath. Trees planted as a windbreak, it will come in strong from Wayka Willki mountain there. A place to invent the Tawantinsuyu."

"Of course, Sapa Inka. *Intindini*, I understand. I will begin today."

"Tomorrow. Inti, Pachayachachiq, and all the other gods need your attention today. Why aren't you drunk?"

"I have had my fill, Apu, all gratitude to Inti and Pachamama. How shall I report to you?"

"Otoronqo Kuy will contact you. Your new place, you sure you don't want the walls plated with gold?"

"Please, Apu, mana."

"Mullu shells? Do you want some pretty acllas sent over? I have more than I can use."

“I have as much woman as I can handle, Apu Sapa Inka.”

“More than you know. Now. Report. You have been speaking with strange and unknown aliens from a distant Pacha. Who are they and what have they told you.” Pachacutiq sat on a building block, motioned for Ramram to sit.

‘He knows. Of course. Yet he doubts me,’ Ramram thought. 'I need to change that.'

"I have seen the wreck of the Tawantinsuyu," he said. "By silver beings, men or monsters I do not know." He began his account hesitantly, not wanting to annoy the ruler with excessive detail.

“More,” the Inka said. “All of it.” Throughout, Chaski Yuyu had been silently knotting khipus with blur-fast fingers. At last Ramram slowed, searching his mind for anything he may have overlooked, then stopped.

Pachacutiq sat stone-faced, hands on his knees, looking out over the valley. Then, eyes still to the south, he said, “Do not fail to apprise me of such events again. You do not need to understand or interpret. I have counselors for that. And a mind. Now, again, these silver asnaqs — stinking demons, from yet another Pacha — were they men?”

“I have been trying to decide, Apu. They looked like men. And they looked like hairy-face demons.”

“The silver that they wore. Was it for the gods, for the weather, armor?”

“I think armor, Apu. But everything about them was strange.”

“And weapons?”

“I think so. Thin silver spears held in one hand. Things I didn’t understand made of wood and silver. They looked dangerous. Whips for the runakuna.”

“And you felt their Kamay?”

“No, Apu. I was with a girl child. We felt only our own sorrow and fear.”

"And you believe that the two men who came to you, and the one woman who came to your Tuya, are from a different Pacha."

"Yes. I can see as they see, and they as I, but not at the same moment. It was our Pacha but not our Pacha. Changes had come. Qoripata and Pinkuylluna were as I described, destroyed, in ruins. There were unknown sounds and smells. The arms and legs of the people wrapped in a fabric I have not seen. Monster insects carry people inside themselves. The Eff Ram boy seemed to be saying that the time is five hundred years yet to come."

"Five hundred years. Too soon. The silver asnaqs, they were from that Pacha?"

"I think not. They were from a Pacha closer to this one. The Qoripata, the qolqas, were damaged but not yet destroyed. And the hatun runa they were beating, they wore unkus like men. I think they destroyed the Tawantinsuyu. I think that you can stop them."

At the last words the Inka's brows knit a little, and lips pressed. "So there are three Pachas, one of them ours, and your spirit-men, they are passing us information about their own Pacha, and another, that is coming to this land. And this ayni karpay, this communication between you and these Then men, what is causing it to happen? How does it happen?"

"It is Pachamama that brings it, Apu. This I know. Pachamama as the consort of Pachayachachiq is in the Kamay of the siq'i rumi, and she is — I believe that she is — trying to tell us something important."

"He, Pachayachachiq, is trying, Q'urpa, to tell me something. Through you. Something I need to know. And you are the only one who has had willay with these asnaq?"

"No, Apu, my intended Tuya has strong willay with the woman Li Li. She has Kamay and is in harmony with Pachamama."

"So not you alone can get information from the other-Pacha-runa, or *machu*, or whatever they are. I will send others to investigate this. And is this siq'i the only one with this power?"

“The only one here with strong enough Kamay to meet the future strangers. Although I think they are more like *ankhari*, spirit messengers of the Apus. But I believe there are more to be found. Great Inka. With each time my own Kamay becomes stronger. I can sense the presence of more waka and more intensely and clearly. I am changing, Apu. I am afraid that soon I may not be a man anymore, a human.”

“I know the feeling, Wakacuraqa Ramram.” Now Pachacutiq turned his face to Ramram. “Don’t fear. You are only becoming an *Amauta*, a wise man, and an Umu. A wizard. It won’t kill you, yet, and you can still get married. You are learning the khipu?”

“Ari, Apu.”

“Good. I may send other teachers to you. Find my place of retreat, return to your siq’i, learn more. Much more. Learn to converse. Do they speak Runasimi?”

“A little only. I think the hairy-faced one has more. They have another tongue.”

“And you know their names?”

“Eff Ram and Bean Um.”

”Ask them about the silver men. Find more wakas with this power of willay. Continue finding wakas as before.” Pachacutiq rose, walked back down the hill. Since he did not look back or beckon, Ramram and Chaski Yuyu waited until he was gone to follow.

Walking away, Sapa Inka Pachacutiq Yupanqui compared what Ramram had reported with what he had heard of the Tarpuntay Qachu, his thin sharp son, and his divinations with the Umu Nikniman. He would keep them apart for now.

Birds, The River, Wind

Ramram found the site for Pachacutiq’s river retreat. He sat cross legged on a long stone of quiet but strong kamay looking out across the land. Workers still hauled stones up the ramp to the Qoripata, far and high across the Qalicantu river. He could see others building andenes on the far side of the Urubamba, but all he could hear were many birds in their morning calls, and the sound of the river below, and the wind.

A group of men had gathered at the intersection of four fields below, three of maize, one of quinoa. He could see them laughing together, relaxed, drinking akha corn beer from ceramic jars; their voices did not carry.

The planting was done for the season. The farmers would have free time now. The census was taken, most mitmacs in place, so the curacas too would have little to do but to enjoy life in Pachamamatambo.

He saw the wives of the drinking men at a corner above, laughing and weaving rich textiles. The woman always worked, weaving even as they walked, but it was second nature to them, a pleasure more than a chore.

Birds, the river, the wind. Healthy crops, good weather; what a beautiful place to live, what a good life. *Kusi kawsay* all around.

Pachamama was everywhere. Eff Ram's bad pacha was far away in time.

CHAPTER TWENTY now

Welcome to the Core

Noe Kroeber debarked her taxi in a little black dress with a two-lobed silver and amethyst pin and a megalithic piece of luggage. The three Temporal Displacement Research Technicians — Ephraim, Lily, and Bingham — were still waiting to hear that she'd left SFO when she hauled her massive rolling suitcase into the plaza at Ollantaytambo and called Bingham.

"Nice pin,"Lily noted after introductions, "Does it have special meaning for you?"

"Special? It's an amoeba in mitosis."

"Nympho," Lily murmured, elbowing Noe in the ribs. Noe looked at her as she did most people in casual conversation, as if she were an inconvenient statistical outlier. Eph and Bing volunteered to carry her suitcase, one on each end, and regretted the offer upon testing the weight against gravity.

"It has wheels," Noe pointed out, looking at them as she looked at most people trying to do things.

"They dig into the dirt," Bingham groused, "See? No pavement." But Noe was right. Bumping along making wheel-size ditches in the dusty road was better than playing two-man pallbearer.

They continued in silence to the mud brick house.

"Do you mind sharing a room with Bingham until we can get the one on the end set up for you? Ephraim watched her study the place, first from outside, then the inside. She checked the outlets.

"Fine. Bingham and I tried sex once, with no distinct negative outcome."

Bingham sighed goodbye to his one-night-in-three with Lily. Lily picked up on that and volunteered her foam mattress so that Noe could occupy the middle room. She and Eph would resume their original musty old bedding until their next Urubamba run.

They now had six plastic Italiano stools, a two-burner gas stove, and one small folding table. Ephraim served his homemade stone soup. Noe ate, recognizing it as food, in silence, eyeing her companions new and old.

Fed, she got a copy of their notes, scanned them rapidly, then they got down to business.

"All right. What's not recorded here is how this displacement experience presents, what parts of the body register the first symptoms, and what are they?

The three looked at each other. It hadn't occurred to any of them to document that.

"It always starts low in the intestine," said Ephraim, looking to the others for confirmation. "Then a strong throb above and between the eyes. Some would say pineal."

"That's right," said Bingham. "It does. You're right. Every time."

"Yes!" exclaimed Lily. "And don't forget the light going on in your head just as it hits."

"Okay, I confirm that," Ephraim nodded.

"And you have the most experience?"

"He does, by far," said Lily. "He's been having these episodes since childhood."

"But not with the present intensity. Still, yes, I have had more contact; but Bingham and Lily have both had unique variations."

"Yes, I see. With an adolescent male, grown to maturity, and an indigenous female, both preterit. Very good. And the next stage?"

"The experiential exchange takes over," Ephraim went on, "All the senses, emotions. It's not you anymore, except up off in one corner."

"Affectual, sensory, somaesthetic, tactile." Noe was taking rapid notes.

Bingham spoke up. "And there is this sense of benevolence coming from the ambient environment, if that's not redundant. I call it the Pachamama effect. You get that too, right, Lil'?"

“Yes. Strongly. Or you can think of it as ‘the Presence.’ From the We Live In You vlog.”

“Right,” said Bingham.

“Me too,” confirmed Ephraim. “You may want to check out this video blog, by the way, Noe.”

“I am familiar with ‘the Presence.’ Alright. And that’s all? No more identifiable effects?”

The twilight filled the windows with a yellow-pink light from above the southern ridge line. A rhomboid of fading light folded over the four on their stools or splay-legged on the floor.

“I guess,”Bingham shrugged . “For me.” Noe looked intently at Lily.

“Oh all right,” Lily admitted, “It goes right to my butterfly. On and in the vulva, a really nice sensation, not especially sexual.”

Noe nodded.

“That is consonant with distribution of the microbiota in the human. Perfect. Excellent. Thank you all. Especially you, Lily, I sense a certain pudeur. All right. This fully justifies leaving my laboratory.” She smiled, and her colleagues in intellectual crime saw an eternal child prodigy, full of the joy of vindication, and something more.

“My friends, except for the stimulus of the *epiphysis cerebri*, on which I have no data, I hope to prove what you have experienced to be microbiota-specific, in interaction with corollary prokaryote colonies which I expect to find concentrated in lichen, that I surmise from your description are largely crustose placodioid coatings.” She cast her eyes around the group. “You see what this means.”

“You got your superorg,” Bingham ventured.

“You *see what this means*! I believe your experience implies a vast network of lichen-hosted interacting bacterial communities. Yes, superorganisms. And if you are transcending linear time under its influence, then it exists, and perceives, in a medium on an axis approaching the vertical to measurable temporal onflow. But this isn't proven, only indicated.

"At the very least, it will be a new form of symbiosis, involving unprecedented interplay between nondescript strains of bacteria, and possibly archaea, and novel lichen forms. And unrecorded psychoactive effects on the human CNS."

"That," Bingham said sadly, "says we're crazy."

"If that's all it is, a psychotropic response. Such instances of shared hysteria are documented. But look at what you are describing. This macrobiotic network seems to propagate communication between coterminous but not connected nervous systems. Not improbably through your own microbiota. You were in sensory and cognitive contact with non-present human subjects in another time. You have a vertical vector through stacked horizontal temporal coordinates."

"Just what I was thinking," Lily said, with maybe a touch of sarcasm.

"So either we're all demented," said Ephraim, "including you, or we're the bull in the china shop of contemporary physics."

"No, physics remains intact. It doesn't choose to conclude on this issue. But we are going to get significant resistance from the Biology establishment. And, well, everybody else in the world."

She looked around. Lily had placed a lighted candle on the folding table. Bingham got up, stretched his knee tendons, got a liter bottle from his backpack. "This was for special. I don't know where this is going, but I think it qualifies. It's cheap rum to be drunk straight from the bottle. Apropos, or no?"

"Darn skippy, Prof," Lily said. Normally, neither Noe nor Ephraim took much alcohol, but when the bottle came their way, they upended it and drank. Somehow the threat of other people's bacteria didn't phase them."

Noe Kroeber nodded to Lily. "Tomorrow," she said, "I observe, take samples. If the samples do not thrive in my makeshift laboratory — or if they do — I set up a laboratory *in situ*.

Meanwhile, I subject myself to your bio-tele-immersion experiment."

Lily smiled. "And welcome to the Core."

Noe was up into the night, scouring the room with cleaning products, preparing a laboratory.

Noe Zoe *In Situ*

Noe Zoe stood inspecting the split rock. The others stood off, watching. She carefully removed her microscope array from the foam-padded carry case. She slid the complicated complex of modular lenses and lights on their movable hinges and bearings into the night vision goggle mount of the US military-issue kevlar helmet. It seated with a satisfying click. She settled the helmet over her black hair, swung the optic array up visor-wise, and gingerly mounted the rock. She waited a moment, tense, for anything paranormal to happen, and when it didn't, she dropped the scopes over her eyes, slid a lens selection into place, and bent to the lichened surface, pursing her lips and murmuring into the voice recorder app on her cell phone.

"Nothing much so far," she observed. "Just the most rudimentary strain, probiotic, resembling *Bifidobacterium longum* but adapted to open air." She moved the lens across the surface a few millimeters. "Wait. This is Xanthoria. And it abuts this...what is it? Rhizocarpon? Oh god."

Noe on her knees on Split Rock — she's been there for an hour, recording aloud what she saw through the lenses. The others stand at a distance, careful not to distract her, mesmerized. Lily was taking cell phone videos.

"Astounding polyads of disparate strains in concert, right now I'm looking at a cluster of bacillus, coccobacillus, vibrious, spirillas, in constant transformation from chains to palisades to regular and irregular formations.

"Gorgeous colors, look, they are forming interlocking circles, mandalas, and spinning in counter-directions, now re-forming in a mirrored neisseria. All emitting rapid-fire transmissions of autoinducers, of an unprecedented variety of signals — a barrage of ion channel protein emissions. How am I going to keep these alive?

"I see bacillus here with six, seven different receptors for different instructions — these bacteria are upregulating for highly complex operations. Now all those luminous blue fusobacterium are separating from the rest, they're spore-forming! The others are organizing as a single, complex receptor.

"Now the blues are rejoining and the whole system is rapidly kaleidoscoping, they are going totally fractal. This is unbelievable enough, but it is just the first level. Oh lord I have to micturate. But not yet. I'm going to switch lenses now, pull back a few microns."

They watched her rhapsodize on and on. "Epic Poetry," Bingham whispered to Lily. "I don't know who."

Noe's voice rose toward a crescendo. "My god. What exquisite choreography, a chain of corynebacteria has broken off and is snake-dancing through, emitting assemblies of messaging proteins, and the receptors are combining into sophisticated arrays to accept them.

"At this level it is already beyond mere intelligence. What then, when these forms affiliate with fungi, coral, algae, insect colonies, with animals — with us? Let's pull out one more level, but we know what we'll find. This paracluster will become one module in a greater system. As below, so above.

"Yes. There it is. And it is bioluminescent at this magnitude. At the macroscopic level it will not be. But...but...the luciferins are performing as autoinducers, they are passing message ripples across their own fields into multiform receptors. Incredible. But too environment-dependant. I've got to transport these somehow, to replicate.

"It is real. It is here. Everything I didn't dare publish is real."

At last she sighed, pulled away, slid down the side of rock and sat splay-legged. She had long since wet her pants, then integrating that contaminant as a control.

“Well,” said Lily at last, “are you in?”

"Of course. Let me get my transportation kit. Here, hold this please, Lily, it is sterile saline. Going to aspirate this....try agar..." She peeled off her white underpants, cleaned her hands with sterile wipes, and was off again.

At the mud brick house, around midnight, Noe sighed through her nose, let her shoulders slump, on the verge of tears. "Nothing survived but the most blunt and isolated cultures. All gone. But," and she smiled at the wooden rafters, "it is still there. Still out there. Everywhere."

Noe dispatched an email to her list of colleagues, among them Louise Minor at the CDC in Atlanta. “Forgive my informality. This is simple. You cannot study the prokaryote holobiome or its corollaries in a laboratory setting. It won’t exist there. It must be seen *in situ*, in the wild. Technology must be expanded to accommodate this imperative.”

It was her final unencrypted communication of this order.

Now This is Real

“I’m terrified," Noe said to Bingham, "I never realized how much I have always counted on being wrong. Now this is real. I have seen it. We all have a right to our personal vertigo here,” she said. “And I am dizzy. We are stepping off into terra incognita. We don’t know what is out there. We are about to realize — I mean to make real — two very threatening propositions. One: the superhuman intelligence. Two: communication through time."

Bingham looked up from typing notes into his antique laptop. She went on.

“The first is the essence of the theory I have been developing for decades. You could say my whole life. Nothing that you have experienced, nothing that we now propose, falls outside the parameters of my speculation.

“The second, the time travel aspect, didn’t precisely occur to me, but that is subordinate. The hypothesis that the holobiome exists in a matrix other than time is implicit. And there is a manifest presence of telepathy, also beyond the frontiers of accepted reality. But physical, biological.

“One thing I have learned from life is that if I am afraid, there is something to fear. I have been experiencing a nonspecific panic since I got your call, Bingham.The moment we are taken seriously agencies will descend upon us. They will confiscate your rock, move it to a quarantined laboratory in the northern hemisphere, and the waiting list for access will be years long and restricted to certified military specialists. I might get in but none of you would.”

"Or possibly out." Bingham clawed at his beard. “And about a hundred agencies capable of murder would move to gain control of communication channels to the Scary Thing. And the same ones and or others, to access the past. And they will come for us and we will never see the sky again.”

Ephraim, leaning against the doorframe, spoke. “Noe, is it possible that in a laboratory setting the rock would be isolated from the Presence and lose all function? That they won't believe in it?"

Lily raised her palm. “Noe will make them believe it, whether she wants to or not. It's too real. Everybody’s going to want to use it to mess with time. And space."

“What if they can’t make it work without us?" Bingham was up and pacing. "We would be chained to a steel table half a mile under some mountain and not even know what continent we were on. The IMF, WTO, Interpol. Google? Every intelligence and counterintelligence agency in the world. Every government that feels it has a claim or a stake in this — every corporation that thinks it can sue for intellectual property rights. Dreamworks? The schools we work for, Noe. Who knows what rights we signed away when we took our positions? We are small, we are weak, we possess very valuable, very volatile, information.”

“Getting a little ahead of ourselves, aren’t we?” chided Lily. “But you’re all right. We need to take precautions if this starts to go live. So, like, online, on the phone, we use your Pachamama word to throw people off the scent. Or put them to sleep. Sound like new-agers. Don’t call it ‘the Presence,’ per the We Live in You dude, ‘cause he’s already in everybody’s sights.”

“Maybe we should come on like his groupies, make ourselves sound harmless. But no, if they get onto your research, Noe, we're cooked. Encrypt everything. Starting now,” said Bingham.

“Oh my oh my,” mourned Noe, “is the world really this unfriendly? Science has always been the one truly transnational community. I have never had to worry about academic politics at UC, or at Beard.”

“That, Noe,” Bingham leaned toward her with a tight little grin, “is why you have tenure and a professorship. You are too disengaged to be a threat to anyone there. If they thought you were politically aware they’d burn you at the stake. With green wood.”

“People,” Ephraim exhorted. Let’s go to the mercado, get food. Then we demonstrate for Noe. First me. I would like to establish a common goal between Ramram and me. Us. If I fail due to my weak Quechua, then Bingham. Then Lily tries with her BFF, if she’s there.”

“My Runasimi is” warned Bingham, “far from fluent.”

“I need clothes,” Noe said, gesturing at her dress and shoes.

“Agreed,” agreed Ephraim. “At breakfast, let’s compile a list of the most important questions we have for our ancients. And be ready for their questions to us. Or anything they want to get to us. Then, in following sessions, we present the most important information we want to convey to them or to their time. And we start looking to recruit a Runasimi speaker. Agreed?”

“Eat. Talk. Decide.” That was Lily’s synopsis.

Noe’s New Threads

As they crossed the Patacancha bridge toward the market, weaving through schools of tourists, Ephraim whispered to Lily, “They’re academic professionals. We’re kids. We could lose all this.”

“We’d still have each other,” She twinkled. “Just kidding. Be serious, Eph. You are the one with the power. They take over this place, and you’d just go off to another valley and start over. The fact that we’re too small to bother with is our best protection.”

The Briarpatch man-spreader was there, in the mercado. He followed Noe and Lily up the stairs to the second floor where the clothes and camping gear were, his face at their ass level. He pretended not to know them, elbowing in close to check out a camo thermos. Lily elbowed him back. He looked at her, nodded politely and went away.

Ephraim and Bingham were already on the third floor where the señoras offered cheap meals on trestle tables along murky aisles. Bingham ordered for them all.

Lily and Noe Zoe came up, Noe in men’s cargo shorts, an orange t-shirt emblazoned with a phony Nazca-Line 'Inka calendar,' a quilted hunter’s vest, yellow and black trainers, and a fedora of the sort worn by the señoras with the colorfully wrapped burdens on their backs. She studied how they did that, having acquired a manta of her own.

Noe walked up to them from behind, slapped Bingham gently on the back, twirled around once to show off her outfit.

Lily, with loud pigeon-Spanish and wide gestures (though she had two semesters of high school Spanish), talked a Ministry of Culture worker into selling her his official bush hat, which she gave to Bing to replace his lost head cover. He grinned and pulled the brim down over his eyes.

Ephraim spied the Briarpatch guy, sitting down around a corner, elbows on the table, muscles bulging, giving him the eye.

Ephraim tilted his head with a quizzical expression, got a wink in return.

"Hey," exclaimed Bingham, sotto voice, "there's the tough guy again."

"Old Chief Twisted-Nose?" Lily said, shooting the agent one of her flash-bang smiles. "He was downstairs with us too. Eph, I think you are still hiding something from us, boy."

"What?" he said.

"You said he is alone. A coincidence. But he doesn't look like a stalker. He looks like police."

"Or military," agreed Bingham. "And here he comes."

The man pushed his bench back from the table, paid, swaggered straight across, looking down at each of them as he passed, brushing Ephraim's shoulder. Lily tipped her manzanilla tea, still hot, onto his pants leg.

"Oops?" she cooed.

The guy just grinned, eyes slitted and glittering, passed on.

Nick Nieman Knows Names

'I don't think I'll go online with this' Nick Nieman came down the trail from Olympic National Park, striding tirelessly, energized by what he had learned from Qachu in the Twist. 'I have names. Eff Ram — that would be Ephraim, not much used in this century but I think I know where he got it. Bean Um. Bingham. Are they using screen names here? Lily. And they are in Pachamamatambo now. I think I know where that is in the real world. No, I don't think I will publish this just yet. I don't think I'll tell anybody. I don't want them to know I know just yet."

CHAPTER TWENTY-ONE now

The World — You Are Not (All That) Alone

No, they are not entirely alone, the Core, Nick. Along the Demilitarized Zone between the Koreas, animals, left unmolested to thrive and to breed since 1953, began to approach the no-entry zones from the inside, staring at the MPs with calm recognition. Red-crowned cranes, an Asiatic black bear, spotted seals, musk deer, all seemed to know how to avoid the countless landmines along both borders. A family of Amur leopards showed no fear of the sentries. Two great tigers, whose existence was considered apocryphal, paced along the coils of razor wire, watching. Stumpy bullheads thrust their whiskered noses out of the rivers, breaking the surface tension and fixing pale eyes on combat boots. Naturalists with their binoculars noted a significant increase in mushroom colonies, fungi, lichen, and algae beds crawling past the fences and under their feet.

In Papuan and Indonesian New Guinea, a reverse cargo cult upsurge occurred. Young tribals were throwing away their cell phones and radios, finding communication deeper without them. The jungle airfields, both the cultist and the functional bush strips, were given back to the rainforest. In *tok pisin*, the Papuan creole, the politically obsolete American shibboleth ‘hope and change’ emerged everywhere, morphing to ‘hopey-changey’ with no trace of the sardonic.

In Tokyo a salary man at a major insecticide manufacturer decided to walk to work in the morning. The distance was about twenty-two kilometers. On the way he met a colleague from the HR department. She too had been taken by the fancy. They arrived at two o’clock. They told their supervisor, ‘We wanted to walk.’ He told the Deputy Division Director who told the Division Director who said, ‘They wanted to walk. *Hai.*’ and went back to his spreadsheet. That was all. The next day the two walkers woke at midnight, walked faster, arrived on time. The Division Director arrived at three-thirty-five in the afternoon, smiling.

At Iowa State University, a third-year electrical engineering student doodled bored in his seat during a lecture on quantum computing, dreaming idly of changing majors or maybe just dropping out, when he looked at what he had scribbled on his graph pad and blurted, "Holy shit. I've just solved the No-Cloning Problem!" Other students looked at him with disapproval. A girl one row up said, "You too?"

A marine biologist gliding in scuba gear over a threatened section of the Great Barrier Reef looked in wonder at the rich colors and teeming life below. "This was dead a week ago," he whispered into his mask. "All these polyps were dead. I did the count. And the fish were gone." He checked his wrist GPS unit. "It's back. It's alive again. They're not going to believe this."

A grizzled old hunter outside of Predporozhnyy, Siberia, lay under a snow crust with a gray wolf in the sights of his ancient bolt-action rifle. A wolf he had been tracking for three days, a wolf who had run off with the hunter's prime breeder billy goat in her jaws. The wolf turned its cruel yellow eyes on him — at two hundred meters the hunter could look into them — and gazed at him in calm acceptance. The look went on. The hunter tenderly squeezed the oiled trigger. Then the old, frostbite-scarred finger relaxed. "All right," the hunter said, "go, old enemy. I am old too. I can get another goat." The she-wolf opened her craw, let her tongue show. The hunter believed that his goats would be safe from her now. "You don't know that, old fool," he said to himself. But he did.

In 1527, Francisco Pizarro, captain of conquistadors, stood on the afterdeck of the caravel winging south from Panama, and felt a shiver run through him. "Que pasa?" he asked himself.

CHAPTER TWENTY-TWO now

Six Days a Week

Something wrong was happening. Ephraim noticed that it was getting harder to feel the Pachamama effect on the lower slopes all around. He found fewer rocks with the tug of that magnetism. Noe said that the concentrations of complex prokaryote life seemed to be rapidly diminishing along the valley floor. The lichen colonies were becoming inert. You had to climb higher into the mountains to find anything.That was hard on the city-bred microbiologist.

Noe Zoe collapsed at the foot of a ruined qolqa low on the side of Pinkuylluna mountain, fighting for breath. Ephraim, Bingham, and Lily waited for her, a little winded from the soft life in California but ready to go on to the summit, Lily's project. Noe stayed behind.

The next morning Ephraim woke at six to find a note from Noe, 'Gone up the mountain. Be back by lunch.'

She forced herself up the hill trails six days a week. She made the summit on day five, coming back down feverish with triumph, face smeared with coca leaf juice. By August she would be going up the toughest slopes in the valley.

Flipping with Tuya, Noe inspected the life forms on the surrounding rockscape in Inka Times. "I wish I could get a microscope back there," she told Bingham, "and take samples. It is different there. Richer, but more primitive."

Ephraim's tics and twitches came back, sometimes in full force. Then the spirit of the mountains would calm him. But their protection was no longer guaranteed. He began to look into himself to find his own resources.

Someone To Tell You Everything

Lily pulled her top over her head and sat naked to the waist.

It was a cool day on Pinkuylluna Mountain, and Ephraim felt the warmth from her body waft across to him, took her heated scent into his nostrils, down to his taste buds. He looked at her and waited for an explanation.

She smiled. "Look, old Briarpatch is spying on Bing. I don't think he knows we're up here."

Lily and Ephraim were sitting on the broken wall of Qolqa Number Five, the rockfall behind to their right, the Crown of Tunupa, downhill overlooking a dizzying cliff.

Bingham was inside the watchtower below, taking measurements. Briarpatch was behind a rock down to the left, binoculars on the archaeologist.

"He won't see much." Ephraim leaned his shoulder on Lily's bare one. "Bing's just doing studies down there. Trying to see what it looked like in fourteen fifty." They fell quiet for a moment. Ephraim scrutinized Lily's profile, puzzled. She was looking uncharacteristically serious. She noticed, slid her eyes his way.

"Ephie."

"Lil'."

"You told me everything. Now I want to tell you everything."

"Is that why you are half naked?" She lifted her buttocks, pulled her skort off, set it aside.

"Yes. It helps me to be naked in deed as in word, Arrowsmith."

"You have my attention. Of this you may be sure."

"Eph, there is something wrong with me. More than one thing. I think I may be sociopathic."

Ephraim just tilted his head her way, listening.

"I don't feel anything. About anything, really. I don't care about anything. Everything comes to me too easily. Ephraim, I don't love you. I don't love anyone or anything. I just enjoy getting what I want, but it doesn't mean anything." She coughed. She still had a swollen throat. "Do you ever wonder why I wanted to come here with you?"

Ephraim was now on full alert. She rarely spoke of herself. And she was enunciating intently, as if she had trouble speaking. "Sure. Of course. You have other, better, lovers. Better places to go. I know Kevin Lee wants to take you to his family estate in Hong Kong for the summer. I thought maybe Bing was the reason?"

"No. You are the reason. I have other lovers of course. They are more like me. They think they feel things, but they don't. Not really. They register jealousy, anger, lust, fear, win, loss, all in reaction to what happens to them. You are quiet and calm, despite all your twitchies, but you come from the center of yourself, you go all the way into anything that interests you, and you have many interests, all your own, not other peoples'."

"Wow, Lily, I didn't know you thought that. I didn't know you could even talk so long."

"Am I boring you?"

"No way. No way."

"All the things you study on your own. And you bring them together, like everything's connected. Eph, you love this Inka stuff don't you?"

"Yeah, I guess it's love."

"And you really want to bring them back, even if it changes the world. You always said you were sorry they got destroyed, and now you are going to really truly try to fix that."

"Well, the opportunity seems to be here, crazy as it sounds. But Lily, what do you mean, something's wrong with you? I don't see it."

"I want to love something too. Maybe you will rub off on me. I want to love you. I want to love my mom and dad. I want to love life.I want to love myself. Forget the last one. I want to feel something about all those silly boys I screw. I mean, screwing is as close as I get to being really alive." Tears ran by her mouth. She licked at them. "And it isn't close enough."

"I don't know what to say. I don't know how to help you."

"Just let me be with you." She punched him lightly in the shoulder. "This is the most intense thing I have ever done. I don't care about the Inkas, if they come back or not, but the quest is real. I want to, at the very least see where this goes. I met Tuya! I saw the impossible! But it's still not enough. There is something wrong with me. I want you to know that."

She surged to her feet, stood balanced on the wall, legs apart, arms spread, her little merkin dark against gold skin. "Hey world! I am bareassnaked for Ephraim Arrowsmith! I tell him everything!"

Her voice carried. Bingham looked up. Three tourists in the Qolqa Three complex below looked up. Agent Orange turned his optics her way, lost his footing and slid off the path, kicking scree downhill.

She sat.

Ephraim made an explosive sound expressing amusement. "You just did that to make me laugh, didn't you? You don't want to be taken seriously." He shifted his weight, pulled her skort and shirt to himself and shook the shorts out to hand to her. "There's a breeze. You'll catch something. You have that strep already."

"Eph..." her voice was soft, pitched high like a child. "I don't have strep throat. I have..." He shook the skort to get her attention. The rustling hid her voice.

"What, Lily?"

She shook her head, lifted her leg to slide her foot in. "Nothing. Later. That's enough for now."

"Okay. I won't press. But do tell me. And Lily, thank you."

How Many of You Do You Think You Are?

"We have everything we need." Bingham smiled, skirting cautiously around an antsy black bull, "Even I have enough cash, saving rent with you and all." They were taking trails across the fields along the side of Bandolista Mountain, sneaking into the main ruins the back way. "We're getting really good stuff out of that rock. We have a mission."

"I have two sweet boyfriends," Lily added, letting herself down a heavy-bouldered andene.

"And we have one of you." Ephraim smiled. "With no major conflicts so far." He followed, lowering himself by an exposed tree root. "And no real problems except maybe — "

"Being stark raving mad." Bingham landed on both feet, knees bent like a paratrooper.

"And me." The guy from the plane materialized in their path, some Green Beret type trick. "I'm your problem."

Ephraim took a rapid look around. There was a eucalyptus-lined creek on their left, a stubble field on their right, the terrace behind, a big rock and the man in front of them. Nowhere to run.

"Nope, nobody else around," the man mocked. "So what you going to do? Be Karate Kid again? Wax on, wax off? Or you, baldy, want to try for my nose, with no stewardess to hide behind? You forgot about me? I'm not a problem?" He was grinning, looking straight at Lily. "I think I'll start with you. You boys might have to put your man pants on."

"Flight attendant," she corrected him in a weak voice. "Not stewardess."

Ephraim was standing on soft, uneven ground, bad balance, staring at the ninja rabbit on the polo shirt where the crocodile would traditionally be. Underneath was embroidered 'Briarpatch." Bingham, short and untrained, stood between Ephraim and the Briarpatch man, who was between Bingham and Lily. "What are you going to do?" .

"Don't ask that," Lily's voice was small and urgent.

"Wal." The man slid around to Lily's far side, "I might just make you watch." Lily backed against the terrace wall. Bingham stepped forward.

There came a rustling on the left, and motion.

"Permisa," came a husky voice, "en passant," and a big-eared septuagenarian inserted himself between Lily and the Briarpatch dude, an oblivious look on his snub-nosed face.

The Briarpatch-shirt man looked toward the creek, as if to say, "where'd he come from?" The wiry man stood poised mid-step, facing the bully, back to the three of them. The look seemed to go on for a long time. The big man's expression faltered, then turned annoyed and contemptuous.

"Next time," he said, "I lost the mood." He climbed easily over the terrace behind them and sauntered away.

The old guy followed, scrambling up over the old stones, grabbing the same root that had helped Ephraim down.

Silence. Then, Lily said, "T-shirt Head. From the first day here. Don't we see him around a lot?"

"Maybe," Ephraim said, "in peripheral vision."

The round head popped back over the terrace top. "As for being crazy," he said. "Ask yourself, how many of you do you think you are? And which one is real?" Then he was gone.

Lily stood looking, mouth open. "It's him," she said, pointing at Ephraim.

The General Gets Specific

"More money." The General slaps an accordian file on the desk of his superior at the USMMRD. "And we need to move to State." His boss pushes his spectacles up on his forehead, sucks air in through his nose.

"What?"

"Turns out this is real. The dots connect. The bumblefuck blogger in Washington is validated by our man on the ground in Peru, there actually is a guy talking to a dead Inka, and that crackpot germ theory may hold water, and together they pose a possible threat to US sovereignty."

The boss pulls the file toward himself with two fingers. “How much money and what for?”

“We’ll let State crank out a number. Maybe a couple of snipers will shut this down. Or a drone. Or a few billion for new construction, tech, and a trained staff.”

“You say there are named targets in here?”

The General swivels the brown cardboard file his way, pries open a tab with thumb and forefinger, pulls out a sheet in a clear plastic three-hole cover, hands it to the director, who brings his glasses back down and peers through the reflection to the text beneath.

“Bingham Bowchamp Bonnaterre...”

“You say it Beecham. The middle name.”

“...Ephraim NMI Arrowsmith…”

“He’s got a girlfriend and an archaeologist sideboard. Auxiliaries.”

“...Noe Zoe Kroeber. She’s the microbiologist. I know her. Of her. Didn’t you associate her with Hatman, the suicide at Detrick?”

“One meeting. Turns out his wife was having him followed. But his craziness ramped up right after. Turns out he wasn’t crazy.”

“Okay. I’ll see if the State Department wants you. And General. If you bring this to me again, I don’t want to hear anything about snipers, understand? Or drones. And I didn’t today.”

CHAPTER TWENTY-THREE then

The Ñusta Misk'i

Four Acclawasi guards, two men and two women, stood just out of earshot of Qachu and Misk'i, making sure they didn't get up to any funny business with the Virgins of the Sun. Misk'i knew well what it would mean to be caught enjoying a man, she had watched her big sister Qantuta thrown from the brow of Tunupa, and listened to her long falling wail. She had been given leave from the Acclawasi in Qosqo to witness that terminal aria.

Sapa Inka Pachacutiq Yupanqui had ordered that, and she would not forget. Now this stringy priest — like she would fuck him — offered her revenge. There were too many hot acclas in Qosqo for one, bewitching as she was at thirteen years, a *sumac imilla* to the tender tasty bone, to get close to the man. Here, in Pachamamatambo, it could be arranged. Preparations were being made for the Inka's return from the Colla Suyu, where he had led men to more victories over the Lupaca, Aymara, and Colla peoples. He would rest and plan in his new Mayu Wasi retreat by the river.

"You will be there," Qachu told her. "We will see to that. He will see you and want you. You will see to that. Can you convince a man you hate that you are on fire with desire, when he is between your legs?"

"Want to try me, priest?"

Qachu emitted a little laugh. "Try me and die, you mean? Do you know why I don't use the many women due to me?"

"Because they do not not fool you."

"Could *you*?"

She gave him a look that dropped his solar plexus into his testes.

"Good," he laughed. "Oh, good. Next time I will tell you what we need from him. And from you."

She would get what she needed from Qachu. Into the presence of the Sapa Inka Pachacutiq.

The House of the Virgins of the Sun

Tuya followed Lily through the wonder and horror of Ollantaytambo's streets.Tuya was mesmerized by the wheel in its many forms and struggled to bring the idea into her time, but it wouldn't quite come with her.

Tuya wondered why Ramram was so upset. Yes, this was dirty and chaotic, but it was also amazing and wonderful.

Tuya reciprocated, showed Lily what Pachacutiq built on the mysterious flat approached by the flying staircase of massive oval stones leading to what was now the municipal garage of Ollantaytambo. “Acclawasi,” she said, peering over the newly raised cyclopean terrace wall. Lily knew about the house of the Chosen Women. She, Ephraim, Bingham, and Noe had almost argued about it. Lily saw a trim three-sided compound with a single entrance closely guarded, walls plastered in wasp yellow, red, white, and black. In the courtyard, women young and old weaved on backstrap looms, made akha maize beer in great jars.

One such long-necked aryballos seemed to waddle by itself across the white sand of the courtyard, only tiny hands and sandaled feet showing at the edges to betray its bearer.

The headmistress hustled up to Tuya. As a woman, Tuya was shooed. Had she been a man she would have been killed.

As she turned to go, the walking jug lay itself against a row of its sisters, and from behind stepped an exquisite adolescent. She fixed her great black eyes on Tuya, and spoke softly but with clarity, "Qantuta."

"Misk'i," Tuya said.

"Qantuta," the girl repeated. Tuya nodded. They turned away, Lily puzzled, Tuya thoughtful.

Kambo Frog Attack

Ramram waved vaguely at some whining twilight insect by his head, then jerked violently forward as he was slammed from behind. He picked himself up slowly, looking over his shoulder to see Otoronqo Kuy standing with his shield held up where Ramram's head had been, the soldier's eyes peering wide over the edge of the square buckler.

The general's orderly stood broadside, blocking Ramram from view, his shield covering Chaski Yuyu's head. The khipucamayoq stood agape, looking at the strange tableau. The four of them had been walking back from the Qoripata together, having arranged a chaski messenger to carry a routine update to the Inka now back in Qosqo. Otoronqo slowly lowered the shield, turned its face to himself, plucked something from the surface. Held it to his nose and sniffed. It was a feathered dart.

"Kambo frog venom," he said. "I did a tour in the jungle. Meant for you." He looked at Ramram, still half crouching, hands on his knees. "Who did you piss off now?"

"You?"

Otoronqo laughed. "Not that much. This stuff's hard to come by." He looked at his orderly, the young man keeping a military face. "You didn't throw yourself in front of me to save my life?"

"Sir no Sir! The corporal believes that the Colonel's job is to die, Sir! The corporal believes that Sapa Inka's Wakacuraqa is directed to live until otherwise instructed, Sir!"

"Corporal, you are promoted to Iskay Chunka Curaca. And you may fuck my daughter."

"Sir, your daughter says not yet, Sir!"

Mayu Wasi

"You are virgin." The Sapa Inka's intromissive organ stands hard against his hairless belly. Sun and looping birdsong waft through the window of the Mayu Wasi riverside retreat. He sits stone faced.

Misk'i stands before him in her fine cumbi-cloth aksu, eyes glossy black.

"You murdered my sister for being no virgin. I have had so many fingers in me, testing. And they liked it, too."

"Did I. So now you will murder me?" His expression doesn't change.

"No. I want to, but I have other orders."

"..."

He is seated on a small platform, she stands below.

"I am going to take you away from yourself. You will forget who you are, you will believe what I say." She lets her dress fall.

"What will I believe?" He stands, looks down on her. Her eyes are level with the corona of his penus, pushed above his prepuce by a surfeit of hot blood.

"That the Umu Antarqui is a liar, a traitor, and an enemy."

"I already doubt him." He puts his calloused hands upon her waist, lifts her easily until her scant-fuzzed pelt is level with his eyes.

"I am not the first."

"Mm. What do you know of me?"

"Everything. I am from the Acllawasi. Women talk." She lifts her legs over his shoulders. "There is a story. You knew the Chanka would come into your trap because of their arrogance. I know you will come into mine because of yours."

Her fused slice presses against his lips. The scent is wild in his nose. He lets his tongue out.

"No! Later." She writhes free, surprising him. He lets her slide to her feet. She pushes him toward the stack of soft blankets in the pool of sun by the stone wall. He takes a measured step backward, watching her. She pushes again. There is nothing cute about it.

"Down." There is hate in her eyes. For the first time he allows himself the hint of a smile. He lays on his back, erection still touching his navel. She straddles him, pulls it toward her tiny hole.

"Easy, child," he says, "take your time." She glares at him, jaw thrust.

"*This* is my time." She sits hard upon the head of his phallus, pushing down, her juice already running along the shaft. Her soft aperture tries to open, making little fish-mouthed twitches, but it doesn't know how. She takes his wrists from where his hands rest lightly on her hips, moves them to her shoulders. He looks at her quizzically. She lifts herself high on her toes, his hands close by her delicate neck, together they ram her downward with all their combined force. She makes an abrupt animal yelp. Her blood sprays his abdomen and thighs. She throws her head back, eyes shut tight, breathes out long, then looks down on him.

"You are going to fuck me with your arrogance. I am going to fuck you with my hate. We are going to be lovers like the world has never seen."

"The world has seen a lot, little girl."

"The world has seen a lot of men who think they know the world."

He has climaxed twice. She has brought him quickly back. She turns her ass to him.

"No," he says. "That is for later."

"There is no 'later.' There is now. Do it."

He tries to rein in his emotions, to control his anger, but tenderness overcomes him again and again. "Ñakasqa!" he thinks, "She wins."

Now his head is between her legs. She pulls his ears, the gold discs reflected in her immense pupils. She begins to make sounds, gutturals, whines, whispered labials, non-aspirated glottal stops. She sings. It goes on. Finally she emits a wail, a howl, a shriek. Farmers fields away lift their heads.

He cannot know this, but that is the sound her sister made, falling.

Aurora at the Tether of the Sun
Pachamamatambo

The Hatun Villaq Umu, High Priest of Inti, in flaming vermillion robe and golden breastplate, lifts a deep shining saucer of dry tinder, anticipating the cardinal instant. The rising sun caroms off gold, silver, through transparent stones, illuminating the finely calibrated surfaces of the Intiwatana sun temple. All around the voices rise and ululate. The sun climbs, filling the mountains with light and heat. The voices shrill into crescendo, the rays careen from surface to gilded surface, the entire temple is suddenly enveloped in a brilliant corona of shimmering radiance.

Ramram sees Inti come over the shoulder of Pinkuylluna Mountain to hit the tip of the tall twisted obelisk on the terrace high over the Qoripata. This is the Plow Field Moon, celebration of the Earth Mother.

Within a concentrated nimbus of light and heat, the central ray of the rising sun, focused by the polished gold of the incurvate disc, ignites the tinder. Flame shoots upward to greet its creator.

Through Ramram's eyes, Ephraim, Bingham, Noe, and Lily, watch in stunned silence, arms around each other, huddled at the gateway of the ruined temple, witnessing a phenomenon never recorded in any account, the Aurora of Inti.

The sphere of voices expands and mellows into a harmonic synesthesia, becoming sound, sight, scent, color, vibrating the core of all present. No one is a watcher now; all are intimately organs of the event.

And in the heart of this fandango of the senses, the flow of communication reverses and with a grunt as if rabbit-punched in the solar plexus Ramram is seeing through the eyes and nerves of Ephraim Arrowsmith.

The once gilded wanka is fallen and stripped, lying at the edge of the andene overlooking modern Ollantaytambo. The whole town is striped and boiling with a color that has no name, no handle by which to process it. It enters the nose and mouth before the eye. The closest Ephraim would come later to describing it, was a blackish snot-green.

For the first time, Ephraim is seeing through Ramram's eyes as Ramram sees through Ephraim's own eyes in a dizzying feedback loop. Their perceptions are interlinking Ouroboros style, the snake that eats its tail.

To Ramram, to them both, the jittering mototaxis, motorcycles, trucks, tour busses crawling through the town — monsters to the Inka — excrete a foul-colored smudge, rising in a gritty haze, full of the stench of death. The houses, too, give off putridity from their alien material, from the demonically invoked electricity. The power lines vibrate with a worm-like nimbus of bloody pus. The relay towers on the Bandolista ridge above seem to emit one long smutty farting of corruption, darkening the sky.

All around, the living Pachamama, the vital spirit of the land, is being murdered. This is beyond what Ramram has seen in previous travels to this Pacha.

Pachamama fights the pollution. From the mountains, from the rivers, from the surviving greens of the fields and hills, most intensely from the hidden ruins of Kunturpunku, comes resistance; but weakening. Far to the north and west, the sky is clear and the mountains are clean; but their blood lines, the rivers and canals, carry venom downstream to the Amazon. The poisonous roads stab into dwindling forest. The dominant force of Certainty, invoked by the priests of Ilyapa, has awakened. It knows now that there is a rebellion to crush and is counter attacking. Pachamama is losing. A breaking point is coming.

To Ephraim it is a revelation. He had no idea it was so bad. People in his time just did not see it. It was the triumph of Certainty, Nick Niemann's technocratic enemy of The Question.

Ramram tries to force himself to keep studying the battlefield, but his inner self wants out, and out is what it gets. He is back in the ceremony. But what is this feeling he has, against his forehead?

It is falling. Otoronqo Kuy and Chaski Yuyu see Ramram topple forward and catch him. He retches, crawling. His internal visitor is knocked away. Chaski Yuyu, torn from his trance, glances nervously about to see if anyone notices this blasphemous failure of decorum.

Only one gaze turns their way. That spindly acolyte of Ilyapa, the bastard son of Pachacutiq Inka. Qachu's eyes narrow thoughtfully. To the Khipucamayoq's eye, Qachu seems disturbingly unsurprised.

Otoronqo's orderly, Choque Anka, also notes Qachu's interest. His eyes meet the priest's, turn hard. Qachu smiles subtly back.

Observing the ceremony from his private belvedere a level above is the Sapa Inka Pachacutiq. Beside him is his principal wife Qoya Anawarkhi. Hunkered below are a few favored guests. At his feet, flushed and succulent, is the Ñusta Misk'i.

A Golden Goblet of Earthy Brew

Over her shoulder, without looking, Misk'i passes Pachacutiq a golden *qero*, a goblet of pungent brew. It is slightly intoxicating, earthy, and enhances sexual potency — among other effects. It is called *hampi*, medicine.

Qachu watches.The Inka has fasted for this ceremony. His body is cleansed of the spirits that live in his stomach. The brew will replace what is lost with Qachu's own concoction. It will create an inertia in the emperor that will suppress interest in any impulses subtle or refined. Over time Ramram's reports will seem foolish and trivial tales. War and Misk'i will remain real to him. Ilyapa's agents will subtly undermine Pachacutiq's trust in Ramram. Misk'i most of all.

The Slip of the Grip on Everything

Ramram didn't know how to tell Ephraim that his grip was slipping. That Pachacutiq Inka was distancing fast. He was increasingly distrustful of Ramram, and skeptical of his information. The Sapa Inka's lust for conquest was stronger than ever, but his interest in Ramram's reports, weakened with every communication. He either didn't believe or didn't care that his newly created Tawantinsuyu would not last a long lifetime.

Pachacutiq had to listen. He had to hear, to know, to act. Otherwise the bad future would come true. Ramram needed to know much more, to have more to tell. This was real. Everything could go. The man, the god, Pachacutiq was always so firmly onto everything around him, but he could not see this at all. Anymore.

CHAPTER TWENTY-FOUR now

Stay Professional

Through Steiner M830r military binoculars, Agent Orange watched the lights go on in the mud brick house, Lily Tran passing across the south window, shrugging out of her jacket. He was keeping tabs on the subjects.

The controlling bitch Tran was with Arrowsmith again, still about two nights for him to one for that nose-twisting son of a bitch. And she was spending more nights to herself in the kitchen room.

He tried to keep his heart from tripping as she pulled her top over her head then bent to pull her pants down. Stay professional, total fail. Then there were just candle shadows on the wall.

The light went off in Bonnaterre's room, poor bastard. Kroeber's shadow still bent over the patch of blue that would be her laptop. Bing and Noe Zoe had been tight in Berkeley, too, so feelings must be getting pretty twisty in there. Didn't show though. No bickering, no snubbing.

He adjusted himself behind the pile of rocks that was his blind across a fallow field. Not much to do since they found the new place, the one in the news. He couldn't follow them up there — too obvious and too much work. He'd gone up once by himself, took eight hours, couldn't find a damn thing, had to come down in the dark.

Screw it. Guess he'd go back to the hooch. Do notes, send in a report full of nothing. "Subject C for Core T for Tran still sizzling hot."

Then the light went out in Kroeber's room The door to the hallway opened in Bonnaterre's. He stood. His silhouette blocked the view in the doorway. It closed behind him. Half a minute passed, then the door to the long house opened, and the two stepped onto the dirt road, walked together to the corner, disappeared.

Agent Orange pocketed his binoculars, followed, and caught up in time to see them ring the bell on the outer gate of the tourist hotel on Calle Turistas.

That was his lodging. "Are they onto me?" He gave them a moment to get inside, followed, and used the key he insisted on carrying. He saw them climbing the external stairs side by side. Turned out they took a room together. What do you know.

The next morning, he watched them leave, arms around each other.

Just as they did, the Tran ho came back from the corner store. He hastily focused the binoculars on her face. She definitely saw her man number two and the scientist lady together, and she did not look happy. No 'Good for you, bro,' face. No, her usual smooth, smug expression had tightened up. What do you know.

It Kind of Sneaks Up On You

Lily Tran fought down a strong urge to duck into a doorway. No need, they didn't notice her. 'Lily girl,' she thought to herself, 'what is going on in you? You should be happy for him. For them. It's like, you have to have all the men in the world and they can only have you? Two nights out of ten?'

Then she said out loud, enough that a nearby dog lifted her head, "When did I become such a cunt?"

"It kind of sneaks up on you," came a raspy voice behind. She started. A barefoot man with a turban-like thing on his skull trod by, eyes on the horizon.

"Great," she muttered, "T-shirt Head. Again."

In Cold Water

Daniel Boone Cooper, call him D.B., thirty-nine, thin, John Lennon spectacles, leans over the gray Korean Conflict era steel desk in his office in a sub-basement of the sprawling National Geospatial Intelligence Agency complex, dropped into the middle of a mosaic of vermiform suburban developments south of Arnold, Missouri. From the satellite view, the surrounding 'burbs' might look a little like the computer-generated images of the bacterial superorganism described on the crackpot website of a Western Washington University dropout in Port Angeles, Washington, and whose birth certificate name is Nicolas Nieman. The website is called *We Live In You*, and D.B. has just been assigned to this task as his sole project.

D.B.s office is crammed between the heating unit room and the server center. On the door is a sign reading B.D. Looper, Office of Microbiological Geomapping, NIMA. NIMA had been renamed to NGA in 2003. The NTT does not support signs on doors.

Doctor D.B. Cooper has been exiled to this assignment for the crime of being the lawful wedded spouse of Mary Ann Cooper, née Poupore, the current mistress of D.B.'s supervisor's Division Director's boss.

His assignment is to focus on the video blogger, who has suddenly become a priority. Not high, but worth his salary. He is diligent in this task.

He calls, on an encrypted phone, Agent Elmer Theodore Thomas.

Thomas is his counterpart in the Office of the Geographer and Global Issues (AN/GGI) under the Bureau of Intelligence and Research (INR) in Springfield, Virginia. Thomas is old in government and has been shifted from office to office until being assigned as liaison to D.B.. Who knew what *he* had done wrong? He oversees, despite having no military experience or expertise, the contract with Briarpatch Security, S.A., a civilian paramilitary company made up of former special operations soldiers nursing at the golden teat of Defense Department contracts. One of their operatives, code named Orange, has been on the ground in Ollantaytambo, Peru, for a while now.

"So you have the Briarpatch report from Peru?" Twenty-eight hours had passed since their last conversation.

Came the reply:

"D.B.. Yes, I have read your report. They redacted the names of course, including the town, but I surmise that our sacred national security is being threatened by two teenage kids from California, an archeologist nobody likes, and a female bug scientist who watches our guy Nick's rants and is possibly the source of the data that a scientist at the Detrick infectious disease facility killed himself about."

'Not in a receptive mood,' guessed D.B..

"Go ahead, be dismissive. Those four, put together with their possibly actual power to talk to the past and cutting-edge knowledge of the microbic Presence thing — what that woman published is a fifty-megaton nuclear strike on bioscience — have just triggered an armed probe by our civilian contractors into a sovereign nation. They have also tripled our — well, our boss's — budget.

"I mean to say, Elmer, we have now identified a real conspiracy of enemies who really want to do what our target mission, We Live In You, says is really happening. The Inka thing and the Bug thing have gotten together and are doing things, apparently, that are scientifically impossible. They want to send a squad of black ops guys down there to capture their source of power. That magic rock."

E.T. came back:

"That was blacked out on my copy. So it is a rock? Is it magnetic meteoric iron or something? Are they down there now?"

After a minute or two, he got D.B.'s reply:

"Your next report won't be redacted. We are equally liaisons. We don't know what it is made of. That's part of why we are sending a team down to kidnap it. And it looks like it will be your contract boys. I'm drafting the orders now. Me. I wasn't ever in even the Cub Scouts, much less Special Forces. But the General says do it, so…"

"So?"

"My orders will have you get your mercenaries down there. Better give them a heads up. Get back to me on Google vid, I hear they assume nothing real happens there."

Ten minutes later E.T. gets back. "Briarpatch Security was expecting my call. They were informed before we were, and they're supposed to be my guys. Send your orders, I'll dispatch them to Inka Land."

"Great. I hope we don't wake up without pensions because 'your' guys just screwed the pooch."

"Yeah. We'd be the goats. I'd miss my pension. Living on Social Security and Alpo."

"You know, these are just kids and teachers down there. We're not merely the fall guys. We are the refined solution. The General is perfectly capable of sending a team to just kill them."

"You know, that un-redacted report you promised still isn't in my in-box. What are their names?

D.B. said, "I'll send the profiles. One is Kroeber, of course. The archaeologist is Bingham Beauchamp Bonnaterre. Two high school students from California, Lily Hoa Tran and Ephraim NMI Arrowsmith. He's the original perp, the time travel kid."

E.T. answered, "I wouldn't want to be any of them. They just woke up in cold water."

CHAPTER TWENTY-FIVE now

Feet Tangle in Cactus

Beard College found evidence that Bingham was sexually involved with a student. He was fired in an emailed PDF copy of the original mailed to his US address. He shuddered at the possibility that they would learn that Lily was jailbait, but so far they accepted the fake ID included in her documented request to audit his class.

He now had no income to contribute to rent at the mud brick house, and refused their charity, however sincere. Secretly, he was finding it ever harder to endure Lily in bed with Ephraim just two rooms away. He set up his patched dome tent on Ministerio de Cultura property near some unrestored Inka storehouses above the little clam-shaped hamlet of Rumira, set at the bottom of a wide arroyo folded away from the main ruins.

He consented to come down to share one meal a day, to plan and to debrief. A local bakery gave him bread too stale to sell. He chewed on it in the night under the stars or deep cloud. He explored in the rough country above.

One day at sundown he lost the trail and found himself near panic as full dark fell, testing inch-by-inch for purchase along the cliffs, feet tangling in cactus, slithering on loose rock.

While Bingham was clinging to a rock wall, Ramram came to him. In Ramram's time, the moon was full and the night clear. With his chin, he pointed insistently upward into the canyon. "Kunturpunku," came his voice. He said it several times. "*Chaykama*." 'Up there.' Far above in the velvet dark were many soft amber lights.

When he was returned to himself, Bingham saw the sky clear and the moon out in his own Pacha. He turned his eyes up the canyoned mountainside.

Come the misty morning, he bushwhacked up the gorge, crossing a sere pasture where scrawny goats grazed. He pulled himself up rocky shelves by sinewy bush grip, the sensation of something ahead tickling in his chest. Panting, straddling a crumbling fieldstone corral, something like a dazzling white light burst in his skull, making him cover his eyes with his forearm. It faded, leaving him dizzy and disoriented but still sensing some strong signal from above.

"I ain't got the juice to go after this shit today," he admitted breathlessly, "I'll get the Core together and come back in force."

The Ugliest Girl in the World

"You know what?" Bingham asked the morning after his assault on the gulch, as Ephraim cooked a pot of banana and mango oatmeal, "Do you ever pull back and look at the Inkas through the eyes of the rest of the world?"

"How so?" asked Ephraim, adding more water because he had over-salted.

"You mean," Lily interjected "that all they did was put a bunch of bare rocks together under a grass roof? Their stuff looks a lot like some Scottish peasant's house."

Ephraim's chest filled with betrayal. He shook his head. The feeling subsided.

"Okay," he said, "I don't like to hear it from an outsider, but sure, I can see it that way. They could barely go two stories high. Compared to say, the Mayans, their temples and palaces look crude. The temples in India, Burma, Sri Lanka, all make Inka architecture seem rustic, like, gauche. To the conventional eye, Egypt, Ur, Babylon, Persepolis, all humiliate the finest Inka works. And medieval castles and cathedrals dwarf them."

"I mean," Bingham added, "their imperial palaces consisted of one-room structures. A Viking chieftain might live there. And Vikings at least had sleeves."

“And tables,” said Ephraim. “And chairs. And candles.”

“Poor boys,” Lily cooed, putting a hand on each of them, “In love with the ugliest girl in the world.”

“Well,” Ephraim sighed, “any superlative has class. Anyway, I hope this oatmeal is eatable.”

“And bear in mind, Lily,” Bingham teased, “we love only you."

"Not too salty," judged Lily. Noe squinted at it as if she were thinking of getting out her microscope.

“I want to show you something,” Bingham said, standing and stretching, “It may be nothing, but Ramram got through to me and seemed to be hot for me to take a look up past my camp. Let’s take a day and go.”

“Okay by me,” Lily said. “I got flipped too, into a Spanish rider in a, like, cavalcade along the river. He and his conquistador bros were whipping a line of cringing natives like slaves. He was always scanning for hot babes to rape. It was yuck.”

She didn’t mention that she was also sexually aroused. He could take any woman he wanted however he wanted without request or apology. Now there would be a man she couldn't play. “But I’ll tell you all now, all of this, playing with the past, inventing tiny gods, playing chicken with the powers that be, is making me a little uneasy. I’m just a girl. I just want to have fun."

She cut her eyes at Ephraim. He met them. 'I know,' she thought at him, 'I said that I want passion for something. But it hasn't happened. And fear, well, that's easy.'

'I know,' he thought back. 'It's okay.'

Bingham watched their 'significant glance.' ‘Do either of them have any idea what the other is really thinking?' he wondered.

“Well,” he said, “this may drive you away for good. It is going to be a ball-buster hike, with maybe nothing at the end. But I gots to know."

Bingham’s Find

"It is going to happen," the old woman said. She and her man and their goats watched the four fight their way up the quebrada. "The Lower World is coming to the Upper World. The tourists are coming." The old man spit coca juice.

"*Allintaqmi*," she said, "It's all good. We're ready."

They were almost there, all four of the Core, fighting for breath but feeling strong.

"It's going to happen, Lily said. "I can feel it."

"Yes," agreed Noe, "my interoception is highly sensitized, I'm trembling inside."

"You, Eph?" Bingham asked.

"No, I don't feel a thing, except out of breath."

Bingham led the Core following Ramram's moonlight directions. He struggled with himself, and he won. If there was anything up there, he would share the discovery with his friends. They hiked up the wide, jumbled ravine above the deltaform hamlet of Rumira.

It was a hard climb. Noe wore shorts, showing off her ropy, muscular legs. Her ankles would be dotted with insect bites in the morning. Lily would not be stopped despite a fear of heights that had crept back into her. Ephraim and Bingham were compelled by a tachycardia of hope.

"It is close," asserted Bingham, "and it is big." The slope was steep, the thready trail kept disappearing into scrub, bare rock, scree.There were scary places where a wrongly placed foot could be lethal.

"Scary place!" Lily gleefully announced, taking the lead from Noe. "Normally I would be soiling my drawers, but now I feel like I have...I don't know what to call it. Grace. I have total grace. Whatever is up there likes us."

"Yeah. Every place I put my boot down is perfect," agreed Bingham. "The mountain is on my side."

“Do you feel heat around your temples and cranium?” Noe asked, “and as if the sutures of your zygomatic and temporal bones are pulling apart, just opening up?”

“Is that your cheeks and face?” Lily asked, “Because I feel like my head wants to be part of the sky.”

“I don't feel it," said Ephraim. “I guess I'm not the Chosen One today?”

“Or we're victims of," Bingham leapt over a five-foot chasm, "autosuggestion."

“I'm losing it,” Noe came in. "The signal is diminishing. Are we passing it?"

"There's a path here,” Bingham pointed, "going in. Wait. It is here. Stop. Everybody please stop.” It appeared to be a standard issue Andean mountainside.

He looked around, alternately squinting and widening his eyes. He spied a small tower of stacked rock dominated by a tall stalk of agave sprouting wild curlicue whorls. He approached, stood on a clearing just above, arms akimbo. He scanned the feral cuts and planes of the landscape.

Noe thought he looked like some mythic figure, maybe Norse. Bingham began to nod his head in funereal rhythm. “I can almost see it.”

“See what?” Lily.

“Whatever it is. I can al...most...see it.” He shrugged took a long swig of bottled water, adam's apple bobbing. He wiped his mouth on his sleeve. "Well, it's here or it's nowhere.”

Lily scrambled up. "Nothing but thorn bushes and cactus. And the big feeling is gone."

"I never felt anything," Ephraim said regretfully, although a little vindicated. He wandered a few meters up what might have been a trail to piss against a pile of rocks stacked against a standing pillar of natural stone. "Hey Bingham, isn't this an apachita?" He finished, took a few steps away.

Bingham goat-footed up, cocked his head. "Yeah, it's man-made. Hey, it's a wanka." He laid an arm against the long, thin stone, hand stroking the thick crust of lichen. His eyes sprung wide and his jaw dropped.

"Holy shit! It's here! Oh my god. Look. Look!" He was pointing out over several level planes above the ravine, suddenly visible through the confusion of plant life and geology. "Do you see it?" He forced his head to turn and look down at his companions. "Come over here."

Lily and Noe joined him, each leaning a hand against the six-foot tall tapered stone stela.

Like an optical illusion switching faces, an entire Inka town emerged from the rock and vegetation, striding down the planes of the hillside, built on every now evident flat surface. What had seemed natural rock became walls, stairs, fountains, towers. What had been shadows were now doors, rows of windows, collapsing roofs. All the myriad rich greens of vegetation that had masked the construction now displayed a breathtaking vision of exquisite streets and structures descending the folds of the mountain, webbed with freshets of water in stone channels.

"Now I see," tears broke free of Lily's eyes. "Now I see. Your ugliest girl. I didn't know!"

Noe stood wide-eyed, stroking her chin.

Ephraim leaned, frowning, squinting. Lily reached out, put her hand on his neck. He looked puzzled, shook his head. Then, "It's coming. Thank you. There it is. I see it. Holy moly," Ephraim breathed, "Astonishing. We are looking at a wonder of the world."

"Not to rain on your plately streasure...stately...pleasure...dome," Noe pointed out, "but Bingham, this is it. This is your career."

The other three watched her climb onto a suddenly visible terrace, open her arms to the world, eyes closed, pointy chin lifted, and shout out into her own echoes, "This is my good friend

Bingham! Bingham Beauchamp Bonnaterre! *Professor emeritus Bingham B. Bonnaterre!* KISS HIS ASS!"

Kunturpunku
Condor Gate

Long before contact between the continents, Ramram and Tuya climbed the fine narrow staircase, he to monitor the cultivation of wakas he had found along the web of silvery streams that laced through the village, she to learn weaving techniques from one of the Qoya's acclas.

"This is the heart of Pachamamatambo," Tuya stood, hands folded over her heart

"And Pachamamatambo is the heart of Pachamama in the Tawantinsuyu," Ramram answered.

A condor, a brown female, soared low over the highland community of Kunturpunku, hidden in a deep quebrada across the ridge from the Qoripata ceremonial center of Pachamamatambo.

Whereas the lion's share of Pachamamatambo was Pachacutiq Inka's personal estate, Kunturpunku belonged to his primary wife, Qoya Anawarkhi. She in turn dedicated it to Mama Killa, mother moon. Its small population rarely descended to the valley below, living in a quiet tranquility that would survive the conquest by several decades because its existence went unnoticed by Spanish conquistadors deconstructing the Inka town below. They could not see it.

Eventually the terraces above could no longer support the population and in a night they filed down the overgrown trail and melted into the Vilcabamba mountains where their descendants still farm and husband livestock. They know where the gold is.

"They have been here," Tuya said. "Li Li has been here and seen this place. It pleased her."

"Yes," Ramram" said. "Good. He heard me. I will try to find him here. I would like to know if Pachamama has survived in this place. Bean Um would like to see it now. As would Eff-Ram."

"Do you like him? Bean Um?"

"I am closer to Eff-Ram. He feels the Apus, and I've known him longer. But yes, Bean Um is funny, and brave, and sees. And he loves, in a broken way. He came to us too late. His Pacha has done him injuries we cannot know or heal."

"But maybe he can heal ours." She let her palm rest lightly on his butt.

The condor stooped down to roof level, gliding to where Tuya and Ramram watched pure water flash over a ledge into a canal. The bird's shadow fell on them. They looked up. The great wings backbeat to hold her in place as her black marble eye looked into Ramram's. Ramram looked back. Satisfied, she looped into the sky and vanished over the eastern ridge.

I Was Blind But Now I See

"All right," Noe called, "I think I have isolated the strain that causes the psychological blindness. There was some of the same at Split Rock. It is a permutation of alphaproteobacteria. It is known for inhabiting the human cerebral cortex. It was your rock stack that counteracted the effect. It hosts a thriving colony of another blend of strains. Apache cheater?" She indicated a four-foot tall sliver of andesite rooted in a circular foundation of smooth worked stones beneath a cone of rough fieldstones.

"Apachita," corrected Bingham. "Propping up a wanka. That's what the Inkas called an upright stone of spiritual power. I think this is the only specimen still standing. The Viceroy Toledo and his church boys tore down the rest of them. So how does it work?"

"A colony of bacteriophages targeting the invisibility strain. There is a direct correlation between increasing visibility and the reduction of the psychoaffective biofilm. We can control that. What is totally beyond my comprehension is how it controls the visibility of the architecture in photographs."

"I was blind but now I see. The Polaroid effect," says Lily. "Like, first there is no Inka town, then there is one?"

"You have heard of Polaroid?" asked Bingham incredulously, "That's from the like nineteen fifties."

"Polaroid is back, granddad," Ephraim laughed. "It never really went away. I have no idea how this works, but once the ruins show up in the photo, it sticks, so you can submit them to *National Geographic*."

"All right," said Bingham, "let's pack up and get down before dark. One more climb up here and we'll have enough to release to an admiring world."

"The admiration of the world," said Noe under her breath, "Has a short half-life."

Two Papers
Kunturpunku

"What the fuck?" Bingham dropped the pottery shard he was examining. A few meters away, a misstep had rolled an ancient jar into a nasty-looking stagnant pool, and now a stench snaked across the ruins, outracing a greasy black cloud boiling up from the dark water.

The other three froze, staring at the weird miasma roiling in from that upper edge of the ancient town, throwing off black droplets. One landed on Lily's bare forearm.

"Ow! Shit!" She smeared at it with her hand. "Agh! Ow, it burns, damn it! Now it's on my fingers!"

The cloud reared overhead. Both Bingham and Ephraim gripped Lily by the shoulder, pulling her away. Stumbling backward, Ephraim's heel caught in the stone lining of a brush-choked acequia, bringing them all down as the cloud's tattered edge wheeled toward them. Noe, running to help Lily, stopped and crouched, covering her eyes with her arm.

As they cringed, Ephraim shielding Lily with his body, a brightly varicolored fog surged thickly up from a rectangular stone bath from which the channel flowed. The rising mist cut into the darker brume, consuming it as it rolled over the four cowering humans, blanketing them. Gobs of black stinking grease arced toward them, but hissed away in the swimming glinting haze. The colored cloud seemed, from below, to overwhelm and devour the dark murk and to melt it away. In seconds, both evaporated as if they had never been.

They lay frozen, paralyzed by fear, until they were sure the dark fog had gone.

Noe was the first to act. "Let me see your arm, Lily." She turned it in her hands, squinting and sniffing. "It appears to be infectious, not corrosive." She dipped a bandana in the water, dabbed at the black-ringed red spots. "Whether that is good or bad is a function of degree."

She opened a fanny pack on her belt, pulled out an aluminum tube of strong antibiotic, squeezed cream onto Lily's skin, pulled on a surgical glove, and gently rubbed the emollient onto her wounds.

"Feels good. Hand too," Lily said. "Is that thing chemical?"

"No, I think it is alive."

“Was that one of your microbe things?” asked Ephraim.

“Yes, I think it is microbial. I think they both were. There are bioaerosol clouds of airborne bacteria,” Noe answered. “*Pseudomonas syringae* for instance. And airborne plankton exist. But those, no. Those I don’t recognize. I will take samples. I think she will be alright."

“We’re burning daylight, pilgrims,” Bingham said. “We better mobilize. Noe Zoe will handle the germs. Don't kick any pots into swamp water."

Ephraim asked Noe, "Do you think that thing could have killed us?"

"Yes. I think that was its creators' intent. And the other one, the pretty one, was the cure. I think they were man made. Centuries ago, by the Inka."

"Part of a defensive system," Bingham guessed, "Probably by Manco Inka, as the Spanish approached. You notice we are on the border of the site?"

Noe found three more of the black ponds on the periphery, one in each direction, each with its antidote pool nearby. She and Bingham carefully removed the jars of liquid catalyst and filled in the infectious holes after drenching them with antibiotics, archaeological value be damned. Noe got her samples. Bingham took her to a small stepped pyramid, still obscured by rough brush and approached by a crumbling staircase. On top, he pried away foliage to expose a chest-high stone carved into various planes and angles and fronted with a symmetrical step design. Projecting from the flat top was a quadrangular pillar, part of the natural stone, about a meter tall, sheathed in moss and lichen.

“It’s beautiful, in a Japanese sort of way, Noe said.

“Yes. Even more so than the intiwatana in Machu Picchu. But it is more than that. Ephraim says that it is the most powerful siq’i stone he has ever encountered. It knocked him on his ass. He is saving it for later, to flip with Ramram. Can you do your microscope thing here, check it out?”

“Most gladly. So it is a, how you say, “hitching post of the sun?”

“No, not this one. This one is keyed to the moon. To the perigean full moon, the harvest moon, the blue moon, and most cool, to the blood moon. That implies that the Inka could predict a lunar eclipse after all. I think this whole settlement is about the moon. I need more data though, and consensual validation.”

Later, Noe Zoe reported to Bingham and Ephraim.

“Yes. This is the most intense concentration of sentient prokaryote life I have identified thus far. This Pachamama effect,” she asked the others, “the ambient force of the holobiome. Is it like this anywhere else that you know of?”

“This is the strongest signal,” Ephraim said. “Here. You would know if anything is found around the world, if any of your colleagues know how to find it and are willing to share with you. But here, if the blight ever gets up here, it’s over.”

Ramram did not come to them. They began the descent. As the air warmed, Noe squinted at a kind of stick figure observing them from a goat trail. Its bared teeth might have indicated a smile.

They got back just before full dark. The photographs were excellent. Bingham cropped them to remove any view that would identify the location.

Noe studied them. "I'm impressed. I assume the scarecrow we saw coming down, the guy with the thing on his head was not an hallucination?"

"No," Lily replied, "I saw him too. That was T-shirt Head. He walks and talks. To himself, mainly." She looked at Bingham hunched over his antique laptop. "Whatcha workin' on, Bing?"

"Paper for the Institute of Andean Studies meeting in January. Then I'll modify it to break the news for the rest of the world. Including the fucking Beard College Department of Anthropology, Archaeology, Paleoanthropology, Paleontology, and Alternative Medicine. They will be gnashing their pointy little teeth."

Noe embarked on a brief paper that would be the unveiling and vindication of her life’s work, presented as a modest complement to an archaeological study. With peer-reviewed validation it would make much of current biological science obsolete. If the government didn’t classify it as top secret for national security.

In preparation for releasing her paper through her professorship, she sent her current findings to an obscure server at Beard College, embedded in a thick cover of innocuous material. Consummate rationalist although she was, she crossed her fingers to ward off any attention directed toward that transmission.

The next time they went up Ramram and Tuya were waiting, and showed them the living town of Kunturpunku. “I am changed forever, “said Ephraim. “Now I can never be sorry I was born.”

That’s Big

"Shit." Agnes Bodkin looked up at Iris Lubbock in the Beard College cafeteria, cell phone in hand. "Bonnaterre just struck gold in Peru. And we fired him."

Bingham called an archaeologist friend at UC Berkeley.

"Heads up. I'm sending you a package. The same one I'm sending the department. I have uncovered a major Late Horizon site. I want you to be my liaison to the University."

"What kind of site? How big?"

"Around two hundred and ninety hectares — over seven hundred acres — including two lakes above. It's smaller and less densely built than Machu Picchu, but of the highest quality, beautifully conceived, and untouched since the conquest. Some of the plazas have been cultivated or used for grazing by the locals, but no one has looted the structures."

"That's big. And, seriously, untouched by huaqueros?"

"Virgin. It's like, somewhere around the conquest, the whole population just up and split. I call it Kunturpunku."

"Condor Gate. Well. Bing. Thanks. I'll see that the right people get this pronto. It's about time you stepped into the light."

To the government of Peru went this package accompanied by the official application to commence archaeological investigation. He knew it would be rejected initially, but would probably be accepted contingent to participation of the Ministry of Culture.

"Well, if they don't," he told the Core, "we won't let them see it, will we?"

Within sixteen business hours of receiving the couriered package UC Berkeley funded Bingham from a provisional account.

Beard College warned him that his findings were theirs under signed contract. “Fuck that,” he replied, “Read your own language in the termination document. All obligations: Null. And. Void.”

When two papers published, both would blow the windows out of their respective fields.

The Data Dump

Cable internet finally installed, Noe, Eph, Lily, Bingham, heads almost touching before the screen of Lily’s iPad, watched Nick’s face vanish in an iris out. They had just viewed the post titled *Superluminary*, a long rap on the intersection of quantum physics and the transmission of information across time.

“Wowser,” said Noe. “Lucky that he sounds so silly. I mean, if the holobiome has superluminary communication, why does she need spaceships? I wonder if anyone in power is taking him seriously? At least Nieman is still alive and posting."

She lifted her head, looked at each of them, brow furrowed. "Listen, friends, I sent a major data package to Beard College today. It’s part of my requirement. And more yet to my home server. It’s encrypted and is always running. There is backup power.

“But be aware. No science like it exists anywhere else in the world, as far as I know. None of you are mentioned at all, much less by name.”

“But they can track this IP,” warned Bingham. “And they know we are here, don’t they?”

“Yes, they do. So heads up.”

Convergence

An IT technician at Beard College, in Oakland, California, noted a sudden data dump into a server dedicated to the Biology Department, and asked the database wonk over there to look into it. The database administrator tugged at his waxed mustache, got reluctantly up and shuffled to the Biology data analyst. She logged boredly on, scanned the top entry, jumped to another random file in the middle, was about to enjoy saying something dismissive, then frowned, leaned into the screen, stiffened, and asked "When did this come in?"

"IT says two days ago." The data analyst took a deep breath and called the department director. "Chrissy. Sally. Who do we know who is on top of Kroeber's field?"

"Nobody. Is what she does a 'field?'"

"I think it is about to be a volcano. We need to get someone to look at this. She just dropped a ton of insane field research results in the department server, buried between a few thousand lines of innocuous stuff like she doesn't want anyone to notice. Maybe I'm wrong and it's routine. Look for yourself."

"I know someone at UCSF Med. Thanks for the heads up, Sally."

"Sure thing. Hope it's nothing. See you Saturday."

In Port Angeles, Nick Nieman checked in on his vlog stats, noticed a surge of new traffic sources in various parts of the globe other than the inevitable Russia, looked deeper, found many of the IPs masked, some were forbidden 403s, and one traffic source whose email address he recognized. Noe Z. Kroeber.

"Peru." The fat L-shape of the nation of Peru was suddenly dappled green on his stat tracker, a rush of traffic. He ran a search on his system, tracked the email address to a biologist who had published a paper in the 2000's. He had kept a copy in his research file on a 2-TB remote drive.

'Right. One short paper. But it was one of the sparks that got me going. *Meta-Quorum Sensing, Ion Channeling, and Potential Prokaryote Biocybernetics*. Noe Z. Kroeber, UCB, Beard College. Nothing since. And she's following me.' He also noticed new traffic from Virginia and D.C. In fact a lot of upticks looked federal.

Gerrymandering Lily Tran

At the approach of September, Lily stepped out of one of her long, if weak, showers, to hear Bingham addressing Ephraim around the corner.

"You're not going to marry her. You're just using her to get through your millennial teen years. She's done too many men too well. Sometime in grad school you'll pick up a virgin, or whatever passes for a virgin in your generation — some freshman in Anthropology 101. You'll be a Big Man by then, wrapped in all your Diffident Dignity. Lily will be a fond memory you can patronize in some annual ecard on her birthday. Maybe a video call, kids crawling up her leg."

"But not your kids? Bing, that's your fantasy. I probably will explore a little in university, fair's fair, but Lily and I go deep. You don't. She got to you through me. You're the one who's going to catapult from penury and obscurity into the limelight. As soon as you are vindicated by publication on Kunturpunku, you'll be a god. Indiana Jones. You'll publish a big coffee-table book of photos of the site, maybe by Sebastião Salgado, and slick super-realist illustrations, a hardcover book for professionals, full of architectural drawings, measurements, and proofs. And a young-adult novel about yourself, ghost-written, optioned by Spielberg. You'll have grad assistants lining up to be your next honey, or one of them, for the upcoming field season. You'll tell yourself that Lily was just the first to see your true value. But not the best."

They both tensed at the sound of the door opening.

"Are you guys done gerrymandering me?" Lily stepped through, still wrapped in a damp, printed manta from the mercado. They looked up in shock. Neither knew she was in the house. "I'll get a place in town for tonight, be out of here on the first flight tomorrow. I've had enough of these kitten-piss showers, this town with its rice and potatoes and so-called 'cheese,' the natives and tourists cannibalizing each other. And you. And your little rivalries. I'll say goodbye to Tuya, then get my used-up ass back to Pleasant Hill where I belong. I want to see the horns of the moon point right again."

They stared at her, stunned.

"That's right. Neither of you have ever talked me into or out of anything, and you know it." Her eyes were wide as a mad cat. Now they narrowed. "I'm smarter than both of you, you know. And more competent. I can do anything I desire. My father codes for the synchrotron at Lawrence Lab. My mother is an M.D. in Ob Gyn. Maybe I'll go there. For sure not psychiatry, I'm not going to spend my life rooting around inside skulls like yours. *Mmmbyeee* little boys."

"Did you ever feel so helpless?" Ephraim asked, when she was gone.

CHAPTER TWENTY-SIX then

The Bad Cave

Ramram found the bad cave behind chaparral in a fold of Pinkuylluna Mountain, hidden in the shadows below a towering rock outcrop. He started feeling uneasy a hundred rikras below, but his job was to track Kamay and it didn't have to be good.

The cavern pulsed malice, and it stunk. Like the plateau of the siq'i stone, the place was difficult to perceive, it reflected thought. He cautiously entered twenty or thirty paces into darkness of a wide chamber before the tunnel pinched off to a fissure too tight to pass. Through the crack in the rock came that powerful vibration of evil, and the rotten stench. He sent word to Pachacutiq, advising him to send engineers to seal the entrance.

Qachu's spies must have reported his find. Before sundown, he saw the Cult of Ilyapa come to claim the grotto and occupy the first chamber.

Ramram watched from a newly built qolqa above as Simi Apaq the Hurin Villaq Umu, and his entourage, Qachu in the lead, labored up the slope with masons and workers, not waiting for the Sapa Inka's response. Later, from his dwelling enclosure below, Ramram could hear them chipping away at the entrance in the night and the dark of the morn, in a hurry. Steps were being carved out of the friable stone slope below. Couldn't they feel the malignancy coiled in there? Or was that what called them? The morbid animus of the place reminded him of what he had seen in Eff Ram's Pacha.

The day after the equinox ceremony, Ramram had walked heavily, shaken. He had asked Chaski Yuyu how the sun had been lured into dancing in the Intiwatana. He had sensed no Kamay in that happening. Chaski investigated, returned with the tale that a Chimu goldsmith, captured in a chaotic and abortive campaign to the northwest, had studied the technique in

Pachacamac and passed the knowledge on to Pachacutiq's goldsmiths. 'Just tricks,' thought Ramram, 'empty of truth. What Eff Ram showed to me, that was the truth.'

He needed to tell the Sapa Inka that this was the horror that was coming. And in the cave was the horror that was here.

Kunturpunku was the center, the heart, of Pachamama's life and power. If the blackness of Ilyapa ever reached her there, it would be over. Death would win.

Eff Ram, Bean Um, Li Li, that strange, complicated woman No-ii, had all been at the ceremony. Pachamama was bringing them together, nudging them toward a clear, undeniable conclusion. If only he could speak their language, or they his, fluently. If he could show them to his ruler.

If only Tuya had been there to see what Pachamama showed him, to help him show Pachacutiq that what he saw was true and real. She thought that the future looked like fun. Better that she didn't see. She didn't need to feel what he felt. But you did not lie to Tuya, and not to tell the truth, that was lying.

'Ñakasqa,' he cursed, 'this is breaking my mind.'

In the Teeth of the Hole in the Hill

A rank stink woke Ramram at false dawn, slithering down from the cave. From his kancha below, he could see torches in the dark mouth in the hill under the zodiacal light. Gut trembling, he pulled his unku over his head without donning his loincloth, and crossed to the new staircase. He could hear hammer stones clinking against rock above, see shadows cast by torchlight. He got to the newly widened cave mouth at the same time first light hit Yana Urqu peak across the Urubamba River. Inside, workers were chipping away at the narrow neck of the cavern. It was from there that the *asna* smell, a fetid odor, snaked from the grotto's mouth; and, stronger, a nameless danger, like the ancient evil spirit *S'uqa*

Machu, finally broken free and roiling down the hill to drag him from his warm blanket.

He had sent three khipus to Pachacutiq, in the hands of an illiterate. This was for the Inka only. Silence in return. No surprise. His job was to give information and to receive orders. Not to ask information or give orders. He climbed the hill to the work site.

"Don't you feel that?" he asked the Uma Runa crew boss.

"I smell it, yeah," he said. "Nothin' I can do about it but pretend I don't."

"But you don't feel anything else coming out of there...like, bad spirits?"

"Nope. Not yet. And if you do, don't spook my boys, got it? 'Cause, you know we're going in no matter what. I work for the Hurin Villaq Umu and he works for the Hatun Villaq Umu and he works for Apu Pachacutiq Yupanqui Inka and he is the Son of the Sun. So if there's anything back in there, we'll get the Thunder Priests to fix it."

Ramram departed with dread that shook him in his teeth. He woke up with it every day, and went to bed with it at night. Sometimes he found himself turning to squint at the watchtower from which Qantuta had been thrown to sing her last long note.

CHAPTER TWENTY-SEVEN then and now

Yana Turmanyay — The Black Rainbow

Through Qachu, from his perspective in the Twist, Nick Nieman watched as priests of Ilyapa and their conscript workers died, penetrating to the third chamber of the cave. Died badly, puking blood, bile, and mucous. It was the *Yana Turmanyay,* the Black Rainbow, that took them. And there was a fourth grotto.

He knew Qachu wanted to turn his face away from the reek that emanated from the fissure in the rear of the second chamber. He gagged on his own bile on his knees under cedars dripping in the misty rain.

The villaq trembled in his narrow chest as if freezing. Nevertheless, he and the other acolytes stood stiffly obedient as the local chief priest, K'anchay, in his purple and black, raiment directed the drugged children into the stinking blackness beyond the crevice in the stone of the grotto. Not so anesthetized as to stop weeping, quaking, and trying to turn back.

The flame-shadows of the drummers swayed wildly on the walls of this chamber. The pounding and chanting ricocheted concussively, the flutes snaked in the dark.

The children were smeared in a sacred salve that burned their eyes and noses but was promised to be an antidote to the oily black fluid contained in the copper-lined pool beyond, and begot in the horror of the dark fourth chamber. The mouths and nostrils of the priest and other ranking divines who approached the crack in the rock, were also covered in fine cloth soaked in scented water and that protection.

The young ones vanished within. The pandemonium went on. The priests at the back now began to dance in synchrony, heads and knees lifting and falling. The Hatun Villaq Umu, tall and angular, lifted his face to smoke-stained ceiling, arms spiked high. Smoke from the fire was sucked deep into the cavern by a constant inner draft.

The children returned circling a pot of vaporizing fluid at the length of their trembling arms. It was set in a stone-lined hollow between the fire and the entrance to the first chamber. Before the depression stood a shallow basin of clear water.

At a signal from Simi Apaq, whose name Nick knew, Qachu and the devotees, escorted the sniveling children to the front of the cave, where acclas of Ilyapa washed their faces and gave them *aqha* corn beer to cleanse their throats. Maybe they would be all right. Qachu returned to the ritual.

The Hunan Villaq Umu turned to face the fire and the container of black liquid. He gave a bombastic speech full of Ilyapas and Pachas. After a while, Qachu's comprehension began, with the assistance of Certainty, to seep into Nick. What Nick thought he heard he later recorded as:

"Ilyapa has has warned us that there are evil beings who work to undo what Ilyapa has done.

"This enemy will come against us on every level, from the smallest insect to the Apus themselves.

"Some of these are men, and they are here now, to attack, to destroy. Today, with this sacrifice, our defense begins.

"With all honor to the perfection of this child of Ilyapa, with all honor to her Ayllu, we dedicate this sacrifice to Ilyapa's gift to us as guardian of the True Heart."

A thin girl, bemused by coca, aqha beer, and perhaps the blood of the cactus wachuma, was brought forward.

Two masked priests lifted the urn of greasy fluid, poured it slowly into the basin of water. The girl, her ankles and wrists bound, was gently nudged forward to face the bowl.

The Hatun Villaq Umu himself tied her to a standing pole by a soft ribbon. At a gesture, all others in the cave were guided away, backs to the cavern wall, now smoothed and niched by master masons. Wetted cloths were passed from hand to hand, to cover the mouth and nose.

The dark liquid spread over the surface, sunk slowly below. All watched and waited. The girl swayed, knees giving way.

A priest stepped out to pull her erect, hastily retreated. At the center of the pool, a bubbling upsurged.

A wisp of dark vapor corkscrewed upward, mushrooming at its apex. The column of blackness thickened, glints of dark color sparking as it roiled. The cloud spread, stinking, fire-lit from below. The points of color flashed like bits of pearlescent lightning.

The witnesses recoiled against the wall of the cave.

It expanded, spreading out over the terrified waif, no longer intoxicated, staring wide-eyed and open mouthed at the billowing fumes looming over her as she cried and writhed, until it suddenly broke into noxious droplets that fell into her open lips, coating her eyes and face, running down over her silken dress, soaking it darkly.

Her jaws snapped shut, then gaped wide, eyes closed. Her bound hands tried to lift to her face. She began to choke, her tongue thrusting unnaturally far into the poison rain. Her thin body writhing and twisting, slid down the stake, her feet kicked, blood gushed from her mouth. From her eyes and nose too, blood squeezed.

There was harsh coughing, followed by convulsive vomiting of blood, bile, mucus. Her bowels and bladder emptied explosively. Violent spasms lashed down her spine. Her head whipped from side to side, her legs cramped visibly.

The mushroom cloud disintegrated, falling to the floor in fine droplets. It took the girl a long time to fall still.

Afterward, as the attendants cleaned the mess inside and then carried the small corpse gingerly out on a litter, Nick witnessed Simi Apaq as he stopped Qachu.

“What you saw today? We have more of it. The Pachamama cult, they don’t know who they are defying.”

Qachu stood stiff, wide eyes dry and burning, lips a thready line. He nodded. At that Nick was set free.

He lay on a cot in the dark, shivering. The cat lay over his heart, giving heat.

The Rainbow Cloud
Ollantaytambo

The day after Lily abandoned them, walking to the plaza, Ephraim felt a tugging at the top of his head, looked up, and saw a shimmering ovoid of prismatic vapor overhead, hovering above the Manyaraki plaza, as if suspended droplets refracted sunlight into iridescence. Nobody else seemed to notice. It looked vaguely like what they had seen at Kunturpunku. The particles were in constant motion, coruscating as if by an eddy around an invisible rock. It wasn't the colorful visuals that impressed him though. It was the sense that the rainbow cloud was a nexus of times and places, as if in its roiling center he could see faces and places almost resolving into recognition. As if it were an agent of the Split Rock. He climbed Pinkuylluna to just above the Crown of Tunupa, at the top of the Old Man's rocky profile, where Lily had once stripped naked for him, and yes, it was still visible. In fact, even more vivid. He crossed beneath it again, craning up through it to Bandolista Mountain, climbed the trail to the 'Inka Watana' ruin. It was just as there, just as real. It pulled him.

Now Ephraim felt like a tuning fork, as if he had no identity except as a receptor for the vibrations of the microbial entity that coated the earth around him. He was perpetually stoned by the presence of Pachamama, in the presence of concentrations of prokaryote superorganisms, now intensified by some awakening. In ancient stones once held in awe by the Inka. It heightened his vision, so that the landscape glittered with signals that were not exactly colors but seemed to Incandesce wherever a concentration was particularly acute. If there had been any doubt that Peru had done something to his head it was gone now.

The rainbow cloud must have done this. “I want to get in there,” he told Noe, “I don’t want to sound like a dork, but it seems to be calling to me.”

“I need to see this,” she replied. “It has to be prokaryotic.” They returned to the vantage point. She couldn’t make it out until he put his hands on her shoulders. “Astounding optical phenomenon. Some form of parhelion. I’m running out of locutions for ‘surreal.’ How can I get a sample?” There was an acerbity to her tone that reminded Ephraim of Lily’s tone in the days before she deserted. Noe walked back remote and distracted, casting glances over her shoulder.

Later, it became visible from their east window, and Bingham could see it too, as he served rice-noodle tomato soup.

Noe Zoe shook her head. “I feel like one of those women who have uncontrollable spontaneous orgasms in the middle of board meetings. Everyday I get sucked further into this Presence phenomenon. I am traumatized and exhausted. I’ve compiled so much material that I could spend a decade parsing it. I've got twelve terabytes of data on remote drives. This place is a vortex. I will find similar concentrations in other locations, and at least traces everywhere, now that I know how to look, but this is one of the, and maybe the, global epicenters of the prokaryote overmind. Colleagues are sending me significant findings from around the planet now. And I’m afraid. There will be some form of draconian response when the significance of this phenomenon leaks.”

“What are you saying?” Bingham asked.

“That I’m thinking the end of this month or early September, if I can stand it that long. Then back to Berkeley. Where I will surrender. To whom I can only speculate.”

“Then,” Ephraim said, “before we lose you, we need to document the rainbow cloud.”

Before We Could Cancel Your Key Card

Katari Kuntur now had money, friends, a job, and an office in Lima. She was astounded by how fast it had happened, given the corrupt bureaucracy. Still, if there's anything a tourist-based economy loves, its a superlative, and Ñawpa Ñawpa was the most superlative: the oldest monumental site in the Americas, and the earliest proven contact between the coast, the highlands, and the Amazon rainforest. By some criteria, the oldest of its kind in the world.

She lifted her eyes from the dark glass of the desk, clean but for a wrinkled greasy lunch sack from which she was sure she could get six more uses, through the window of the towering black glass monolith of the Banco de la Nación building overlooking the freeway. Within which dwelt the headquarters of the Ministerio de Cultura.

She had a title now — what was it again? — and a salary with the Ministry of Culture, the government entity tasked with, for instance, maintaining, restoring, supervising, and guarding the many archeological parks and sites upon which much of the Peruvian wealth depended. At any dinner party, in her best clothes, she felt like a dog dropping. She could afford to shop now. She wished she were back in the mountains with a worn-out camel's hair brush and a *lampa* to dig with.

She jumped. What was that? It was her new phone. It had more buttons than a cavalry jacket. "Hola?"

"Doctor Kuntur?"

"In truth."

"I am Director Juarez, Cusco Region, we met at your welcoming party, you recall?"

"No, I don't. I remember almost nothing of that. And nobody."

He laughed. "So success has not ruined you. I have been warned about your inability to lie."

"The day is young. How may I advance my career at your expense?"

More laugh. “In a few months you may not be joking. I have field work for you. What do you think of that?”

“I think, *gracias a dios*.”

“There is a Department in Honduras named that, you know. I wonder what they have to be thankful for. But you? You have this. A gringo archaeologist has submitted a request to dig in Ollantaytambo — you know the place?”

“I have read Protzen.”

“All right, but this is not in the park. It is on the other slope of the mountain at around four thousand meters. He sends photographs and plans of an extensive, pristine, late-horizon architectural center and is being cagey about the source of his knowledge. We sent local agents to the coordinates without his knowing and they found nothing. It was cloudy. We would like you to meet with him, evaluate his claim, and if anything is there, see the project through its initial phase.”

“Doctor Juarez…”

“Director. I know you have your own pressing concerns, your life’s work. But you are in exile from that site right now while the Ministerio team checks it out. You will get it back, I promise you. And all glory will stay with you, none to be stolen away. Likewise, if this affair here bears fruit, you will be credited as Peru’s discoverer, and once established, we here in Cusco will take over and you are free to return to your beloved child, with a new charge on your escutcheon. Now you may ask the question foremost in your mind.”

“Why me?”

“Because your desk is empty — what would you do in Lima? And so that, if we deny his application, the North Americans can’t say that we saddled their man with a clueless bureaucrat. Right now you are omnipotent. Do you know how much the Institute of Andean Studies wants diggers on the ground at Ancient Ancient?”

“Who is this Americano?”

“An obscure archaeology graduate from Berkeley. Barely published. His name is Bonnaterre.”

“When?”

“We will send you a ticket — first class — and arrange lodging. Any time within the next month. He will be expecting delay.”

“Well. Send me a copy of the request, and whatever you have on the *Norte Americano*. Do you have independent photos of the site?”

“That will be part of your job. We can assign a photographer to you if you like. And a secretary and field crew.”

“Just the field crew. On standby. What’s the distance from Cusco?”

“Hour and a half. We could probably put a helicopter down there somewhere, a government bird goes right over Ollanta twice a day. Maybe on the futbol field.”

“Ah, Director Juarez. Fine. No. Send the materials, I will give you my answer within forty-eight hours.”

He laughed again. Katari decided she liked the sound. “Doctor Kuntur, if we insist, will you resign?”

“What does my dossier indicate?”

“That you would hitchhike back to Huarochiri before we could cancel your key card.”

Now she laughed. The director found it surprisingly light and feminine. “Forty-eight hours,” she said.

The Raid on the Data

Lily got a call from an unknown number on her third day back in California. It was Noe Kroeber.

“They got to my databases,” came Noe’s tense voice, “The hard drive at work was wiped clean. The IT tech said it looked like a professional hack, or even a physical attack on the drive, but the school is claiming it was a power surge. I can’t get through to my home server, which I leave running at all times, with backup power in case of outage. I had it put in by a very reputable, and expensive, hardware technician from LBNL. He knows your father."

"'They?'"

"Bing Bing's 'They.' Conspiracy theories are rarely keyed only to psychology. He points out that we put our findings on the Beard College system on one day, the first time we've let any of our dangerous theories be confirmed by data in an open forum, and zam, we're hacked. Lily, if this isn't just some quotidian coincidence, people or institutions who are capable of recognizing the implications of what we're on the verge of proving may now have everything we have except the experience itself. I'm afraid."

"What do you want me to do?"

"Go to my house. The key is in back under the tongue of the cement frog in the rock garden. It's for the back door. Go downstairs — the light switch is at the top on the left — see first if anything looks, ah, weird, out of place. Like the whole place has been ransacked with chainsaws. If not, the big hard drive under the bookshelf full of data binders should show light. If it doesn't, press the button on the front top. If it doesn't turn on, check the plug. If it is plugged in, look for signs of damage — is the back panel in place? If so, is it coated with dust? If so, does the dust show prints, disturbance around the screws? If it has been opened, is the hard drive — lower left — still in it? If anything's suspicious, shoot it with your iPhone. After that, just use your judgement. I know this is a big favor, and I know you don't need money — although this is worth five thousand dollars to me if you want it — feel free to haggle. Maybe your sense of adventure will be tickled. And I will owe you. I don't forget a debt."

"All right. I'll check it out. Are you on your cell phone?"

"A new chip. Not traceable. Look, you're right, check out the house from the outside before going in. I don't have any idea what to look for."

"All the Deep Government guys on TV lurk around in vans full of surveillance equipment. In real life they could probably do it from a bicycle. I'll be careful. Are we really talking like this?"

"I am. They could have all our numbers, all our email addresses. Except this. Getting into my cell would be easy. My emails won't reference you or Ephraim, but Bingham is on my contact list and Bingham leads to you and you lead to Ephraim so they could have a lot. Luckily, none of us have discussed our work in detail with anyone. But, and this is why I'm on high alert, why I'm so nervous, all of our notes are in the cloud. We all use Google. And our whole story is there. So if they take us seriously — and my data is strong — we may have attracted some very serious adversaries."

"Or maybe just people in your school, academic rivals?"

"I hope so. But they wouldn't get into my basement, I think."

"Okay. How do we communicate?"

"Get a throwaway cell, call this number. I won't bother you after this. In fact, it's better that you stay away from all of us. I'm already on Tor on my laptop and the two boys are teaching me encryption. I'm, how you say, going dark. Into the dark net. I don't know how much protection that offers."

"I have a friend who is a full-blooded cyber paranoid. Maybe this will get interesting. I will do this for you. After this, I don't know. But Noe. Don't tell the boys, okay? I don't want them knowing I'm still playing in their sandbox."

"Thank you, Lily. Truly. Keeping those two out of your hair will be the least of our problems."

"Yeah. Noe, I'm not mad at them. I just got scared and ran. I'm back up now."

The next night Noe's cell vibrated in her shirt pocket. "They got your hard drive," said Lily. "Your Neighborhood Watch guy called in a burglary. The first floor front window had been obviously broken. From, I note, the inside. Drawers opened, vases broken, mattress slashed, mayonnaise jar smashed. But your computer tower had been carefully opened, the hard drive pulled, then the back replaced but not screwed in. The screws were neatly placed under a strip of Scotch tape on your desk. The back plate and tower case were wiped clean, no dust."

"They allowed you to enter a crime scene?"

"No yellow tape. Investigation closed. For all we know, the cops took the drive."

CHAPTER TWENTY-EIGHT then

The Far Seer

As Ramram watched the workers on the disquieting cave above his kancha, a chaski runner came from the Inka Pachacutiq, far to the northwest where he was establishing an administrative center at Vitcos. The message runner looked almost dead. Wordlessly, chest heaving, he handed Ramram an imperial khipu.

The Inka's monks had found, the strings informed, a great white stone in a significant location, but could not agree as to whether it had powerful Kamay. Ramram's presence at the Sapa Inka's quarters would not be resented. Unless he was late.

It was five to ten days walk to Vitcos, for a job that would probably take Ramram less than a papa pun. He had an idea.

Ramram had been feeling his rapport with Pachamama growing. Now, with the chaski's khipu seeming to burn in his hand, he and the runner climbed to the Kamay-rich monolith standing in the Intiwatana temple, stood in its aura, felt this power about to take on life. He closed his eyes, fingered the location knots against his palms, directed his face toward the faraway place, and sent a question to Pachamama.

It was answered. His inner eye opened and he saw, as if he were present, a high meadow, surveyors at the edges lining out andenes-to-be, and in front, a house-sized hump of white stone.

He was looking through the eyes of a minor priest in divinatory training, who was straining to pick up some message from the big rock. He lacked the knack.

But Ramram did not. The waka was patched with black rumi qara, from which great Kamay vibrated. This was it; but none of the villaqs, clearly, had enough insight to be certain.

Ramram could picture them trembling before Pachacutiq, whose narrow gaze would be asking, "You *think* this is the one? With your *head*? And if I dedicate an offering to Lord Inti, and Lord

Inti says, 'My son, why have you spilled the blood of perfect brown llamas on this inert thing of no Kamay?' Will your head then answer? From the point of a stick?" The Inka's look would say that.

He took bearings on the surrounding landmarks at that far place, returned to this place, and went to work on the blank return-message khipu the chaski runner had brought for him.

The chaski was on his feet now, ready to run, masking impatience. His huge thighs tensed and relaxed, the ropey muscles in his calves clenched, while his face was forced into a parody of unconcern. This was an earplug man he stood before.

Ramram handed the dispatch to the runner. "Bring this answer. 'The White Rock is the one. Great Kamay. Have it carved.'" The messenger archived it behind his eyes, which opened wide, in a kind of horror, at the subtext of the message: Ramram was not coming. Then he made mocha, turned, and vanished down to the Qapac Ñan.

"That's right," said Ramram quietly, "I just refused an imperial summons. We'll see how that works out."

A Conversation

"So you have been promoted to *Antarqui, Umu Phawaspa*. I don't think there's been an Antarqui appointed since Qapac Yupanqui's reign. You must be wrestling with vanity about now."

Ramram, testing a big rock on the bank of Qalikantu river for Kamay, looked over his shoulder. It was the villaq Qachu. "Oh hullo Qachu. I'm not sure it's a promotion. I used to be Pachacacamayoq. A hundred household boss. I don't know if I can still be that and be a Flying Wizard too."

Qachu was clearly out of his element off the road, trying to keep his fancy unku clean and dry, not to disarrange the many feathers of his headdress, while holding a fat sack under his arm.

"If you can still identify wakas, you still qualify. Can you?"

"I guess. Not on this one, though. But I can still feel the bad vibes coming out of your cave. You need to get out of there. It's a bad place. It will hurt all of you."

"It's Ilyapa's place. I guess that would make you Pachamommies nervous. So you can still read Kamay. What I wonder is, Umu Phawaspa, can you fly?"

"Never said I could."

"It was for some far-seeing trick you pulled, right?"

"Just another Kamay, thing, Qachu. Hey, careful, it's slippery here. You wouldn't want to fall into the river and get all those feathers wet. And whatever is in that bag."

"It's for you. Your soldier boy, Otoronqo Kuy, asked the Inti villaq to get him into one of the Apu storehouses, I was there and volunteered. I think they both thought it was amusing, given our adversarial relationship. So here it is. Your formal Umu Phawaspa Flying Wizard outfit, two of everything in case you lose one in the river. They're having an Antarqui staff sent over, nobody thought to store one of those."

"You know, you can be a pain in the butt, but Qachu, I'm not your enemy. We're just doing our jobs."

"Sorry, Antarqui, but you are way out of your territory. I'm warning you. We know what you're up to. You need a lot more feathers to be playing with this kind of fire."

Qachu handed Ramram the sack, lost his balance and teetered toward the fast-flowing creek. Ramram pulled him back onto his feet.

"Thanks," Ramram said, "For the costume and the heads up. But about that cave? That *is* in my purview and I'm telling you, get your people out of there."

With an untraceable Chanka Spear

Qachu gripped the feathered javelin until his thumb knuckles hurt, heart writhing in his chest like a snake. The darkening sky had a volcanic light, the rope of smoke from the pyre in front of the cave an anaconda twisting into the lowering clouds. He peered through a stunted thorn thicket at Ramram, who stood on the stone lintel of the gateway to Ilyapa's cave, face grim as the black stone, staring up the long staircase to the chaotic fire-shadows and cacophony of the wild rite above. If Qachu was to make his kill, it would be now.

Ramram was arrayed in full Umu regalia, the very vestment that Qachu had delivered to him at the river in the bright day, gold-headed staff of power in one fist, star-headed macana mace in the other. His lip curled in disgust as he stared at the chanting dancers above. "Turn around," Qachu growled in this throat, "turn your back, damn your eyes."

And then he did. Passing his left foot behind his right, Ramram about faced, as if showing his back to a despised enemy.

Now.

Qachu clenched his teeth and ran full out, his footfalls buried in the drumming.

He slammed up against the massive stone wall, backed along it until he reached the shelter of the gate, took three deep breaths, bent his knees for the attack. He would have one chance.

He leapt from the portal, swiveled, javelin cocked back for the throw, eyes on…

Nothing. Ramram was gone. Qachu peered through the trapezoidal opening to his target standing now on the ground, three paces away, back to, scratching his august wizardy ass.

As Qachu threw his arm forward, an image flashed in his mind, a memory. It was Ramram grabbing him by the shoulder as he, Qachu, teetered, falling off the rocky bank into the river, Ramram pulling him to safety. Qachu's fist tightened reflexively on the haft of the lance, the arc of his arm driving the spearhead into the sill stone.

He watched Ramram walk away. Qachu pictured the Villaq Uma's face as he explained the Umu Antarqui's continued survival. "Weasel shit," he said to himself, "I just won't tell him how close I came."

Later Qachu would kick himself. "The son of bitch didn't save me from anything," he cursed, "The river was shallow, the current was weak, I wasn't going to die." What he didn't think aloud was that that little talk, adversarial as it seemed at the time, was the only truly friendly conversation Qachu had experienced in...the great god Inti; forever?

Two Thousand Virgins of the Sun

"Move fast. Block them. Turn them around. Get them off the mountain."

Otoronqo Kuy looked into Ramram's eyes. The boy wasn't joking. He looked down the slope. Thousands of important people dressed in their finest were filing up the new staircase to the Ilyapa cave, under the eye of the Inka.

"Check," he said, and turned to his troops.

Three months after Ramram brushed off the Inka's call, Pachacutiq came to Pachamamatambo. He was on his way to Qosqo, first resting for a few weeks in his new river retreat, Mayu Wasi.

One of his first acts was to honor Ramram with the title Antarqui, Umu Phawaspa. Antarqui, Wizard Who Flies. Ramram would now wear, on formal occasions, a circlet of vicuña wool, fitted to his personal skull, with a crescent moon above his eyes, horns up, topped by a triad of brilliant feathers from some tropical bird. And a spare, in case he lost or broke the first.

His defiance of the imperial summons was not mentioned, and the Sapa Inka wore a mask throughout the affair. Still, Ramram imagined that he saw a dangerous glint in the eyes behind the eyeholes.

Later, at the new moon, Pachacutiq decreed a triumphal ceremony celebrating his conquests to the northwest. The Cave of Ilyapa was due for dedication, so the Sapa Inka combined that with his own spectacular, the Son of Inti laying claim to the lesser god.

Resplendent tens of thousands filed onto the green at the foot of Apu Pinkuylluna, with its new-cut stone stairway edged in gold, gathering for the procession to the cave with its winging pavilions of sumptuously dyed fabric, its wide portal sheathed in thick sheets of gold inlaid with silver and emeralds. It was rumored that the Inka had reserved this place for his eventual — a very distant eventual — transformation to mummy.

The Sun's Son watched, from the Qoripata solar dias on Pututu Mountain, the glittering file commence toward the cave. And, leaning forward with a perplexed frown, he saw a file of soldiers cross the staircase to block the procession.

Colonel Otoronqo Kuy, at the head of his company of hardened veterans, was accustomed to following Ramram's curious requests; one of his core functions was to humor his ward's impulses. Otoronqo had seen him save Qosqo and thus the Tawantinsuyu, and anyway, Pachacutiq had told him, "he knows what he's doing. So far. If no one else does."

So when Ramram told him, "Move fast, before they get to the first landing," he did.

As the troops fell in, Ramram looked the colonel in the eye. "We may all die for this."

"With any luck, it'll just be you. But who cares? My wife is dead and my daughters ignore me." He gave a nod to his adjutant, who signaled the lieutenant colonel, who rapped an order to the major, who passed it onto the captain, who snapped a curt word to the lieutenant, who saluted, about-faced, and signaled the sergeant major, whose leather-lunged voice lashed out even unto the Emperor's gold-studded ears far above, commanding:

"Ten HUT! By the left flank! Forward HARCH! Double TIME!" and all dog-trotted across the lateral walkway to deploy directly in front of the ascending procession.

At the head of which, even before the Hatun Villaq Umu, treading with immense and stately gravitas, was Qachu, befeathered in his finery, holding forth the Golden Rod of Ilyapa.

Ramram stood in front of the phalanx of spearmen now in battle formation. Feet wide planted, palms out, halting the whole display of solemn majesty, which ran back-to-front into itself like a drunken tent worm. Behind Ramram at stiff attention stood Otoronqo Kuy.

Before him, face white, mouth tight, eyes black points of fury, was Qachu, whom Ramram now knew to be Pachacutiq's bastard first born son by his first love.

Qachu hunted frantically for the right words to dominate this upstart. Maybe, 'do you dare defy…' or would it be, 'Be so kind as to…' or what of, 'You WILL stand aside…' What came out was, "What the *fuck* are you doing? This is Pachacutiq Inka's big fucking day!"

"Sorry, Qachu, you just...you just can't go up there."

"*Ñin pip, akka siki*," says who, asswipe?

Ramram held forth his "*Obey This Sign*" khipu, given to him long ago by the Sapa Inka Pachacutiq, overriding any official who did not have authorization more lofty than the emperor's. Ramram had, of course, never used it, or expected to use it in his lifetime. "Sorry," he apologized again. "But says this."

Sapa Inka Pachacutiq Yupanqui watched from on high, carefully controlling his expression before the gathered luminaries of the empire, as his triumphal procession shuffled around, having no protocol for reversing direction on a staircase, colliding with one another as the leaders curled around to the rear on the narrow path, some sections trying to back-step while others about-faced as a unit while still others tried to follow the lead of the Ilyapa contingent at the head of the line.

Finally Otoronqo's soldiers' day was made by seeing the rear of the column, two thousand Ñustas, Virgins of the Sun, the loveliest young women in the world, parade their rears around in their fine clinging *cumbi* cloth as they about-faced back down the grade. Out of the corner of his mouth, one survivor of the Hunchback Hill forlorn hope massacre whispered "Ari. *Now* I can die."

"And now," his equally hard-bitten comrade replied, "you damn well will."

The Imperial Guard came for Ramram and Otoronqo Kuy. "Stand down," the colonel ordered his troops. "Go on home boys, the fun's over."

Antarqui, The Wizard Who Flies

So Ramram was to die now, not because he had failed to present himself in Vitcos. For that he had been elevated to the office of Flying Umu, a powerful tribute to his far-seeing ability. No, he was to die for spoiling the emperor's triumph at the Cave of Ilyapa.

Ramram was twenty years old when he climbed to his execution. He was a man. He had competed in the *Warachikuy* race and earned his loincloth and gold earplugs. The Sapa Inka had made him officially *Intip Churin*, Child of the Sun, a True Inka, had valued his advice and even his company.

But it is dangerous to be loved by a king. Or by Pachacutiq Yupanqui, were he no more than the ragged army scout Ramram had first taken him to be.

The triumph of the Sapa Inka Pachacutiq, and the opening ceremony of the Grotto of Ilyapa had been, for no good reason, stopped. The newly-named flying wizard Antarqui did that.

Ramram was an hour later being pushed roughly up Pinkuylluna toward the Crown of Tunupa, the *arawa*, place of execution, that doubled on most days as a watchtower. His ch'uspa had been ripped from his shoulder, its khipus dumped on the ground, and the *Imperial Warrant of Indisputable Dominion* khipu torn from his fingers. He would be thrown off the cliff. Now Otoronqo Kuy marched by his side, breathing through his nose.

"Damn lucky I'm not going with you," said Otoronqo Kuy. 'You were just following orders,' he says to me." 'My orders, thanks to that khipu.' The Sapa Inka doesn't forget his own commands. Or anything else. He dispatched me to ask you if you have anything to say to get yourself deeper in trouble. He said he is aware of your portentous warnings about the cave and that they had undermined his faith in all your other judgements, including that white stone."

"I can't help it. It just happens. Glad you're okay."

"Goodbye, Q'urpa. I'll miss the weirdness."

So Ramram, The Wizard Who Flies, prepared to demonstrate his distinctly limited ability to do so. The ceremonial array remained down by the river, awaiting Ramram's atonement to ascend once again.

Qachu, in his capacity as Witness for Ilyapa, was not smirking at his victory. No, his thin face was pale and his lower lip was trembling. His face screwed up as if in puzzlement at his own emotions. He looked down to his father the Inka in his bejeweled palanquin, its long poles shouldered by strong Rucana bearers in rich blue, far below.

When the Inka lifted his right hand, sun flashing off the raised pike, Qachu signaled to the executioners, whose grip tightened on Ramram's shoulders just as...

The northwest face of Apu Pinkuylluna tore off the rest of the mountain in an immense wall of stone, obliterating the cave, the pavilions, and the shiny new staircase. The roiling edge of the landslide finally stopped at the retreating heels of the Hatun Villaq Umu of Ilyapa, who was pushing his way through the now dust-basted Ñustas.

For a moment the guards stood riveted, still clutching their prisoner.

Ramram too looked at the knife-cut cliff a few dozen paces away where a hillside had once bulged. Dust demons danced in the zephyrs above the rockslide. Someone grabbed Ramram from behind, pulled him away from the vacuum that was still hungrily whispering his name. It was Qachu, a paler shade of white.

The last loose rocks rattled down the slope of the landslide. The mountainside where the procession had been was now buried under earth and stone. Dust wafted off like smoke. As if returning from a trance, the witnesses began to move again.

Qachu and the guards assigned to his execution sidled in front to look below. Qachu faced his father awaiting instructions.

Pachacutiq Inka Yupanqui stood in his litter, held solid by the bearers, and stared up at the watchtower cum execution platform, then, after a pause, clearly and deliberately swung his flattened left hand, palm down, across his chest.

Ramram was shocked at this display of forgetfulness. Pachacutiq, born left-handed, had with granite will required himself to use his right hand for all commands. But Qachu and the guards understood, and Ramram was pulled gently away from this particular death.

On the way down, Otoronqo Kuy spoke low into his ear. “My youngest was down there. She is a flower girl."

CHAPTER TWENTY-NINE now

Briarpatch

"That's them." Agent 'Go Man' Mango, in command, nodded toward where Noe, Bingham, and Ephraim rose up from their bench across the plaza of Ollantaytambo, looking back at the four Briarpatch operatives.

"What's 'them?' asked Agent Ché Guava, swiveling his head in the wrong direction.

"Never mind. They're gone. They made us."

The tourist season was in full force in August but even so Agents Mango, Kiwi, Cherry, and Guava, stood out in Ollantaytambo's plaza district. In their gaudy sports shirts and baseball caps they might have passed, individually, as tourists, but together, with their bulked-up bodies, tense cheeks, eyes scanning faces and hands, and something too weathered about their faces, no.

The local street food ladies, restaurateurs, and *indígena* adventure-tour porters gathering for their next trek up the Inka Trail watched them intently as they passed by with that hyper-aware martial-arts walk. So did the three species of policia: Nacional, Transito, Serenazgo; but their papers were good, so they were, for now, left alone. The other tourists glanced at them and averted their eyes.

"You sure it was them, chief?" Agent Guava frequently needed to be reassured but he was good in action.

Agent Mango slid his military grade fully-rugged 10-inch tablet from the custom inside pocket of his utility vest; the sunlight-readable screen lit up instantly to headshots of the four members of the Core.

"Yeah Ché, except for the cute one. She unassed back north."

"Wait," said 'Garcia' Cherry, looking over Mango's shoulder at the photo of Noe Zoe, "that one's cute too."

“Focus, Cherry. If they’re gone they’re gone. We know where they live.They don’t know shit about us.” Mango switched to satellite view, located the GPS arrowhead, zoomed in, then turned the screen toward Cherry and Guava, Kiwi still craning over his shoulder. A thin red line shot from their location — they could see their own caps and if they had wished could have drilled down to view the tablet screen viewing the tablet screen in that mirror infinity. The indicator line shot from their seats across the square, up the street, through the wooden gate to Pinkuylluna, up the stairs, off the main trail, squiggled down to point identified as the location of Split Rock. He made a two-finger slide and the rock rushed into close-up, in crystal resolution, as if seen from five meters up.

“Nobody on it. Wait, here comes Rango.” On the screen, Agent ‘Orangatang’ Orange exited Lares Street across from the plaza. They turned to watch him coming in real time.

“Agent Orange. You are damn near on time. You got the call on that ATV yet?”

“Affirmative chief. But it’s useless. And a bore to see you too.”

“You look a little trail-worn. The kid beat you up again?”

“He’s got training, Go Man. Somebody might’ve told me that. And I can break him in half. But no, ahm fahn. My Spanish is coming back, I’m over the runs, and I know the ground. And that ATV won’t go up the hill and ain’t got the weight to take a winch. You get that Nissan Armada rental HQ promised us?”

“What are you talking about, Rango?”

Agent Orange put his finger on the tablet screen. “That rock is big. Best we can do is set up the trailer here, run a cable, hook it up, winch the mother down this slope. No way we can roll it ourselfs.”

“You have been to that objective. Hands on.”

“Not quite. Nobody but the mujies go down there. The locals, cops, army and all, won’t go. They say it’s cursed or something. It puts up a shield. You’ll see.”

They referred to the Core as 'mujies,' their shared vocabulary having migrated from Iraq and Afghanistan.

"You haven't got hands on the thing. In all this time."

"You'll see."

Here Comes Twisty Nose

"Ya thank them is us's guys?" Bingham nodded toward the mercenary types in their tourist getups. He, Ephraim, and Noe watched from the darkness behind the balcony of a cafe across from the plaza. Noe had spotted the Briarpatch operatives and called "scat," their code word for 'run away fast'.

"Bingham, I don't know.They look military, or ex-military, and somebody is overdue to show up. Maybe I just panicked."

"Look," Ephraim said, "here comes Twisty Nose. He's walking right up to them."

"That's it then. They are here for us," Noe affirmed, "Our stalker has given them away. I thought I saw the thin gypsy one, and maybe the big ginger-haired fellow, recognize us. That's why I called 'scat.' So we got away."

"You were right," Ephraim congratulated."

"For now," said Bingham. "They're going to know where we live. Probably have for weeks. Nose-twist — Briarpatch — will have been surveilling us. You see that iPad they are all looking at? I bet it has military satellite signal."

"Let's see where they go," Ephraim suggested, "We are low-tech but we have eyes."

The Briarpatch team all turned around and walked back down away from town. Bingham found the nerve to scuttle down the stairs and watch them from behind a hollow fiberglass statue of crouching campesino with his pocket binoculars, then follow them down the street, ducking from doorway to doorway.

"They're in Sumac Ñusta hostel," he reported. "I don't think they noticed me. I took off my hat."

Agent Mango grinned, snapping shut the tablet. “His bald spot looks pretty shiny from space. And he looked pretty silly dodging around after us. He musta seen a war movie once. Well, game on, little man.”

CHAPTER THIRTY then

You Were Lucky Today
Pachamamatambo

Umu Antarqui Ramram was walked under guard before Pachacutiq Inka in his suite atop Qoripata Hill, where he was escorted upward past the temples and through niche'd halls to a long thin building in the depths of the complex, where he was prodded through a breath-fine orange-gold curtain. There he waited, squatting, holding his knees, long enough for a man to walk across town, with no offer of food or drink. He began to wonder if the praise and vindication he had been anticipating were indeed forthcoming.

Finally the taciturn noble re-entered and signaled for Ramram to follow him. He led to a tapestried curtain with eye holes between the shimmering folds. There the man whispered through the fabric, listened, and squatted by the wall, forearms laid across his knees. "I will relay the words of the Sapa Inka," he said. "Look at me, do not look at the curtain."

They waited a hundred or so breaths, hearing rustling, behind the curtain. Several of the most beautiful visions he had seen or imagined, Chosen Women, passed through and out, wrapping silk-fine aksu dresses over their nakedness.

Finally came Pachacutiq's voice, deep and flat.

"You were lucky today," the Inka said, "that the mountain chose that moment to shake off her unwanted skin." Ramram was squinting at the curtain. The lordly escort wiggled his fingers to get his attention, then pointed to his own mouth.The voice hollow and base

"You were lucky today," the interlocutor repeated , "that the mountain chose that moment to shake off her unwanted skin." And so on, every word echoed.

"Trust has deserted you. Your word is infected with doubt. You will continue your work as instructed. Others will confirm or negate your statements.

"The White Rock is verified, the mountain fell, but doubt remains. Nothing has been proven against you, still, doubt remains. For the Son of the Sun to doubt is Inti speaking.

"You will continue to live, and to be called Antarqui. You will be given a house within the suyu of your ayllu. You will report to your Khipucamayoq nightly.

"You will marry. If you cannot find a willing woman one will be issued. Do this during the moon of Distributing Surplus Land.

"On the morning of the first day of Plowing Fields Moon you will be banished from Pachamamatambo and sent to what was once Chanka land and beyond, to learn what becomes of those who defy or betray the Lords of Cusco.

"You will be stripped of all tocapu insignia. You will be supplied with clothing appropriate to your merit.

"Your reports will be evaluated by qualified authorities. Where credible and significant they will be relayed to the Tocoyricoc, Imperial Investigator, for application. Do not make further jests regarding 'haunted caves.'

"Here Apu Sapa Inka Pachacutiq Yupanqui provides no further counsel."

As Directed

He married Tuya as directed, receiving a headband and cape woven by her hand, giving her sandals in return, also woven by her hand. They had been making love for three years but now they were also authorized to make babies. They moved into a small but trim wasi in his father's kancha and he was content.

They discussed her accompanying him in his exile, at which her eyes lit up with an enchantment that dimmed the light of those acllas just deflowered at Pachacutiq's pleasure. The hope that he had already made her pregnant cast doubt on that journey, but in the end she won.

Before leaving this town that had brought so many unexpected experiences, he took Tuya up the long sinuous staircase to Kunturpunku to show her a small prismatic cloud that had appeared over the town. "A *Kuychi Puyu*, she exclaimed, "The rainbow cloud! I have heard of them but never known anyone who has seen one!"

"It just materialized in the night over the killawatana. To be near it is to make your heart sing. I saw it here once before, briefly. It was the day we felt the presence of Eff Ram and Li Li here — the day the condor came to me."

"I remember that," Tuya said, taking his hand, "So sweet. That was the night I finally got you to fuck me in the ass."

Going West

On the day of Ramram's departure, Otoronqo Kuy, now a lieutenant colonel, came to him. "You are under my care for the first part of this journey," he said. "We will be traveling under Major General Topa Qapac. He is Pachacutiq's son by an accla, and a hard man for one so young. He will be leading an army of forty thousand. The Apu Sapa Inka will be heading south into the Collasuyu with two hundred thousand. With us will be Princes Amaru and Tupaq Yupanqui. Tupaq will take the *Borla* when Pachacutiq is done with ruling. They are fifteen and six years of age respectively. You will answer all their questions and not lie."

"I thought my word was, ah, not valued."

"Q'urpa, you defied Pachacutiq's desires and commands, as well as those of the Hatun Villaq Umu and various governors and generals, under the eyes of sixty thousand of his subjects. He is not going to forgive you publicly for a long time."

"But privately?"

"Privately, you saved the lives of all those dignitaries, three of his bastard sons, a thousand of my soldiers, and two thousand acllas, two hundred of whom were Ñustas of royal blood. You are whispered of with respect and affection for eight days' journey in any direction. But do not expect the Sapa Inka to act on any of your reports. He truly has felt doubt of you, and despite all reason, he states, he cannot forget that. I suspect the Ilyapa priests have been at his ear. But," and as they stepped out onto the Qapac Ñan, where rank upon rank of armed men waited, he gave Ramram a sharp look, "Amaru and Tupaq have nothing against you at all. And one of them will rule.

"And oh. The Apu Sapa Inka doesn't believe anything you said about the hairy-faced silver sickos. He thinks you made them all up to scare children. And he wants you to find out where they came from, who they are, and if they're human. So make up a good story."

An Army Marches No Faster Than its Slowest

An army marches no faster than its slowest element. Climbing the steep switchback of the Vilcaswaman Ñan up the gorge of the Apurimac, Lord Speaker, river, the slowest element was a lame, pregnant, officer's wife carrying twin babies.

The thirty-three thousand soldiers and their seven thousand more porters, wives, consorts, priests, and all the camp followers, labored upward, the hanging bridge below shrinking too slowly. Tuya sidled down against the human current until she came to the woman. Smiling and cooing, she took one of the twin girls from her mother, anticipating but not receiving possessive resistance.

She took the other from the shawl slung on the woman's back, and thrust it onto the sergeant leading the rear guard, whose brows came together in anger. Seeing the lovely woman, he softened, and nodded when she said, "Would you like to get up this hill before dark? I'll get a woman to take the baby. Please help us for a short while." She returned with two unburdened wives, a medic, and a stick. One of the wives took the baby from the soldier, the other took the injured woman's arm over her shoulder, and the medic took a strip from Tuya's aksu hem to wind a support around the sprained ankle.

Forty thousand travelers climbed faster.

Ahead of the army but behind the scouts, Ramram ranged searching for waka, blending into the landscape in Pachacutiq's tattered unku and worn cloak, now thoroughly cleansed by Tuya. He was a puzzle to those in the army who were aware of him, and who heard him mocked for his rags, called Q'urpa The Lump, caught whiffs of the rumor that the Sapa Inka himself had exiled him for crimes unknown, saw that he had no insignia of even the lowest status, yet noted that generals and priests seemed to consult him, and that he was allowed to move at will, answering to no one. But the most impressive contradiction was the attention shown him by the two crown princes, Amaru and Tupaq.

Ramram, hands on his hips, looked up at a slender standing rock, towering over his head by more than a rikra. Jagged, coming to a crooked point at the top, it was furred with every manner of growth. Mosses, lichen, fungus, and algae. It hummed with the strongest Kamay he had ever felt, stronger than the Split Rock or the wanka in the Intiwatana at Pachamamatambo. Honey bees and hummingbirds circled it. The sky seemed to revolve around the sharpened apex, clouds spinning in a lordly gyre overhead, pearly veins of color shimmering with intelligence in its surface. He marked the location in his mind, orienting to peaks in three directions, the position of the sun relative to the length of his shadow, and entered it into his scouting khipu. 'This is coming to Vilcas,' he decided. 'The ultimate wanka.' He could feel it pulling in his *ñawi chakata*, pineal gland, and he knew that when he was ready the Pachamama would have something new to say.

As he turned to hike down the high bluff, he saw Amaru and Tupaq coming up, Tupaq's six-year-old knees pumping, Amaru carrying the water-filled gold bowl that was his latest project with improbable finesse, spilling nothing.

Tupaq, feisty, bright of eye, squat and solid, came up grinning, blowing breath, elbows in the air, ready for anything.

Amaru, sixteen years old, seemed to levitate, so fine was his coordination, as if the world carried him lovingly. Solemn and serene, his pupils always filling his whole iris. He had run, and won, his Warachikuy race at ten years old, defeating every other son of the nobility, all trained from birth in fighting, throwing, wrestling, and most of all, running. He had reached puberty, winning his loincloth, sandals, and gold earplugs that year, three years before the rest, taking every prize without seeming to try. No boy in competition resented him, because in Amaru there was no contempt, he held everyone his equal, eyes repealing all judgement though knowing of its existence and source. As in athletics, he was in scholastics. He completed his four years at the Yachay Wasi university in one, leaving with full command of the khipu, of religious ritual, myth, and memorized history. Engineering, architecture, agronomy, all the miracles of number, came to him as a gift.

He had been given his first woman as soon as his initial erection displayed — a Ñusta of the highest rank, a young widow. From that encounter a wondrous phenomenon emerged. She left his blanket with pupils as large as his own, all her grief erased, and from that moment on she never needed another man between her legs. Merely to breathe deep gave her a shuddering *yumachiy*, thighs clenching, head thrown back. And when she raised her arms to serve Inti, for this was her life now, an Accla of the Sun, great tremors of ecstasy convulsed through her body, and the surrounding atmosphere would turn burning gold in her eyes.

This happened to every woman who came to him. That was every woman who could, because for a female human to stand in his presence was to melt for him. Blind, mean, conceited, sapphic, ancient, bereaved in black sorrow, or in love with another, none were exempt. He gave himself only to those whose lives would not be deranged by his influence.

He was in line for the Borla but he would not follow Pachacutiq in expanding the Tawantinsuyu to the ends of the world because in Amaru there was no violence and no greed. He perceived

Pachamama everywhere and in everyone. He could see the nacreous threads of color intertwining in the clouds, and the tiny beings that live in the sky.To Amaru, power was illusion. Pachacutiq had sighed, nominated Amaru into the circle of his chief counselors, and begun grooming Tupaq for the Tiyana seat. The younger brother would do well.

"See this," Amaru said, and set his gold basin on a dip of loose soil with flawless balance. The bottom of the vessel was coated in fine black lichen; the inner surface was sheathed with green algae. The water itself was thick with various hues and forms of minuscule life that Amaru had gathered and cultivated. He drew a complex khipu from his ch'uspa and held it spread over the bowl. In the water, the tiny diatoms of algae began to shift into patterns, swirling and aligning until they came to tremble in a mimicry of the khipu's knots and cords. "Yes," Amaru said, "Now watch."

The mirrored khipu in the algae colony began to sprout new shoots and the shoots to synthesize new knots, generated with shades and hues not seen in the original. The knots, too, took configurations not known to Ramram. Amaru copied the new extensions onto his own khipu, fingers whirring. Sometimes his brows came together in concentration, striving to duplicate an unknown ligature. The structure hovered in the trembling water for long enough for Amaru to get most of the knots, then transformed again, shifting into layered skeins connected by vertical threads, a three-dimensional system of cords and knots.

"See that?"Amaru indicated. "It is speaking now in threes, not twos. Our khipus are founded on polarity, Hanan and Hurin, black white, man woman, good bad, me you, zero one, twist left twist right?

"That polarity is the very base of khipu recording — it's also the basis of life, seeing the world, knowing. The seer and the seen. Now everything here is in threes. Before, the world was flat. Now it has depth. See how the knots are in threes on each plane. Then the lines rise to meet at a single point in the next level? It forms a pyramid. And knowledge is contained in that in a way we cannot understand. Understand? But *it can*. The Pachayachachiq is talking to us by this new khipu. So I ask it a question."

He pulled out a blank khipu in standard colors. His fingers flew. He held it above the dish. Again the algae reconfigured, reorganizing at great speed. Then it reduced itself to a single, simple, two-dimensional khipu. The khipu read, "The man Ramram and the Mother Lake."

"You and Mama Qocha." Amaru rocked back on his heels, looking satisfied.

"I don't know what that means."

"But you will. From you I learned how to talk to Pachayachachiq. Before that I could only see him." He made a row of knots on a new string and held it over the golden bowl, which shifted to a new message. "You will grow now from two dimensions to three. You have found a new *punku*, a new gateway to Pachamama."

Ramram looked over his shoulder at the wanka he had just left behind.

"Maybe so." Amaru smiled at him, eyes black, and deep.

Tupaq hunkered on his heels, watching them, sometimes lodging his fists in the dirt and lifting his whole body free on his knuckles.

"Tell us more stories," he said. "The ones Father Inka says are lies. They're the good ones."

Before the sun set, Amaru ordered men to carry, carefully, the encrusted rough-hewn obelisk back to the moving line of travelers. By next nightfall the advance guard would be in Vilcaswaman. So would Ramram and that stone.

CHAPTER THIRTY-ONE now

Rumble at Split Rock

Five men filed carefully over the jagged boulder toward Split Rock. Four were big and one was wiry, dark, and in the lead. All eyes were fixed on their prey.

"I wish Lily were here," lamented Noe Zoe.

"What would she do?" Ephraim asked at the Rock, watching the mercenaries descend. "All right," he admitted, "she'd get mad, not scared. Scared is better."

The five swaggered down the overgrown plateau, each with their own menacing smile. Ephraim set his feet apart, hands at his side, dropped his weight into his feet. He heard Peewee Kiwi, the biggest one, laugh.

The other two stepped up beside him. Bingham began to snap his fingers in 2/4 time, and to sing: "When you're a Jet you're a Jet all the way..."

The Core had gone up the Inka stairs, carved from living rock, hoping to thank Ramram for Kunturpunku. Now, before they could try, the squad of special operations types was coming at them.

Noe stood by Ephraim, who waited, eyes on the oncoming Briarpatchers. Her hands shook. Bingham stepped up beside him.

"Thanks," Ephraim said, "but please take Noe back. I need room." Bingham looked at Ephraim's profile, saw he meant it, took Noe by the arm and dropped back behind the stone.

Now, smiles gone, the five moved in around Ephraim like a river around a rock. The lean one faced him. Ephraim recognized the flaming bomb tattoo on his forearm. From *La Legion Etrangere,* the French Foreign Legion. As a kid, Ephraim had kinda sorta wanted to be one. He was going to lose. It had nothing to do with attitude.

Agent Mango swiftly scanned his squad. They were all in place, stances good. This was just a skinny kid but Mango knew better than to underestimate an enemy. He relaxed a little, looked the kid in his root beer brown eyes, smiled to put him off guard, and got a jodan-zuki fist right in his mouth for his effort. He staggered backward, and by the time he had regained his balance, he saw Kiwi and Guava doubled over and Cherry on the deck curled up clutching his junk. Orange had stepped back, avoiding the kid's snap kick, and was moving in. From the ground, Mango signaled Orange to hold off, to ready for a coordinated attack. Cherry was clearly whore duh combat.

Mango ran his wrist under his nose, it came back bloody. "Ishmael — is that what you're called? Stand down. You get one chance. I hope you don't." The kid looked right at him. He was somewhere other than in this world. He would fight. "No breaks, no vitals," he ordered his crew.

At Mango's nod, the four stepped in. The kid didn't land a shot. Mango did, the kid's head snapped back, Kiwi got him in the jaw, Che's kick to the solar plexus knocked the wind out of him, and as he hair-pinned, trying to keep his feet, Guava unleashed a lightning quick spinning back kick that took the boy in the left temple and put him down.

They all stood back, helping Cherry to his feet. They let the other two mujies walk the scrappy little snot away from the rock site.

Let's Go

They had come up on the place led by Orange. W□hen they hit the ridge over the flat part, some strong reluctance stopped them all in place for almost a minute. "See?"Orange said smugly.

But the inhibition vanished, as if a door had been opened, and they were free to pass. They had watched the three perps go up, they could see them below. Agent Mango saw the eager foretaste of vengeance in his men. He led them down. The fight was short.

Now they stood off, looking at the oh-so-special hunk of stone. "Well, it's pretty well planted, looks like," Cherry mused. He had the most experience at moving shit. "We might could winch it down that declivity though. We got right of way from the yokels?"

"Easement. Yes. I have been assured of this." HQ had been arranging contacts and paperwork, keeping Mango informed.

"So this hunk of junk is supposed to have some voodoo to it?" Guava looked a little unsure.

"For them. The mujies. They have 'sensitivities.' Or they use drugs. I don't think it's got anything on us. Except Orange — hey 'Rango, what do you think now?"

"You felt it too, chief. I know you did. It just let us through."

"I don't know what I felt," said Kiwi, "but I don't feel a thing now but wanting to get it done. I'm hungry."

"Okay then, let's get Oscar Mike here. You got the choker cable, Peewee?" Kiwi went into his backpack, pulled out a coiled carbon steel cable with end clips.

"I got fifty feet here. There's more in the vehicle."

"Okay. Give me an end, Kiwi, Guava, you take the other end, let's see if we can pull it underneath. Cherry, you got that folding shovel?"

"Word, chief. With a pick end, I think you gonna need it."

"Check. Let's go."

Pachamama Plays

The remaining Core observed from a Qolqa above and east of Split Rock. Bingham focused his cheap Tasco binoculars through a clump of agave. He saw the contractors' heads bob below the terrace edge, mill around, produce gear, step up to the rock, go still, then, one by one, disappear from his line of sight. Twenty-five minutes later he watched them struggle slowly back behind the outcrop, rise into view, stumbling and dazed, supporting each other, carrying one inert between them. Furtively navigating the stone steps, waiting for passersby to pass by, they lugged their casualty through the portal, loaded him awkwardly onto the Jeep, wrangled that down the narrow cobbled street to the plaza, where a parked SUV, now loosely surrounded by curious Peruvian kids and more circumspect adults, waited.

"Well," Bingham observed, "I guess they met Pachamama and she met them back."

"I would surely like to take some biosamples from their skin and clothes," Noe added.

Voodoo Rock Clusterfuck

"*Borracho,*" Agent Mango explained to the skeptical locals as he dumped Orange into the back. He drove both vehicles to their hostel on the edge of town.

Foremost to lay hands on the rock had been Agent Mango, always a First-to-Fight man. He gripped the rock as he tried to work the cable under the end. He spasmed violently, threw himself off the stone, projectile vomiting and flopping like a fish. Guava too was incapacitated. As soon as he tucked the cable around the other end of the larger boulder his head snapped back and his tongue shot out of his mouth like a turtle head. His back arched, his shoulders converged as his scapulae pinched together. He let out a gargantuan belch and fell forward onto the rock, which seemed to catapult him off itself, where he hiccupped convulsively. Cherry, who had barely touched the boulder, was sitting in the dirt doubled over, bawling, snot running down his chin, moaning "I'm sorry Momma, I"m sorry, I'm so sorry."

Steeling himself not to show hesitation, Agent Kiwi stepped in to pull Agent Mango away from further danger. In doing this, his rear touched the smaller section of Split Rock, and he was sucked onto the grainy surface as if by an octopus. He rolled around to pull himself away. His eyes went wide and mouth opened, threatening to dislocate his jaw. He shot spasmodically off the rock, face distorted, tearing off his shirt and pants, clawing himself fanatically. Cherry, still tearful, tried to restrain his buddy's scratching hands. "Jesus, Peewee, you'll tear your fucking skin off!"

"Let me go, cocksucker, let me go! Get it *off* me! It itches! It fucking *itches!*" They wrestled until, panting and emitting tiny treble whines, Agent Kiwi subsided into semi-conscious relief. "Oh momma, never again. Oh, don't let it come back." He got some panting control of himself. "I got kneecapped by a sniper in Kandahar and I'd trade this for that in a hot minute." He looked at Go Man Mango, who seemed to be marginally back in service. "Boss, we got anti-inflammatory in the kit? Oh damn, make it stop!"

Go Man shook his head in disgust. "Affirmative. Let's get the fuck out of here. We can't touch this bastard, much less lift it."

Avoiding contact with the stones, Orange pulled both Mango and Guava free. He looked at the writhing Kiwi, then at the offending geology. His brows pulled down and his jaw thrust out.

"No," he said. "You each had different responses. I'm going to see if it can take me down." He stepped over the coughing Mango, turned around, and hiked himself to a sitting position. Kiwi watched as the tension drained out of Agent Orange's beefy face, his eyes rolled up into his head and his mouth opened in some charismatic transport, as if suddenly seeing The Risen Christ or Willie Nelson. He let out a deep sigh, his eyes shut, and he slipped off the rock, conscious but too limp to move. Of them all, it was he who could not self-propel himself back to the street.

On the flight out — the Briarpatch company jet met them in Cusco — Agent Orange was silent. All he would say about the experience was, "I'm okay."

What he didn't tell the others, or the company debrief team, was that he had converted. He saw the light. Life on earth was ending in a black mist of shit and somebody had to stop it. He resolved to learn what he could about the countermeasures of his government and its allies, and report to the miserable defective pencil-necked snowflakes who seemed to be the only boots on the ground dedicated to saving the Good Whatever It Was that had opened his mind and heart on that rock. And, weirdly, turned him left-handed.

This was the first harbinger of what would come to be known as Eye Kay. Certainty had looked into the total equation of human consciousness on earth and had an idea.

CHAPTER THIRTY-TWO now

It Is a Peruvian Tradition Now

Bingham was dimly aware of a small dark woman sitting alone two tables over, glancing up from her lawyer's pad with increasing hostility. He lowered his voice a little.

Bingham was messaged to be on alert for the arrival of his liaison with the Ministry of Culture, who would make a determination as to the value of the site and his qualification to work it, and if positive, would represent Peru in the dig. They would be subordinate to Bingham, but effectively in charge since access to property, labor, and tools would filter through the Ministerio. If a permit were to be issued, Bingham would be free to solicit private funding.

Ephraim continued. "I heard a tour guide on Temple Hill say 'One word. Anti-gravity.'"

Bingham shoved his bush hat down over his eyes. "Well, if I were going to move big stones downhill, the first tool I'd use is anti-gravity. There must be some around here somewhere — isn't there a Lemurian hardware store around the corner?"

Eph and Bingham were idly mocking what they took to be stupid theories about the Inka, while eating lunch in a working-man's restaurant by the market.

"True, just using gravity wouldn't work. What if it quit on you halfway down?" Thus spake Ephraim.

"Right, I mean, this is an 'emerging nation,' you can't count on the utilities. I like the Ica Stones theory, too — ya can't let go of that just because Basilio admitted that he etched all those dinosaurs himself, and sold them to Javier as 'ancient' then demonstrated how he did it on camera for BBC. That don't mean nothing."

"And all the dinosaurs look like nineteen-fifties plastic toys. Proving current paleontology all wrong. Who likes dinosaurs with feathers anyway?"

"Yes. And how the tour guides tell you that irregularities in the surface of the 'sun temple' monoliths are carven condors, llamas, pumas. So the tourists stand there squinting, looking puzzled, until one of them says, 'O yes, now I see it.'"

"Yes," Ephraim came back, "and the emperor's new clothes. And what about how all the Pachacutiqs with long Conan the Barbarian hippie hair?"

"Right. Despite how every chronicler who brings up hair at all agree that it was both law and custom that Inkas had their hair cut above the ear."

Now Ephraim was becoming uncomfortably aware of the woman's inimical eye. He felt forced to speak sotto voce. "And that it was death for anyone not of the Intip Churin to wear their hair short. And we already roasted the chakana myth. Like, where did this symbolic information come from? Three-by-five cards found tucked into square Wari hats? Audio files embedded in Ica pottery? Bing, that lady is glaring at us."

"It does look kind of stink eye. Do you think she speaks English?" Bingham finally stopped avoiding her gaze and looked at her. The woman carefully closed the cover on her notebook, shouldered her Peruvian knit purse, stood and approached.

"Of course I speak English, you arrogant imbeciles," she seethed, "I'm an Andeanist. The global center of Andeanism is in Berkeley, California. It got appropriated there along with a few hundred thousand pieces of our patrimony. And one of you is Bingham Bonnaterre?" Bingham tentatively raised his hand.

"Good. I'd hate to think that there were more of you cultural saboteurs in this town. Understand this: if the Chakana was an invented tradition in two thousand three, it is a Peruvian tradition now, because we have made it one. The narrative spoke to us and we embrace it. If Guaman Poma portrayed the Inka elite with short hair in Fifteen Ninety, we portray him with long hair now because it conveys virility and our men were virile. As of now they have long hair and always have had.

"Your scholastic truths are thin, weak, and bloodless. Our heritage is deep red and will be here when your people are scratching in the bones of your ten billion dead for edible dung beetles. Never forget, your view is etic. You are an outsider. Mine is emic. My blood is of this land.” She glared at them, weighed the degree of their abashment, and said,

“I am Doctor Katari Kuntur. The Ministerio de Cultura has sent me here to assess your request to dig around in an Inka cemetery that has been preserved from desecration by the ‘locals’ since the sixteenth century.

"They sent me, instead of some other archaeologist, on the supposition that I will advise denial. I probably will. But if I don't,” and here she smiled a little for the first time, reminding Bingham of Peter Sellers doing Doctor Strangelove, “I will get first name on anything we publish in Spanish, and you on publications in English.”

“Um. Agreed.”

“And we split revenues from anything in film, television, or video presentations of any sort.”

“To be discussed.”

“You understand that you live or die by my recommendation.”

“You understand that it is my discovery.”

“Your RFP substantially pinpoints the location and what's to be found.”

“Did your guy stumble onto anything when he went up there? Anyway, we can work together and our agreemeadvise denial. I probably will. But if I don't,” and here she smiled a little for the first time, reminding Bingham of Peter Sellers doing Doctor Strangelove, “I will get first name on anything we publish in Spanish, and you on publications in English.”

“Um. Agreed.”

nts will be in all three languages. Doctor Kuntur, allow me to present Ephraim Arrowsmith, my partner in research. He will be returning to the States and not involved in the archaeological side of things here.”

"*Mucho gusto, Caballero.*"

"*Igual, Profesora*. So sorry to seem officious, but do you have papers? These are insecure times."

"Yes, I have been informed that various governments are interested in how you came by this information, if it is authentic. In fact, they escorted the raiders on your 'Split Rock' onto their company jet." Now her eyebrows raised. "You left that part out of your proposal. All right." She slid a faux-leather ID wallet to Bingham, who scanned the contents in silence for a full two minutes, then slid it to Ephraim. Katari's hand shot out to stop the transfer, then withdrew short of its target. "Fine," she conceded. "I'll contact you officially in the morning. After you've Googled me. Can we inspect the site by, say, four a.m.?"

'Now I remember him,' she told herself later, 'He gave that lecture in Lima. He is actually sort of a mensch. It was a good talk.'

Ancient Air

Katari hardly felt the killer uphill hike. Rations and sleeping bags hit the ground at the foot of the rising stone that Noe had ID'd as intensely infested with the prokaryote cocktail that made people see the otherwise invisible lost Inka town.

Katari saw only stone and vegetation. Bingham walked her toward the apachita of stacked rocks basing a small wanka, waited for the biofilm to rise and envelope them both, and since it didn't take immediate effect, getting explicit permission just short of a signed document, stood behind her with one hand on the top of her head and the other on the small of her back. He let his own bioelectric film transfer to her. When her knees began to give, he held her up until she regained her foothold. In Spanish, she breathed:

"Mother of god, there is still thatched roofing extent here."

"Five buildings with near complete coverage, traces on seven more."

"That alone is worth...well, there is no system by which to quantify. This is *asombroso*."

"*Asombroso*? I guess that doesn't mean 'boring.'"

"Astounding, in your mongrel patois. Bonnaterre, I feel like rolling around in this place like a dog in his own shit. This discovery will change everything." She turned to him, shaking off his hand that still rested on her neck, and drilled her black eyes into his. "How did you find this? What hides this place from others? It is impossible that this has gone undiscovered since the *nakba* of Peru."

"Basically intelligent microorganisms. I'll brief you later tonight. Later, we'll show you everything." He barked a mocking laugh, and said in English, "Hang onto your hat, doctor, it's gonna be a brand new world."

"If the new one has this in it, then I am ready."

Katari scrutinized Bingham's satellite photograph superimposed with a numbered grid in ten-meter squares. He saw that she approved. "Here, 56A, the sealed grotto in which large pottery jars and metallic reflections have been identified, may pay off." He tapped the photo with his forefinger. "Are you sure that the man that owns this property will not chase after us with a machete yelling '*Propiedad privada*?"

"Woman. She has been neutralized with Law 28296 protecting the National Patrimony and with good land elsewhere. Show me."

"With pleasure. And, Doctor Kuntur, there is a killawatana."

"A gnomon measuring phases of the moon?"

"Yes. And it will knock your socks off."

"I am even now entirely unsocked, Assistant Professor Bonaterre."

He led her around over a springy ground cover that felt like a trampoline, among vine-hung crumbling stone walls, ducking into a beautifully masoned chamber. Seconds later she was peering through a small slit in the thick clay plaster sealing a slanted fissure in the living rock of the rear wall. The break was too narrow to line up a flashlight and an eye. Bingham stood as close to her as he dared.

"So you smell that?" she challenged.

"Mildew?"

"Ancient air. It has been trapped in there for centuries, I have smelled it before. Maybe we can get an electromagnetic conductivity instrument system in here. Even try a Molecular Frequencies Discriminator, they aren't totally useless, we will see what's in there."

"We'll just go in. Carefully, but in through the seal." He rolled an eye her way. "*Con permiso, maestra*."

Bingham heard Katari make four calls. One to the Ministry of Culture, one to The National University of Saint Anthony in Cusco, one to the National Police, and one to TV Peru. She described the situation to all of them in the most sensational terms.

"I want them here immediately. All of them. I don't want any single agency taking over the site and looting it. Everybody turns *huaquero* when they smell gold."

They camped onsite that night. Bingham brought out a plastic water bottle containing a liter of cheap rum. Katari took a hit. "Okay, gringo. How did you find this place? I can't figure it out."

"I don't think you're ready. You're not *bastante borracho*." Drunk enough.

"Do you want that authorization?"

"It's already in my pocket. They can't see this place without me."

"How much more will you make me drink? Look, you're going to tell me, this you know. So. Here is a good night in which to do it."

"All right. But it'll take you a week to begin to internalize what I'm going to tell you." Bingham closed his eyes and marshaled his thoughts.

"Okay alright. There's this rock down there on lower Pinkuylluna. We call it Split Rock, it's covered with green, black, and orange lichen, and when you touch it..."

Katari didn't ask a question for the next forty-five minutes, although Bingham paused to give her a chance to call it bullshit, or just to walk off muttering. When he ran out of breath, they sat silent for minute. Then she said, "N. Nieman. *We Live In You.*"

"Damn. Seriously? Five thousand meters up in the Cordillera Negra and you are tracking some nutball blogger in Washington State?"

"Did you all not google me? And find my website about Inkas?"

"Right. Right you are, there's your wishful The Inkas Win alternative history blog. So you found him through that angle."

"Yes. And the rest of it seemed like inane tonteria. But it gives the concept, so you are not so difficult to follow."

"Or to believe?"

"All the bacterial 'Presence' BS? But it is just what you described, no? And your microbiologist friend, she arrived there by her own path? And you have all experienced this personally multiple times? That is your story?"

"Yep."

"And look, here we are. Let us see what is under there."

"You are taking this pretty well."

"I have been, how you say, prepped. I was not myself believed for fifteen years. Until two weeks ago." She reached for the flask. "So. We'll see. I will see for myself, this siq'i rumi of yours. This enchanted stone."

"And if it works on you?"

"Then, *caballero*, we bring back the Inka Empire and you gringo dogs can smoke my farts!" She held out her fist. Bingham squinted at it, then bumped it with his own.

Katari and Noe

Morning. Katari explored the site in the new light, gobsmacked by the wonders around her, muttering, controlling the shaking of her hands to take notes. Then they went down for supplies and to confer with the various invitees — the Ministerio boys were eager to go back up with them, but were told to wait for the appointed hour.

The morning after that, Ephraim and Noe joined them on the return hike. Katari listened with respect as Noe briefed her on her research and conclusions. At the Killawatana stone she put her eye to the microscope, just shook her head.

"This is not usual?"

"Not at all."

"And this is world-wide?"

"I have only investigated here, but colleagues report other concentrations."

"And it is Pachamama?"

"To you, yes. You are seeing a phenomenological link to your version of the Earth Mother. To, I believe, the source of all human mystical experience."

"Mother of God. I thought this was no more than the greatest archaeological discovery of the century, after my own."

"You have a surprising grasp of my revelation."

"It was in an episode of *We Live In You*. Yes, I also follow him — one of his threads is the redirection of Peruvian history."

"As another is my macrobiota. So that's why you seemed familiar with my narrative."

"Yes, demented he could be but he seems to bring a lot of sane people together. And, have you noticed, his presentations are growing quieter, simpler, more dignified? I think it is no longer a game to him." They descended before dark. Katari moved her scant baggage into Noe's room.

Breaking the Seal

The next morning, as a helicopter leaned up off an open pasture near the ruin, blowing hats and hair, twenty-two people from seven institutions stood restlessly while Katari briefed them on the protocols of their introduction to Kunturpunku. Each of them was passed through the aura of the coated cairn, until they too could see the ruin. Four failed and depended, disconsolate, on the breathless description of others. They were led awestruck through the elegance of the Inka *marka*. At last they entered the edifice sheltering the grotto.

A plastic tarp was strung across the sealed entrance to the treasure room. The TV crew set up lights and cameras as Katari and two archaeologists from the Ministry and the National University carefully documented and removed *embarro* plaster from the fissure. Katari, then Bingham entered, sidewise, refixing the plastic tarp behind them to preserve the inner atmosphere. Noe would want samples.

She began detailing, in Spanish, her discoveries into a video camera linked to a web recorder monitored by those waiting without. "My light shows aryballos...metal artifacts...textiles...unidentifiable detritus fallen from a broken ceramic vessel. Khipus. That is a spillage of khipus. I see they have lined part of this cave with fine masonry." Bingham carefully filmed everything *in situ* before any item was touched.

The impatience without was palpable. The wait was over two hours. Then the removal began.

Gold objects were passed through to Ministry of Culture archaeologists at the opening. Beakers, dishes, breastplates, crowns, masks, mimicked plant life, idols. Each item was described aloud to electronic and human recorders while television crews blasted LCD light onto the glittering hoard. The various agents shifted on their feet, looking at each other with barely constrained suspicion. All firearms had been left behind by mutual agreement.

Later, lock boxes were lowered by army helicopter, filled with the finds, chained to one another and guarded by multiple agencies. A hybrid crew of the stronger invitees cleared a campground among the cacti in the main plaza, and as dark fell, a fire was built from the root-clump of a dead tree. Porters had carried camping gear from below and a soup was prepared and served.

"We stay up all night," Bingham said, 'kudos to Noe and Ephraim, for packing in these warm clothes and blankets."

"And you brought your signature," Noe Kroeber nodded, "rum."

Portable klieg lights were set up with a generator chugging away, illuminating the entrance to the treasure chamber, only partially emptied. Flagging ribbon was strung around the perimeter, three police departments, paid triple-time, and the military, were there to watch each other.

Ephraim, Noe, and others trailed back down before full dark. Katari and Bingham, wrapped in blankets, stayed huddled by the bonfire, passing rum around the circle when the chill got through. The sky was clear, the moon came up orange, the Southern Cross glittered, pointed out by the finger of Rigel Kent and Hadar.

By dawn, all the guards, a network camera crew, and six andeanists sat slumped in a circle around the smoking embers, feet to the heat. Bingham's bottle and four others were empty.

Bingham and Katari were quiet, thinking, cold outside, warm inside. The edge of the solar disk rose over the shoulder of Bandolista Mountain.

"Inti," a sergeant of the *Policia Nacional* called, scattering coca leaves to the breeze.

"Inti," came a ragged chorus of voices. A few meters away, bottled under a stone roof for five centuries leaked ancient air.

Back to School

"What can I say?" Ephraim waited for a colectivo van headed for Cusco, with the same daypack and wheeled carry-on he'd come with. "I just want life to be regular again. And Lily." Bingham and Noe nodded, hands in their pockets. "I didn't think it would turn into this."

"Funny thing is," Bingham said, "without you, it wouldn't have."

"You have done your part," Noe assured, "we have made contact. Soon Doctor Kuntur will find a way to speak to our Inka friends in their language and we will tell them everything they need to know."

"Unless she's stopped." Ephraim shuffled nervously. "Or Pachamama doesn't like Chanka girls."

"That's our problem," Bingham said. "You go back to school. We will brief Ramram, he will brief Pachacutiq, and that will be that." Katari came up behind, listening.

Ephraim replied with a kind of grin. "Roight."

A car pulled up to the curb. The driver eyed their little congregation, called "Cusco?" sounding like "KOOkoh?" Ephraim thumb-hooked his pack strap, smiled at all three, crossed to the ride. "*Diez*?" Ten sols?

"Diez," affirmed the driver about the fare. Ephraim got in with his baggage and that was it.

As the car pulled out, Katari Kuntur suddenly seemed to come awake. "*Waynalla kanki*," she called. "Stay young!"

As they walked away, Katari said, "Bingham. You are about to be edged out of our Kunturpunku project. So sorry, but the Ministry is going to take it over, and everybody else will have to re-apply for permissions."

“I told you that would happen. When? How long do I have?”

“November. You can come back in the fall — your spring — as an independent. I argued for you.”

“After a fashion and to a degree,” he retorted somewhat cynically.

“Damn you Bonnaterre, I don’t play.”

“Yeah. I know. Siento mucho. So I’ll go back up pretty soon too. Berkeley is offering me a full professorship. It is on you, Doctor Kuntur."

"And you, Doctor Kroeber?" Katari asked.

"I have been planning to return to Berkeley, you know."

"Yes."

"But now that the paper is out, I don't know. I came here in part because I was afraid to be in the US, where my own government will want to contain and control me. Now I know that they will. I am also afraid to be here. I might be easier to eliminate here than there. More, this is an epicenter. That rainbow cloud over the bridge is attracting attention. I don't know. I may just have to be afraid and do what I came to do."

"That is true courage," Bingham said, putting his arm over her shoulder.

"No. True courage is knowing what you are going to do."

"You are right," Katari said. "You cannot overcome fear by an act of will, not for long. And your government will want to shut you up and take you over. So stay here, bruja, until this is over. It won't be long. Be welcome in our land where there are corners without cameras."

"Actually, Ollanta has CCTV cameras all around the plaza," Bingham muttered. They ignored him.

The Trick to the Trick

Noe became more and more obsessed with the ultimate reality of what she had pulled the bandage off in her research. What, really and finally, was the holobiome?

With this question in mind she went alone to the Split Rock at night, stripped naked, and, shivering, swabbed herself with a probiotic nutrient gel she had composed in her ad hoc laboratory.

"This," she said to herself, "is what real witches must feel like."

She didn't expect much. Maybe Tuya, maybe Ramram. She might channel them for their experience with Pachamama. She went in straight, no green goo.

She got the holobiome raw and naked. It began with the Pachamama experience, that sense of earthy communion, that then expanded suddenly beyond anything she knew, tearing her away from herself and throwing her into a consciousness that had no borders and no definitions.

Then it took her beyond the Earth Mother, into the spaces between the things between the things, to where she could perceive, was pulled toward, a being that she later determined must have been Certainty. A hunger, a desperate need, to escape the loneliness of this place, this isolated family in its desert settlement, on its impoverished island, Earth.

Then with a velocity that filled her with helpless panic, with a terrible desire to escape back to her self, it took her into a crazy mob of beings, each with their own longings, certainties, commands. The Question, Certainty, Pachamama, Ilyapa, these were only tiny faces in an endless crowd.

Then she was above them all. She was with the holobiotic Nameless One. She was at the highest level, where life and death were the same, where being and nothing were the same, where agony and ecstasy were indistinguishable, where time and place were gone, where yearning was laughing and loneliness was love. Everything changed and was always the same. She herself was a question. The question was 'Why?' And the answer came. The answer was 'Why?'

Then there was no more question and no more her.

Then it was morning and she was dressed again but everything was on backwards. She hummed to herself to keep from letting her mind back in. It was a beautiful melody and she could not later bring it back.

She went back again and a third time. Each experience was different, yet the same. Each time the tune would return and each time disappear before she could remember to record it.

Katari worried about her. She looked into those eyes and there was something there that had not been there before. Noe Zoe looked back until Katari became uncomfortable and had to ask,

"What?"

"The trick," Noe replied, "to the trick is, that there is no trick." Then she laughed, and slapped Katari gently on the back.

"I know," she said. "Never mind. I won't go mystical on you. I am still a scientist."

It Is Done

Ramram slammed Katari in the back of her head — medulla oblongata or hypothalamus, whatever, she thought later — splattering hot tea on her pants. She was in Kunturpunku, leaning on the Killawatana, bundled in her parka, hands wrapped around a hot metal cup, when he took her to his place in Vilcaswaman.

She found herself at the foot of a tall twisted stone, propped in a cone of sand and cut rock, hunkered, arms around his knees, breathing evenly. It was full night and but for shadows in the few torchlit windows below there was no one else. It was warmer than where she was. He introduced himself, allowed her to get used to him, to what he felt like, where he was, and then he turned the vehicle over to her, saying, "Tell me."

She did. Speaking quietly and clearly she first outlined the danger they were in, framing it in the succession of Sapa Inkas...Pachacutiq, Tupaq Yupanqui, Wayna Qapak, the plague, the civil war. She described the abduction and assassination of Atauwallpa.

She told the story in a widening spiral, outward to the stars. She had been practicing, organizing her lessons for this moment.

She paused for questions. He had some. Thankful that the signal towers were so close, she showed him Google Maps on her smartphone. She got up to piss her tea away, the thread did not break.

She asked where they were. Vilcas. She knew the place well. It was still dark in her time, the Southern Cross long gone behind the hill, when dawn came. He held up a hand, and began to give her back in spare phrases the critical points of what she had told him. Then, in soft awe, he read back some of the outermost facts. That the world was round and floated in nothing. The size of the oceans. The wheel. Airships. Men on the moon. The Web.

As the Priests of Inti filed onto the levels of the temple of the Sun. Ramram stood, thanked her, and gently set her back in her own time.

"It is done." She smiled, weary and glad. "It is done."

The agreed upon code phrase was *ama imaypas*. Never. She emailed it to Bingham, Noe, Ephraim, and Lily. She had no other confidants.

Sinister People

"Have you noticed," Katari said to Noe and Bingham, "that we are all left-handed? Lily and Ephraim too."

"And Ramram," Bingham added. "He's leftoid."

"So is Tuya," Katari said, "I flipped her more than once."

"I have observed," Noe said, nodding and frowning, "that bacteria, void of external stimuli, veer to the left."

"Are you making that up?" asked Bingham.

"Yes," said Noe Zoe Kroeber.

CHAPTER THIRTY-THREE now

Something Did Something to Our Team

A report to NTT HQ by the CEO of Briarpatch SA:

“We have definite verification the site exists as described and that they are dealing with potentially toxic materials.”

“Did they retrieve samples?”

“Not as such. Some good material was acquired from epidermal, oral, anal, and pulmonary sampling.”

“Identifiable strains of bacteria?”

“We have yet to bring in a microbiologist, or maybe a xenobiologist, but yes, we got some live cultures.”

“Any indication of intelligent micro-organic systems? Of potential consciousness, volition?”

“Something did something to our team, but it didn't speak to them. ”

“Casualties?”

“On our side? One of our contract assets seems to be afflicted with an anomalous form of PTS. He is now rated combat ineffective and is on medical leave.”

“Symptoms?”

“He looks at you funny and smiles, mostly, I’m told.”

“What about their side?”

“No, no direct contact was made. Well, our guys brushed them off on the approach but no significant dialogue is recorded.”

“And the stone is still there.”

“They call it Split Rock, we surmise from intercepted electronic transmissions.”

“Gmail?”

“Yeah. Until they encrypted up with PGP. Listen, it was a clusterfuck, but it worked. The NTT knows it is in over their head, they kicked it up to IARPA, which has delegated elements of this to…”

“Yarpa?”

“Intelligence Advanced Research Projects Activity — they coordinate intelligence missions that are too weird for any one agency to deal with or that involve ah, it says, ‘*high risk, high-payoff research that delivers innovative technology for future overwhelming intelligence advantage.*’ They’ve clued in the CIA, FBI, NSA, and Homeland, of course, but also the National Geospatial Intelligence Agency, the Defense Clandestine Service, and, now that your contact has been alerted, the CDC.

"One outcome is that the President now has memos from multiple intelligence sources regarding a possible non-human intelligence with global presence that may have been, and be, influencing the past, present, and future of the human race, and of which the United States may be the only world power to know or have contacted. Also of a possible threat to our sovereignty over the continental west coast. That ought to poke a stick in the wasps’ nest.”

“Wait a minute. I’m stuck on ‘innovative technology’ for — what was it? Definitive advantage?”

“Future overwhelming intelligence advantage.”

“That’s what they have. Not us. Their team just ate our team alive. So the executive branch has been fed old We Live In You’s theories as fact, as well as being told that US citizens are aiding and abetting an extinct Bronze Age political entity in an amphibious invasion of US territory, pre-Plymouth Rock. Has Canada been advised that British Columbia is at risk?”

“I think someone texted Justin Bieber.”

“Right. So it’s out of our hands?”

“That, or the NTT will expand to head the freakiest task force since MK-Ultra. And get bags of money and power. And, oh, I hear that the NTT is holding Nick Nieman in a basement somewhere wringing him dry. There was talk of renditioning him to Uzbekistan.”

“Joke.”

“Not the part about him being in custody beyond Habeas corpus. Well, the other shoe has to drop soon. We’ll see if either or both of us will be invited to the party.”

Mmmbyeeeee

In Hayward, California, the CEO of Briarpatch SA called his Personal Assistant into his office.

"Have HR put together a severance package for Agent Orange. The minimum Legal will allow. He's been useless since Operation Voodoo."

"No."

"*No?*"

"He quit this morning. The letter is on your desk. I tried to tell you but you waved me off, remember? And I quit too. I'm done letting your maggot into my filet mignon. And I'm talking to my lawyer. She thinks we can get all Me Too on your lily white — uh — cafe au lait ass. My last check direct deposited at eight thirty this morning and your benefit package isn't worth pissing on so Mmmbyeeeee."

The President is Briefed
Washington, DC

“Sir, the NTT — it is now subordinate to the State Department — will oversee all other agencies involved in this project, as listed in your briefing packet.”

“Just tell me.”

“So far, the Intelligence Advanced Research Projects Activity, the Bureau of Intelligence and Research. It oversees the Office of the Geographer and Global Issues. The National Geospatial Intelligence Agency, the Center for Disease Control and Prevention, the Defense Clandestine Service — that’s an arm of the Defense Intelligence Agency. The Defense Advanced

Research Projects Agency. The CIA, FBI, and NSA have liaisons. Offshore, Peru's Ministerio de Cultura, and France's external intelligence agency, the General Directorate for External Security."

"France?"

"Their intelligence people have put together a theory that falls pretty close to our own view, through observation of biological anomalies within their territorial borders and of similar phenomena worldwide. We want them under our wing rather than reaching out to other governments."

"Other governments?"

"Well, there are outbreaks on every continent and all oceans. Other states are beginning to listen to their scientists. But only we have solid knowledge. So far."

"And our sources are?"

"It is all in there…"

"Just tell me."

"Well, the phenomenon — we are calling it the Entity — will not communicate with any of our resources. Nor can our biological technicians reliably and thoroughly replicate the results obtained by the Kroeber woman. So, with the exception of the vlogger Nicolas Nieman — who we will be recruiting within hours — all our sources are rogue."

"And what of the bozos we sent down there to steal their rock?"

"We brought them on board, Sir. To keep them close."

"Instead of killing them."

"Approximately. Sir."

"Christ in a body bag. The world is covered in a slime that is smarter than we are and wants to change the past so that Las Vegas disappears."

"Not Las Vegas, sir. That's on our side of the Sierras."

"So now we have an umbrella agency in control of this gibbering fuckaroo. I hope somebody knows what they are doing. What does 'NTT' stand for?"

"Nothing, sir. It is just a name."

"Then tell Just a Name that I think this whole thing is a crock of horseshit."

A Call to Legs

Elmer answers, "D.B.."

Daniel says, "E.T.."

On video, they each look to the other as if they were in shock. "From your face I guess you got the call to arms?"

E.T.: "More like call to legs, Dan. I want to google places with no extradition treaty, but I know they'd know. I'm mobilized to Berkeley to infiltrate the goddamn eco underground. I checked my contract. I gotta go."

D.B.: "Why you? You are an old middle-class white guy?"

E.T.: "Pal, my folks were radicals in the 60's. People's Park, Chicago, exorcising the Pentagon. I was born off the grid in Humboldt County, didn't have a birth certificate until I was twelve. My mom screwed Abbie Hoffman. My dad said Jerry Rubin was a bourgeois phony. At seventeen I had hair down to my ass. At eighteen I got a buzz cut and had my name legally changed from Zarathustra Free Man to Elmer, and went for a degree in Business Administration. But I'm still named on old hippy commune nostalgia websites as a wild boy, and the NTT wants me to grow a beard and play eco-terrorist. But the first thing we all learned as kids is how to sniff out a nark. So good luck to me."

D.B.:"Yeah. Me too. I'm bound for South America. I mean, after Nieman went AWOL into that Bermuda Triangle place in Washington, they assigned me to tracking volcano chasers. Then this."

E.T.: "Volcano chasers?"

D.B.: "Like storm hunters without the tornadoes. They rappel into hot calderas at the last minute and live-feed it to the web. We try to stop any US nationals doing that."

E.T.: "So Nieman — I thought he was our boy?"

D.B.:"So did they. So they pushed him. He said he was tuckered out and wanted a three-day weekend in the woods, signs off online, and just whoof, disappears. So after a couple weeks on volcano detail I get a visit, they tell me the real threat now is the Kroeber woman. Her paper got intense response in her field, and that went underground just as fast. The NSA didn't even pick up on keywords because they were babbling in biotech on obscure proprietary academic websites. Then the Saudi *Mabahith* disappeared three top microbiologists off the street in Riyadh, some international conference, and now everybody's gone black. We know they're communicating but nobody knows how yet. She told everybody that she is back in California, but she's not. She's still in Peru. She got tight with a local female archaeologist down there and we think they're weaponizing. You know her from WLIU." He pronounced it will you. "So I go down to play spy."

E.T.: "You mean after my team tripped over their dicks? Sorry D.B.. That it blew back on you. You warned me. Same up in Cali. It looked for a while like the kids and the prof got scared and decided to stand down. The NTT sent some agents to put the fear of god into them but that Eye Kay thing boomeranged it on them and now there is some kind of eco warrior movement going on in Berzerkeley.

"The biological anomalies in Ollantaytambo — and other places — have popped up in the East Bay hills. Even stronger. We are countering it with our own biowar stuff, all top secret — I hear we call it the 'bug war' — and, jesus, D.B., is this really happening? They are making you a field agent in the Peruvian Andes and me a nark in Berkeley?"

D.B.: "Looks like fact."

E.T.: "Yeah. I wonder if my retirement is on hold. Although the grandkids apparently think it's 'badasstic.' It seems there is a 'Peacock cloud' there now with magical properties."

D.B.: "Yeah. There is one in where I'm going too. Part of my assignment is to check everyone who is too interested in it."

E.T.: "This is political, Dan. The general just wants to look active. The real money is going to military assets. So how do you feel about going down there?"

D.B.: "I think it is an excellent mission, E.T.. I am happy to risk my life and the lives of my colleagues — especially yours, Zoroaster Freak or whoever — to accomplish it. I am certain that our leaders are brave, competent, and inspired, and that our tax money is well spent. I only wish that my sentiments could somehow be known to those we serve."

E.T.: "Right. Of course. Stay well. May all your medals be prehumous."

Eye Kay

It showed up in Ollanta first, to Operation Voodoo. It turned the doers intent back onto the doer. The action was blurry at first, unclear, hard to define. It took on clarity, and force in the San Francisco East Bay. An off-duty Berkeley peace officer, drunk, tried to club a young non-student ecological activist who was walking down from an illegal camp site in the Berkeley hills. The cop slammed himself repeatedly in the head with his service baton and was hospitalized, still believing that he had beaten the kid up. The phenomenon began to manifest throughout the eastern sections of town, including the U.C. campus, until its presence was undeniable. It operated on many levels, both blatant and subtle. A snide remark would leave the one who spoke it feeling humiliated while the target looked on puzzled, unfazed. A man determined to drown his wife drowned himself.

Before long it took on a name, Instant Karma, swiftly shortened to Eye Kay.

It was associated with the Peacock Cloud phenomenon in the Oakland/Berkeley hills, which in turn was claimed by some of the followers of Will You as a manifestation of the Presence.

CHAPTER THIRTY-FOUR now

There is a War in Heaven

It is night in Port Angeles, Washington. Nick Nieman reviews the draft of his next post. He records.

"There is a war in heaven, between what happened and what didn't. I hear you whisper, "I'll take the other one, please. I'll take the one where I stayed in school, instead of bumming around the globe; or the opposite. The one where I said *yes oh yes* to the quiet guy instead of the bad boy on the motorbike. Or the other way 'round. I'll take the one in which the honest politician got the nomination. But that's not how it works, dreamers. Your lost world is not what is at stake. In the world of men, it is power and territory.

"I have been there, to the war, carried by what your government now calls The Entity. Because now Uncle Sugar believes me. Do you?

"Now, where they once just watched me and smirked, they are sitting straight up in bed, eyes wide. My once pathetic fantasy has suddenly taken on scaly and taloned flesh. It is not a joke, not even a nightmare. It lives in you and everywhere else on earth. Now they know.

"Strange things are happening around the globe, Eye Kay not the least, and they can all be tracked back to microbiology. Lense-like clouds drop almost to earth, swimming with color. Wild animals come out with hypnotic eyes. Calm falls over battlefields, uninvited. I told them so.

"I told you so. But really, I always assumed I was wrong. This is true of most conspiracy theorists and iconoclasts. They expect to finally close their eyes in some assisted living facility, in the same old workaday world they have always railed against as delusion. The Men In Black finally at their bedside, but they are only from the funeral home."

Nick leans back in his swivel chair, eyes hooded, a sleepy smile on his pursed lips. The cat is draped blissfully over his shoulder. He is looking smugly content tonight, instead of his usual gaunt and hag-ridden self, because now The They have finally stepped into the light.

"But they are real. Yes, and they have come for me. So far only in sheeples clothing. Men in Zegna pinstripes have contacted me, bought me lunch overlooking the Juan de Fuca strait. Now they take me seriously enough to direct deposit substantial funds to my little bank account, to up my bandwidth.

"They represent taxpayer supported agencies with long strings of initials, they carry deeply embossed badges in soft leather wallets, plastic cards with embedded chips.

"They are very interested in conversations with my Quechua monoglot back there in pre-Colonial Peru, up with whom I team to preserve the Reality that has earned its reality by being real. They want to know what I know about their Entity, my Oneness.

"In exchange, they make a few suggestions, just if I feel comfortable with them, you understand. This talk of this...call it what you will...might it fall by the wayside a little? Could I turn the volume down a bit? All voluntary, of course, just a hint of menace in their tight little smiles. But mainly, they want to know what I know, and how. And I tell them.

"But first I tell you. I couldn't have done it without you. I need to believe someone needs to believe me. Someone with soul.

"Because there is a war in heaven and it is being fought in the Sacred Valley of Peru, in the fourteen hundreds, and the twenty-ones, between gods of the Inkas, as two spacetimes go head-to-head to decide whether what happens next in their time is what has already happened in ours. Or not.

"It is heating up in the north, too, in the Golden State. Men with guns and boots debark from armed aircraft in the dark. Kids in sweaty t-shirts exchange glances in the hills. Something is messing with natural law. Eye Kay, Instant Karma, bacteria come from above, not by the hand of man. Cannibal microbes are frankensteined in laboratories below and released into the wild. The They hate that Eye Kay.

“Viewers, soon curious and seemingly unassociated news items are going to be connected for you in language carefully constructed to make it all seem tediously scientific. Not your problem. Superluminary entanglements and cats in boxes, a microbiological collective, please let us dumb it down for you, and if you object to being patronized, we’ll shoot you an equation or two to shut you Art History majors the fuck up.

"They will not exactly tell you that closed-door senatorial committees are shaking hands across the aisle to assure that you are in a world that knows if not where it is going at least where it has been.

“So, speaking from the front lines, let us pray that we do not wake up in Jubilee to find that the golden throne is occupied by a bronze-faced, hawk-nosed, Son of the Sun.

“So stub out that Spirit cigarette, empty that square-bottom glass in the sink, the seven dollar sauv blanc has gone stale. Tell yourself, ‘The next post better be better, if he wants my 'Like.’ Shrug into your ex-BF’s t-shirt, and curl up with your corgi under your duvet. Nothing can take this night away from you, not even never having existed. Sweet dreamlessness all.”

He sighs, rubs his temples; the cat, indignant, runs down his body to the floor. “Crap,” he says out loud. “What sophomoric drivel. Grow up.” He turns on his webcam, begins again:

“The Government came for me. They believe us now. They are in the war. I am a recruit. Or a conscript. Or a collaborator.”

Kwee, sphinx-like below the flat screen computer, lifts her head, tail switching, stares fierce-eyed down the hallway.

He goes on. The product is simpler and shorter. That is good.

Now it is the hour of the wolf. He makes last edits, and then he posts. There is a machine gun of knocks on the door to his studio. Who has gotten past his front door, with all the locks?

The one-green-eyed cat, almost big now, hisses.

He opens. There are men with badges in wallets of soft leather, and shoulder holsters.

CHAPTER THIRTY-FIVE then

Antarqui and the Snake Condor Woman

"I told you that my friends in the Dark Future were trying to warn me, but could not get across." Ramram watched the rough twisted obelisk he found on the march into Vilcaswaman being wrestled across the plaza by five hundred men. Amaru and Tupaq watched him attentively.

"There is a new one now, a woman who studies things past, including us. I stayed up with this wanka last night and she came to me. She speaks Runasimi and has told me in plain language that we are to be destroyed, and how, and when. And that we must stop them, and how. And for that your father's will and power is essential. The whole Tawantinsuyu will be needed."

From stone windows, Ramram, Tuya, the princes Amaru and Tupaq Inka, watched the shaft being ported through all the construction around the new-laid plaza of the bureaucratic and religious center being built to control the heart of old Chanka country.

The twisted monolithic siq'i, its coat of life-forms scrupulously preserved, was hauled toward the waiting shaft sunk into the center of the civic expanse. Amaru had ordered it installed where it would catch the sun rising and setting, as well as the eye of man and god. This was no inert monument, it was a living thing.

Amaru hefted the heavy gold bowl between his palms, muscles contracting like anacondas. "Ramram," he said, a touch of impishness in his eyes, "do I understand that you want your wanka set up someplace else?"

"I was thinking that hill." He pointed through the window.

"I see. To tie the earth to the sky. Let us first share its Kamay with the people, at least until we can find another waka on which to center all this pomp and magnificence. And moreover, my bowl of *qucha yuyu* — until now it answered only to a khipu, and to me — is attracted to your wanka and piles up on the lip of the bowl, pulled in the direction of that monolith. I walked a full circle around it before dawn this morning, and it followed. We are about to learn something significant."

"If we do, will you tell your father?"

"He won't credit anything coming from you. Not even through me. He doesn't take me seriously either. He thinks my head is in the sky."

"Well, it is. And that is good. From the sky you can see much more than you can from the Tiyana on which your father squats."

"There is one direction from which we can approach him. We need hard proof. We need a Silver *Suq'a* alive, with his strange possessions, to prove our point." Amaru held a string of algae up to the light.

"I have no idea how to do that. They are only visions so far, and not even my own."

"Until then, keep telling Tupaq your stories. He thinks you are a messenger of the Apus. And very funny. Have I ever heard you make a joke?"

"Fart."

"I see."

"Amaru. The Pacha is much larger than we know. And it is a round rock."

Prince Tupaq was fidgeting, eyes alight as always with curiosity and too much energy, lifting Ramram's heavy bronze-headed macana over his head, ignoring the trembling of his elbows, forcing it beyond his strength, until, with a whoop and a grin, his arms straightened and he prevailed over mere gravity.

Amaru gave a quiet smile as the goldsmiths carried his new, larger, deeper, bowl, into his tapestried, gold-corniced chamber, the basin's depth already lined with red algae. Phytologists followed with containers of living specimens selected and cultivated to Amaru's specifications.

Ramram looked behind now, toward Tuya, conferring with the wives and daughters of the governors and generals — she had been accepted through some mysterious process of selection as one of their own — watching the train of pregnant women and new mothers being guided to their new-built homes in the residential district below the square. The high-born ladies in their scented finery were sneaking glances, not always so veiled, at Amaru.

And Ramram saw that his wife was among them, and that she was fully smitten, beyond infatuation — Tuya had never been trivial in any aspect — and he knew that he would have to answer to that.

Green Flash

The sun set with a green flash. Ramram settled himself cross-legged in the thrumming magnetism of the monolith, resisting until he was ready. When he submitted, it took him from within and seemed to throw him into the sky. Then the seeming became reality. He was flying, faster than an eagle, into the last thread of sun. He had no control and rushed headlong with more velocity than falling. He soared across the dark mountains, into the night, away from the moonrise, over lifeless desert, then the desert quit and he saw an infinite wrinkled silvery blue flatness glistening with moonlight. It was a thing he did not understand until the wanka lowered him swooping to its surface, where he was splashed with wetness and tasted salt. He was over a vast moving qocha, a great lake, and he recalled the prophecy Amaru had given him of Mamaqocha, the Mother Lake, that no Inka he knew had ever seen. He was lifted again and sped on. He knew that the air was very cold but he felt only warmth. He breathed a keen salty wind. He flew all night. The stars wheeled. The moon set before him. He flew away from the rising sun, which struck white-gold sparks from the moving water below. Then, when the sun had passed overhead and dropped into the west, he smelled rank life, vegetable rot, and clouds of brown and white birds with hooked beaks surrounded him, eyeing him in outrage.

He was moving more slowly now, seeking. Then another sunrise.

He flew into hot wind full of scents. Below he soared over the circular tops of many deep green trees, and he descended, and saw dark people, men and women, on the white sand beach, in bright colored skirts and hats. On the beach and in the surf were long floating things, like floors, carved out of logs, some with great cloths on poles. He saw them fill with wind, pushing the floors through the water.

"What a fantastic idea," he whispered to himself. He flew low but no one saw him. He rose, went on over high green hills, some of them smoking. Then, the land speeding by almost to a blur, he came to Mamaqocha again. Here there were more of the floating floors with wind-catchers, carrying people. Some threw nets over the sides. He knew nets from fishermen on the Urubamba River.

'What am I doing here,' he asked himself, 'why is Pachamama taking me here? Who does this help?' But in his stomach there was deep warmth. For the first time he realized that he has a body, but he had no body. He could not see himself flying but the birds sensed him. He began to consider trying to return to himself and the land he knew, as the corrugated water sped under him. Then he saw land again, and began to slow and to descend. He saw the vast lake making great billows, then breaking into whiteness and sliding up onto the tawny edges of the deep green forested land. Then, speeding parallel along the white sands, he came to a curve, an arched indentation where the water was still, and smoke rose from wasi's of thatch, and there were people on the sand, and floating things as big as a kancha, with great square cloth wind-catchers, that carried people — and, against the edge of land and water, another of floating things, wrecked, ribs showing through its wooden hide, the cloth-carrying sticks stripped of fabric. On the bank of the land, he saw beige men in different clothes, away from each other, and he sensed suspicion, difference. Some were brown here. There, further, some were black as charcoal.

And there, meeting a delegation of the black ones, carrying bags of something, were the silver demons. Now he saw them clearly, not through another's eyes, saw the fatty hairy faces as he dropped silently and softly to earth. Saw the puffy blue and red cloths at their shoulders, saw the ridged silver helmets on their heads, saw long black things on their feet and legs, saw, held by ropes, great brown and black llamas, kicking the sand with uncloven round toes. Saw too much to understand or remember. His invisible body breathed deep. He concentrated. They were trading. Silver things and colored beads and metal pots, for food. Their clothes were faded, and becoming ragged. The light-skinned hairy men further back by their huts were mostly naked but for fabrics covering their legs and hips. Black hair shows on their chests, their pocked faces, arms. And, amazing, orange hair and yellow hair, yellow as flowers. There were no women. Among the blacks were women, wide-hipped, heavy breasted, round-haired. Among the browns, farther down, women, long black hair like his own people but with small noses.

And from the hairy ones came a smoky, oily, peppery, fecal sense, a melange of diseased alienations from the earth and its unity.

From the black ones, suppressed threat, barely contained, a desire to take by force, a fierce, joyous, dancing love of their own strength. And a suspicion against the hairy ones.

From the browns, a gentleness, a sweet love of the water, of the trees, of eating, of each other; and fear and distrust of the others.

The Inka, thought Ramram, would use these distrusts. He would absorb the browns and blacks into himself. But the hairy silvers? They are to be taken for what they know and otherwise thrown away.

Everything he had learned from Eff-Ram, Li Li, Katari the Poisonous Snake Woman — who would name a daughter that? — in Pachamamatambo and Vilcaswaman was true and more than true.

Those pale ones were his friends, but their people were not.

These ones, these silver hairies, that he had seen walking on his good land as masters, they were danger. Danger danger

danger. They could cross this vast Qocha in their great wind-pushed floating forts.

Just before he pulled away, satisfied that he had seen what he came for, he saw something else. Prisoners. Under guard by the silver asnaqs, in cages of bamboo. Small, pale golden men, naked, thin, wretched. Some sitting cross-legged, with their heels on their thighs and hands cupped in their laps. And from them, hunger, misery, anger, despair, shame, terrible desire for their own land, and an inconceivable intelligence, knowledges of wonderful things, of beauties that Ramram could not name. And then he felt himself pull away, shooting high into the air, and the long journey home began. Through day, through night, into morning and again.

Shadows in the Torchlight

His eyes came back to him, still open, dry. He found himself sitting cross legged in the shadow of the wanka, and around him, standing, watching, carefully distanced, were Amaru, Otoronqo Kuy, Chaski Yuyu, his love Tuya, Tupaq just now standing, rubbing his eyes. Amaru stepped forward, fluid and tireless, eyes deep, looking into his, seeing, lids dropping in satisfaction.

Tuya's eyes left Ramram, full of relief, and rested as if against her will on Amaru, yearning. With effort, she pulled away and looked to Ramram. In a world of eyes only theirs existed. Tuya's met his without pleading or demanding, but open to him as ever, hiding nothing.

That night, after a long day of recounting, remembering, interpreting, guessing, discussing, he and Tuya retired to the wasi assigned to them in Pachacutiq's compound.

She cooked for him, not allowing Amaru's servants that privilege, and sat with him, back-to-back, Inka style, in the courtyard. They went inside to hold each other, silent, on their blankets. To Ramram, it was as if for the last time.

Then, without excuse, he got up and went out, wondering if Tuya knew where he was going.

A few minutes later he watched Amaru cross the courtyard and enter his and Tuya's quarters. Amaru did not argue or demure to Ramram's request. Ramram sat on a terrace gazing on the wanka below, now quiet and restful, the peace of Pachamama sifting down upon him. Across the square he saw, now and then, shadows move in the torchlight of his wasi. Then the window and doorway went dark. The moon moved a forearm's length across the sky, then a tall figure slid past the wicker door and returned to Pachacutiq's great domicile.

When a Woman Has Been

She was waiting in the dark, on the blankets, hands in her lap. Ramram untied his cloak, folded it onto the shelf of a wide-bottomed niche.

"They say," he said at last, "that when a woman has been with Amaru, she never again needs a man under her blanket."

"It is true," she replied, "I will never need *salinakuy* again. But I will always need you." And she held her hand to him and when they woke in the morning sunlight, he ran the tongue of his mind over the most moving salinakuy of his life gone and to come.

CHAPTER THIRTY-SIX now

All the Flies On One Windowpane

In Port Angeles, Washington, Nick Nieman worked under the eye of the NTT, the controlling agents of the Defense Clandestine Service, the INR, the IARPA, and agencies none of the other agents could identify — were they even ours? — because it had been decided that to change his location might disconcert his contacts in the fifteenth century. They paid him, fed him, walked him when he became restive, controlled and monitored his communications. His vlog was now geared to bringing any new independent players into the open.

Despite a strong temptation to revise history according to their own agendas, word had come down from 'the highest level' to concentrate on keeping this historical outcome intact. As We Live In You once vlogged, "The future is a done deal, already happened, can't be changed, so let's keep it that way."

Nick did not lead them into the Twist. He took them to a rock pile in the National Park, sat on a boulder for a while, reported that he was unable to make contact. Strangely, Qachu did find him there once, dimly, peered out of his eyes at his handlers, and went away.

Other eyes were on Ephraim, Bingham, Lily, watching for their next move, pushing their counter-options up and down the priority list according to shifting circumstances.

"Bonnaterre's back in Oakland," it was reported, "That is all of them on effectively one windowpane. We should choose our flyswatter."

Just to kill would be so easy. But they would be killing the only ones who knew what it was that they were killing.

The Interested People

The NTT were concerned when the surveillance MP3s of Ephraim and Lily together turned up none of the keywords on their list. The kids weren't talking about their adventures in South America. They sent people around to test the waters, accosting them after school, on the train, at lunch break from the Happy Heart Acupuncture clinic. Lily called them the interested people. They were assigned to encourage disengagement from further Peruvianistics.

The General wanted to send someone to kill them. The staff pushed back. One whistleblower could put them all in prison. And these were kids. So saboteurs and provocateurs were sent.

"Ms. Tran. You have been recorded as using false identification with federally funded institutions. That can be prosecuted as a felony."

"Do you ever intend to apply for government work, Lily? University? Corporations with federal or state contracts? Any job at all?"

"Do you hope to get into a good university, Mr. Arrowsmith? Any university? I see here you have applied to U.C. Berkeley, Anthropology. Any news from them so far?"

"You seem to be in excellent health, Mr. Arrowsmith. You are a fortunate young man."

"I like you, Eph, you're a smart boy. Let me be frank. Things can change overnight. Hell, in a couple of seconds. And never be the same again. What do you think luck is actually made of?"

"Professor Bonnaterre — no? Not yet a full professor? Some sort of delay? Well, we have it on good authority you will have your professorship soon. I see your new book is coming out this winter, in time for Christmas. Eighty bucks a pop, and more than half of them pre-sold! That Amazon Dot Com, pretty useful to a man like you. Got a new girlfriend, word is? Or, rather, three? Just lining up for you, pretty little undergrads. Life's good, isn't it? For now."

"Pretty squirrelly stuff your friend Kroeber wrote in that paper, wasn't it? Do you really believe in it? But you're out of that now, aren't you, what with your King Tut's Tomb type deal? You know, you were making some important people pretty nervous for a while. Glad that's over, aren't we?

Seed of the Sun God

When Lily Tran huffed back to the US, she traveled with ten bleached paper seed packets labeled '*semillas Intis: quinoa y mezclas*.' In English, 'sun seeds, quinoa and mixed.' They were products of Pachamama-crop strains. She planted one envelope — in her palm lay a wild mix of germs, kernels and sprouts — in her backyard garden in Pleasant Hill. She was delighted by the speed at which the plants — which included choclo maize, peppers, melon, squash, potatoes, dominated by quinoa — took off. She brought the rest to a couple in the tiny beshadowed community of Canyon, parents of a school friend, who had a hole-in-the-wall organic gardening shop. Not long after, the friend tugged her sleeve at her locker and said, all fry-speak, "Where did you get those seeds again? They grow amazing!" The father bought a ticket to Peru.

Two weeks later they were being marketed by a mail-order raw foods outlet in Emeryville as Sun God Super Seed Mix. By spring an eco-guerrilla group had broadcast them throughout industrial corn fields in Iowa and Nebraska with remarkable results: they took over acres of the vast oceans of inedible ethanol-producing corn plants, choking the grown stalk, stifling the seedlings, and replacing them with mixed varieties of fast-growing quinoa, sweet corn, potato, amaranth, squash, yucca, fava bean, and melon. They shared the same soil, each plant synergizing with the others to create a symbiosis frightening to the high-fructose corn concerns. The corporate growers complained. The USDA dispatched agents to investigate, eventually acquiring a third-generation packet of the Sun God product, and finding it crawling with unidentified strains of bacteria. Meanwhile, more plains were purpled by the tall, vividly colored quinoa seed panicles. Soon a new species of agri-tourist appeared, parking along the farm roads to photograph and sample and to purloin the seeds. Then the media caught on, and video clips from helicopters taking low rolling long-shots above the profusion of subverted monocrops memed the web.

Lily blushed, and prayed they would not track the phenomenon back to her.

In Runasimi there is no way to say goodbye forever

Ephraim got out of the cab of a produce truck in the square of the old Inka stronghold of Vilcaswaman, Sacred Hawk. He gave the driver ten Sols, found the cheapest of hostels, and checked out the ruins.

He'd had no plans to come here. He'd seen the blue and white sign, Vilcaswaman, on the road toward Lima and called "Baja!" to the driver. Getting off!

Terribly restored, the top of the usnu pyramid was filled with concrete, but still he could see the grandeur of the site, breathing through the centuries: in the gravity of the building blocks, in the towering gateway, in the sun temple now sat upon by a church that sucked up the power still coiling in the muscle and bone of old stone.

A strong urge to get out of town came over him. There was something wrong in the air. The people here didn't like him. Why had he come? He had no reason to be here. He had no idea where Ramram was, except gone. He resigned himself to one of those long nights in a desolate place. He climbed to his second-floor room, looked out the small no-glass window. Something out there pulled on him. There was a hill.

'All right,' he thought, 'let's take a walk.'

The round top was half a hundred meters off the road coming in. As he neared the crest, an old woman, bent, leaning on a crooked stick, firewood on her back, peered beady-eyed from beneath her worn black fedora, and, shaking a finger, called, "*No entra! Fantasmas! Espiritus malos! Peligroso*!"

Don't go in, ghosts, evil spirits, danger.

"Hola," he said, waving a hand like a dumb tourist, continuing on up. 'Geez, I'm in a Blair Witch remake,' he thought. But, so, there was something there. Or so the lady seemed to think.

The barren crest was circled by a fence of dead cactus, and fallen there was a long, twisted stone, mostly buried at the big end. That was the dynamo from which this humming signal came, the familiar vibrations in his gut and forehead. Strong. He stepped high over a gap in the cacti, walked slowly around the Ozymandian spike, feeling its bioelectric current, then knelt on it, palms laid on the lichened shaft.

"*No toca!"* called the woman, now silhouetted by the rising moon, shaking a clawed hand.

Ramram appeared. The stone stood tall now, dark against a clouded horizon. They, together, were wrapped in an old cloak that ruffled in the wind. The fabric was worn but intricately colored. The world seemed strangely flat. Ephraim realized that he was missing stereoscopic vision; Ramram was one-eyed. The hands were older, calloused, and one was shy two fingers. But it was him, Ephraim knew the feel of the self as he knew his own. This self was picking cactus spines out of his forearm.

In Runasimi, Ramram spoke slowly, simply. "I spoke with Katari Kuntur. She taught me."

"Good." Ephraim replied in the pidgin Runasimi he had worked up with Katari, whose name and the verb "to teach" was all he had gleaned from Ramram's statement, "I go now. I go far place/time to. See you later." There seemed to be no way to say 'goodbye forever' in Runasimi.

"I understand," said Ramram in Runasimi. "A happy life to you, peaceful but stimulating."

Ephraim said Thank you for everything, at least he hoped he had. He had probably massacred the phrase but with luck it got through. Ramram had been his teacher, his guide, his friend. His entry to a breathtaking world.

"*Imamanta*," said Ramram — for what? Ephraim knew that one. For maybe the last time he looked at the world through Ramram. The last chance to see an Inka reality. Venus, *Chaska Quyllor*, was already out in the west. She was not a rock in space here, she was a powerful spirit. They stood until she set. Neither wanted Ramram to flip to Ephraim's century.

Ramram let him go. Ephraim was alone now on the old hill. He braced for intense sadness, but it didn't come. It turned out he already knew all that. He was prepared. He was just happy to have found Ramram at all.

'Maybe I'll just forget all this back home. I mean, it was hard work. Or maybe I'll go up to Washington and check in on old Nick. Wouldn't that be a kick? Does he know who I am? What we did? But I really don't like war. I'm not that kind of kid.'

He turned away toward a thin mattress and a cold toilet down the hall. His cell chimed. It was a terse message from Katari to them all, relating her contact with Ramram.

"We did it," he said aloud. And the tics and twitches that had been coming back by the hour lifted away. "I think maybe we really did it. If that old curmudgeon Pachacutiq will just play along."

There ahead in the street, the bundle of kindling on her back, was the witchy old woman, shaking a finger at him and laughing. "*Te lo dije, chico turista,*" she said. I told you so, tourist boy.

Let's talk about *Inkas*

When Ephraim called Lily on his first morning back, not knowing what to expect, she hung up on his opening line. His heart power-diving in flames Ephraim sat stock still on the edge of his bed, fingers entwined. At last he emitted a deep sigh.

There was a scraping behind him; Lily came through his basement window, as of old, and threw herself up into his arms, bare legs hooked over his inner elbows.

“Jesus I’m glad to see you,” she said, nipping his arm. You may be clueless, but you are never BORING!”

Later she whispered, “I’m sorry. I was scared.” Her voice slurred a little.

"I know. Me too, Lily." He looked at her curiously. "Are you drunk?"

"No, it's just that throat thing hanging on. It's doing something to my voice.

"You had it checked out?

"Of course. It's a little different than I thought. Boring. Later for that. Can you think of anything to do that isn't boring?

"You bet. Let's talk about Inkas!"

Brace Yourself

The Interested People kept coming around. One man/woman tag team intercepted Ephraim and Lily walking home from school, showed them some screen shots of them together, taken through Ephraim's basement bedroom window.

Lily: "Big mistake, babies." Ephraim and she hugged their knees on a Berkeley hill, considering their situation, inspecting cumulus clouds. There seemed to be something in the air these days. In fact, a pointillistic shimmering over the canyon below.

"What do you think, Lil', "is this the worst they can do? I mean, potentially, it is bad enough, if they carry out their threats. I'll maybe have to work harder, but I'll be okay. My life is good enough."

"Me too. Though my situation is a little different."

“Yeah, you are a beautiful woman with a genius IQ. I’d hate to be in your shoes.”

“Eph, I don’t have strep throat. Brace yourself.”

“You just wanted an excuse not to kiss me?”

“I have ALS.” There was a long silence. Ephraim looked out across the valley. A wind picked up.

“You mean that thing where you end up communicating with your eyelids then your lungs collapse? The incurable one?”

“Amyotrophic Lateral Sclerosis.”

“How long do you have?”

“Not long.”

There was another silence. Lily looked at her lap, sidelong at Ephraim, then at her lap again. “I was going to say that time on the mountain. I wussed out.”

“I can see why you didn’t tell me," he said. "I don't think I can handle this. God, what a crime. You going to Oregon?”

“Mom’s got contacts. There will be hospice. We will have an Aloha party. You will come. You will hold my hand.”

“Fuck on a stick.”

“Ephraim! Language!”

"What do you want to do with what time you have left? I'll do anything you say. Anything."

"You already do, my sweet man. I guess it is no surprise that I don't feel like doing much." She elbowed him in the abdomen. "I have disentangled from all my other silly boys. As gently as I could. You I'm keeping."

"This is the first time you ever called me a 'man.'"

"Slip of the tongue. Speaking of tongues, do you want to go over behind those trees and talk about *Inkas*?

By October, Ephraim seemed to get more emptied out every day. He was tired, listless, his schoolwork suffered. The same seemed true of Lily, and when she and Ephraim got together, they would sit side-by-side doing and saying nothing.

"Is this one of those 'comfortable silences?' he asked.

"What could be more comfortable than total apathy?" she replied. Her symptoms had flattened out, but there was no cure, there would be no relapse.They were giving her a maximum of eighteen months, and she was doing nothing with that time. Her death sentence was mentioned only when there was a significant change.

Then Ephraim got sick. The symptoms were easy enough, debilitating fatigue, loss of appetite, and, when he closed his eyes, nagging hallucinations recalling the hard ascents he had made in Peru, always unfinished, needing more. There was always some problem to solve, and when he woke or came to himself from the half-dream it would take a minute or two to realize that there were no such moves to make in the real world. Prescribed antibiotics made the symptoms worse.

Lily came down with a similar indisposition, diagnosed as unrelated to her ALS.

On the ninth day of the affliction, he dragged himself into his backyard, where his father had built a Japanese rock garden, working from a book and notes from Kyoto. He closed his eyes and took in the sun, lying back in the aluminum and plastic jelly lounger. After a few breaths, a new energy came into him, as if he had inhaled pure oxygen.

His eyes opened, he sat up, looked around the garden. Wedged between a mossy rock at the end of the small pond and a twisted bonsai cedar, was the chunk of lichened stone he had smuggled home from Ollantaytambo. He went there, lay with his cheek against the green-furred rock, and his lethargy left him.

After a few minutes of testing effects, he concluded that the prokaryote colony he'd transported here in his luggage was alive and active and had spread to the mosses on the surrounding stones, and to the decorative algae in the pond. He called Lily.

"Lil'. Come on over. I have the cure to our slough of despond." Later, after a long slow erotic encounter, they video-called Bingham. He looked moribund, face haggard.

"Did you bring any Split Rock back?" He had not. "Can you afford a cab, now that you're born to sweet delight?" He could, but wondered, what is this about? "We've got the cure for what ails you."

Later, over pizza, they broached the elephantine topic. "So we just let it go now?" asked Lily, "As if it never mattered? The whole Inka thing?"

"Maybe it does, maybe it doesn't," said Bingham, "but look. We did our job. We — well, Ephraim — well, Katari — clearly communicated every significant fact necessary to gear up for Pizarro's appearance in fifteen twenty-eight. That was our assignment and it is completed. It's in their court now."

"Did you get a visit from the interested people?" Ephraim had picked up on Lily's sobriquet.

"Several."

"And…?"

"Fuck it, Eph, they can screw us up beyond redemption just on their retainers. One of them put a laser dot on my chest and told me it was a sniper. It wasn't, but it sure as shit could have been. Life is good for the first time since I got my Ph.D. and I like it this way."

"Yeah. I know what you mean. Lil'?"

"My life has been sinking into the ooze since the diagnosis. I'm wasting my last days. No energy, no interests, no inspiration. Do you know what the Zen monk said to the hotdog vendor?"

"Shoot," said Bingham.

"'Make me one with everything.' Boys, I miss the Presence. I miss Pachamama. I miss the feeling of being one with everything. And I do. Not. Appreciate. Being…"

"Messed with by Deep Government?"

"Limited. In my choices. And those vipers threaten us. And...you guys know Sisyphus?"

"Guy pushes rock uphill, it rolls down, he pushes it back up, repeat loop," Bingham offered. "Sentenced to that by the celebs on Olympus for being an all-around dick."

"So let's say," Lily takes over, "he gets the rock to the top of the hill, gets one instant of relief and triumph, then, bang, repeat loop as you say. But," she holds up a finger, "what if one of the gods, say Loki, gives him a reprieve. As long as he stays on top of the hill, he's okay. Sanctuary. The cycle is broken."

"I'm picturing it," Ephraim said, "I think I've got it?"

"Well, that's how I feel right now. I'm fine just as long as I stay on top of this nice safe hill."

"Right. And you hate it."

"Death sounds like a tourist destination. Even barista-ing at Starbucks. Arrowsmith, if we still feel this way tomorrow, energized an' all, let's skip school and see if we can jack into Noe's biota, the equivalent of what we had in Peru."

"I was thinking something like that. It's around here somewhere, I can feel it."

"And if it is?" queried Bingham.

"Then I put out feelers to anything in it that wants to make contact," said Ephraim. "Maybe some old Ohlone medicine man. Beyond that, maybe, nothing. Let's just see."

"Let's," agreed Lily. "And I know Loki isn't Greek, so stop thinking."

CHAPTER THIRTY-SEVEN then

Ramram the Spy
Western Frontier of the Tawantinsuyu

Ramram recorded his flight over Mamaqocha on khipu, Chaski Yuyu doing the same, and conferred with Amaru, saw Tuya to her new wasi next to the wide, hermetic Acllawasi compound, bid farewell to Tupaq, calling him a *supisiki supitulu*, a fart-ass bag of farts.

"I will be Apu Sapa Inka someday, you know, Q'urpa."

"I know. And then you will be a great *Thasa*, O Immense and Silent Fart."

"And you will be a Lump of *Supi*, and you can *akayta mikuy supiyta pitay*, Ramram-Supi!"

"Ari, August Crown Prince Tupaq Yupanqui, with great relish will I eat your shit and smoke your farts."

"You never will, Umu Ramram. You will be my Chief Advisor and Governor of your own Suyu, which I will conquer for you."

"I will be an old man who doesn't remember my own name. Now become educated and don't forget to be you most of the time."

That morning Otoronqo Kuy came to Ramram with orders from the Apu Sapa Inka Pachacutiq. He was to leave Vilcaswaman, alone, to scout out the unknown lands and spy on the fabled empire of the Chimor, said to be as great in might and domain as the Inka, and far greater in knowledge and culture. He was to report back to Chaski Yuyu in no more than two years, and not to lie to him as he did to everybody else.

Otoronqo Kuy and a company of the guard walked Ramram to the end of the Qapac Ñan's westward spur; there the Tawantinsuyu petered out. Ramram wore a military cloak and helmet. They stepped off the cobblestoned road. He stripped to his worn brown unku, seen first on the hard-eyed Inka scout, handed the uniform to Otoronqo.

“I’m a spy from here on out. I hope none of theirs are watching this little ceremony.”

“We cleared the area of every last herder. No eyes in these hills except weasels, puma, and things with their own feathers.” Otoronqo handed him Pachacutiq's threadbare old cloak.

“Chay hina kachun, Tayta. See you later, General.”

To Amaru, he had said, “If I don’t come back, I know that you will see that Tupaq knows what to do when he takes the Borla.”

“If it’s not too late,” Amaru replied. “Learn everything you can about the sea-going rafts that are said to travel the coasts and even the Mamaqocha herself. I would build those rafts today if I could. If we go there and bring back what you have seen, the old man will be free to take action.” He handed Ramram a knit pouch with shoulder strap.

"In this ch’uspa are Ayawaska, Vilca, Wakacachu, and Wachuma, plants of spiritual power. I call on those spirits at need. Here is a khipu in Chimu style that contains the secret pass of the cult of *Naymlap*. Don’t flash it at anyone in the cult of *Al Paec*. The Founder and the Sky God are anathema to one another. Secretly. In public they are best of friends. These are the secrets we have gleaned so far. You will increase our knowledge exponentially, this I know. See you in a year. Two is more than you need.”

“Yah. I’ll try to do all that. Especially the part about coming back.”

“Supposedly they know things about sex that we can’t imagine. And certainly wouldn’t allow. We could use a khipu on that.”

“Yah. *Tupananchik kama*, Snake Man.” See you later.

Ramram turned west, neutralized in his mission to convert the Sapa Inka to his purposes, and Pachamama's. Tupaq was too young to be of use in this, and Amaru, always ready to help a friend, would not involve in politics. For this he had given up rule of the land. So for as long as Ramram was gone spying, no work would be done to save the Tawantinsuyu from the future.

Black Sand, Waterless and Chill

Ramram staggers dying of thirst and wounds through the waterless desert under a cold sky, lowering and dark. Stumbles up hills of black sand, down rocky slopes brown and blue, he has not seen a growing thing in days. The agony in his face never stops throbbing, his hand, too stiff to close, drips puss. He has been taught how to ignore thirst, pain, and fatigue, but he knows also that he will be dead before sunset. When what he knows dies with him he fails. Everything he wants for the world is gone.

He crosses a crest, faces a stony drop. Too much. He will have to go around. His head droops. He would rather just fall. Then his face lifts. There is a far tinkle of music. Is it real? Away, across the alkali flat, coming down a distant slope, shimmering, is a column of polychrome figures. He falls to his hands and knees, shuts his eyes. His mind goes into whirling darkness, vague images come of things he once loved.

When he opens them, the music is louder, the people are closer, men, women, dancing, chanting, carrying a festive palanquin bearing a woman in a great spreading headdress that shimmers. His mind goes dark again.

They are there, surrounding him, poking him with carven staves, curious. Incense and perfume waft from them. A tall man in sorcerer's gear — they are Ychsma people, he knows the raiment — lifts his feline mask and looks, eyes wide and lips parted. He gestures, speaks to the majestic lady in the litter, points at Ramram, at what he is wearing, at his injuries. He is explaining something. All around the people begin to bow, murmuring.

Now he is bobbing in the palanquin, the queenly woman walking beside, carried over the high rolling rise of sandstone he thought he would never live to touch. Beyond the summit are a lush valley, cultivated, a silver river and canals. Delicate dwellings, tall pyramids.

Amaru, in his wide chamber, now a laboratory of bowls and basins of various fluids supporting still more botanical organisms, received a message that a stranger had come to the checkpoint of the newly extended western Ñan. It was a man of obvious status but alone and who would not answer questions.

Lianas and other trailing plants now ran from one bowl to the next, connecting their miniature ecosystems. Chaski Yuyu and a couple of apprentices stood by, learning and recording. In a sunlit corner Amaru's principal wife, Uca Uma, stood at her loom, deftly weaving intricate designs into the finest chumpi cloth. She was short, lumpy, bow-legged, had a head like an unwashed potato under thinning hair. Her pupils had from birth been as large as Amaru's, and Amaru was never more than a few sikyas away from her. She was rarely heard to speak, but now she was laughing, a clear, unselfconscious burbling. Beside her, kneeling at her own loom and studying Uca Uma's technique, was Tuya, laughing too. They exchanged a glance, full of understanding and carefully modulated joy. Tuya had woken up lighthearted two days before and remained so.

"What insignia is this silent stranger wearing?"

"Unknown. We sent for a Tocapucamayoq, who said his raiment is enigmatic. He believed the headgear, that is square and depicts strange and menacing gods, may be Warqo. He is wearing much gold, silver, and mullu. Apu..."

"*Ari?* Details please."

"The man is missing two fingers on his right hand and one eye. The eye seems to have been replaced by a clear green stone. He had been standing at the guard post for a night and parts of two days when I left. If the guards relax he takes one step forward. When they cross lances again, he takes one step back. He has not eaten, slept, or taken a piss since arrival. He has been seen to take a sip from a gourd at his side. He has a shawl-pack on his back, not heavy but large, and will not allow it to be inspected."

“Chay hina kachun,” Amaru said, ‘so be it,’ spreading a complex network of strings and knots over an ironwood bowl, whose contents stirred, “Send the Amauta Huku Tuku to the outpost.” He turned to Uqu Uma; “He was ambassador to Cajamarca, and knows the Mamaqocha peoples as well as any Inka.”

Return of the Exile

Two days went by. A messenger came again. Again, Amaru stood at his studies, holding a deep scarlet strand of tiny ear-like growths to the sunlight. Again, Uqu Uma and Tuya wove at their looms.

“Apu,” the messenger said, making mocha, “Apu Huku Tuku follows. He will arrive before midday.” Amaru nodded. The women did not look up from their work. The messenger left.

The amauta arrived, dusty, winded, and stoic.

“Apu,” he began after proper greetings, “the man wears a gold breastplate of ancient Mochica workmanship. His unku is Chimu, of the finest quality. His cloak is Paracas, his *uma qatana* headdress is Chachapoyas from the cloud forest, his sandals are Cuismanku, he carries a tumi knife of Huancas provenance, and a five-bladed Chanka macana. His ch’uspa bag is Huamachuco. His false eye is an emerald from the far north, as is his staff, inlaid with polished mullu shell and silver wire. He will not allow anyone to open the fine-weave Ychsma chumpi cloth he is using as a pack.”

At this, Tuya lifted her face to Amaru, questioning. He smiled subtly back.

"Rumors are that it contains the head and hands of an Inka spy." Tuya raised her head again, listening intently. Uqu Uma laid a hand on her shoulder. "When I arrived, he had been standing silent for nearly five days."

Two days later, Tupaq Yupanqui and Otoronqo Kuy entered. Tupaq was chattering. “We will have all the guards crushed under big stones. Yes. And their commanders. Or no, we will have them stand at attention without food, water, or sleep, until they *die*.”

"For obeying orders, Apu Tupaq? Of course. It shall be done. Then will a soldier ever obey another order? That will be so much fun to watch."

"Hah," Tupaq said, "The question game again. Answer: Yes. They will obey mine." The young prince had given up fart jokes and was working on wit.

Ramram stood in the door, thin, still, waiting, taking in the room. He moved his head just far enough to rest his one eye on Tuya. She suppressed her own smile, eyes glowing back at him.

"Oh," Amaru said, over his shoulder, "it's *you.*" With his heel he kicked the Puma-carven wooden tiyana stool across the floor, where it came to rest perfectly at Ramram's feet.

It was death for anyone not the sapa inka, his coya, crown princes, or one of the very few given express Imperial permission, to lay buttock upon a tiyana. Ramram lifted it with the end of his staff, threaded through the room so that the circle of algae-bowls lay between him and Amaru, and plunked down on the stool, legs splayed.

"Eighteen moons," Amaru said.

"Ari. And one eye and two fingers. You know I was offered a kingdom?"

"Hadn't heard. Did you accept?"

"No. Nor did you, Apu. Tupaq will take it soon enough." He unknotted the folded manta, pulled it around back-to-front, carefully lowered it to the smooth plastered floor.

When he opened it out by the corners, Amaru leaned over and saw a beautifully crafted model of a raft with people aboard and a wicker cabin. Ramram pulled on a fine thread and two masts, crossed at the center, stood, opening a pair of triangular lateen sails. Tupaq, Otoronqo, and both the women came close to view.

"Oh wow," blurted Tupaq, "how awesome is that? Can I have it?" Ramram lifted his eye to Tupaq, appraising.

"You will have many more than this if you are a wise Inka," he said. "You will have a thousand of these, and you will cross the great Mamaqocha, and see and do things all will hail as awesome." As he turned to Amaru, he folded what was left of his right hand over Tuya's, now cupping his shoulder.

"You see how this works," he said. "Those tiny man-figures? They are in scale. The base is *llampu* logs, a light buoyant wood, always an odd number, in this case nine. The waves just roll over these logs and pass through, running back into the sea. There are two lightweight but strong bamboo floors above, on cleverly designed blocks, keeping the cargo and crew dry. It is bound together by ropes that flex with the motion of the waves. It won't fall apart in a storm, it won't sink. It water logs at around two years, but can be dried out in four months of good sun. The wind-catchers are called 'sails' and are of cotton. They need to be replaced twice in a year of hard 'sailing.' They are light and easily stored. These crafts are called llampu, after the wood. Some are three times this size.

"We will need to cultivate llampu forests. It will grow deep in the Chinchaysuyu, in Quito territory, and where the Chachapoya live. In the Collasuyu, in hot forest land. Your father or Tupaq will need to push the Tawantinsuyu to annex those lands."

"Try to stop them."

"Exactly." He looked at Amaru. "I've been to sea. Not far enough. Chimu traders have made landfall three moons out, they name two big islands, Avachumpi and Ninachumpi. There are men there, gold, strange animals. I have been that far and farther on my wanka-travels, as I recounted to you. And there lies our work. Or, Tupaq's."

"We'll all go. When we're ready. And the rest of your eighteen moons? Did you learn anything beyond how to stand sleepless for five days? Why did you do that?"

"I learned how to sleep standing. I told the captain of the guard that I would speak only to you. He said, 'We'll see.' He saw."

"That conversation wasn't reported. Tupaq may get his wish."

“Mana. One thing I learned on the road, Apu, is that the world is full of people with too many masters, and some of them are us.”

"Yes. And the fabled sex?" Amaru questioned.

"Tediously artificial, most of it."

Tuya dropped her spindle.

To Fly

A colony of bats — they often came out to witness Ramram's clumsy nocturnal attempts to fly — flocked head-on into his face. He flinched, his wings spun upside down out of control, he crashed into a cactus bed. He dragged the wreck uphill under his right arm, picking spines out of himself with his left hand.

The act of flying in his spirit-form had caught Ramram’s imagination, so he undertook to learn to fly in this world, the Kay Pacha. On the steps of the ancient and sacred temple of Pachacamac, overlooking Mamaqocha, he had seen the brightly colored Umus in their long robes mesmerizing their congregation with flights of colorful flying gods, lifting and stooping in the warm breeze, chased and caught below by bare-legged boy acolytes. He had schemed his way into possession of three of these magical beings and discovered that they were constructed of llampu wood frames supporting cunningly designed winged devices of lightweight cotton cloth.

He camped, with the authorization of Amaru and Tupaq, on the slopes of his wanka hill, experimenting with materials, designs, and weather. He worked in a makeshift hut in the days and took the results out after dark to test in secret. The outcome was typically bruises and contusions.

“To fly,” he told Amaru, arms full of broken bamboo and torn chumpi cloth, “is not for men. Wizards, whatever we may claim, are men.” Now, as he stood in the cone of power from the shaft, he felt the approach of Eff-Ram, his friend the alien stranger.

CHAPTER THIRTY-EIGHT then

First Blood for the Young Prince

Tupaq Yupanqui, fifteen years of age, sturdy, sharp-eyed, vibrating with energy, ever leaning into the next challenge, faced his first battle line.

He could just make out the eyes and set jaws of the enemy, sensing their resolve in the way their feet dug into the crusted snow on the high pass between the Inka and their enemy's mountain chiefdom.

The Inka army stood on a hard bunch grass moor, wide behind, narrow ahead.

The enemy's main force was on the other end of the bottleneck guarding a swinging bridge, but first, the defenders would funnel the invading force into this cramped wedge where boulders would roll down on them from the cliffs, plowing into the vanguard, destroying the formations, demoralizing the forward elements. And Tupaq, under the watchful eye of Otoronqo Kuy's aide de camp, was unleashed to the front rank. The slingers stepped through the shield wall, thousands of stones peppered the sky. There was a battle cry, a standard was brandished, the line of infantry stepped forward through the slingers, the enemy grimly braced for impact. Tupaq Yupanqui's teeth gleamed in the pale sun.

Pachacutiq's armies had gone north, run into tough opposition, lost their Chanka component to desertion, triumphed over Cajamarca, but did by crossing the forbidden Yanamayu, Black River into Chimu territory, too soon. Pachacutiq executed the commanding generals, one of them his brother. Now his armies went north again, eyes on rich cities and fertile land.

On this campaign, Prince Tupaq Inka Yupanqui would face his first battle. He was ready.

He would rather have gone after the warlords and empires of the coastal Kuntisuyu, the snake's' nest of powerful opponents blocking his way to the far islands Ramram had seeded into his imagination.The fibers of his young being hungered to see the Mamaqocha of his childhood tales. But first, to redeem the Inkas' humiliation in war. And to taste blood, even if only his own.

He saw massive rocks bounding, careening, tearing gouges through the Inka lines. Men were cut down by sling stones, then spears, then he was upon his enemy. He could smell their alien sweat and there was a youth like him, flanked by, he guessed, a father and an uncle. He wanted the boy, but his training told him, the uncle. He was the dangerous one, and guarded the flank. Then the boy. He didn't wait for an opening. Don't dance, he told himself, elated, trust your training, trust yourself, go straight in. His spear was his heart and his heart was his spear.

Then came the muscle, the struggle, the blood. His lance lodged in the uncle's ribs, he saw the boy's courage flee his face, but Tupaq's foot slammed into the kid's chest and his club came down. War.

Defying Certainty

The Cañari Capital of Guapondelig in the Chinchaysuyu. Tupaq Yupanqui stood on a hill beyond the smoking ruin looking toward the setting sun. Cañari captives, guarded by fresh Inka troops newly arrived to relieve those whose mita service was completed, faced their future according to their strength. The generals, surrounded by staff officers, gathered nearby, planning, smiling, looking along their line of march toward Quito, the next major conquest.

But Tupaq gazed toward the sea, fingering a newly delivered khipu, talking with Otoronqo Kuy. He had known war and proven strong.

“According to this message, the Umu Antarqui has learned that we will go on and take Quito, and then further, to the endless forest. That is what occurred according the reports from the far future, and that is what this army, and my father, intend."

"It is." Otoronqo eyed Tupaq suspiciously.

"And then come plague, and war for the Borla, the Silver Asnaqs, and defeat, and the end of the Tawantinsuyu."

"There is already famine, disease, and rebellion back home."

"But we get through that. The Tawantinsuyu is strong, well organized, well thought out, not in real danger now. But you have read this khipu. Do you believe it?"

Otoronqo poised to say, No, no. Your father says it is folly, all lies, Antarqui cannot be trusted.

"Yes."

Tupaq spoke with controlled passion. "Then let us not do what was done before. What will be done if we let it. We have waited for my father to give us orders to defy fate. He has not."

"He has not. He has given orders to take Quito and beyond."

"Let us — not the army, just your twenty thousand. Or half that. Go to the coast. To that town of the Tumpis Ramram visited — where he lost his fingers — take it, and their llampu wood, and build rafts and go to sea and bring back Silver Strangers and whatever else we need to convince the old man."

"Disobey his orders."

"Yes. Change fate. Save the Tawantinsuyu."

"You recall what he did to his brother who defied his command."

"You are not afraid to die."

"But I do not relish dishonor."

"And where does your honor lie? To a king deceived by wizards, or to the future of the Inka people and of our world?"

"Antarqui is a wizard."

"He?" laughed Tupaq Inka Yupanqui, "He is a storyteller. He's going to make this one come true. So he promised. And so am I."

He Who Knows Little of Farming Tubers

Stone faced, Otoronqo Kuy informed Ramram that he would be escorted back to Pachamamatambo. Pachacutiq had sent orders that he was not to be admitted to his kancha, reunited with his *ayllu*, or supported from the communal qolqas. He would pay his taxes in bedtime stories. Amaru was recalled to Qosqo, and Tupaq gone to war.

After a week's journey to the town he had helped nurse into life, Ramram was taken to a deserted herder's hut, high on a barren hillside in the sterile mountains, a hovel built before the coming of the Inka. He would subsist on what he grew. It seemed to Ramram that no other subject of the Sun was denied so much of the Ayni, the fair trade between the State and the worker that was the basis of the Inka society. Nor had he the warmth of the Ayni on the level of community and family. He was separated from his wife, his ayllu and his hamlet on the rich lands below. Further, he knew very little of farming tubers.

Tuya was told to stay with her family in New Rumipuqyu. After three days she showed up at Ramram's miserable fieldstone shed. "Just for a papa pun or two," she assured him, "until we both starve to death."

Light on Stone

Ramram's eyes lay unfocused on the bleak mountainscape. In everything that meant anything, he had fallen. What he won was trivial. He had wasted the best of his life, an eye, much of a hand, and stood nowhere. He had learned too little and the wrong things. He could not feed his wife, or give her child. He had been hungry for months, and cold.

Plague, vicious war, invasion, defeat, and subjugation, were coming to his people. Now he knew the size and shape of the world, and how little his own people knew, how weak they were among other nations, and that the hearts of the strong were foul. But he could do, had done, nothing.

Pachamama had given him a job and power to accomplish it, and he had wasted that. He had lost his grip on that tool, gone off the trail, pissed away critical time. The Sapa Inka had been on his side, had listened to him. He had let that squirm away. His allies were a prince who wouldn't fight and a boy years short of primacy who was marching in the wrong direction.

And in his own life, his wife could not conceive with him. The greater his rapport with Pachamama, the less potent his seed, it seemed. And what would become of a child in any case? He had no work, and his home was a crumbling hut. He was an exile and outcast.

He stood, took the badly repaired wooden foot plow from against the porous, jagged and blackened fieldstone wall, returned to his chakra to furrow the stony soil for planting potatoes. A little light, very little, infused his chest when he spied Tuya climbing the precarious trail, shawl bulging on her back. She smiled, and with that came both warmth and chill. How could she still smile? He could not live up to her and never had. Everywhere the land was sour, the few struggling grasses and wiry scrub stood without soul or meaning.

"*Rimaykullayki*, husband," she greeted him. "When is harvest time? I'm hungry for more root crops." She was laughing.

"The day after never, far as I can see. Did Papa Chakra give you any hints about how to make new papas out of old wrinkled blackened papas?"

"Yes, he did. And he sneaked us some good seed papas as well. And I've got some kuy, two of them pregnant. And some *choclo* and quinoa for soup."

"Thank Pachamama your weaving is so popular."

"Yes, I'm pretty good. But no one, my love, has forgotten you. They will be here tomorrow in full Ayni to put our fields in order.

And we will reciprocate at the new moon. Even old Kusi Yupanqui can't keep us from the planting feast. Let me go put these away."

He gave her what little shamed smile he had in him. Where was his strength? Where was the buoyancy of the hills, the land, that he had once known? He listened for the sound of so much as a brown bird.

He listened, and he heard silence.

It came to him, the stillness, so complete, so huge on the land, broken only by the sough of the wind across the edge of his ear.

He listened, eyes turned to the empty sky, and though nothing changed, everything changed. There was a twist in the essence of the world.

The random wind became, had always been, soft, full of harmony. The life in the contorted little stem at his feet turned in its nauseating blunt thingness to something complete and perfect in its balance with the hills where it grew, where it lifted its leaves to precise equipoise in its being, exact in its weightlessness between big and small, high and low, cold and hot. Between being and not being.

All around everything growing was the same, exactly content in its place, in the hush of the breeze, in the pale sun that let the land live just as it was, nothing too much or too little. In perfect equilibrium between rising and falling.

His back straightened, he breathed deep of the air, the beautiful air, so measureless, there to take always, asking nothing.

Warmth filled him. Color was everywhere, subtle, in shadow, in delicate light, and everything was alive.

“Everything is alive.” he said it aloud. The world seemed to lift him to his feet. He felt light, strong, his hunger was a gift, the upthrust rock formations breathed with light. His eyes weren't the only eyes seeing this perfection. Birds saw, bugs have eyes. The grass saw, the rocks saw, he had known that all his life. Nothing was alone.

But that thought blew away. Now there was just the land and the sky and the delicate music of the stream in its bed. The bushes gave off captured heat as he stood near, and a faint spice for his nose. A condor lifted on the rising heat of the morning, canting in a great slow circle. Tuya sung soft around the corner of his stone house. There would be a fire in the night, that magic spirit. Everything was alive.

Above his head, a prismatic mist rippled unseen.

Two Unkus

From the day of the Ayni, when his neighbors came to share their energy with him, Pachamama smiled on Ramram's estate. He found topsoil in a small delta of the creek and carried it to his farm. That, along with the good seed plants brought by Papa Chakra, and a strange microclimate that seemed to settle over their highland croft, brought a fat harvest of big, flavorful oca and potato. Rather than leave the chakra fallow for a season, he planted a hardy strain of choclo maize he had been offered by a veteran of the Chanka war, and mixed that with quinoa. Everyone said it would fail — below, a black blight was eating growth on the mountains and taking ever more of the crops — but his crops flourished. He planted alder and molyay pepper tree seedlings around the house, and they grew. Chonta had brought clay to fill the holes in the walls, and, strangely, a flowering plant burst out of that soil so that the hovel became a curiously pretty, vine-covered little dwelling, as well as windproof. He re-roofed the house, and when there was time, began to carry in stones for construction of a new wasi. Tuya turned up with child.

Under his eye the community quietly removed the pots of defoliating brew the Ilyapas left. There was little violence, just skirmishing for advantage, and fields began to prosper. The hills held their own.

"We are afflicted with happiness," the one-eyed wizard told his wife, "I don't trust it."

Sure enough, not long before sundown a chaski messenger pumped up the hill with a khipu bearing the signatures of both Tupaq and Otoronqo. He was bidden to depart in all haste. A detail of Otoronqo's long-range scouts would escort him. With them they brought a good military cloak and two regimental unkus, one of wool and one of cotton.

"Uh-oh," he told a stoic Tuya, "we're going to yunga territory, hot country. I've been there, on the coast. I don't think Apu Sapa Inka Pachacutiq is going to like that."

"Maybe I should let him know," Tuya retorted with a menacing eye.

"Please do. My head will look good on a stick in our chakra, and maybe keep the birds away." She looked at the ground. But she understood. She had been in on this from the beginning.

CHAPTER THIRTY-NINE then

Dark Chemistry

High in the stone eyrie of Shaqishawana, on the remote heights where the old Sapa Inka Viracocha dwelt divested of his kingship, shadows of the priests of the cult of Ilyapa gyrate wildly in the firelight to drums and wild interweaving modulations of chanting as they dance to enchain the mind of the reigning Inka Pachacutiq in Qosqo, and to counter the influence of Pachamama with spirits of their own.

In Qosqo, a high priest of Ilyapa whispers tales of the miscreant Antarqui insidiously directed toward Pachacutiq's ear. Suborned Ñustas, bewitching princesses from the Acllawasi, infiltrate the Inka's concubines, oiled in a fragrant film of enervating hampi, hovering for an opportunity to poison the Antarqui in the Emperor's mind. A yanakuna servant, in fact an agent of Ilyapa, pretends to be accidentally overheard speaking of Tupaq Yupanqui's detour toward Mamaqocha, the prince abandoning his orders, murmuring that it was Antarqui who made the prince go renegade.

Sorcerers, eyes ruby on poisonous medicines, carry viscous defoliant down to the valley, to Pachamamatambo, where it replicates and devours its way into the living tissue of the earth mother. There is no one there to stop them.

With the Umu Antarqui gone, in exile or dead, the forces of Ilyapa have blocked the progress of Llachaqkuna Kamay and the spread of Pachamama's greeness throughout Pachamamatambo, its travel down the Yucay valley, it's appearance in the fields around Qosqo. The green is driven far back into the hills, chased by morbid black desolation. Pachamama's strong point was far up Pututu peak, the place called Kunturpunku. When Ilyapa got up there, it was over.

Qachu smiles, overseeing the acolytes who carry on a litter with long, long poles, the stinking jar of bubbling black goo that is the YanaTurmanyay brew that survived the disaster of the rockslide. From this steaming seed he will grow more. Ilyapa's triumph is a month away, two at most.

But Misk'i, his most critical agent, was she under control? Where the Emperor was, she was. He had seen them exchange looks, hers full of barely veiled hatred, his of amused contempt, her sister's death forever between them. What happened to her sister could happen to her. But when they turned away, what were those hidden smiles?

Pachamama is always here

Waywash looked at his feet. Something was wrong. The purple flowers there were withering. There would be no tarwi seeds to gather in the hills this season.

He spilled *akha* corn beer from a jug onto the earth of his field, thanking Pachamama for her bounty. The Inka had taught them all to sacrifice to Inti, to Killa, to Pachayachachiq and Ilyapa. He did, gladly, sincerely. The Sun, the Moon, the Creator, Thunder and Rain, ruled; but he knew, his wife knew, the village knew that under their feet, here in the chakras, not in the temples on the hill, was their nurturer and protector. Pachamama gave them their everything. She was the earth and the earth was life.

"Yuquy, *munaqi*, look at this."

His young wife, a widow whose first husband had died fighting below Hunchback Hill, looked up from where she was offering coca leaves to the founder stone in the center of their terrace field.

"I don't have to look, my man, I know. The purple chocho, the yellow wildflowers, the big-eared cactus, many more green spirits are dying. Something is attacking the Earth Mother, blackening her, chasing her up into the mountains. Until now, our chakras have been spared. But the tarwi is dying. It's your ñakasqa wizards and their stupid quarreling." She came to him.

"They are not my wizards, sweet thing. And look, never before has her power been so strong. N□ever before has she spoken to us so clearly, sung so loud. See: maize, quinoa, papas, oca, pasto grass, fine harvests!"

"This time. Maybe. The clear water in the acequias protects our chakras so far. And Chonta's crazy son Ramram, he isn't your idol and hero? And isn't he sticking his wizard staff into the nest of those storm god bastards?"

"He has not only found — speak this softly, woman — but he has brought to life, the wakas that have made our fields so fertile. And you too are fertile, my fine wife."

"And he has brought disharmony to this fine new town. You know what they are saying. That there is a war between Pachamama and Pachayachachiq, with his killers from the temple of Ilyapa. One is mother of all life, the other is the creator of all things. And if either wins, if either loses, what will be left? For this *wawa* in my oh-so-fertile belly?"

"They are saying that the Creator God has willed a *Taripay Pacha*, a new and beautiful time and world, that will take us to the stars? To the llama and her kid, to the fox, to the qolqa, the white river that moves across the night sky. Does that sound so bad?"

"Do you listen only with your left ear, my strong-thighed war-hero husband? Your right ear will tell you that Ilyapa's Taripay Pacha will also bring a great pachacuti, the overturning of the world, full of monsters and cannibals to tear down the Tawantinsuyu and bring disease, destruction, hunger, poverty, slavery, and death. That the end of this age will come in less than one long lifetime, to take everything from our children. Even from ourselves. And Pachamama, his daughter and sister and wife, fights against him to stop this. And so he fights back against her, and the growing things die."

Waywash leaned on his long wooden foot plow. "That's what they say. Because if Pachamama defeats Pachayachachiq, if he fails, the stars will disappear. Chaska Quyllur, the star of morning and of evening, will fall below the earth forever. Chakana, the three stars that bridge between the upper world, this world, and the lower world, will vanish. Not good. Yet if he wins, pachacuti: destruction, misery and death. Big talk. So, my fine smart strong beautiful woman, light of my life, who I can never deserve, do you really believe any of this *mankata akka*, this stupid crap?"

Yuquy laughed, washed her hands in the canal, shook droplets off. "They say a lot of things, big dumb husband, as do you. They say your boy the great Umu Ramram is lost or dead, or on a mission for the Inka. That he is the favored advisor to the king, that he is banished, condemned, honored, despised. That he would come back any time now, and never. It is getting so you can't believe anybody anymore. They can't all be right. But they can all be wrong."

"Well, my lovely pussywilllow, it's not my business. I cannot by the law of Ayni be called to war again. We can only hope the Sapa Inka and his amautas are wise enough to handle these matters."

Yuquy came to him, wiped her damp hands on his cloak, leaned her head against his shoulder.

Waywash watched the foamy liquid soak into the rich topsoil. “I know him,” he said. "Ramram. He’s just a boy. He can’t even grow potatoes or build a qolqa like his dad. If this is all about him, it can’t be that important. Kings, gods, wars, so what. Pachamama is always here. We will be fine.”

He put his arm around her, she hers around him. Together they gazed at the blackening that climbed the mountain from below.

Oily and Dark

The priest of Ilyapa and his cult faced off against Rumi Uma, the Head of Fifty Households, effective chief of the new Rumipuqyu community in Pachamamatambo. Una Uma stood solid with his hands on his hips, flexing the muscles of his big shoulders and thrusting his massive jaw. The hawkish villaq's arms were spread as wide as a condor, gold-incised staff in his right hand, a thin khipu waving in his left.

“This is Inti land,” growled Rumi Uma, “We pay our third to Inti, our third to the Sapa Inka. T□his pata is ours. That is the law of Ayni.” He gestured to the patch of open land, where the *camachicus*, town assemblies, were held, as well as the informal markets and ceremonies for the wakas of the ayllus and other seasonal rituals. In its center was a small head-shaped stone Ramram had found for them. “Ilyapa has his suyu up there, in the Ocobamba valley. You have your cave on Flute Mountain.” There was a mischievous glint in the headman’s eye at this, and the Rumipuqyus behind him smiled, backing him up. The Ilyapa cave had been buried in the landslide that had interrupted Chonta’s boy Ramram’s public execution.

Ramram had gone west.

At Rumi Uma’s left shoulder, assuring that he did not waver or retreat, was Tuya, eyes hot and jaw set, hiding her fear. She, and the rest, valued the power that emanated from the central stone. It was a good waka and they took pride in and strength from it.

The Villaq straightened, summoned his authority. “By decree of the Michu of Pachamamatambo, the House of Ilyapa has the right and prerogative to commandeer non-producing land in this sector as offerings to the Apu of the Rains to assure the fertility of the land and abundance of the harvest. You know there is a blight.”

“Our land,” replied Rumi Uma, “is as fertile as any in this region, and our harvests are superlative. Many think the black crud is Ilyapa's tool. Pachamama has shown a particular affection for us, and we give our thanks to her with every breath, and in many ways. How do we know what those strings say? Do you come here with a Khipucamayoq?”

The villaq straightened, raised his voice. “Tiwla Simi, come forth.” Twenty men in black and purple stood behind the villaq. One, large and apparently well fed, stepped out. “Here is our khipu reader.”

Rumi Uma, a man given more to consensus than conflict, hesitated. Tuya poked him in the kidney. He started.

"Mana. Not your man. A neutral authority. Isqha Chaki, go to the Pachaca Kuraka and ask for a khipu reader to come *ñapas*. Isn't Sinchi Amauta still in town?"

"We do not have a day to waste waiting for decisions to be made and journeys taken," the Villaq spoke low. "Any khipucamayoq will bear out this directive. Brothers, remove the old stone, begin work." The Villaq knew that Sinchi Amauta bore authority, at least moral and popular, beyond his profession. He was trained by Chaski Yuyu, who was a minor legend, and people listened to him. He was also a friend to the Antarqui.

The monks of Ilyapa stepped toward the waka in its circle of planted flowers, a little twitchy. The stone was a partisan of Pachamama, and they could feel its threat. The crowd behind Rumi Uma, led by Chonta and Papa Chakra, moved to intervene. Tuya spoke into Rumi Uma's ear.

"I read some khipu."

"Wait," the headman said. "Let me see that order for a minute." The villaq lifted a hand to stall the confrontation, then, with a skeptical look, handed the knotted strings to Rumi Uma, who passed it behind his back to Tuya. She squinted over it, laboring to descry from context what she could not read from her lessons with Ramram. The Villaq waited with exhaustible patience. The opposing gangs parenthesized the stone. Tuya spoke low to Rumi Uma.

"Yes. This seems to support his claim. You must by law comply." She handed the khipu back, he conceded it to the villaq, regarding at it as he would a rotting fish.

"The hell we will," the headman objected. "I killed a Chanka awki before the brother stones came. I head this village and this is our waka and our land. Chonta, form a line."

"Unu, my friend," replied Chonta, "you didn't kill him. So I hear. You just broke his knee. And I will not see you tossed off the arawa for disobeying legitimate orders. Let them have the plot of land. For now."

Rumi Uma looked over his shoulder at Tuya. She nodded. "All right boys," he said in resignation, "stand back." There was a low snarl from the crowd. Half of them were female. "And girls."

The monks moved in. Reluctantly, slowly, the locals moved back. With trepidation, three of the monks reached for the waka. Instantly, Waywash and Papa Chakra interposed, a battered macana club appearing in Waywash's fist. Knives flashed in the hands of two of the monks.

"Not our waka, stated Unu. "Touch that and we shove those potato peelers up your ecclesiastical ass, Your Holiness."

Just then, Isqha Chaki ran up from behind. "He was just up the path, coming this way. Here he is."

Sinchi Amauta, in the unku and gold diadem of a Hatun Khipucamayoq, ambled affably between the two bands, held out his hand, smiling blandly. The Villaq gave him the khipu. The High Reader barely glanced at it.

"This is from the Michu?" The villaq nodded, the thin line of his lips losing some of its firmness. "This authorization is from the Deputy Michu. And he has been in Qosqo for a month. Has he not? And these knots were tied by a rank amateur. Do you have some khipu training, Villaq Waraqu?"

"The — Deputy — Michu is in Shaqishawana. He authorized me to complete this khipu. I assure you, the Will of the Sapa Inka is reflected in this directive."

"I have your word. Before Inti."

"You do. Before Ilyapa. And Inti."

"All right." He turned to Rumi Uma. "He has the clout for this. Just barely, but that is enough. He can't touch your waka, but you must remove it. We will take this up with the Michu when he gets back from the capital. Come with me, we must speak. You too, Tuya. The Antarqui made you his proxy in relation to me."

A vocal sigh arose from the Rumipuqyus. They dispersed, looking over their shoulders at the priest and his minions, as they swarmed in on the emptied space, beginning to dig.

In the main house of Chonta's small kancha, Sinchi Amauta said, "This is an invasion in force. You are the most visible stronghold of Pachamama in this llacta. They will plant their *yana saqra* there, their evil magic. This is no joke. That stuff will kill you."

"What stuff exactly?" asked Chonta.

"It's called Yana Turmanyay — the back rainbow. It lives in stagnant pools and marshes, planted by witches of bad intent, and when it wakes, it rises as a vapor that expands, then breaks, and rains down on whatever or whoever is below. The death is prolonged and painful. They say now, the villaqs of Ilyapa, that it is a very potent sacrifice. It has no history that I can find in the archives. It is not really a traditional offering. It is a weapon.

"Now that Ramram is gone off on another of his luqt'u missions, they are moving in to take over this region, the stronghold of Pachamama. Walk carefully, and stay away from whatever they put there."

"What will they put there?" Rumi Uma asked. "In the heart of our little suyu?"

"Watch for water. Greasy water. If you see that, a pond or pool, you will know I am right. They plant the bad seeds there, and summon it by some magic that I do not know."

In the morning, the people stood cautiously away from a new pool, ringed with sharp stones, its surface oily and dark.

The Sublimation of the Virgins

When Nick got with Qachu for the last time, the little villaq was overseeing a Qapacocha in which twenty young girls and boys were to be buried alive at the Inti Raymi solstice to allay a fungal crop failure that had been secretly arranged by the Ilyapa crew to manufacture a crisis for political motives, when he experienced something that changed his life.

Nick understood that Qachu, for the first time, felt the presence of the Apus. They told him that, as Ramram had revealed before the battle, Inti didn't want those deaths, nor did Ilyapa. And Qachu saw something that Ramram hadn't.

Pachamama did.

'This is a kick,' Nick thought, tucked into his cockpit in Qachu's head. 'I don't think anybody knows this.' His integration into Qachu's point of view had never been so complete or so clear.

The ceremony was staged in Pachamamatambo in the fields between the town and river, where villagers' crops had blackened and died. It was there that Qachu, who never had truly felt the gods, met Pachamama.

He was high on both the cactus and Ayawaska, Vine of the Dead. He didn't enjoy these influences, they frightened him, but they gave him power, visions, and he had guts.

But as he watched the trenches full of flawless children being filled in — those girls who would never have wanted him — as he saw their eyes recognizing through the veil of coca leaves and chicha alcohol what was happening to them, he felt for the first time, sadness for them in their tenderness, their fright, the beauty of their beings.

As they died, that beauty became the wonder of the land itself, of the sky, of the fields that were dying, and a shivering descended over him. He convulsed briefly, then a soft sweetness suffused him, an unfamiliar easiness came over him, some tension he had never realized was in him because it *was* him, lifted away. He saw Pachamama everywhere; in the fields, in the sky, in the swallows overhead, in the insects of the earth. Even in the priests of Ilyapa who knew nothing of her, and in the children he was killing.

He saw her as a gentle vibration, in tune with the world, as a rhythm thrumming of the soft beating of insect wings, the breath of the wind coming down from the snow peak Apu Wayka Willki. But what he saw most was that Pachamama wasn't so much *in* the world, or *of*, it, but *on* the earth. Disposed across her and swimming over her, always moving, always alive. And that she was on and in all the people, himself, and those children.

He saw that she was attacked, and was weakening.

He saw that Pachamama needed the vitality that was in those children, so much more alive than in the grown men and women, much more vigorous than any other source, more comprehensive than any other animal, and, as it passed from the dying children, the Kamay flooded into the world, into Pachamama, to revive her, empower her to counter the curse that was killing the fields and the hills.

Above their grave appeared a wavering ovoid of pulsing points of color, rising into the air, billowing and surging with the breeze, expanding, growing more luminous, numberless sparks of brilliant light in reds, greens, blues, yellows. It burst, dissipated into the breeze, nourishing the world. It lit up especially the river and the canals. Qachu knew the chakras were saved. A god would need the purest, most intense energy to vitalize her. That is the soul of a sacrifice.

A sacrifice. But not to Ilyapa. He needed all his discipline to wade through the rest of the ritual. Afterwards he found solitude and assessed what he had seen.

'The guy is deserting,' Nick thought. 'He is going turncoat. Fine with me. Ilyapa is an a fucking asshole anyhow. And so are his priests and monks. Well, not Ilyapa himself, he's part of Certainty. Just his cult. It was not about rain, thunder, lightning. It was about the power of men.

Watching through Qachu, Nick saw that Ilyapa himself was small compared to Pachamama, to her care of the earth. Inti was great, without Inti there would be no Pachamama. Inti wasn't going anywhere, or doing anything he wouldn't do anyway. Pachamama was here now, loving, giving, protecting.

And in trouble. She needed help. Ramram was gone. His wife was here. Qachu needed a gentle heart and a woman's forgiveness and strength; and to understand. When he had freed himself from the Priests of Ilyapa and their soldiers, when he was ready, Qachu would climb the ridge to Tuya's wasi.

This time Nick was able to separate from Qachu by his own will, without a struggle.

“Wow,” he said to the cat that lay on his chest like a sphinx, gazing into his eyes, “I finally break through to the guy, I am like, one with him, I understand everything he thinks and feels. And he jumps ship on our cause. I don’t think I’ll be seeing him again. But, you know, he has a point. What do you think, Kwee kit? And that bit with the sacrifice of the lolitas? To the Presence? Kind of an ethical thing there, huh?”

The Bastard Son and the Good Wife

Tuya, spinning fine chumpi cloth in her yard, watched a boney little man in a frayed unku and the scuffed tiara with its jeweled antenna of a Villaq Umu of Ilyapa huffing up the trail to Ramram’s farm. It was Qachu, bastard son of Pachacutiq Inka and storm god priest. She had heard rumors that he had disappeared. She greeted him courteously and curiously, offered food and drink.

“No word from Antarqui?” he asked. She shook her head. He nodded. “I come from Qosqo. We are no longer enemies, your man and I, you and I.

"I have been hiding among friends in the service of Pachamama. They are not in favor there now. My news is, the Cult of Ilyapa has subverted the mind of Pachacutiq Inka against Antarqui and now against his own son and heir.

"It didn’t help that they disobeyed him and went off onto Mamaqocha seven months ago. More each day, every hand is turned against us.

"They will come for you and your ayllu. The Sapa Inka is considering giving the properties of Pachamamatambo to the cult of Ilyapa. If that comes to be, the center of power of Pachamama in the Tawantinsuyu will disappear, and with it, the hope of salvaging the future of the Tawantinsuyu and the Inka people. The

Silver *Pishtacos* will come and we will fall into slavery. I have seen it."

"As have we all, poor Qachu." Tuya smiled. "Know this. Ramram is alive, and so is the Heir. And so is Amaru. But they are on deep water somewhere, I cannot know where or how far from shore." She turned her face upward, pointing to the sky with her chin. "The spirit of Pachamama is still strong here, but grows thinner. Where will you go?"

"I am hunted. This *chullu*," he rolled his bloodshot eyes up toward the gold ringlet on his head, with its upshoot insignia of Ilyapa, "along with a passage khipu I was given in the Sacred City, gets me through checkpoints so far, but not for long. The cult of Ilyapa does not love apostates."

"Stay with us. Our Rumipuqyu ayllu are together in this."

"No. So far you are deemed innocent. That is good. I will go to Mamaqocha, as Ramram did, and wait for his return."

"No. Do not. We need you here. You are the only one on our side who had seen into the heart of the Ilyapa-Pachayachachiq being. You have power, and knowledge. There will be a struggle here and right now I am alone in defense. There is an old herder's hut above, Ramram's power has made the land there fertile. We will put you there off-khipu."

"And if the Tocoyricoc comes? When they say 'He Sees All,' they are right."

"Yes. He sees all. He passed here not so long ago. He signaled to me that he has seen what we have seen. He will not report you."

"He kept information from the Apu Sapa Inka?"

"No, I asked the same. He told the Lord Unique Inka the plain truth, and the Lord Unique Inka waved it away. He is not a friend of the plain truth right now."

Qachu didn't spend much time in the high safe herder's cottage that Tuya offered him. He came down among the people in the daytime. He was trained in disguise and had an identification unku for the Rumipuqyu ayllu that Tuya provided. But she didn't know what he was doing.

He was at war. In the light, he sought out and marked the places where the cult of Ilyapa was poisoning the land with their brews and potions, the potions he had helped them discover and manufacture before his conversion and defection. In the night, he destroyed them. They found their sentries unconscious, clubbed, drugged, bound and gagged. The villaqs hid this from the people. The fact that there was a war was secret, and the fact that they were made fools even more so.

But they were winning the war. There were fifty of them, one of Qachu. Every day Pachamama was pushed farther back into the hills, every night her powers weakened. The canals that carried her life force were being choked off, sometimes to feeble trickles. The fine blanket of living force that was her body and spirit was countered by a corollary film created in the compounds and caverns of Ilyapa by the priests and monks. Qachu never forgot the deadly threat that puddled in the center of the Rumipuqyu suyu of Pachamamatambo. Some villager always on guard, always watching. He knew, because he had devised the trick himself, and taught it, that a single flick of the wrist could trigger the Black Rainbow.

The headman Rumi Uma passed an advisory on to the Storm Priest Simi Apaq. "'If the black rainbow comes, you and yours start to go. Maybe I don't know what that means. Maybe you do." Ten days later the black rainbow came.

The Rainbow War

Qachu turned to see a black fantasm below, rising like smoke from the cluster of five small houses that surrounded the plaza of Rumipukyu. He ran headlong down the trail heedless of loose stones, cactus, and bad ground.

In the early dawn the monastics of Ilyapa woke the locals and brought them, cobweb-headed, to the dark little pool. The young children were seated around the perimeter.

The Hatun Villaq, High Priest, glared. “This is the power of Ilyapa; lest you forget.” He made a two-handed palm-down gesture over the greasy pond, and from it arose a wisp, then a shadow of darkness. It fleshed into a roiling column and rose. The children watched open-mouthed. They had not been warned. It is a parent’s job to protect a child from such knowledge.

“Get them out of there!” the village headman Rumi Uma exploded into the tiny village square in time to see the Yana Turmanyay mushroom overhead. “Run!” he shouted, yanking three children by the arms. The other kids sat stunned. One girl began to get to her feet. The grownups shuffled around, uncertain. It happened too fast.

Three adults found the wit to move. One of them was Tuya. A wall and a house stood between her and the Black Rainbow, and rather than run around she grabbed the overhanging thatch and scrambled up over the roof. Two other parents got hold of their offspring just as the cloud released a sudden flood, spilling greasy black fluid, drenching everybody below. The effect was immediate.

Rumi Uma fell to his knees, shoving a girl and a boy before him, out of the flood. The first girl to move escaped. One of the rescuing parents managed to throw their youngest out of the circle of death. Those still in it flopped and bucked in paroxysms of mindless reflex.

The villaq seized a pubescent girl, too old for that ring of youth, from the arms of her father. His militant monks in purple and black filtered through the crowd.

“Who is it?” he howled. “Who is assaulting the faithful of Ilyapa? Who is pulling the teeth of Apu Ilyapa?” He swiveled his head, eyes maddened. “Tell me or she dies!”

At that instant, the cloud expanded, darkening the square and the surrounding houses. The priest and his functionaries backed out of the perimeter, taking the girl with them.

Qachu raced on, wheezing. He was a few rikras away when he saw the smokey darkness balloon.

Above it, no more than a few heads, a scintillation appeared in the air, thickening, sparkling, dissipating the greasy blackness below. It was trying to descend, but it could only ride the breeze, it had no weight, no propulsion. But its touch had broken the surface tension and the thing discorporated in a last splatter of black gouts, dropping threadily back into the pool.

Tuya came across the roof into the rainbow cloud, and leapt, following the black slime down, twisting her ankle as she hit the greasy dirt. She pulled the prismatic fog down with her. She took the nearest child in her arms, struggling to her feet as the girl, her unnamed daughter, coughed lung blood and mucous over her neck and chest. Tuya staggered, fell outside the steaming mess.

The Villaq, still clutching the young woman, turned toward the massacre, to see Tuya and her toddler englobed in a glistening pointillist penumbra of tinted lights. He tensed to lunge in their direction, then imploded to the ground, his throat's blood on the half-moon blade of Qachu's bronze tumi knife.

Qachu whirled the girl out of range with one wiry arm, and slashed the face of a monk deeply enough to part the cheekbone and sever the muscles of the jaw. He punched the long handle into the solar plexus of another, reaching into the hollow with his right hand and pulling the ribcage away from the spine. Neither would respond to treatment.

Tuya survived, suffering only a twisted ligament and hairlined fibula. Her child would be hag-ridden by a debilitating cough for the rest of her life, and would never run or find the breath to laugh. Chaski Yuyu took her into service and her male line would be khipucamayoqs for as long as the Tawantinsuyu was to perdure.

All others touched by the Black Rainbow died within a week. The town refused everyone sent to replace Rumi Uma for over a year, until someone counted worthy by the Camachicu meeting was accepted.

Tuya named her daughter Kuychi Puyu, Rainbow Cloud. She lived through the reigns of three Sapa Inkas to see the Spanish sails appear on the horizon of Mamaqocha. She died the only female Khipucamayoq in the empire, and the oldest of her profession.

The regional governor sentenced the surviving Ilyapa monks to public execution. The cult leaders in Shaqishawana repudiated them as rogue and offered unassociated replacements, approved by the Michi. They were worse.

No more were Ilyapa's agents found beaten, bound or drugged when planting their brews. The lesson had been learned. They were found throat-cut, gutted, garroted, blinded, castrated, dead.

CHAPTER FORTY now

In The Corridor

They found it almost immediately, the Presence. Ephraim fixed his piece of the Split Rock to his handlebars like Spielberg's ET when they biked east out of Pleasant Hill into the Lime Ridge Open Space. Ephraim discovered the network of trails soon after his parents relocated to California from D.C..

From there Lily and Ephraim followed the paths through the dry grass hills and sparse live oak groves into Shell Ridge Open Space and down to Diablo Foothills Regional Park, where the groves thickened, threading between communities, and in the arroyos they found madrone, buckeye, dogwood, willow, blue witch, and of course poison oak. Two kinds of alder. These Ephraim identified by cell video with a botanist friend of his dad's.

They searched the satellite view maps for a way through the Interstate 680 suburb belt, with no luck. Lily stopped her bike, tipped her head back, eyes shut, breathing deep. Breathing, still breathing.The next day they biked west, into Briones Park.

Everywhere, as soon as they left the city they were back in the arms of the holobiome, the Presence — a different feel, not as strong as Ollantaytambo, diminished by the surrounding urban sprawl. It was the inverse of Peru where the man-made settlements were surrounded by the wild mountains. Here the cities ringed the parks. But the Pachamama effect was strong, with its own character, full of that benevolent enveloping and enfolding. And expanding rapidly.

"One With Everything," Lily breathed, and Ephraim saw her smile, truly smile, for the first time since his return. Even her effusive greeting had been a message, practiced for effect. This was real. She pulled a long leaf from an overhanging tree, gently broke it, inhaled the scent. "This is a spice, I know it," she said. "What the heck is it?"

"California Bay," came a husky baritone. A long-haired, soaker-hatted, utility-vested, bespectacled and gray-bearded man clambered through the brush into the light. "*Umbellularia californica*. And this stuff trying to take off my hat is straggly gooseberry. Kinda rare. What brings you kids this far out into the corridor?"

"What corridor?" Lily asked.

"The corridor of wild lands that runs all the way from Los Padres down by L.A. up there to Crockett Hills by the Carquinez Bridge. You know, a Puma could chase a mule deer just about four hundred miles through these hills and not see a human being, except for crossing a few roads. The only real obstacle is right here, this strip of towns between Pleasanton and Martinez."

"Yeah, we were wondering," Lily said — Ephraim usually left the socializing to her — "is there a way to cross the I680 mess anywhere? For kids on bikes?"

"Not really, until you get way down by Verona. Not for people. But," and he laid a finger satirically along his strawberryesque nose, "the animals know the secret paths. Culverts, underpasses, creek beds, fire trails — they somehow seem to pass the information along. I think they do it interspecies."

He waved a hand at the surround, "You know, this land has a *mind*. I don't know how it does it, but I know that it does. It may be eat or be eaten, it may be Darwin proving his theory, it may be red-in-tooth-and-claw, but it's also 'we're all in this together.' It's the land against man." He snorted a laugh. "Yup, another crazy old coot. Think what you want."

They chatted a little, shook hands, and as Ephraim uprighted his bike, pushing off on the pedal, he called over his shoulder, "Bacteria. That's how they do it. It's a superorganism."

"Now who's the coot?" the man laughed back.

They went back to school, aced their tests, and on the weekend they went back out to the Corridor to try to make some kind of contact with someone in the biota, maybe an ancient native of the land.'

They did. But it wasn't a red man and it wasn't in California. It was with Nick Nieman, hiding out in the Twist.

Double Swirly Hill

"Okay. This is no joke," Lily said one late October day, leaning her scooter over. "Something is seriously happening in these canyons. The Pachamama effect is up like three notches." She elbowed Ephraim in the ribs.

Ephraim didn't go back to Peru at the end of the school year. Summer passed as they wandered the hills. Lily delicately disengaged from her other lovers, including Bingham.They studied together, enjoying the comfort and safety of school work and their own interests. Ephraim found a part-time job at the Phoebe A. Hearst Museum of Anthropology at the University of California, Berkeley, receiving and cataloging artifacts and maintaining the collections. He was hired partly through the influence of Bingham. Lily was now assistant manager of the Happy Heart acupuncture clinic. They rarely spoke of their time in Ollantaytambo and drifted away from Bingham and Noe.

Bingham accepted an appointment as Associate Professor at Berkeley. He returned to the site in Ollantaytambo a few times, but found that it was in good hands and that his absence from that project had no observable effect on his career. His wardrobe improved as did his love life. He found promiscuity uncomfortable and settled in with two young women, both blonde and often taken for sisters, who seemed to enjoy sharing him. He discovered the admiration of students and colleagues to be cloying and that he had liked himself better as an outsider.

Ephraim and Lily hiked the hills in all weather. They bought motor scooters for wider range but found that they preferred their bicycles and feet because it kept them slow and close to the ground, and it felt better. Closer to the Kamay.

So Lily elbowed Ephraim in the ribs.

"Yes," he replied. "Okay yes?"

"But you didn't want to say. Something in your gut told you not to."

"Right." He looked at her, eyebrows hiked.

"Like the psychological blind over Split Rock and Bingham's find. Where did we feel this most? Briones?"

"Uh, no. Berkeley. That chocolate drop hill. Remember, the air kind of shimmered?"

"Double Swirly Hill, that guy called it. The skinny guy you said looked familiar. With the thing on his head. That was July. Let's go back and look again."

They parked their scooters on Grizzly Peak and walked the fire trails in. They could see it through the trees half an hour before they got there, but but when they panted up to the crest, scribbled with two stone spirals put there by who knew who, they saw that it had grown big and vivid. It wongered pointillistically over the arroyo. A dozen people, young and old, stood looking at it.

"Wow," Lily breathed. "There it is."

"The rainbow cloud. Same as in Ollanta."

"But bigger. And brighter."

"High luminosity. Many joules?"

"Looks like jewels."

Off to their left they heard a young man's voice raised. "There they are! They came!"

A young woman: "It IS them! For real!" The scattered watchers, off to the west, coalesced into a group, coming their way, led by a brightly dressed girl with a gypsy head scarf holding a cell phone before her at arm's length.

Lily and Ephraim poised, wary, as the people stopped barely three feet off, some craning over the girl's shoulder at the cell phone, then at the objects of their interest, heads bobbing. Others winged out to the right, forming a composition reminding Ephraim of some Renaissance masterwork.

The girl turned her iPhone toward them. "See?" she declared, "It's you!" Ephraim and Lily peered at the screen displaying a photo of the two of them descending the steps from Split Rock. A thirty-something man in loose cotton clothing, quiet, sharp-eyed, stepped forward.

"You were in South America, right? With the original Peacock? You are the Corps? First in the fight?"

"Peacock?" asked Lily. "Fight?" The man indicated the prismatic cloud with his head.

"That. And all of this." He swung an arm over the hills. "Against that." He nodded at the city sprawl below.

"You see, we've been waiting for you. The stupid head rag man said you would come. He sent us the pix. You and the beardy dude and the woman with the glasses. He wouldn't tell us who you were, just that you were the Corps and the protectors of the Peacock. And to wait for you."

"'Stupid head rag man?'"

"Sure, you know him don't you?" This from a kid with hair cut high and tight, and a slide rule slung from his belt like an old school engineer. "Wears stuff on his head. Sometimes shirts. Kind of talks sort of literary? Says he knew you in the Andes."

Ephraim and Lily looked at one another. "This is all about that cloud? ventured Lily."

"No," an intense young man, also holding a cell with the photograph, "this is about the war to save the planet. The Pachamama upsurge. The Presence. We," he looked around at the others, "most of us, are deep ecologists. We have XR up here, ELF, Green Peacers, Sea Shepherds — this lady was an Earth Firster." A woman with white hair pulled back and tied off nodded.

"And a Hardesty Avenger," she grinned through clenched teeth.

"I'm a nothing," said a brown haired girl in a calico blouse, "I'm here for the Peacock."

"I'm a nothing too," said a long haired boy, "I'm here for her."

"You are? Why didn't you say?"

"Scared is all."

"Fuck that. This place makes always me hot. Let's go over there somewhere."

"Whoa," said the boy, "but first, let's see about these two."

Someone in the back murmured sotto voice, "Don't ask their names. We're not supposed to ask their names."

"What," asked Lily, "do you expect from us?"

"Nothing," the first man said, the sharp-eyed one. "Just be here sometimes. Something is going to happen and we don't know what it is. Apparently you don't either."

"But you're here," the girl with the cell phone said. "You came."

Lily and Ephraim walked away alone, a little stunned. Later, they called Bingham and Noe to let them know about this development.

The next weekend, after consideration, all three got up early and came back to the hill. There were already people there, an even larger crowd. The boy and the girl had somehow become, very informally, leaders.

"We are all nothings now," she said.

"Yes," a very tall, very thin man with straight hair to his waist and a full length duster said, "we are nothing."

Nick Signs Off

"This is my last post. My handlers here, the NTT, are not my friends. And if the wind blows my way, I will slip from under them into the Twist and there I will stay until this war goes away."

Nick faces the camera. A small window above shows a dim gray. It is morning or evening. The light seems more north.

He is shaven clean. To his left, your right, is a cot and leaning against it, a full backpack, the old, external frame kind. On the cot are hiking and camping clothes. In his lean face is an expression light and relieved.

Snuggled up to his shoulder is something dull black, furry, with one blue eye and one green. He says:

“This has always been about the Presence, one of the countless names of that being who whispers to us in our fear and hunger and to whom we call throughout the ages for strength and wisdom and money and luck and life and love. Who is sometimes known as The Infinite, but who, really, is measurable and visible by instrument and is only a slender thread in the weave of whatever whatever this is is.

"Within it, there will be war and adversity and intentional infliction of discomfort, but in our story there will be no villain among men because here we are all just looking for love, in whatever contortuplicated and evaginated manner that meanders into our bewildered minds.

“Here the villain is certainty, because in certainty nothing moves. In certainty, everything has already happened, is frozen in its completeness, a hologram, a four-dimensional painting, except that a painting requires a mind to view it and a mind must be in motion and in certainty nothing moves. There mind is a sketch on a napkin.

“It is Uncertainty that sets time free.

"Beautiful time, the wind in the leaves, the surf on the sand, your will in the world.

"Uncertainty, the dark secret of science, the switchblade of the bad boy Werner Heisenberg who whupped kindly old Uncle Albert Einstein in every game of rock paper scissors, whose god does play craps with existence. Uncertainty that coils at the pit of every lullaby science sings to us.

"Uncertainty says that the universe is *weird*, wherever you turn. Did your physics teacher tell you that when you look at something, you change it? This is at the center of everything. The observer affects the observed. This is not physical effect, an observing photon dislodging an observed quark. This is intrinsic. It *just is*. Peering into the world will change the world. Thinking on the future will change the future. Observing the present — well, the present is timeless so cannot change. Do not look too closely at that."

The cat shifts, looks up at Nick's chin, then straight at the camera with a knowing eye.

“The advantage Certainty has in the world is Inertia. It has already happened.

“The advantage of the Question is momentum. With enough she can roll over anything. Her secret weapon is Uncertainty, that slippage in the universe that says everything is to some degree up for grabs.

“I have been an advocate of the first. Certainty is for science, for discovery, for 'progress.' It presupposes my personal existence, and yours, and of this town. And because messing around with what has already happened is unpredictable if not impossible.

“Now I have switched sides. I go for The Question, Pachamama. She is a pacifist, her primary weapon is Instant Karma. Whatever you would do unto another, happens unto you. Violence becomes highly impractical. You will hear more about that. Bullies of the world, your time has gone. I like that.

"But more deeply, because in Pachamama’s world, uncertainty gives us something certainty does not.

“Free will.

“Yes, with her, perhaps one tenth of one percent of the choices we make, or hey, maybe fifteen percent, let’s kick out the jambs, is really our choice. Can change the way things go.

"In the universe of certainty, that Möbius sphere where all times exist at once and destiny is real, the outcome on every level of every event has been determined since the first zeptosecond of the Big Bang. Since the Word. The dominoes fall. Of course there is the sensation of free will, the psychological requirement to make decisions, but it is illusion. The arrow of time is a trick of the mind. And the mind is a trick of the arrow of time.

“Yes? No? Yes. In certainty, nothing moves.

“With uncertainty comes being free.

“What kind of universe do you want? Don’t answer yet. Think. Because an enemy of freedom is security, so to which bank will you trust your retirement?

“So I go. I am the dog you do not have in this fight.

"If we lose, nothing changes. If we win, the world may be Inka. And that may be good, because with the Inka comes green energy and instant justice. Maybe. But maybe we go away.

“But we don’t know that, because the Presence tells me something else. In every timeline, *What Is* has an inertia of its own. Entities incline to persist, states tend to stasis. A few steps away from the point of change all is samey-same. Why not me, why not you? Am I not an entity?

"I bet the Inka State of Not California would like you. As you are. Living free in uncertainty. You might like it.

His eyes drop to the inky animal cupped in his arm. She has grown. She seems almost well groomed. "Kwee. What will I do with you?" He shrugs, spoons the cat from him, she slides down like mercury.

“Well. Ciao, individuals.”

Nick smiles. It is a young smile. You move the cursor onto the pause sign before YouTube can shuffle you onto whatever they have chosen to be the next video. Probably something to do with Hitler. You have always done this and you will always do this, it is written. Unless…

Kwee

"There's nothing I can do. You are on your own. You found me, you'll find someone else." Nick looks Kwee in her one blue eye. Kwee looks back.

He has left gallons of water, eighteen kilos of dry cat food in various containers.

He shrugs into his pack, opens the basement door. Rain falls hard onto the lightning-struck madrone. "Good. They won't be watching me now."

The doorbell rings above. He readies to run, then stops. "They don't ring." He waits. It rings again, and again. He unlocks the hall door, climbs the stairs, peers through the rain-washed side window. A woman. He opens.

She steps into his hallway, sidling past him, pulling off her red sou'wester. She has stringy blond hair and no makeup.

"I hear you have my cat."

"Your cat?"

"Yes, a neighbor says he saw it on your YouTube thing. Several times. He has one green eye?"

"She has. One green eye."

"Oh! There he is! Schrodinger! Schrodie my love!" Kwee sits staring at her for a moment, then opens her mouth wide. After a few seconds, she emits her kwee, and crosses the carpet to the woman, who scoops her up.

"Schroodie-poodie! Oh! You are so BIG now! A BIG kitty!"

Nick would swear the cat rolled her eyes at him. But she stays in the stranger's arms, and begins to purr."

"She never purred for me," he carps under his breath.

"He is a she? I'm sorry, I am Jenny. Jenny Williams. I have been in Switzerland for an operation. My aunt volunteered to take care of him...he is a she? Oh goodie. But she ran away. Wait. What are you doing with her?"

"She came. She wouldn't go away."

"She did? She was fine where she was." There is accusation there.

"But you left her. I kept her. And I'm allergic."

She melts a little. "Oh god, you are right. I'm such a bitch. You probably saved her life. Thank you. Oooh Schroodie, I missed you! You sweet girl!"

A few more niceties and she departs, cat tucked under her slicker.

Nick stares out into the rain in his own storm gear, pack on his back.

"Ingrate cat," he says, and shuts the door.

Nark

Nothing surrounded Elmer Thomas in the dim light of the teepee hidden in a live oak grove in the gulch below Stonewall trail above Berkeley, California, in the shadow of Double Swirly hill. Young and old, man and woman, they eyed him. One of them spoke, thumbs in her belt. "What do you call the kid of your sister?"

"Niece."

"Well, I know yours. She's one badass vahini. And she says her mom says you must be a nark."

"Her name?"

"Mona."

"Ramona. Yes. No, I'm not a nark. I'm a bureaucrat. What are you? An outlaw? I'm here to infiltrate your affinity group, so I need to know."

She laughed. "No man, I'm nothing. We're all fracking nothing. Her dad told me you are a sleeping dragon and not to fuck with you."

"Chaz? The boy of the Black Panther couple?"

"Yeah right. Don't call him 'boy,' boy. He says you started out rebelling against mommy and daddy, then against the whole hippy-dippy thing, then against the educational system — didn't bother to pick up your PhD — then got shunted from one government job to another, always ten minutes from getting fired, and they put you in a basement somewhere counting toothpicks. And now you're here."

"Wait," said a guy with a beard. "He's federal?"

"NTT," answered Elmer. "Here to see if you kids know what you're doing. If you do, then what it is."

"Wait," objected the guy with the beard, "you *are* a nark?"

"No," spake Ramona's friend, "he's Zarathustra Free Man. Call him Zardo. Ramona says her mom says he doesn't lie, he doesn't cheat, he doesn't do anything. She says he prob'ly did more to bring down the US Government just by doing nothing from the inside than the whole Youth Revolution did from the outside bombing banks and smoking LSD."

"You don't smoke..." interjected a nothing. "Oh."

"So," beard guy said, "who wants to be boss of this?"

"Me." The sharp-eyed thin man stood. "He's in."

"We just turned away maybe ten guys who've been fighting the good fight all their lives, and we take in some old fart who says *out loud* that he's here to rat on us to our main oppressor?"

"Well duh."

Beard guy grins, bumps fist with sharp-eyed nothing. "Props, Angus my man. Nothing, welcome to nothing.

Either Everything is Funny or Nothing Is

Katari called Lily.

“You talked to Noe about a prismatic vapor?”

“They call it the Peacock, but yes. Why?”

“I ‘flipped,’ as you call it, over to Tuya in Pachamamatambo. They had a horrible attack in her village. Fanatics of the Thunder God Ilyapa used a terrible thing, some airborne black slime, on the people there. Twelve died. I know of the legend from the Inka side, it is called the Black Rainbow. Zoe says that it sounds like a prokaryote biofilm, used as a mass murder weapon."

"Should we watch out for it up here?"

"Yes. It may be in government hands. But this is the point: your fog appears to be the antidote to the Black Rainbow infection. There's one in Ollanta. Arrowsmith knows it. The full bloods here call it Kuychi Puyu, the rainbow cloud. It covered Tuya and her child and of those exposed, only they survived. So harness that if you can." Katari's eyes were intense on screen.

Lily shook her head.

"So far no one has come close to it. It hovers over a deep valley far from either side. We are thinking about getting a parasail or hang glider or ultralight aircraft up here. But not very hard. Still, Ephraim did it once, and if he did it, anyone can."

"Don't be flippant. This is serious."

"Professor, either everything is funny or nothing is. And something had better be."

"I'm not sure about the logic of that. If I ever get a sense of humor I'll try it out."

"I'll FedEx you one of mine. Okay, so we have a bad rainbow and a good mist. I'll pass it on. How you doing?"

"Losing a war, so far. The dig's going well. Did you watch *We Live In You*?"

"Adios Mister Nieman. Not much of a swan song. I don't know whether I'll miss him or not."

"There was always information in there somewhere. Now there's not." They looked at each other's faces on screen. Katari thought, in Quechua, 'She's ok, for a viracocha.' Viracocha was more or less synonymous with gringo. "One more thing. When Tuya got rainbowed, she said for a moment there, she didn't know what Pacha she was in. It seemed like multiple."

A Shadow Falls

Something was happening to all three of the Core now in California. The final paperwork on Bingham's professorship was delayed, and his colleagues seemed to avoid him. He felt whispered-about. Lily was dismissed from her position at Happy Heart Acupuncture. The owner was coldly apologetic but would not explain. "You are no longer needed. That is all." Ephraim's hours were reduced at the Hearst Museum and his acceptance to UC Berkeley was "under review."

"It's the goddamn NTT," Bingham speculated. "Too much coincidence, too little explanation. Them, or some other agency."

"There are twenty acupuncture places in the East Bay and I can't get hired at any of them."

"Yes. They have turned people against me too. No one will talk to me about it."

They received occasional encrypted messages from Noe Zoe Kroeber, who was said to have returned to the US but to have gone to ground. In fact she had remained in Peru. Bingham would sometimes, late at night, receive a phone call; they would talk for hours, never broaching their work together in Peru. She was suspended from her position at UC Berkeley for absenteeism.

Lily called Katari Kuntur, but although Katari was friendly, the conversation didn't take wing and trailed off. That was okay with Lily; there wasn't that much in common anymore. Until something new happened with the Peacock.

CHAPTER FORTY-ONE then

Balsa Launch

Ramram, now decked out in the long crimson, indigo, and black robe of the haughty Hatun Umu Antarqui, sporting the annealed copper and silver mask and crescent moon headdress, oversaw the initiation of the first balsa raft of what Tupaq intended to become five hundred. There was incense and chanting and stately line-dancing and the sacrifice of camelids, and then there would be drinking and wrestling and laughing and dancing and the sacrifice of modesty.

Behind, the glowing white harbor town of Tumbez, formerly an outpost of Chimor, now under an uneasy agreement to be Inka as long as it took to build and launch the fleet. Queen Capullana, regional ruler, sighed. If all went well, and their mentors to the south didn't come up in arms, they would be allowed to be Chimu again. For a while. Along the clean white beach were the fresh skeletons of many more craft, rapidly fleshing out.

When the ceremony was over an old fisherman sidled up to Ramram. "So, Q'urpa," he said in Chimu, keeping it simple, "you are all going out into the Beyond, like the legend of Viracocha?"

"And a little farther, Naymlap. And then we come back. I hope you are here and alive when we do."

"O Great Wizard so do I. We got back alive last time. Barely. You wouldn't have without me, I think."

"Nor you without me. Look, old friend, when the Inka come for real, keep your head down. You'll do fine."

"I'm already doing fine. But yes, O Great Lump. I hear you. Didn't you used to have more fingers?"

Pushed through the surf to the open sea, two long, deep red and yellow wedges of sail unfurling, the balsa bobbed on a wave, and turned to the horizon.

A towering black hump of water billowed under Ramram's balsa as he clung to the ichu-grass ropes holding the fat logs together. Wind screamed and pounded. The raft slid sideways down the briny spume, throwing men toward the merciless dark sea as they groped desperately for any kind of grip. The twin masts, crossed and roped at the top, were crawling with men grasping them and men grasping the men grasping them. The cabin at the rear center was empty of human life but for the armed guards protecting the critical supplies within, water, rations, spare rope and sailcloth, and the few who had managed to crawl over the sprawling, tooth-clenched soldiers to take shelter within.

The captain was aloft, knees and elbow wrapped around the juncture of the masts, maddened with fear and fierce exaltation, one arm brandished like a demented snake at the gods of weather and wave. The rain came so hard that Ramram had to keep his face down not to drown in the driven gouts alone. Still, he saw two men, men he knew like brothers from their months together on this flat insult to natural law, dragged away by the suck of the sea, gone. And yet.

And yet, so buoyant were the balsas, component logs moving freely in their ropes, water running free between them, that at the black squall's end, eight hundred and six of the original nine hundred and four craft, were still afloat. And of the twenty thousand men who had cast off, more than eighteen thousand were still aboard. Thirst, hunger, storm, disease, ice, suicide, and hostile natives notwithstanding.

One raft over, in a mellow beam of post-gale sun, Ramram saw Tupaq Inka Yupanqui standing legs apart, swaying confidently with the sea, arms crossed at his chest, laughing. Near him, cross-legged, Amaru smiled up at him, fingers working as he repaired frayed rope. In the cabin were the prizes, prisoners, and proof they brought back from lands unimagined. The Intip Churin brothers didn't mind giving up their quarters to captives and booty. They had always slept on deck anyway. They were *INKA*.

Landfall

When Tupaq Inka's fleet made landfall at Tumbez, two thousand-man Inka battalions were waiting to arrest Ramram, to the annoyance of the Capullana, queen of the Tumbis. Tumbez had fulfilled its contract, and now here the Inka forces were again, trampling their ground. She sighed. Submission to these yokels was clearly an inevitability. But not yet.

Three young captains, heading the delegation under the eye of the colonel in command, stepped forward with the imperial khipu commanding the arrest of the Umu Antarqui. Tilca, Chalco, and Achachi, school friends of Tupaq, accompanied by Chaski Yuyu, under guard and charged with the identification of his former co-worker Ramram, stood forward to take the Antarqui under arms. Ramram had debarked from the second balsa to land, joining in to haul the hawser to ground the raft, then coming up the beach, slapping sand from his faded unku. The three young officers and the guard moved forward.

Tupaq Yupanqui stepped between them and Ramram, smiling affably but with feet apart and planted firmly. The captain of the guard stepped forward, a grim look in his eye, but Chalco, recognizing his old classmate, prince heir to the empire, stopped him with a raised hand.

"Tupaq. Yaw! I barely recognized you!" The three boys, and for all their military gear they were boys, looked in awe at their prince, who was now anything but a boy. Sun-darkened, rope-muscled, lean, relaxed and assured, he inspected his coevals. "You boys here to welcome me home?" He lifted his regard to the ranks of armed Inkas behind. The three genuflected, made mocha. Achachi, always the gutsiest, came to the fore.

"Your Dad — Apu Sapa Inka — sent us to escort you home."

"He is a little peeved," Tilca chipped in.

"And to apprehend the Antarqui," Achachi concluded.

"The Inka knows none of this was your fault," Chalco said, "The Wizard Antarqui bewitched you."

"Oh?" Tupaq said mildly, "Am I under the control of a rock-collector? Let us move up the beach a little, boys. We need room to unload."

The ranks of crisp, impeccable, Inka veterans, all two thousand, watched eighteen thousand rough-looking, hard-eyed survivors of nine months' inconceivable tribulation crowd onto the shore, some of them hip deep in surf, all land-born military discipline long eroded to nothing. They leveled their gaze upon those who stood between them and their own country, their own solid ground at last. They shifted on their feet and from them came a low, almost inaudible, growl.

From among them in his bleached checkerboard unku, Otoronqo Kuy emerged to stand beside Ramram, who observed these proceedings attentively. Ramram turned to Otoronqo, spoke quietly. Otoronqo nodded, approached Tupaq.

"August *Inkap Sapay Churin*," he said. Tupaq raised the nearest eyebrow. "The Umu Antarqui requests permission to voluntarily remand himself into the custody of the representatives of the Apu Sapa Inka. Lord." Tupaq turned to Ramram, then to the arrayed Imperial forces, then to the delegation.

"One field-rank officer, two guards, no bonds. Your troops will stand down, mine will come ashore. I will meet with Queen Capullana — she is still here and in office?"

"She is," Achachi nodded.

"Arrange that. We will thank her — that includes you and whoever is running this show — and apologize for the intrusion. Get me the appropriate raiment."

"I don't think 'appropriate raiment' exists for who you are, what you've done, where you've been, and what you are about to become. But we'll get you some fancy threads." Achachi, knowing the prince from birth, had run out of formality. "Where the living fuck have you been, Tupaq? You know we all thought you were dead? Until news came of a herd of balsas coming in from the hotlands?"

"There are civilized people over there. A great kingdom called the Mexica. We will have to deal with them. Food and drink for all my men, good stuff and lots of it. Let's go."

Otoronqo Kuy walked beside Ramram, as the one-eyed, eight-fingered Umu Antarqui ambled up to the arresting personnel, not looking very apprehended.

The Inka officers saw strange men under guard by the seafarers, too black to reflect light, others small and golden, yet others tall and pale with hairy faces. Strange articles were carried behind, following Tupaq Inka Yupanqui higher onto dry land.

See To It

"My men walk, I walk." Tupaq Yupanqui cast a contemptuous look at the glittering palanquin carried by blue-clad litter bearers, ported down to meet him from Vilcaswaman. "I'll have to ride in that thing the rest of my life when I'm Sapa Inka. Put Ichu in it." Ichu was a private soldier whose amputated leg had left him fevered. His squad had been carrying him since the coast. "See to it, Colonel Otoronqo Kuy."

The Inka column curled down the transverse ñan from the west, past the standing stone obelisk, the nearly completed usnu pyramid gleaming with gold below. "We take two days here. My father can wait. There will be medical facilities, and we have sick and wounded."

While Tupaq endured the official reception from the gold-plated throne, Amaru inspected his laboratory and Otoronqo conferred with Chaski Yuyu, who had been overseeing their affairs for the past year, now back in Vilcaswaman from his brief assignment to the coast. “Do you have Ramram’s project ready? He is remanded to Qosqo under arms.”

“As he left it, and insofar as I understood his instructions, some improvement.”

“Of course. We will want it forwarded to his wife in Pachamamatambo. Are you free to accompany that delivery, and to explain? She has learned some khipu, so says Ramram, but not enough for delicate work.”

“At your service. In fact, I would enjoy a little walk. Life here is slow.”

“Were you not married? Was that not stimulating enough for you?”

“Lost her. Childbirth. The girl too. Since then, dinner parties and social intrigue.”

“All right. Put your affairs in order, we leave in two sunups. Anything from Qosqo?”

“The Sapa Inka intends the Umu Antarqui’s death upon his return, if rumor holds true.”

“We have a plan for that. Almost half of my plans pan out. We’ll see.”

“Speaking of rumor, did you really find the lands across the Mamaqocha that Ramram’s strangers told him of, and bring back the silver asnaqs?”

“Yes. Time enough for that on the road. Go see Ramram. Without the guards. Here’s a command khipu from Tupaq. I’ll go see to our sick and injured.”

Two days later, thirty thousand Imperial soldiers and returned voyagers marched out in the chill dawn. Chaski Yuyu left them at Izcuchaca, bound for Pachamamatambo.

CHAPTER FORTY-THREE then, then now

Llachaqkuna Kamay

Chill gray dawn over Qachu's hut high on the ridge. The ropy little man stands naked by the rivulet running through his withered field, splashing cold water on his armpits, over his head, making his assassins wince.

They have been hiding in the hills all through the interminable Andean night, wrapped in dark woolen cloaks against the wind. The cloaks and their faces and hands are coated with Hukwa as a shield against *Llachaqkuna Kamay,* the power of Pachamama to turn a hostile act against its actor. Now the three watch from hiding as three others descend in stealth down the grade between the house and the stream, armed with spears and bolos — three stone balls on leather thongs tied in the center — to throw and tangle the arms and legs of their prey. They are masters of silence.

A single morning bird makes its call, three notes in descending tones.

Now Qachu pulls his charcoal gray unku over his head, blinding himself. The Ilyapan monks rush, the bolos whirling through the air, spears lifted on atlatl throwers.

For months the minions of the cult Ilyapa had carried the viscous slime extracted from the brew of Yana Turmanyay to the mountains, blackening on the lower slopes, then higher, and higher again. The spirits that cupped the valley in their protection withered. The bonds of Pachamama's symbioses decayed.

The Rumipuqyus in their village, Qachu in his mountain, countered. Men and women died. So did sons and daughters. It is dangerous to kill the parents and leave the children alive. It is dangerous to kill the children and leave their parents alive. Chukuri, who had declined the fight on Hunchback Hill, caught monks poisoning his maize, objected and was killed by Ilyapa militants. His wife, who had lived with the shame of her husband's cowardice, tried to murder the priest Simi Apaq in the town center and was taken to the district governor, who spared her life but denied her the right to remarry. That was all right. She didn't want a different man. Pachacutiq sent officials to investigate. Their reports were inconclusive.

Then from Pachamama came Llachaqkuna Kamay, the Administration of Justice. Suddenly each malicious act rebounded on the doer. Every kindness brought peace to the perpetrator. It mutated from the mind of the mountains. It came born by the wind and the rain, and it spread like fire in dry grass. The agents of Ilyapa were baffled. The followers of Pachamama were delighted. Those who carried the defoliant plague would find their own flesh rotting. The attacks stopped. The blight didn't. It was self perpetuating.

Tuya wondered what would happen to Ramram's plans to bring the emperor Pachacutiq to his cause. Was that a bad act, or good? What would the Llachaqkuna Kamay judge? Would that turn around to bite him?

Qachu knew something else. Before he deserted the Ilyapa cause, he had prepared an infusion that could, with a little refinement, locally disempower LLachaqkuna Kamay. Were the priests sharp enough to see the potential? He called it *Hukwa*, 'to reverse.'

Pachacutiq was aware. He kept braziers of Hukwa smoking on Qoripata. The Llachaqkuna Kamay effect was so far confined to Pachamamatambo and the Yucay valley. His armies could march on.

The mountain bird — the wife and mother Tuya — is on the three watchers before they can shift their weight. A sling stone murders the leader as he lifts himself on his elbows to better view the death of his apostate enemy. The long sharpened tang of a bronze tupu shawl pin stabs into the base of another's skull, into the ancient lizard brain, terminating his motor functions. A foot comes down hard onto the back of the third man's neck, pinning him as Tuya spins on her heel, right foot swinging rear in a dancer's move, and the pin enters the base of the priest's spine, paralyzing him. Qachu had trained her well. Tuya whistles a bird call to Qachu. The same as had alerted Qachu to the presence of the attackers.

The spears vanish down the gulch, their target gone. The first two assailants drop through a thin weave of ichu grass into a trench lined with cactus, some toxic, and floored with sharp stakes smeared with human feces. A shit spike trap. The last is already dead, a spear through his eye. One uses his comrade's back to push himself out of the spiny pit, and is speared in the throat. The one in the bottom, whimpering in pain, is blinded and sent back down the mountain with passing herders.

When the Ilyapan assailants oiled themselves to deflect Pachamama's spell, they hadn't thought that they themselves would lose the protection of Instant Karma.

It takes Tuya's two wounded another hour to die. Her daughter still hovers between life and death under the care of the Inka's healers.

Still, the withering climbs the hills. Llachaqkuna Kamay has fingers too big to touch at the level men and women act.

A Cat Walks Into a Bar

"Cat goes to eat a mouse, instead he bites himself in the balls. 'Shit,' says the cat, 'Instant Karma. I hope this kibble crap isn't alive."

"What? What are you on about, Junior?"

The son of D.B. Cooper, a low-level data tracking asset of the NTT based in the midwest, tried to explain to his old dude.

"Cats are from another planet. What happened to your Briarpatch bros? In South America? The kids call it Instant Karma. What you do is what you get. It shows up even around here, it gets raw on bullies if they catch Eye Kay. Don't you ever check out YouTube?"

"I've seen those phony videos where some guy tries to jack an MMA fighter. And there's the Lennon song."

"Well, thing is, Dad, it's real. It's in the water or the air, some kind of virus, and it is showing up all over in patches. More and more. I mean, it's part of the general weirdness attack."

"Weirdness attack? Is there more than usual?"

"Dad. We live in Iowa. Don't you look out the window when you drive to the airport? All the funny stuff in the fields where the corn you can't eat used to grow? Some peeps say it's just another meme that Scopes will debunk, but negative, bro, it's happening. And Eye Kay is part of it. Max Angersmith tried to punch Noodie Underwood in the parking lot and instead slammed himself in the face like ten times. He had to go to the school nurse, he was hamburger. And all the time he thought he was whaling on Noodie. And that's just one."

"How did you know about Peru? You know about not listening to my calls, you could get me fired. Worse."

"Father bro, you used my gmail account to email your boss's boss's assistant — Donna — in the Saint Louis office. You were telling her about the Voodoo Rock op, what happened to those guys, then you started to get sexy all over the place, then you sent it, then you deleted your copy." He couldn't look at his father's face. It embarrassed him. "You didn't empty the trash, though. I have a Donna too, at school, I thought, 'why am I texting her, and why did I delete it?' I was halfway through when I realized I was reading your stuff."

"Don't tell your mother, okay?" His father's voice was raspy.

"Dad dude. You told her yourself. You got in from your flight like two weeks ago, she asked why you were held up in Seattle, you told her about Donna. Don't you remember?"

"I did? No. What? How did she take it? Is she back with her mother now? Where is she?"

"At the hairdresser. I guess you don't remember what she told you back. The whole world knows what she is doing with your boss's boss's boss. You two better talk. You're even, don't worry. And the baby is still yours. Jeez. I do believe you Eye Kayed yourself."

"What was that about the cat?"

"I'm going to be a comic. A cat, an Australian, and a televangelist walk into a bar..."

Rain

It was September, the second season of the Sun God Seed multi-crops. The industrial farming entities learned to cohabit with, and profit from, a mild shortage of corn oil and with harvesting and processing the plague of invasive food plants. Marketing was no problem. There was a strong call for what had grown to be sixteen species of edible vegetables now sharing the same fields in rapid growth cycles. For the strawberries, honeydews, butternut squash, and blue corn, people would pay prices well over cost. The seeds had been thoroughly patented by a couple in California under the name Moon Santa. The USDA had found the new crops to be safe and highly nourishing and, in the case of the rare Glass Gem Corn, an effective cure for the common cold. More, although this could not be quantified, these foods made people feel *good*. They were natural euphoriants. And to the wonder of Dixie, kudzu disappeared. Several species of succulent berry found their way down theah and ate the Plant That Ate the South.

Each crop had to be harvested separately, by hand, from the mixed fields. This meant that people had to be paid to do it. Visas were issued to Mexicans, Central Americans, and South Asians. Strangely, the corporations found that middle-class Caucasian-Americans were willing to stoop and pick too, learning from the imported agrarians, for low wages. Some enterprising concerns charged for the privilege of working their fields. The profits, which had driven some smaller companies almost into bankruptcy, began to rise.

So did the mist from the fertile soil and the bounty of growing things. It rose into the humid summer atmosphere, entered the water cycle, and through evapotranspiration made rain, and the rain carried bioaerosol bacteria and archaea, and rendered unto the land what had come to be called, as it emerged around the living sphere of earth, Instant Karma.

Eye Kay in Thumbs Up, Oklahoma

Ygritte Wurmz was the ugliest girl in Thumbs Up, Oklahoma, High School. In fact, wherever she stood, however dense the crowd, she was the most universally shunned.

She was bug-eyed, weak-chinned, pallid, slack-muscled, boney, flat-chested, knock-kneed, fashion-challenged to a Lovecraftian degree. Her knuckles were cracked and knobby, her face blue-veined and mottled. She smelled, even on those rare days in which she washed herself with gritty Lava soap, distinctly off. She dressed in long calico dresses that came to her wrists and buttoned at her throat at white peter-pan collars. She wore heavy leather shoes and plastic butterfly clips in her thin, dry, corn-silk beige hair. Her eyes, transmitting the self-contempt, despair, self-pity, venomous spite, stale-piss-flavored misery, and immeasurable loneliness within, were a dull milky blue. She did not seem to be intelligent. She was clumsy. Her more cultured classmates called her Pig Blood.

Sitting alone in the local Denny's, she spasmodically elbowed over her sticky soft drink, which now spilled across the table, soaking into the thin pages of her red-cover Gideon bible. She was still damp from the sudden rain that had hit just as she crossed to the restaurant.

Rick was a semi-popular boy, temporarily included into the window booth with five members of the ruling clique, known as The Winners. He was walking back from the men's room when he saw the pop spill.

He was going to take a wide berth around the pariah girl when something in him just broke. It took him over. He watched himself push past a janitor with his steel cart, swipe a towel from the push-bar, and beeline for Ygritte. As he approached, in the corner of his eye, he could see the five faces of his momentary friends turn his way. He almost veered off, but the demon in him told him no.

He saw the desolation in her. A contempt came over him, for everything he was, for everyone he knew, an anger. He came to her table, looked down at her averted pale face, gently moved the book and the toppled cup, spread the frayed white terry cloth over the spill and began to mop it up. He smiled, in case she found the guts to look at him.

'I am going to help you,' he silently said, in words he would never have spoken, 'I am going to take your hate, I am going to take your shame, I am going to take your loneliness, I'm going to take it into me. Give it to me. For just now, for just a minute, be free. Feel no pain.'

When the towel was soaked, he took off the sports shirt he wore open over his tee, wetted earlier by the warm rain, and sopped up the last of the drink, wiping off the bible and placing it carefully in front of her. He didn't plan or anticipate any of this, he just did it. Then he sat across from her, folded his hands in front of himself, wet shirt in his lap, and looked at her. He noticed that the tiny flower pattern on her cornflower blue calico dress was quietly beautiful.

Ygritte saw him coming. 'Oh no,' she thought, 'he is going to try to help.' Every now and then, pity or guilt took control of someone and they would try to alleviate her condition. She hated that. She loathed them. 'He doesn't know how stupid it is to even try.' She looked away as he wiped the table. In her peripheral vision, she saw the five popular kids looking their way.

'Poor Rick,' she thought, 'now he is smeared with me.' She thought of the hardness within them, the cruelty that made them The Winners. She felt the hardness, the rancor, in herself, resonate to theirs. An understanding came to her.

‘It is fear,’ she thought for the first time, ‘the hardness is just fear. That’s all it is.’

She knew she was not very smart, but suddenly she could see that. She let her eyes lift a little toward Rick. ‘He is going to sit there,’ she thought, ‘and try to help me. Like my auntie. Like the church lady.’ She despised them both, the few so-called helpers. ‘Poor boy,’ she thought. ‘Poor Rick. How can I get him out of this horrible thing we’re in?’ She didn’t recognize it, but at that instant, the hardness within her dissolved. The fear dissolved, and with it, the misery, the self-hatred, the aloneness.

“It is just fear,” she said to him in her high mousy voice. “That’s all it is. Just fear.” She reached out with her thin left hand and lightly touched his wrist.

The moment Rick decided to try to help, all the blocks of psychological machinery within him fell away. The buried self-contempt, the insidious nausea, the whimpering terror, and he was free. When he sat across from her, he surrendered everything he was to this moment. ‘It’s nothing,’ said the whisper within him, ‘it’s all nothing. They are all nothing. She is everything, right now, she is all there is. I have always wanted to help her. I have always been afraid. I will take it all into me,’ he telegraphed to her, his eyes on her dead-dog gaze, ‘pass it to me. I will take it all in.’

“It is just fear,” he heard her say, “that’s all it is. Just fear.”

“Yes,” he said back. “That’s all it is.”

He saw her eyes clear, the dull film melting away, he could see far into them, into the world of rods and cones, into the now crystal deep blue, into the intelligence, the knowing, that came into them. He opened his hands on the nacreous laminate surface, let them relax. They regarded each other. The tension was gone. He forgot who he was, who he had ever been. He forgot who she was. They were just there. There was no message. Nothing to say. It was over. They were free.

That was Instant Karma. It was in the rain. What they had tried to do to the other, had been done to them. And what each had tried to do to the other was kindness.

The five Winners looked at them. What they saw was just wrong. By intuitive agreement they stood, formed a squad, fixed their eyes on the loser and the traitor, macked arrogantly toward them, aiming close enough to sideswipe the outcast girl.

As they approached, before they could form some deadly comment, something happened in each of them. Their moral rigidity vaporized in a flood of systemic humiliation, in a certainty of their own incurable nastiness, weakness, repulsiveness. Emptiness. They saw that they had always known that no one had ever loved them, no one ever could. Their pathetic delusion that they were admired, cared for, sought, cherished, had been a sickening spectacle to everyone who looked their way.

They were nauseated by the smugness that had hung on their own faces, by the falsity of their laughter, by the garish braggery of their clothing. They were broken by their infinite lameness, by the sewage of their souls. Their mothers, their fathers, their sisters and brothers, had never loved them. They had never been nor had a friend. They loathed each other only less than themselves. They had been ever mocked and despised. They were alone, and deserved to be alone, and that would never change. In sick shame they rushed toward the glass door.

Someone behind the counter said, “Hey, the bill?” The queen bee among them, in terror of being challenged, of having to show who she was, fumbled in her purse, dismissing the credit cards, they would take too long, require eye contact. She found some bills. She pushed them onto the counter by the register, were they enough? She added her iPhone to the pile and ignoring the voices broke out onto the street.

None of them had anywhere to go. Home? To what? To whom? To that outhouse of the ego they called their room? Each wanted only to be unseen. Each searched frantically for someplace they could go where no one else would see them. The place by the river where drivers threw their garbage? The shut-down granary? The junk-scattered empty lot by the crop duster airport? Under the overpass?

They had come to make someone feel ugly and it had recoiled onto them. Instant Karma.

The rain brought it to Thumbs Up. It was delivered to other places in other ways. Each person touched by it would be done to as they intended to do.

Tricking Instant Karma

The NTT Situation Room, somewhere in Virginia

The general sat impassively in the back, watching his exec, the director, at the podium push his thick black spectacles back up his nose, clear his throat, begin.

"Instant Karma is the most fundamental assault on social organization in all of human history. It makes all disciplinary agencies ineffective, obsolete, and functionally suicidal.

“They’re calling it Instant Karma because whatever you try to do to anybody, it does to you.”

The attendees sat around the long table surfaced in black glass, funding recently enhanced, mirrored sunglasses in their sports coat pockets, eyes grazing over the national and global maps on the screen behind the director as he spoke. The maps were vivisected into colors indicating levels of concentration.

“It showed up first in Peru, the Briarpatch Voodoo Rock incident. You all know what happened there. They got off easy. There were other episodes. You may have heard the rumors. A federal agency we will leave unnamed sent two close combat personnel to remove members of the bio-terrorists that call themselves the Core, in California. They put each other into intensive care. One lost a tongue, the other a kidney, through their own acts.

"The heaviest concentrations appear to be in the Cusco region of Peru, and in California’s San Francisco East Bay. Gang warfare in critical districts of Oakland has tapered off. You try to cap someone, you cap yourself.

“Police now have to send scouts into a situation to determine whether they will be able to use force. Seven peace officers nationally have killed themselves with their own service weapons in pursuit of perpetrators. Mostly unarmed, mostly African American or poor or both, no surprise. Black Lives Matter is laughing its ass off.

"There are reports of outbreaks around the globe, mostly subequatorial but creeping north.

"Suicide statistics are unaffected, Instant Karma does not operate reflexively, your intentions toward yourself do not trigger its effects. Stand up comedy has become more gentle, in some instances funny.

“It spreads outward from center points. It hasn’t reached everywhere; the east coast of the US is largely unaffected. It is less present in urban environments, possibly because it is bacterial in nature and it breeds in rural ambients. Chicago and Detroit are however infected, we suspect that it comes in off the lakes. Projections have it on all continents within eighteen months.

“It is slippery stuff, it has its subtleties, but it hates weapons. Anything so designed will turn against the user. And you can’t trick it. It knows what you are thinking, even if you don’t. It knows your intent. It is you.

“Various work-arounds tried to send agents unaware of the intent to target persons in hope of striking before the Eye Kay becomes aware. Total fail. Eye Kay traces the intent back to the source.

"Now, motive isn’t everything; we have learned that if your intent is to do good for bad reasons, for instance, to test the parameters and mechanisms of Instant Karma, it lets you do it.

"But apparently you can’t do harm disguised as good. We have tried suicide missions, sending in an agent willing to absorb the consequences of their hostile act, provided they can do damage to their target. Fail. It recoils onto the dispatchers as well.

“We are, of course, working on defeating Eye Kay by identifying the offending prokaryote organisms and eliminating them in the breeding grounds, but this effort is in its early stages. Eye Kay does not seem to be a strain, or even a simple combination of strains. It is born of highly complex eusocial microbiological systems, involving symbiosis with other life forms, such as fungi colonies and insect swarms. And it takes many incarnations.

"Besides, Eye Kay sabotages the research efforts. Taking the theory of the global superorganism called The Entity to be valid, it seems that the Entity is dedicating a large part of its resources to manufacturing Eye Kay.

"However. We have an ally within the Entity itself. Our one active sensitive, the video blogger in Washington State, who has since gone dark, gave us one piece of critical information. Using this, our operatives in South America have come across a microbial cocktail called Hukwa that is an effective counteragent against Eye Kay. Stops it dead. This is a local solution but that is all we really need for this mission complex. USAMRIID has transported it north and is enhancing its application.

"The primary mission is now under the aegis of this task force, the NTT. We will pass our findings and product output on to you here in the Intelligence Advanced Research Projects Activity and associated groups.

"We have the antidote and the cure. Currently it will protect our agents. Before long, applied as aerosol, liquid, and an airborne biocide, it will eliminate the threat at its source.

"Ed, thanks for coming tonight as rep for the DCS. When we fully weaponize against this threat to our national security, you will be first to receive and deploy all armaments.”

As the meeting broke up, the DCS invitee approached the director. “What happened to that expendible you sent on the suicide mission to the west coast? Referred to in the footnotes?”

“D.B. Cooper? The remote-detonation nerve gas bulb he was unknowingly carrying turned out to be the training dummy. He got along fine with the local archaeologist. The live one was left in his controller's car, where it went off spontaneously. The controller is in a paralytic coma in Walter Reed. Scratch that ploy. *Aller angfang ist schwer*, Ed, All beginning is hard."

Cockblocker Comes to Double Swirly Hill

Instant Karma came to Double Swirly Hill in a dry wind. Sharp-eyed Angus saw that nothing girl was having problems with nothing boy, so he told her, "No worries, he feels just the same for you. You can have all of him you want," and he got a full-body frisson of good feeling, much stronger than he should have, as if he just realized he had completed a dreaded project without even noticing.

Nothing girl snapped back, "What do you know about it, man-'splainer, you think you know me?" and he saw her face stricken with shame and dismay, 'just what she wants me to feel,' he intuited, and he told her, "Quick, say something nice to me, something true." Like someone with a bad burn who knew she needed help fast, she said, "You are beautiful, you are the real leader," and her face and shoulders filled with relief, and she smiled. "It's Eye Kay," she said, "It's here! Thank you."

"You are right," Angus said back, "that's why we look to you and nothing boy. You are in tune. Let's tell the others. Test it out, for it's limits."

That night four armed Berkeley Police came up the hill to harass the nothings, to make sure there were no fires and to push them around until one of them sassed back so they could take him in. When they got back down the hill, they found they had put cuffs on two of their own, who were somehow convinced the shackles were on the other two.

"Well, now we know it's real," said the lieutenant, "We can tell the feds their memoranda are confirmed. Cockblocker is real, and it's here. Everything new comes to Berkeley first."

"So what do we do about our sweep plan? To take them all in before they can launch their hang gliders into the weird cloud?"

"We'll have a bunch of meetings and waste taxpayer money and if it's what I just said we go to the feds for ideas. Meanwhile, send a probe up to see where it starts and ends and how strong it is."

"You mean they are going to get away with it? That anti-American conspiring?"

"Maybe. Maybe not. If their motives are as passive-aggressive as they look from here that hill might clear off by sundown."

"Dang, El Tee, here comes one now, crying like a baby."

"Uh, no," said a sergeant of detectives from the periphery, "He's my C.I.. I have eyes up there. Had."

Everybody had to figure it out. The people with motives too mixed did pack up their sleeping bags and trail disconsolately off the hill. The Peace Officers methodically worked out protocols for assessing their own intents - it was a university-educated police department - and gingerly put their toes into the murky waters around what they used to call Fuckhead Hill. They found that the circle of no-no was a little bigger each day.

On the hill it was the same, except for an elation in realizing that their fear of the cops was gone.

"They can't hurt us," said beardy guy, "they can't come up here at all without they bring candy and flowers. And," he looked at E.T. Thomas, "you are still here. Angus was right. You are our kind of nark."

"I just report it like it is," E.T. smiled, "and it is fine by me."

News got back to the NTT right away. "Good," said the General. "Let them let their guard down. We got black rainbow glorp now, and we're working on aerosol and particulate for air drops."

CHAPTER FORTY- then

Pachacutiq Despises the Proof

Thirty-six outlanders captured on Tupaq's sea voyage crouched on the terrace of Pachacutiq Inka's Qosqo kancha, dressed in crisp Inka unkus. Their demeanors ranged from sullen insolence through proud defiance, fearful submission, curious wonder, to calm acceptance. Their skin colors ranged from blue-black through nut brown, olive, pasty beige, to pale yellow.

Old Urcu Waranka, the docent of the Imperial Museum atop the gigantic Inti Wasi center on the hill above the capitol, still under construction, oversaw the artifacts Princes Tupaq Yupanqui and Amaru had brought back with their captives from the sea voyage to Avachumbi island. Among them were a brass throne, the skeleton of a horse, matchlock muskets, steel swords and armor, a dugout canoe, a scale model of an Italian galleon, strange clothing. Other outlandish objects.

The two princes stood at the massive gate to their father's compound, awaiting a response to their request for audience. "We have brought you proof," they had sent him to know. "The threat is real. They have weapons, trained beasts, floating fortresses, and knowledge dangerous to us, and they will come."

Their messenger returned from within, bowing. "The Sapa Inka replies that he thought of these things when they were new. If his interest returns to these trinkets he may inform you."

Amaru nodded. "All he hears is 'Ramram was right.' The Ilyapa priests have our mighty progenitor bemused."

"He will call for Ramram," Tupaq judged, "probably to order his death. When the Wizard Antarqui is dead, he may listen to us."

His brother nodded again. "If we could be sure of that, Ramram would die in peace."

In the wide Wakaypata plaza below, hundreds of women, noble and servant, gathered, as always, to gaze yearningly at Amaru.

The Corpse of a Hairless Dog

"Every man who comes before me, comes alone."

Apu Sapa Inka Pachacutiq Yupanqui sat in the depth of his long reception hall, fists on his knees, wearing a painted mask depicting a happy man, eyes crescents of mirth. Hunkered before him in gold and scarlet was his interlocutor, who would pass his august utterances on to the petitioners. A brilliant burst of feathers radiated behind him as if they were the rays of his magnificence. The walls were lined with courtiers and Inka elite glistening in their finery, each bearing a symbolic burden on their backs to signal their submission, but in fact competing with each other for extravagance and originality. Before Ramram and his guards was a long line of solicitors. Behind, many more.

The weight on Ramram's back was not token, it was the corpse of a hairless dog. Everyone tried to make distance between him and themselves, even though the carcass didn't stink much yet. The line moved slowly. At the lift of an imperial knuckle an advisor would step to the Sapa Inka's left ear with counsel as to the case before him. Somehow informed, two beautiful women came from behind a curtain to place a golden bowl under the unku, woven of thousands of hummingbird feathers from months of exquisite labor, to be worn once and ceremonially burned. When invisibly signaled, the Ñustas removed the receptacle, and glided away, actually sniffing it as if delighted connoisseurs. Two more women came with a silver container of water to cleanse the majestic fundament.

There was a rustling at the door far behind. Heads turned, mouths and eyes annoyed, then swiftly went blank. Tupaq Yupanqui and Amaru Yupanqui came up behind Ramram and placed themselves at his sides, left and right. A yanacona servant rushed to Pachacutiq, lifted his laughing mask so that he could squint at the disturbance. The mask came down, the servant vanished, the woman took their flashing dish and left, the line in front of Ramram parted, bowing.

The pair of Princes, Ramram, and his guards, moved forward with a minimum of decorum. One of the guards trembled like a sick dog. The other guard, weathered and scarred, set his face for death.

The interlocutor lifted his cheek to catch the emperor's words, but Pachacutiq lifted his mask, leaned forward, right forearm on one knee, left fist on the other. His eyes were black as oil, glittery as volcanic glass. He spake not.

Amaru and Tupaq made mocha. Ramram knelt, forehead down. The scents of hukwa and hampi stung their nostrils.

"Father," Tupaq said, being the heir, "we bring our friend Antarqui before you to hear his fate. We would not have him face that alone."

"Then you are ready to die?"

"At your slightest whim, O Son of the Sun."

Trained since birth in revealing no emotion, the Inka visored the mask over his face and just as swiftly lifted it again. "Whimsy is not in me. And every man who comes before me, comes alone. Ramram, once Umu Antarqui, hear your death."

Ramram pushed himself to his feet and straightened, head still bowed. A gasp passed through the room and everyone but the two princes took two steps back.

Pachacutiq's eyes widened microscopically. "Look at me then." Ramram lifted his head and his eyes.

"It is known that your magic worked to save the Tawantinsuyu. For this you will die intact and beautifully. Once you escaped death-by-flying by keeping your feet on the mountain. This time if you escape death-by-flying, it will be by flying. On the day of Qapaq Raymi, from the Tunupa watchtower in Pachamamatambo, at the height of the Sun. Whom you have affronted. Under my eye."

The princes made mocha. Ramram made mocha. They backed away down the aisle. The interlocutor leaned into a whisper, signaled a befeathered captain. A squad of golden soldiers came for the trembling guard, who was dragged whimpering from the great chamber. A soldier does not show fear before the Sapa Inka. The other guard was later promoted to Awka Pachaka Curaca, captain of one hundred soldiers.

"You heard that?" Tupaq laughed, once outside in the entrance plaza, "If you can fly, you are saved. Our dad does not often make a mistake like that."

"Our father," corrected Amaru, "does not make a mistake. Like that. You had better fly, wizard."

As they walked toward the outer gate, the condemned guard, suddenly calm, thought he heard Prince Tupaq say, "But he can fly, can't he, brother? You always said that he can!"

"No, that was you."

They Do Not Know Me

Pachacutiq sat on his jaguar-form iron-wood tiyana, inlaid with rosy mullu shell and turquoise, its eyes emeralds in gold. Around him, qeros of hukwa and hampi, gold and silver, to shield him from Llachaqkuna Kamay and enhance his sexuality.

His armies already oversaw the placement of administrators and mitmac population imports far to the south beyond Titicaca Qocha, north along the spine of the Andes, to the eastern rainforests. Humiliated elites of newly annexed kingdoms were trailing the two thousand kilometers to Qosqo where they would be educated in Inka language and Inka ways, and domiciled, along with their gods, to assure compliance. Wounds were healing, soldiers sent home at the end of their tours while replacements marched north to garrison duty or the next campaign.

Across the land, his policies, innovative, and conceived in genius, methodically constructed, were implemented and becoming reality as if they had always been. The most beautiful women in his world, some newly imported from among the statuesque, pale, Chachapoyas, awaited him in scented chambers. Misk'i sat cross-legged in a niche behind him, fulminating in delicious intensity.

What was wrong with him? For the first time, his will turned to mud. As never before, his mind drifted. At last, his eyrie of solitude had mutated into loneliness.

"I am not a miserable old man," he muttered to himself, "I am strong, my will has never faltered, I have outdone my ambitions in a world owned by a cinder-hearted father who hated me, and where I was marked for death by those Chanka bastards. I imagined a land of gods and made it so. One glance at the mightiest priest, general, warrior, the most devious woman, and they piss themselves. If they dare, they look into my eyes and they do not know me.

"They do not know me."

In his mind's eye he took a long shit on a bleak hill in a filthy tunic on the eve of his inevitable death and through the brambles came a thin boy who looked him in the eye and knew him.

His head lifted.

He took a deep breath. Tendrils of smoke came in.

A wall in his mind slammed down and killed that vision.

Everywhere Girl

Small among the tall Chachapoyas concubines Misk'i sat cross legged, smiling like a cat. She was never more than a few paces from His Presence. Her eyes said he was the tower of manhood. Her voice that she was his bed of jaguar fur. Yet every moment with her, every image passing through his mind, every memory of her voice or scent, weakened him. To not see her would be to go blind. To not touch her, to be dead. So he willed himself not to think of her. And still she was everywhere.

"Do you hate me still?" he asked.

"Yes."

"Good."

"No."

"No, you do not hate me?"

"No, it is not good. You cannot hide from me there."

CHAPTER FORTY-FOUR now

Zzyzx, California

In the cool Mojave Desert dawn, Jane and Richard Book, amateur entomologists hiking south of Zzyzx, California in hope of spotting Desert Spider Beetles (*Cysteodemus armatus*), noticed that just over Crucero road the ground seemed to be moving. On closer inspection, it was ants. Billions of them, moving east further into the desert.

The couple approached cautiously until they observed that the flood of insects ignored them, passing around their oiled desert boots like a river around a rock. They called a contact at the Mojave National Preserve in Kelso, who in turn woke up a retired myrmecologist living in a double-wide next to the old Bagdad Cafe in Newberry Springs.

Jane was first to notice that the ants were leaving a sticky residue on the ground and sage growth. They began collecting samples.

Late morning, the myrmecologist, Ambrose, who had been murmuring to himself since arrival, verified that this was a mass migration of Argentine Fire Ants, considered to be the world's largest single superorganism. "The astounding thing here is that we have both the Very Large Colony and Lake Hodges Colony together. Now, they don't fight each other, but neither do they collaborate. Except now. And this gunk on the ground? It's a biofilm. I'll bet my boots that these little devils are transporting bacteria, maybe an offshoot of *Myxococcus xanthus*, and they're generating some kind of synergy. See the oil slick color swirls? This ain't normal. I'm going to put a call in to UCLA."

They were all taking tea at Ambrose's' place near sundown when the laboratory trailer from UC pulled up. They climbed in and guided the driver to the optimum access vantage. They didn't have to point out the phenomenon. From Exit 230 on US 15 they could see that the desert was a teeming sea of purple and green bioluminescence, undulating toward the Colorado River. The multidisciplinary UC team, in biohazard suits, went down into the mass to take samples and record the phenomenon, as Jane, Richard, and Ambrose watched from the road. The coruscating bioluminescence below the suffusion of the desert sunset made for a deep and haunting beauty. It was the twelfth of December.

The ant migration turned out to be laying a self-organizing stigmergic biofilm which was followed by a rapidly expanding algae bed that formed strangely complex patterns. All together, the combination was eating plastic trash and petroleum film, cleaning the desert. When a video recording was played, there was heard a deep hum, resonating somewhere between Mongolian throat singing and the didgeridoo. Filtered, there was vibration at 136.1 hertz, B-sharp.

A similar algae-bearing bacterial biofilm appeared overnight in the vicinity of Chernobyl, Kiev Oblast, Ukraine, metabolizing radiation, cleaning the Exclusion Zone. It too glowed in the dark.

Cheorwon, Republic of Korea, December sixteen. Civilians began to gather on the south side of the Demilitarized Zone between the Koreas. At first it was largely young adults, then businessmen and housewives, then whole families. They were mostly silent, holding hands, encroaching inside the Civilian Control Line, spooking the MPs. South Korean and American military units were mobilized, but formed a skirmish line too permeable to stop the forward-inching, ever growing, flash crowd. Satellite surveillance showed an equivalent popular movement on the north side, meeting with a more draconian opposition that did not entirely deter.

The DMZ sustained one of the most biodiverse temperate habitats on the planet. Animals, including endangered species, had been approaching the demarcation fences for weeks now, looking out, seeming to recognize and to avoid land mines. Flocks of birds were drawn there in ever-increasing numbers. A Japanese tourist swore he spotted a mastodon, but was so nonplussed that he dropped his Nikon F3 camera.

Nick and Lily

Huddled in a dank dirty dome tent in Olympic National Park, Washington, eating cold canned tuna, the mushy stuff, not the meaty product, in the rain, Nick Niemann had struggled to contact Ephraim Arrowsmith. If he could get through to Qachu across time, then he might, just might, be able to lock onto Ephraim across space. They had a lot in common.

Chilled, unwashed, lonely, hungry, torn cold turkey from the internet, but he was free of the government fuckers. They wouldn't find him here. The Twist would protect him. He hoped. But days of trying impotently to thrust his mind into the ether had failed.

Then, mouth palping fish mush, something thwacked him from behind, as Qachu used to, but nothing like Qachu. This was female. This was pure concentrated Yin, hitting his Yang center right in the gonads.

She, he, they, were on a dry hilltop looking across a town to the sea. There were young people there, milling around an anarchic camp.

"Who are you?" she demanded. He felt the breath of her voice; and the weight of her breasts. "Who are you? I feel you there."

"I am NIck Nieman." He discovered that he could speak with her voice. It dropped an octave.

"Nick Nieman! Ephraim, Eph! I have just flipped Nick Nieman! Nick, where are you?" Apparently she was a whiz at switching control of her voice without changing overall point of view. The lag time was minimal.

"You know who I am?"

"Don't be an idiot. Where are you?"

"Do you know about the Twist?"

"Of course. You said you were going there."

“I have a message for Ephraim. For you both.”

“Wait for Ephraim. He’s coming.”

“Can I see what you look like?” She laughed deep in her chest, a little sardonically, pulled out her cell phone, held it at arm’s length in selfie mode.

“Okay?” she said. “That’s all you get. I mean jesus, you are *in* me for god’s sake.”

“I know. Gawd, Lily, you are the most ravishing gynecoid on the planet.”

“Not quite. And we’re not dealing in sex anymore, Nieman. Most of our superorganisms are gender-neutral. This boy/girl mix we have going is just a little creepy. But it’s not your fault. Here’s Ephraim. We’re swapping out.”

‘So this is the chosen dude,’ thought Nick, seeing a brown-haired boy in blue work shirt and jeans stride across the turf.

“Wait,” he pleaded, “before you go. Where are we here?”

“If you insist, sir. We are on Double Swirly hill, looking down on Berkeley, California.” Her eyes scanned a tawny hilltop popping with chaparral, looked out across a cityscape to a body of metal blue water, a towered city on the horizon. Her gaze swiveled back, overlooking a brush-choked ravine. Hovering over the arroyo was a thick mist, lenticular in form, with waves and points of color rippling through it.

“What’s that psychedelic UFO over there?”

"That's the Peacock. Or the Rainbow Cloud. There is another one in Peru. It has something to do with spacetime."

“That’s what I mean. Okay, give me the Prophet Arrowsmith if you please.” Their eyes turned to the brown-haired boy, who laughed. Lily’s hands went up under Ephraim’s shirt. There was confusion in his eyes and guts, the change came and he was plugged into Ephraim, looking at Lily, smiling. She smiled back. Nick felt the steel wall he held between himself and his loneliness fail for an instant.

Nick looked at Lily through Ephraim's eyes. She was even more lethally affecting than through her own. Seen through Ephraim the world was more textured, richer, than through Lily; hers had been sharper, more defined.

“Berkeley. California. Standing in a shaft of light. Wish I was there,” Nick said, striving for lightness. “What is inside that Peacock thing?”

"We can't get there. It is equidistant between the hills." Ephraim’s voice was light, matter-of-fact, pitched low.

“You’ll find a way,” he replied, surprised to hear his voice still coming from Lily. “Ephraim. I need to tell you one thing. What I learned from the Feds before I absconded.”

“Nick Nieman. Good to finally make contact. You are holed up in the Twist? Wet weather there now. Do you need anything there? Can we rescue you?”

“No, I’ve got people sneaking me supplies. The Twist is my shepherd. Even if there is a little too much nature here for me.”

“Good then. What?”

“You are standing in a place of power. Presence-wise. Probably the most intense on earth. You’re on the Coastal Stigmergy there. It runs all the way down the west side of the Sierra range clear along the coast to the Sonora desert in Mexico, but it's thickest right where you are.”

“Stick Merjie?”

“Stig-mergy with a 'g' or two. Google it." He spelled the word out loud. “It means another level of superorganism. If an organism does work, some task, it leaves traces, and the next one to come along — not necessarily the same species or genus — picks up the traces, and takes over the same work. Maybe takes it to another level. And leaves a trace for the next comers to pick up.

“In combination with the biocybernetic intelligences you’ve already got going there, it is a freakin’ powerhouse. And it is thickest right where you are, north central Cali along the coast. San Francisco East Bay.”

"Okay."

"Now that I see that cloud - it is a prokaryote high differentiation node for shizzle - I understand even more clearly. This dynamo, this power point you are standing on. Use it. You are the key player in all of this, in this era. You have the line in to the Inka time, the Late Horizon."

Ephraim laughed. "Late Horizon. You did do your homework."

"I been to school. Dig it. You can't drop the ball now. Your Inka boy, your posse in Peru, they can't do it by themselves. They need you, and they need you there, on that ground. That's all I got to say. Except."

"Except?"

"The government is scared shitless of you. They have already sent NTT agents to assault and abduct you. They got Eye Kayed and beat them own selfs up. Eye Kay is instant karma. You got that down there? It's going around."

"Eye Kay is here but so are government aircraft spraying, probably, bacteriophages. Okay Nicholas. I'm taking you as real. And not working for them and not catfishing. You talk like you, you feel like you. I am delighted to meet you. You have turned on a lot of people."

"But do you hear me?"

"Sort of. I will try to act on it."

Nick felt the thread pulling apart. Something was interfering.

"We're losing bandwidth," Ephraim said. "I'm going. I hope you can check back later. Stay safe."

"Check," Nick said with Lily's voice, "You too. Those people will kill. They take you seriously now. Okay. Later, gator," and he was gone.

Just as Ephraim was standing up to leave the circle, Nick came back for an instant, stopping Ephraim and snapping Lily's head up.

"...see them. They found the way in. But they're..." Through Nick's eyes they saw rain-blurred figures with rifles, down the fir-furred mountain trail. "...damn...here they come..." As Ephraim strained to hear, Nick's voice broke into stutters and mutters. Then he blinked out. That was the last they heard from Nick Niemann.

Aat Na Rama Presides
Pyongyang, Democratic People's Republic of Korea
Seven Years after the first contact with the 15th Century CE

Pyongyang, Democratic People's Republic of Korea

Aat Na Rama Presides

"Gentlemen and Gentlewomen, welcome. We have chosen this venue for our international summit of heads-of-state or their representatives because it offers insulation from the press.

"I am Aat Na Rama, and I will present the introduction and some select speakers, after which the floor will be open to general discussion. The information upon which this exposition is based comes largely from the United States, with contributions and verification from other nations and scientific institutions.

"There is an entity on this planet that is more aware than human beings by multiples of ten to a hundred. It is older than all plants and animals by several billion years, it is the dominant global life form, and it has probably tailored the evolution of mankind to its own purposes.

"It lives in and on every human being and every animal. It inhabits every landmass and all oceans, and the sky. It can survive in space.

"This entity is not hostile to humanity. It is symbiotic with our species, and to every descript terrestrial life form.

"It has been for time immemorial involved in every aspect of human life, but within the last few months it has manifested a level of activity unprecedented in recorded or surmised history. This has been reported on every continent and ocean including Antarctica.

"This entity consists of a hierarchical network of prokaryotic superorganisms and associated eukaryotic eusocialisms. That is, bacteria and related single-cell organisms designated archaea, and allied plant and animal superorganisms. All plants and animals consist of eukaryotic cells. Our cells have a nucleus. Prokaryotes do not.

"Our knowledge of this superorganism, limited as it is, comes to us very recently. Its existence has been verified for less than six months.

"This entity, that we are provisionally identifying as a holobiome, or macrobiota, appears to be conscious on a level that is and will probably always be, largely inscrutable to human intelligence.

"One of its properties is that time does not exist for it as it does for human and animal consciousness. Events do not follow one another from the past through the present into the future. This is not entirely inconsistent with current physics, or for that matter, with long standing traditions of religion and philosophy.

"Our concern here is with a sudden and disconcerting intervention in human affairs. To wit, a subset of this superorganism intends to rewrite human history beginning in the fifteenth century Current Era with unpredictable but significant effects on all of our nations and peoples.

"It is in the process of achieving this through the collaboration of a few human beings apparently selected for their sensitivity to the presence of the entity and their association with each other.

"These collaborators create a base from which they can, with the aid of the Entity, communicate with humans alive in the fifteenth century to provide them with information about the current era, urging them and abetting them in altering events critical to the status quo of our time.

"If this takes place, we may not be aware that it has. This reality, our reality, will disappear as if it has never existed.

"This nature of event may have occurred in the past, if that word retains meaning. Possibly many times. Possibly never before.

"Why, then, would we care? In this case, were the change to occur, the developed nations could lose their current economic and political eminence. The United States could lose its West Coast and its access to the Pacific Ocean. In its place, the now defunct, short-lived, technologically primitive, Inka Empire would become the most influential polity on earth.

"I see many of you smiling to yourself, as I did when I was first exposed to this proposition. Bear in mind that other presumed consequences would be the political disappearance of the nations of western South America, Mexico, and Australia, probably of many African nations, and possibly all of South Asia from Pakistan through Indonesia. The abrogation of all European colonial efforts of the Sixteenth through Twentieth centuries, and the marginalization of Europe, and therefore America, in human affairs."

"These may be the most superficial of ramifications. Would we, any of us, exist as individuals, given the unknowns of the so-called 'Butterfly Effect?'"

"We are here today to exchange any information participating nations may have to contribute to our body of knowledge, and to receive suggestions as to how to deal with these circumstances going forward. May I now present the proxy for the President of the United States."

The proxy for the President of the United States stands.

"Good morning. I will be brief.

"A few months ago information began to filter into our intelligence community, and to this office, as follows.

"Six American citizens were discovered to be involved in communications through the Entity, with the dead while they still lived, and/or to have knowledge of the existence and nature of the Entity not known to the rest of us.

"They were, and are, one archaeologist, one microbiologist, one video blogger, two teenage youths in California, and a private security consultant suborned by contact with the Entity. A Peruvian national archaeologist makes seven.

"Our first response was uncoordinated and frankly inept. A federal agency attempted to co-opt the means of communication with the past, a rock. Actually, we tried to abduct the rock from Peru. The mission failed due to the Entity's resistance to our interference.

"Then we undertook surveillance of all involved. This was fairly successful, if disturbing. We learned a lot and are still learning.

"Then we tried to contact the Entity and the participants in the past ourselves, without success. It seems that the Entity chooses its own interlocutors, and very few of them.

"We had already made contact with one of the original collaborators, the video blogger, who appeared to be in opposition to the others — Doctor Professor Rama hasn't mentioned that there is a degree of schizophrenia in the Entity, a counter-impulse — and we believed we had enlisted him to our cause.

"Our cause requires that history remains history, stays as it is.

"He deserted us, ran to ground in a location that seems to be under the control of the Entity.

"The Entity manifests on both sides of the dispute.

"Now we continue to monitor the situation, that is frankly developing at breakneck speed on a global level, while we firm up contingency plans. Our plans range from cultivating our own players as previously attempted, recruiting the existing players to our side, neutralizing them through coercion, bribery, and psychological manipulation, or termination by blunt force.

"It is interesting to note that the government of the nation of Peru chooses to remain silent on this.

"The President of the United States is himself highly skeptical of all aspects of the theory being proposed here today, but he is provisionally suspending his disbelief for the purpose of this gathering. We welcome any constructive counsel from the distinguished participants of this meeting. Thank you."

(Doctor Professor Rama returns to the podium.)

"Thank you sir. Yes, there is much to tell that has been deferred in the interest of brevity. An internal faction of the Entity appears to favor preserving the status quo. This faction appears to be the dominant force in the fifteenth century wing of this conflict, whereas it is the lesser influence in our own era. Our access to the notes of the 'interlocutors' indicates that history as it stands offers one advantage that a resurgent Inka Empire would not. A space program. We may bring it into contact with others like it in the universe. I now present the representative from the People's Republic of China, Doctor Lee Li Liu."

"Thank you, Professor Rama. The prevention of the conquest of Peru by European national interests is not the sole revisionist agenda of human collaborators with the global superorganism. Within China two hundred and fifty-two citizens, largely students of meteorology and history, were marked for arrest and interrogation concerning their participation in a plot to deflect the Yuan Dynasty invasion of Japan in 1274. Their intent was to either rush the invasion to 1273 to anticipate the typhoons of 1274 and catch the Japanese unaware, or to delay until after the storm season in late 1274 or 1275. The two factions were based respectively around Mount Wutai in the Shanxi province, and Mount Jiuhua in Anhui. In both cases small numbers of plotters appeared to be in contact with microbe-based superorganisms that they referred to informally as the Tao. In truth, our people were more interested in studying the feasibility of this plan and perhaps refining it than in preventing it. However, any agents who attempted to meddle with the key participants — from any distance, incidentally, including offshore — would immediately fall asleep for sustained periods. The rest, two hundred and forty-five of the identified conspirators, were questioned and released as not significantly involved. The remaining seven continue their project, under a watchful eye. Printed reports will be distributed to all concerned. The Japanese Government was informed of our findings in September of this year.

“Likewise, we are aware that a similar project was undertaken by Russian citizens in Mongolia, with the intent of persuading the high command of the Mongol Horde under Batu Khan not to withdraw from the invasion of Vienna upon the death of Ögedei Khan in December of 1241, when Europe was defenseless to the west and south of that city. I here defer to the Russian delegation.”

(The leader of the Russian Federation speaks informally from his seat.)

“Yes. The five Russians involved died rather comically in a natural gas explosion in their apartment in Ulaanbaatar. This occurred before Eye Kay matured. Our agents did not fall asleep, although they did perish when their rental car disturbed a party of wolf hunters near the Mongolian-Russian border. Some Russian nationals, however, in loose communication with Mongolian nationals and a British paleontologist, remain fugitive in the Gorkhi Terelj National Park near Khan Khentii. We have withdrawn all of our interested officials in order to avoid any diplomatic misunderstandings with our brothers the Mongolian people.”

(The Mongolian representative interjects a loud, abrupt, non-verbal vocalization.)

“Well, almost all.”

(Professor Rama resumes the podium.)

“The floor is now open to discussion. Sir, representing the US?”

“General Mack Jackman, NTT. The President of the United States of America will go on record stating that he believes this whole thing is a crock of horse shit.”

“So noted. We thank the President of the United States of America for his candor and acumen.”

Nick Nieman watched the camouflaged, rifle-armed men materializing through the misty rain again. They had passed nearby before but followed a different path. Now they came directly up the devil's club and burdock-choked clearing in the dark cedars and fir, a city block away. Nick watched them through pocket binoculars. He was surprised to see a man stride briskly to the front in a dark suit and tie and homburg, carrying an umbrella. He wore transparent plastic booties over his shoes. He seemed to carry a folded Burberry-style macintosh under his arm. His clothing made the combat dress of the others look silly, rather than the reverse. It made Nick's own dank, smeared, wrinkled clothing seem even more foolish. As they came closer Nick saw the dapper character's pale eyes through his black-frame glasses. They were looking directly down the barrel of his optics. He seemed to be a dangerous man. He said something over his shoulder and the man behind unslung his scoped deer rifle.

Nick pulled his escape pack closer by its shoulder strap, pushed a knit toque onto his head with the flat of his palm, and got ready to run. Then his shoulders slumped. He just didn't feel up to it. He was unfit, malnourished, tired. The mercenary dudes looked like they ran fifteen miles every morning. The guy with the umbrella looked inexorable, as if he would just keep up a steady pace until, like an elk chased by wolves, Nick ran out of vitality and just lay depleted at his feet. Anyway, the other side of the hill he crouched on was basically a cliff. The fort had been built to repel attack, not for escape,

They came on, aiming for the point where the path hit the ancient ruin, twenty yards to Nick's left. He laid the binoculars down and waited. His dome tent was pale yellow and hard to miss. The column of five hiked up to where the first stone stair of the fort stood. The umbrella man stopped, scanned methodically right to left, looked intently at Nick's position, then lead on, passing by, and where they should have continued up the slope, they disappeared downward instead, as if there were no hill but a dell. After an epoch of half expecting them to come charging up behind, Nick released the breath he had been holding.

“Fucking Twist,” he said, shaking his head. “Fucking lovely Twist.” But they got closer this time.

CHAPTER FORTY-FIVE then

The Battle Plan

The two guards stood off watching as Ramram and Qachu conferred on a hill across from the Inti Wasi complex in Qosqo, near the compound where he was being held on Tupaq's recognizance. Qachu had come in disguise at Amaru's request.

"You think he'll run?"

"*Mana*. He won't run."

"Why not?"

"He's only got one eye."

"Well, what of it?"

"You can't run with only one eye. Your balance is off. You fall away from the dead eye."

"You serious?"

"Mana. What's the point in being serious? But he won't run."

"You are funning me about the eye?"

"I guess so."

"Why do you do that? It's mean."

"A little. Not much or the Llachaqkuna Kamay would get me. Gotta watch that." In fact, he had suffered a small injection of humiliation.

"But why?"

"Because it's kinda fun to play with your provincial proclivity for credulity. You are so gullible. Look, I apologize. It is sort of mean. But he won't run."

"They say he already survived one execution."

"Indeed. I was there."

"You were there?"

"I was. We bivouacked in Pachamamatambo, up the valley. There was a rockfall. I was standing where it is."

"You were one of the ones he saved?"

"Check."

"So if he runs, will you stab him?

"I told you. He won't run."

"Not so loud. He might hear us."

"No. He won't. He can't."

"Why not?"

"He's only got one ear."

Qachu spilled a gout of the thick green liquid to the west of the waka, another to the east, and one at its foot. "Thank you Pachamama," was all he said. It was the last of a long prayer. Ramram hadn't eaten in two days, and drunk only water. He took the wooden qero of wachuma cactus juice, held it to the sky, and drank it down.

Qachu began to chant softly, deep in his bony chest, and to tap on a small drum. Ramram had questions for Pachamama, and Qachu knew how to enhance communication with the Apus. Especially Her. Behind Qachu, over his shoulder, between them and the Sacsaywaman construction, a Kuychi Puyu rainbow cloud shimmered, a lens of mist twinkling with tiny points of colored light. It had appeared in the morning and would be gone by nightfall. Ramram was comforted and animated by its presence.

After a while Ramram vomited the scant contents of his stomach, then his eyes closed and he began to sway from side to side from his seat on a smooth stone platform. Deep animal sounds came from his open lips. Qachu's chanting and drumming got louder.

The sun went down. The relief arrived for the two guards.

"What's all that?" one of the replacements asked.

"I don't know. Wizard stuff," the gullible guard answered.

"Is he dangerous? Might he do us some manner of harm?"

"No," the gullible one said. "He can't."

"Why not?"

“He’s only got one testicle." He scratched his nose. "Just kidding. That's the Umu Antarqui.”

At sunrise Qachu’s chant began to tone down, the drumming quieted. Ramram, who had been conversing in guttural, growls and unknown tongues all night, went silent. Chaska Quyllur, the Long Tangled Hair Star, brazen in her brightness, set.

The guards, wrapped in their woolen cloaks, glad for the sun, looked at one another. The official morning prayer to Inti floated over the rooftops from the Qoricancha.

Ramram stood. “All right. Good. I have to speak to the Katari Kuntur woman from the Dark Future. The Runasimi speaker. Bring Tuya.” Amaru had gotten passage for her to be near Ramram.

Tuya got a very clear connection with Katari. She held Ramram into the night as Katari briefed him in depth.

Here is what he told Tuya to pass on to the strangers from the far future:

“I have struggled to find words and thoughts to bring what Pachamama showed me back to you. This is what I have made of what I have seen.

“There is a Pacha in which the Tawantinsuyu is conquered by evil silver strangers. You have shown me this. This Pacha is like a boulder, it has great weight and requires great strength to move. This stone is heavy because it has already taken place in your time.

“If the Sapa Inka Pachacutiq Yupanqui could move this boulder of future time, he could prepare to beat the strangers before they beat us. Only he has the power to do this. He controls the men and materiel.

“But the Priests of Ilyapa do not want the stone to move. They have made the stone just heavy enough that Pachacutiq can't budge it. He can't see what I have told him. He can't see the Pacha in which the Tawantinsuyu is broken. He can't see what must be done to save it. The stone lies too heavy upon him.

"The change we wish to make is a small thing within the river of the Pacha of all Pachas. We would only make a small eddy in the flow as a boy would drop a pebble in a puddle, or a stick in a stream, to make a small change in all Pachas but a great one for us.

"The Apus cannot do this. Their hands are too big and our Pachas too small. We must do it for them.

"In the Kuychi Puyu rainbow cloud all our Pachas meet. Kay Pacha, this one here. The one where the Tawantinsuyu is dead and our friends live in a far land and Pachamamatambo is called Ollantaytambo. A third in that time far away, where Eff Ram and Li Li live now and Pachamama has great power.

"In the meeting of these three Pachas is the lever that can move the stone to create a new Pacha. The one where everything is possible. It is sleeping. It must be awakened. The mind of Pachacutiq Inka must be wakened.

"The Pachas in the rainbow cloud will sleep until they are awakened by the messengers of Pachamama. I am one. Snake Condor woman is one. Eff Ram is one. When we meet in the Kuychi Puyu we will wake the power to move the stone. Sapa Inka Pachacutiq must be present for this to occur. There is a time and day.

"That time will be midday of Qapac Raymi, the Prime Festival. The longest day of the year."

He exhaled, and looked to Tuya.

"Ramram, my love, be simple for me. There is no boulder on Inka Pachacutiq and no boy with a pebble and no puddle."

"Ari. We need to get three people into the rainbow cloud like that one over there, but in Pachamamatambo. The one for which you named our baby girl. They must all be there at the same time. And Pachacutiq must be there to see and feel.

"If we do it right and we are lucky, a powerful force will fly free and it will get through to the Inka and his eyes will open and he will prepare for the silver demon people and we will beat them and time will change and the Tawantinsuyu will not fall. The three people you know. I am one. Others will try to stop us.

"Pachacutiq will be here to see me fly or die at the height of the sun, during the Qapac Raymi ceremony. It must be then. On that day Pachamama will send a signal, a sight and a sound, to tell them when to fly.

"Please meet Snake Condor Woman. Tell her that. She must ask herself, and ask Eff Ram: can they enter the Kuychi Puyu at the signal on that day? If they do, can they fly?"

CHAPTER FORTY-SIX now

She was Peruvian

Katari Kuntur had a cold hard resolve like a gnarled fist in her gut. She wasn't sure if she had thought through what she was trying to do, but she didn't care. She was Peruvian, she was Andean, she was Indian. Her forebears' feet had been on this ground five thousand years before they had known to plant seeds. These were her mountains.

She laid hands on the Split Rock, her face stone hard to hide her racing pulse. Something in her gut drove her to try to connect with the Inka woman Tuya one more time. The rock hummed under her hands. She closed her eyes and waited. "*Dios, haz que pasa*," she muttered, god, make it happen.

Tuya answered, in archaic Cusqueña Runasimi.

"Lady Katari Kuntur." Tuya was weaving on a hand loom before a small fire, facing the stone doorway of her house, the entrance hung with a beautiful multicolored curtain glowing in the firelight. Katari found that she could speak directly into Tuya's mind, her own voice both whispery and echoing, heard in both ears.

"Sister," she answered. "I will not lie to you, I will not steal, I will not be lazy," she swore the ancient Inka greeting. "*Allillanchu*?" Are you well?

"*Allillanmi.* I am good. And you?" Tuya spoke aloud.

"I am good. So glad to find you."

"I have been waiting for you. We have a request," Tuya said. "It may be hard to understand, and more so to do."

"What can I do?" Katari waited, heart full, knowing she would receive what she came for. Instructions.

Tuya stood, walked to the doorway of her kancha, stood on the terrace looking out over the town.

"Qapac Raymi is near. Then we live or we die."

Through Tuya's eyes, through the blood in her veins, she saw the ancient Inka night, dim straw-torches glowing in the windows, llama-dung stove fires through the open doors of the houses. The stars crazy overhead. It was a good place and time. She heard, felt Tuya laugh, tasted the lightness of her heart despite her coming deprivation, her risk, and her loneliness. It was a resilience, a strength wholly unknown to Katari's age.

"You must learn to fly, a little." Katari listened. "And you must tell Eff Ram the same. You must fly from the place where my beautiful friend Qantuta flew for love, so swift, singing."

Katari felt gritty jealousy that a *turista*, a soft unknowing baby *Norte Americano*, had the same mission as she. She knew it wasn't fair, and that Ephraim Arrowsmith was chosen by the Pachamama, and chosen well. But she didn't care. She hated his presence in this struggle.

"*Ari*, sister. Tell me, I will do it. I swear."

Tuya told her.

The Juice to Kick It Over
Antepenultimate Day to the Showdown

Katari found herself on the verge of hanging up the video chat more than once, but the gravity of the situation took precedence, finally. "Good then. Talk it over. When you think you have an answer, please get back to me. The question is: can you do it? Can you fly into the cloud?"

Lily and Ephraim both opened their mouths, Bingham got there first.

"Time difference? We don't even know what year it is there, much less date and time. There's a three-hour difference UTC here. We won't know when to go in."

"Ah. I forgot. There will be a signal. A sight and a sound. It will come from the cloud."

"Okay, Katari," Lily allowed, "we will have to take their word for it. A wheel of fire in the sky or a shining Madonna isn't that different from what we already have here. Thanks."

"The signs will come. Pachamama assures Ramram of this." Katari signed off.

The three looked at one another across the table in Ephraim's breakfast nook.

"All right then," Ephraim said, "We have a showdown on December Twenty One, at noon Ollantaytambo time more or less. Agreed?"

"Looks like it," Bingham concurred. "But I'd be ready earlier in the day. We have no idea when the sign's going to show."

"Check," Ephraim agreed. "What will happen then is, three of us go into the Rainbow Cloud — Katari in Ollantaytambo, Ramram in his time, one of us here."

"Why again do they need us here, at all?" Lily asked over her shoulder, paying a pizza delivery kid at the door.

Ephraim rapped the table with his knuckle. "Okay. This is the crux as I see it. Clearing Pachacuti's drugged-up mind is not enough. It is physics. There is an inertia standing between us and actually changing time. Of course there is. But the Presence has given us that prismatic cloud to overcome that opposition. We've got to blast through the inertia. That's what the Peacock Cloud is for."

"Yeah?" said Bingham, head cocked.

"The Question has some leverage over time, because it doesn't exactly exist in time, but it's not easy and Certainty is going to fight it. That's what this is all about, always has been."

"There is a pain between my ears," said Lily, "The Storm God guys have been keeping Patchie Cutie drugged, Tuya told us that. But we should be able to counter that, just by using the Pachamama effect somehow. Some antidote. That'd be up to Ramram and Tuya and Pachamama herself. We can't help with that."

“Yeah well, that’s it, Lil’. They can’t do it alone. They need our powerhouse thing here. The Question can conjure up enough quantum uncertainty to do the time-flip thing for us, it’s got that much mojo, but not to pry the thing over. It’s fighting the full weight of the inertia of time.

“Thing is, it’s their inertia versus our momentum. We few, we trippy few, whom the Presence brought together through some sort of synchronicity, have set up a shaky, ramshackle, slippery, base from which to try to pull off this hat trick, but it’s not enough. Even if we got...Patchie Cootie, you little iconoclast...off their drugs and onto our agenda, he wouldn’t be able to phlorp what’s needed. We’re skinny feeble old Don Quixote and the current timeline is a humping big carnivorous windmill.”

“Yeah, and because something is wrong with us,” said Bingham. “Something is fucking with our minds. There’s stuff we are just not getting. Including this. And down there too. I feel it. It’s like that psychological blindness field around Split Rock.”

“You’re right, Bing!” Lily peeled a pizza slice loose from its nest. “It’s like a word on the tip of my tongue. I see it there, but I just can’t get it.”

“Yes,” Ephraim went on, “We are feeling resistance from Certainty. And more. The big picture is, the Question has been building a power base for years. All the Pachamama stuff down there and here, the Eye Kay phenomena, anomalous stuff around the world — everything Noe Zoe reports to us. All to do one thing. Stop Pizarro.”

“What,” asked Bingham, “I have to ask, is the science behind this folktale?”

“Yeah,” Lily piped up, “we need Nick’s Shotgun Girl.”

“Quantum uncertainty, I think. Like a hand grenade of free will to toss at the timeline that is already in place. To pry loose fixed time.”

“That’s the hard part to get,” said Lily. “Certainty is biological, it’s just life on the crust of the Earth, but it is fighting with something like physics. Isn't all this entanglement stuff physics? I mean Heisenberg was a scientist, not a theologian."

"He was a fucking sorcerer," said Bingham. "He was a Messenger from Beyond."

"We don't know what it is," Ephraim rapped again. "But we do know that the Presence has some leverage over time. Existing outside time as it does. It does it to us. Like Nick said, even us dumb animals have entangled non-coexisting particles in different times.

"But it's not enough. Even with Pachacutiq fully alert. Even with their rainbow cloud made of Noe's prokaryote supermind, even with what Ramram knows, they don't have the leverage.

"So here is your answer, Lily. Pachamama has power in Ramram's Pacha. Pachamama and the Presence have power in Ollantaytambo, Ramram and Katari have the power of the Rainbow Cloud. They can go into it and combine their powers, synergize, catalyze. Ramram can go in. Katari can go in. When they unite, they bring their powers together, zap wham bam. But Pachamama knows it's not enough charge to bring down that windmill.

"But you know who has the most clout? You know where the Presence was able to put together the biggest force field, the dynamo with the most voltage?"

"Here? Lil ol' us?" Lily lifted a slice of pizza, squinting at it as if she could order it to shed calories.

"Yup. Double Swirly Hill. Nick's Coastal Stigmergy." Ephraim looked from one to the other.

"I finally got this. That's why the Presence brought us all together, with our connections we didn't even know we had.

"Me with Ramram, Lily with Bingham, Bingham with Noe. Noe Zoe with the Presence. Bingham with Katari, Katari with Tuya, Tuya with Ramram, Ramram with Pachacutiq, Pachacutiq with power over the Tawantinsuyu. All of us sensitive to the Presence herself. And left-handed."

Ephraim expected to hear the adolescent interrogative uptick in his voice. It didn't happen. That part of his life was over.

Lily sniffed her pizza slice. “And Nick with Sneeze Monk and Sneeze Monk with the Storm God on the other side. Nick, in fact, with everybody sooner or later. And that brings us to us. Here. Now. Or I mean, the day after tomorrow. December Twenty One.”

“Yes,” said Ephraim. “We are the big guns. We are the catalyst. We are the Observers who rip the lid off Schrodinger’s cat. We are the lever and the key. We are the ignition to the engine of this mother ship. We carry the uncertainty bomb into the cloud with our exercise of free will. We are the juice to kick it over.”

“We are the Core!” Lily hoisted as if it were a champagne glass her delta of yeast-inflated phenolic compounds, ferulic acid, coagulated casein, meat products, and *agaricus bisporus* fungi. “To high noon, Winter Solstice, two thousand and..." the pizza guttled into the teeming Calcutta of prokaryote congestion that was her mouth.

“Summer solstice,” corrected Ephraim, looking up from his cell phone screen. “Down there.”

“God spare us that you ever get a degree in education,” muttered Bingham.

“So that’s our windmill,” Lily said. “How do we get into that cloud?”

“Well,” Bingham said, “Ramram is Antarqui, the Flying Wizard. We need a flying wizard too.”

"That’s you, Chosen Boy,” Lily licked her lips at Ephraim. “ I know a guy. We'll get you your wings. I'll get mine soon enough.

They Say It Is An Angel

“So one of us has to go into that?” Noe nodded at the undulating nimbus of bioaerosol bacteria suspended above the heads of the townspeople. The Rainbow Cloud.

All around among the souvenir stalls were self-appointed shamans, mystic teachers, healers and their followers, burning coca leaves under the lens-shaped pearlescent vapor that had been expanding and amplifying over the Manyaraki plaza below the Temple Hill ruins. Tourists gawked. Katari and Noe were there to study the phenomenon with an eye to somehow entering.

"It has to be one of us, someone who has already flipped back to Ramram's time," Katari said. "And it has to be on December twenty-one, at the solstice." She frowned. "We will be sent a sign?" Then she shook her head, as if to clear it. "Ramram's time will send us a signal."

"A signal," echoed Noe. She stared at the cloud again. "I would love to get a sample from that. Very hard with aerosols.They're among the most delicate ecosystems on the planet. And strangest, and very beautiful. I speculate that their autoinducer system is highly sophisticated. How will you get in? A flying device?"

"One of my former students has a paraglider. He's bringing it from São Paulo."

"So it will be you?"

Katari grinned. "Do you want to go? There are your samples."

"We have to consider it. Maybe. But I think you. You have the mitochondrial connection."

"Yes. I think me."

From the crowd, two girls gave an excited "Ohhhhhhh." Katari and Noe looked their way.

"The chime! cooed one of the young tourists, "We heard the chime!" A susurrus of wondering commentary rippled through the crowd.

"I've never heard it, Katari" said.

"Nor I," agreed Noe, "how would it work? Vibrate suspended water molecules against one another? Collude with our microbiota to create an auditory hallucination?"

“The tabloids say it is an angel. You have to admit, we’d have thought most of this impossible six months ago. And it’s still mostly inexplicable.”

“But a chime? What if that is the signal, and we don’t hear it?”

“Well, we are also promised a ‘sight.’ If we see it.”

Katari

No rain for many weeks. The sluice gates were closed in the irrigation acequias all over Ollantaytambo, municipal orders. A swaggering Brazilian paraglider with great hair brought Katari his flying machine to show her how she might navigate from the Crown of Tunupa Viracocha — Qantuta's leap - into the Rainbow Cloud. He would tutor her in its use from the Pachar Wall, then she would try him out in bed.

She arranged an introduction to the patriarch Francisco Pizarro Komadreja-Quispe, a full-blooded Inka who oversaw a family sprawled over the hills for fifty kilometers up the Ocobamba valley. His lineage still worked the land granted by Pachacutiq for the fight on Hunchback hill. That ancestor’s mummy still clutched his boney knees in a cave high above Markacocha.

After the conquest, the Viceroy Francisco Toledo had systematically suppressed the oral traditions of the Inka people. To pass on any knowledge not necessary to daily production was criminalized. No one alive now could read a khipu. But the old man Quispe still knew all the waterways in the valley, including those lost to official record. He was the last who did. His son, who called himself “Dani,” was worthless and no other boy wanted the responsibility.

Katari had not called on the old man for help. You did not waste his time on trivialities.

“The cops are down there just out of reach of the Eye Kay, watching us, waiting.” Bingham ran his fingers through his cropped beard. “I get the feeling they know something we don’t.”

“We know one thing,” said Lily. “The holobiome explosion, the Pachamama effect, up here, isn’t happening down there in town. It’s late December and no rain. Glaciers are melting. Jellyfish are filling the eco-niche where other life in the seas are gone. The world population has doubled in my parent’s life time and is doubling again, but the Earth’s surface is a constant. Double Swirly Hill is like the Alamo, like the buffalo, like dodo birds and passenger pigeons, surrounded by oncoming death.”

“Like the Incas,” said Ephraim, then he cupped the top of her head in his palm. “Like you.”

“I have months. The human race thinks it has centuries, but it has decades. Maybe.”

“Lily!” Bingham laughed, “You sound like a Public Service Announcement. What’s going on in that pretty little head?”

“Right now I don’t feel like life is but a joke. We feel like we’re winning because this bio-magic shit drove a few cops back down the hill. Because we have a twinkling mist for Ephie to fly into with some plastic wings. Do we really think that’s going to change anything?”

“Do we really think,” Ephraim asked, “that they are going to let us do it?”

Behind, they heard voices rise and fall, singing a line to a cheap guitar and a precious mandolin, "Only kindness matters in the end..." A violin weaved in.

"But you know something?” Lily shook her head. “My favorite fatal disease hasn't advanced an inch since we walked into the corridor. You know that?”

"I didn't want to say. Hubris."

"Except the days when we don't come. Then I feel it like there's a spider in my blood."

"Then be here."

"Right. But it's true. We can't forget. Something is really happening with this Inka thing. we aren't dead yet. Tomorrow is another day."

"Frankly, Scarlett," Ephraim smiled at her, "I hope so." He took her hand, so tenderly that her eyes couldn't lift.

"So we fight back the guys with the defoliants," she gazed downhill into the city. "We keep our nothings together, we look for a plan — I know there is something that we're missing — and keep it together until December twenty-one."

"Tomorrow. Man, that wizard better fly."

"You too."

"I will. Or," he turned to her, "maybe you want to?"

"No. It's got to be you. You got the mojo. You are the chosen boy."

In the background, three voices rose in stoned harmonic counterpoint, "*My hands are small, I know…*"

Bird's Eye View

Eye Kay came down from Kuntur Punku into Ollantaytambo, and climbed the side of Pinkuylluna mountain. Katari, Raoul the Brazilian, and Noe Zoe climbed above to the worn ruins of the Crown of Tunupa perched on the head of the rock face of the old man of the mountain, carrying the parasail in its sheath. "I want to see how you do it," said Noe. "I'm a scientist."

Along the Korean Demilitarized Zone, north and south, military sentries fingered their   triggers nervously as clots of civilians stood quietly at the razor wire and chain link fences, toeing forward, not knowing exactly why they had to be there, only that they did. Some hadn't eaten for days but felt no hunger. Medics reported a baffling enhancement of metabolic efficiency in test subjects: nobody felt the need to eliminate bodily waste. The guards knew that any act of violence would be suicidal. *Jeugseog Kaleuma*, Instant Karma, was there.

In New Guinea tribes who had been enemies for time immemorial shared fires and seemed to comprehend each other's' linguistically isolated tongues.

In Tokyo thousands of people decided to walk to work.

In the Sakha Republic of Siberia the Evenki hunters lay down their traps and rifles, held together by wire and duct tape, oiled and cleaned for generations, and walked into the morning to meet their brothers and prey. Throughout the vast taiga, elk, wild reindeer, roe deer, bear, lynx, wolf, marmot, fox, and sable came into the open to look their hunters in the eye. The branches of the pines and larch, birch and *populus tremula*, bent under the weight of hundreds of thousands of birds. Wolverines, the meanest and most cunning animal on dry land, laid their heads at the feet of men who wore the furs of their grandfathers. The women looked at the sky, seeing Seveki, the guardian of the plant and animal world. The only true shamans in the world sang deep in their throats.

Across the world, north and south, thickest around the equator, the enhanced symbioses of innumerable centillions of invisible organisms achieved a state of self-awareness new to the planet Terra.

But in those locations nothing critical was at stake.

Shooter Suits

"Your anti-cockblocker body suit got here," the NTT controller phoned HQ from Ollantaytambo. "Our shooter tried it on and it fits. All I can say is, it better work."

"It has been thoroughly field-tested and it works," his handler replied. "The bacteria killers in that black rainbow glop are fully counter-effective against the instant karma bugs. It's all just microbiology, it isn't supernatural. Tell your man to take his shot. He's covered."

The NTT sniper was holed up in a private home on the outskirts, his weapons carried through customs by a sympathetic colonel in the Peruvian army.

Agent Mango and his squad of Briarpatch operatives had been ordered to make themselves seen around Ollantaytambo in order to discourage any opposition, then, in the morning, to deploy on Pinkuylluna to throw a wrench into the Core's mission. They were not issued anti-Eye Kay suits.

Within restricted hangers in Hayward, California, and Cusco, Peru, the clawed biohazard symbols designed for Dow Chemical in 1966 were pasted over with decals of showing the spread eagle of the U.S. Department of Homeland Security. The mercenary pilots in both nations wondered to themselves over Styrofoam cups how Eye Kay would reflect against them. They were afraid to test its patience. On the other hand they were paid a lot of money and the orders came from dangerous men.

CHAPTER FORTY-SEVEN then

Capaq Raymi
December 21
Summer Solstice

Dust-coated near the rear of the column came Ramram, under guard but unbound, in the stoic stride he had learned in his months of lone travel. Shadows shortened as Inka Pachacutiq's procession filed into Pachamamatambo. Ahead, the temples and terraces of Qoripata, Golden Terrace, Hill were touched by the new sun. Above them all to the north, the small square tower of Tunupa's Crown waited for Ramram's execution. The air was sweet, birds sang morning songs. It would be a warm day.

Ramram had maybe eight papa puns, the time it takes to boil a potato, to live. The column had been on the road since the sunrise ceremony at the tambo east of town. Villaqs led, chanting and holding fragrant torches. The guard followed in full feather, then acclas of Inti, holding sprigs of qantuta flowers, singing in pentatonic scale. Then came the Sapa Inka's resplendent palanquin borne as smoothly as poured honey, followed by the litters of Tupaq and of Amaru, leading the outlanders and exotic artifacts captured on their ocean expedition. Behind came those of the high elite, then another twenty thousand of the entourage and other assignees. Then in the tail of grit Ramram and his guard.

On the same ground, insofar as sameness exists across space and time, the pureblood farmers of Ollantaytambo, up before dawn, lifted their heads to the east. An unfamiliar sound grew in the sky, growling, nothing like morning birdsong; aircraft incoming, still far. A little like the sound of the tractors that had suddenly shown up to plow the chakras for those who could afford them, bringing a small pain to the hearts of those who could not. People who had been content farming as their fathers had for thousands of years in lifeways that disappeared within a year, forever. Now skies that rarely heard the racket of an airplane grew full of the sound.

In the Berkeley hills, although a red touched the towers across the bay, it was still dark. Ephraim untangled himself from his mummy bag, negotiated groggily through the cocoons of sleeping bags to the designated piss slope. He tried for silence, but rustling and stirring behind told him that he wasn't the only one who couldn't sleep. He had been awakened by a lonely dream which had turned into a hunt for a working toilet. In the arroyo the Peacock cloud pulsed bursts of light. In the city below, all lights were artificial. What was that noise? Planes? For real?

Down the trail in the dark men in kevlar and battle dress checked their gear, made sure their warrants were current in the glow of UV flashlights, spoke low into radios, estimated windage. Across the valley, in their new anti-Eye Kay suits, the snipers' camouflage tooth caps showed dimly in their feral grins. Wouldn't those spoiled snots be surprised when the 7.62 slugs tore their heads off. They thought they were exempt. Sniper three lifted his chin and smiled. He heard air support inbound, lights out.

CHAPTER FORTY-EIGHT now

God Let It Be Over
Berkeley, California

A dozen sleek little yellow and black attack planes whined in, low wing, tiny cockpits, faceless pilots. At first they circled Double Swirly Hill at a distance, waiting for full light. The nothings stood, some with hands on hips or shading their eyes, twisting around, squinting up. A quarter mile off the six frontmost planes seemed to catch fire, trailing smoke. The second six followed. The kids had been telling one another that the government wouldn't spray deadly poison so close to the city.

"Here it is," called Bingham, "Shut your eyes and cover up." As practiced, the nothings pulled wet bandanas over their mouths, and those who had goggles used them.

A Somali exchange student began to tremble, fighting for control, the bombing death of his village coming back to him hard. When the planes closed in his knees gave out and he fell to the ground, shaking and wheezing. Lily pulled the traumatized boy to his feet, tugged his kerchief up.

The lead plane peeled off, dived straight at them, growing huge, howling and growling, billowing malodorous dust from a belly tank; Lily was blinded, choked and coughing, tears squirting from her eyes, snot running over her mouth, gagging, sucking the now mud-soaked fabric into the cave of her mouth. Vomit rose in her throat, blocking her breath. Something grabbed her from behind and she panicked, throwing her arms out wildly, but it was Ephraim's voice saying something comforting, and suddenly it was dark and she could breath. "Jesus," he said low into her ear, "They don't care if they kill us." He had thrown his open sleeping bag over them both.

The racket of the plane dopplered away, the particulate filtered to the ground. Lily wriggled from beneath the bedroll.

"Hoo boy, I wasn't ready for that."

All around nothings coughed and spit, wiping futilely at their eyes and mouths.

"Not chemicals," Lily called out across the hilltop, "Bacteria, anti-Eye Kay, it won't kill you." Then, as a full-disclosure afterthought, "Not counting any delivery agent."

Before they could recover their wind, another single-engine aerial top dresser, banned in Europe, came in strafing them with choking granulate as they crouched and covered their heads. The air tanker banked away, and another whined down, then another, unfurling whirlwinds of smoke-like spray drift on them all, low enough for the prop blast to blow one girl's glasses off.

The planes dropped away beyond the hills.

"Is it over?" someone gasped. "God let be over."

"It's in my eyes, in my nose and mouth. And I have goggles and a surgical mask," said another.

"Yeah? Well I just washed my hair," complained the gypsy-scarfed girl who had first welcomed Lily and Ephraim to the hill. "In the Student Union bathroom."

There was gagging and hacking in the welcome, relative, silence.

"I thought I was dead," came from one of the young men. "Tastes like stale chaw tobacco."

But the first wave wasn't done.They streamed west over the bay, turned, came back for five more passes, until there was no one there who thought they could bear another attack; Lily heard people, male and female, crying, saw them trying to crawl away before they were hit again. "At least nobody is dead yet," she observed.

Then the last flight targeted the Peacock Cloud until their spray tanks were empty.

"At least it's not us this time," said Sharp-Eyed Angus. "But look. The Peacock is shrinking. She's dying. And she is what we are all here about."

At last they disappeared over the hills. Ephraim could make them out going home to the southwest, little black fleas, leaving thick drifts of gritty powder filtering down on the hill, coating everything in dun particles.

Bingham took his binoculars from a pocket, peered at the second flight, ten aircraft, circling to the west. "One of these next guys looks like the Red Baron," he told Ephraim,"Great War biplanes. And they will be coming in."

"That was the first squadron," Bingham called to anyone nearby, "We still have to deal with the Red Baron and his bunch. Good move with the blanket, Eph. Everyone, if you've got sleeping bags, ponchos, tents, put them over you or get inside. There will be more."

"Fuck this," came through the haze at the trailhead, "I'm outa here."

"Yes," called Bingham, "If you can't take it, get off the hill now. There will be more, maybe worse." People, maybe fifteen of the thirty or so there, retreated down the trail. "But be aware," he raised his voice, "the police will be waiting."

"We few, we idiot few," said Sharp-Eyed Angus, "Band of bozos. Listen," he turned to Ephraim, "You three want in my tent? My GF went downhill. It's a standard dome, we'll fit." All around nothings were putting up tents or slinging blue plastic tarps from trees.

"Sure thing," Lily answered, "Why are you dressed up like Ephraim? Blue work shirt and jeans, no hat?"

Angus looked down along himself. "Not on purpose. Anyhow, my shirt has stuff embroidered on the back and cuffs, see?"

"It's a classic outfit," Ephraim defended Angus, "Chambray shirt and jeans. Very proletariat. So let's get that tent up before they hit us again."

They barely made it before the second wing came in.

Airstrike on Ollantaytambo

In Ollantaytambo the first wave dropped leaflets warning people to get inside and stay there, this was a non-toxic government disinfectant. Then they dust-bombed the population center. The planes were older than in Berkeley and there were fewer of them, but they were reinforced by half a dozen military prop-driven models.

"They are targeting Pinkuylluna. Rather pointedly, the Crown of Tunupa watchtower you are planning to leap off." Noe peered over the second story balcony of the tourist restaurant by the plaza. Katari and Raoul drank coffee from the inside edge of the round table.

"And they are hitting your magical fog," noted Raoul in Portuguese-accented Spanish. Sure enough, one hotshot pilot dared to blow right through the hovering mist, pulling polkadot trails of color behind him as he waggle-winged away. The cloud reformed. The pilot kept it up for two hours, migrating out over the river and the valley to dust down the clouds. When it went quiet, malodorous dust drifting down, people began nosing out to see if the strange assault was over, wondering why the mayor hadn't warned them about that. The artisan storekeepers swiped disgruntled at the filth on their wares displayed around the store doors, ponchos, hats, handbags, all coated, maybe ruined.

Then a stubby red and white Fuerza Aérea Zlin Z242 Guru came in low, siren howling, and the town ducked back inside.

This time they splattered the streets with oily gobbets smelling like floating livestock carcases in a poisoned pond.

"*Madre*" cursed Katari. "Your Instant Justice does not effect these flying toilets, yes?"

"That was the purpose of the initial flight," said Noe Zoe. "The dust contained bacteria-eating life forms designed to defeat the aggression-defusing bacteria. That's why they maintained altitude. Except for the daredevil who entered..."

There was an explosive clap as two crop dusters collided in a fireball, burning debris spiraling down into the river.

"¿Es esa tu justicia instantánea?" Is that your instant justice? queried Raoul, then twisted suddenly backwards, toppling his chair, as a wasp yellow bomber whined in at rooftop level and loosed its load right onto the facade of the cafe, blowing the window open and splattering their table. Noe was shielded by the swinging latticed glass, Katari's reflexes threw her to the floor on the other side, but the Brazilian frantically wiped his eyes and mouth with his shirtsleeve.

"Stop," said Katari, "You make it worse. Wait." She dipped the table tissue, passing for paper napkins in Peru, into the teapot and began to carefully dab the worst of the rank pollutant from his face. Noe went to the other two occupied tables to offer what help she could, but those windows had held firm and the tourists were only shaken and bewildered. Outside, the attackers regrouped and came around for another pass.

Second Strike, Berkeley

Ephraim peered over the bay. "Here they come, people. Take cover!"

"Okay Red Baron," Bingham shouted to the sky, "Let's see what you got!"

The blood-colored biplane came in low and slow, its round cowl ballooning huge as it closed in, releasing a rain of thick, brownish-black droplets, passing to the left of their tent. A panicked girl in a straw bonnet clawed her way in.

"'Scuse me but my damn tree leaks and that stuff stinks."

"Welcome," said Lily, "There's room, if you're not too intimacy impaired."

"Grumman Ag-Cat B-Plus double-wing," the intruder declared. "600 horsepower R-1340 Pratt and Whitney nine-cylinder radial engine." The other four stared at her. "My dad had one. We had a crop duster airstrip out by Vacavile when it was still farms."

Bingham re-zipped the tent flap. They huddled like London schoolchildren in the Blitz, eyes upturned to the shadows slashing across the domed roof. Droplets thudded onto the rainfly when one passed close. The new girl curled at the front, peering through the triangular gap at the bottom of the zipper.

"Here comes your red guy again. Omigod, he's coming right at us!"

The landing gear nearly hit dirt as the pilot released his load straight onto the front of the tent, as if he knew who was inside. The PVC fabric billowed in, slapping Ephraim and Lilly in their chest and head before they could cover their faces; then the fly tore free overhead, exposing the mosquito netting, soaking them all with the viscous liquid. The fiberglass struts and guy ropes pulled free, the tent collapsed and the five inside found themselves in a tangled, sopping, stinking, chaotic mess, struggling to get out.

"I can't find the zipper!" the new girl cried. "We'll suffocate!"

"Pardon me," said Ephraim, feeling inane, crawling over her, groping for the pull tab.

"Screw it," said Angus, "It's my tent. I own it clear." He cut through the mosquito netting with the blade of a folding knife, holding it open for the others to escape. Bingham helped Lily though, and followed, holding the ripped gap wide; Angus followed to clear the way, Ephraim helped the crop-duster's daughter out, then stood in the middle of the deflated shelter just as the ten planes dive bombed in over the hills for the next strike.

The hilltop was a mess of wrecked tents and crawling, choking humanity. A dog whined and barked miserably. Someone was sobbing out loud. Another cried, "Oh god!" as half a dozen loud yellow raiders homed in on them. This time, though, they veered down the canyon, targeting the Peacock cloud. They formed up nose-to-tail, drenching the scintillating aerosol entity with a compound of some different color, consistency, and malodor.

"Thank god," someone breathed.

"Too soon," said another nothing, as the other six ad hoc fighters banked in from over the bay, coming in an arrogant, unhurried arc aimed at the people in the ravaged camp.

"Well," said Ephraim, "I can't get any wetter." He stood facing the oncoming assault, hands at his sides. Lilly and the crop duster girl went down crosslegged, hugging each other forehead to forehead, but Bingham, Angus, and a few others, woman and man, stood among the huddled others, defiant or just resigned.

Natural reflex made them hunch and turn away as the slime struck them.

CHAPTER FORTY-NINE now

On the Hill
Berkeley

"Lord what I wouldn't give for some nice, fresh, freezing rain." Bingham stared at the sky. The fliers were gone. The raid was over. Everybody was gluey with the fetid biological napalm. Somehow, the sky had clouded over. There was a strong wind, but dry.

Bingham sighed and scratched his mustache. "Just enough rain to wash off with." Ephraim strode over to him, pushed him hard in the shoulder.

"Jesus Bing Bing, are you picking your nose? That's ultra gross. No wonder your groupie twins ran off on you."

Lily stared at Ephraim, mouth open.

"I don't feel a thing," Ephraim said." Bingham's eyes widened.

"No Eye Kay. It's gone. They successfully wiped it out. We're naked."

"The cops will be coming up loaded for bear," said boy nothing. "If we're going to do anything, we'd better do it fast."

"Look at the Peacock," said girl nothing, pointing, "It's almost gone." She turned to Ephraim. "Everybody says you are supposed to do something with it. Like, you have that wing thing."

Ephraim looked at Lily.

"She's right," said Lily. "It's now or never. Let's set it up." Bingham was already striding into the chaparral where the hang glider was stashed. As he approached, two zaftig blonde women came running to him, arms wide.

"We couldn't leave," one cried, "We turned back just as the police came at us, made it back to the new Eye Kay line, then the planes came with the sticky stuff. We hid under a bush. Here, let us help you with that."

Ephraim, Bingham, and Lily began to rapidly assemble the hang glider, when someone shouted, “Here they come!”

A squad of kevlar-armored, gas-masked peace officers came barrelling up the fire trail, batons out. Stragglers from Double Swirly hill, demoralized and hiking down, turned around to run back up only to be clubbed from behind, stomped on, and left to be processed by following cops.

“Crickey, those troopers are stoked,” said Angus. “You can see the blood fly.” Ephraim was frantically strapping into the glider apparatus.

“Shucks,” he swore, “It’s put together wrong.” He shrugged out of it.

“We have three minutes,” Lily ground out, “until they get here.’

“Come on Boy Nothing,” said girl nothing, “we’ll slow them down.”

Ollantaytambo
The Inkas Loved Two Things

“The cloud is almost dead.” Katari peered at the remnants of the Rainbow Cloud. “And so is your bacterial security blanket. We have two hours to get up that hill, put the wing together, and get me into the cloud. And the target cloud looks like it will last half that long.”

“Yes. It is diminished. And the Briarpatch mercenaries - see them over there? - regard us with a murderous eye. Things are not going well for our plan. Ramram and Ephraim may find themselves in that cloud alone.”

“Unless their luck is as bad as ours.”

“What then will we do?” pleaded Raoul. The two women looked at him. Katari shook her head.

“Wait,” said Noe Zoe. “Ephraim always says, ‘The Inkas loved two things. Stone and Water.’ Well, we only have one. I see a plenitude of stone. A dearth of water.”

Katari lifted her chin, gazed around the plaza. “That’s right,” she said, “Something has blinded my mind.” She gathered herself together. “Yes, Kroeber, you are right. But I have a plan for that.” Her eyes fixed on a dark young man in a Fly Emirates t-shirt. “Abelardo,” she called in Quechua, “Come here please.” The boy trotted across the street. “Where is your uncle?”

Open Everything

Comadreja-Quispe, the patriarch of the ancient waterways, standing with his family in the adhesive slop on the street, saw the Chanka curandera coming. Finally. Her black eyes were intense, she leaned toward him. "I have come to ask your help, Father," she said.

His nephew in the Fly Emirates t-shirt, unable to contain himself, interrupted.

"The Layqa says to open the water! All of the *sikyas*, *parkus*, *yaku ñans*, every acequia and sluice in the mountains, all of them!”

For days Kamadreja had been organizing the communities along the Patacancha drainage to be ready at the hydrological choke points.

"We have an hour and a half," she said.

He nodded to her, then turned to his family, standing respectfully, eyes on him. "It is time," he told them. "Give the word. Open everything."

So Camadreja Quispe gave the command to all his hundred family young and old.

He himself turned back into the hills to squint intently at where the channel hid connecting the network of local canals to high Lake Yanaqocha. Flood the fields, revive the fountains in the places of the Inkas, now ruins for the foreign viracochas to take photos of themselves. It must be done now, before the final struggle. “Call the boy,” he said. He looked at his feet, shook his head.

The nephew speed-dialed Kamadreja's useless grandson who waited at the submerged dam of Yanaqocha, Black Lake, far above. He was, in body, the strongest man in all the ayllu. In spirit, maybe the weakest.

Tarps Pull Off, Generators Hum

From points along the Lawrence Berkeley National Laboratory fence line, tarps pulled off the experimental LRAD sound cannons designed to explode eyeballs at seventeen hundred meters. Generators coughed to life.

CHAPTER FIFTY then

Living Water

Inka Pachacutiq was in a peevish mood hunched in his feather-canopied litter, carried up the long staircase into the temple sector. It was a childish state and he recognized that but could not shake it. He was carried through the long ten-windowed dining hall to a plaza bordered by gold-and-silver studded stone blocks, draped with sumptuous tapestries. He dismounted, took his place on the tiyana as his retinue arrayed themselves around him. Across the flat below, beyond Manyaraki plaza, across the river, beyond the palaces and residences, beyond the annoying gaudy fog, he eyed the execution blockhouse above the rocky profile of Apu Tunupa Viracocha. What was it that rendered him so petulant? Of all the ways he had been in his life, none of them were petty.

He had always been calmed by the music of running water. It was in his Inka blood. Here there was none. Had he heard the chorus of the fountains, passing through the esplanade below? He couldn't remember. He glanced downward for the glint of sun on water, but saw none. Wouldn't the feeder canals be visible from here? Where was the Kamay of the hills? Where was Misk'i? Oh, there she was.

Take This to Tuya

The sergeant at arms gave Ramram an apologetic look, prodding him lightly with his spear when he, Ramram, hesitated to look over his shoulder stepping onto the staircase up Flute Mountain toward the point of execution.

That was what was wrong. No water flowed in the channel along the street. There had always been fresh water there, for the residents to take in for drinking, cooking, bathing, washing clothes. He started up. An imperative call stopped them from behind.

“Halt!” It was Choque Anka, Otoronqo Kuy’s boyish orderly, now promoted to adjutant. Ramram recognized him from days on the march, and the kambo dart incident. Behind him, a full bull colonel, looking for trouble. “A message for the dead man from Prince Tupaq Yupanqui.” Ramram accepted a khipu with Tupaq’s knot cluster on the top string. It forwarded a message from Tuya asking if there was anything she could do for him. He remembered their parting look, her eyes dry but face gray and pupils the size of a grain of ash. He was about to say No, no, but thought better of it.

“Follow us to the first qolqa,” he ordered, “I need to make an observation.” The guards looked at one another, but Ramram’s messenger was a Chunka Waranka Curaca, Colonel of Ten Thousand Soldiers, so they looked to him. He nodded.

From the landing of the small cubic qolqa, Ramram cast his eyes over the scene, without sentiment, looking for anything of use to say. Dying today he might still against all odds have some good effect on what became of the Tawantinsuyu.

Across the river he saw the glint of sinuous silken cumbi cloth where the Emperor sat. Below him, the town, the lowered river, the water temple’s channels were all too dry. He noted the fading sweetness of Pachamama as she retreated into the west, the dark of the encroaching deadness now across the Qalikantu River, climbing onto the Qoripata sanctuary. A wide tendril following the Sapa Inka up the stairs to his seat. Yes, that was what was wrong. He squinted, twisted a crick from his neck.

“Reply?” the colonel asked. Ramram nodded. The colonel fished in his ch’uspa, handed Ramram a blank khipu. Ramram’s fingers flew over the threads, making knots.

“Take that to Tuya,” he directed. “If you don’t know her, give it to General Otoronqo Kuy or Cord Master Chaski Yuyu.”

“I know her,” the colonel said. “Good luck.” He winced, embarrassed at the fatuity of his offer.

“Thanks,” Ramram said, and turned toward the stairway toward his date with the *Hanan Pacha*, the Upper World. “I think I’ll spend it today.”

Be Polite, They're Priests
Skirmish at the Gate

Ramram's message said, set the water free. Tuya watched the crowd of Ilyapa monks and priests winding from the water temple below Qoripata toward the tall portal of the Manyaraki plaza. They were chanting and stepping in slow time, holding aloft gold-headed yauri staffs, drummers beating serpentine rhythms. There Tupaq and Amaru waited in their palanquins, studying the approach, Amaru smiling enigmatically. She gazed at him, recalling their tryst. A honeyed frisson shuddered through her.

A wide space separated her and the other spectators from the elite. She bit her lip. Every nerve urged her to run across, throw Ramram's khipu into Amaru's strong, sensitive hands. She spied the acolytes of Ilyapa posted throughout the crowd. Some of them had their eyes on her. They knew she was the wife of their enemy the Antarqui. She half expected an arresting hand to take her to some dark chamber.

'Don't be silly,' she reassured herself, 'Llachaqkuna Kamay is here. No one can hurt anyone.'

Something touched her shoulder. She started, turned to see long brown fingers rest lightly on her.

"You have something for Prince Heir Tupaq Yupanqui?" Chaski Yuyu asked. "He is waiting."

"Not Amaru?"

Chaski laughed softly. "No, woman. He is not the heir. You may need more leverage than a second son can provide." She bowed her head and gave him the khipu.

"Hurry," she exhorted. Then thought, I promised to see that message delivered. "I'm coming too," she called, unheard.

She followed Chaski Yuyu as he sidled through the crowd, watched by tense and hostile eyes, to Tupaq's litter and handed him the khipu. Tupaq read it and sent it back to Amaru. Tuya watched Tupaq and Chaski Yuyu confer, then the Khipucamayoq went to Amaru's sedan chair. Amaru leaned over to listen. Chaski Yuyu fell into line between the palanquins. Tuya sneaked up behind the Khipu Camayoc to catch a glimpse of Amaru. The beautiful Prince's eyes seemed to flash at her for an instant, stopping her breath. Was it imagined?

Tupaq signaled a green-and-gold feathered High Priest of the Temple of Pachamama, who in turn gestured to his aides.

A dozen of his party peeled off from the queue and hurried quietly toward a side exit from the temple complex to the Manyaraki plaza. The main body Pachamama monastics approached the principal portal, blocked by Ilaypa militant monks. A messenger from Amaru's company ran toward the rope bridge on another mission. Something was up, Tuya decided, something the Ilyapas wouldn't like.

Tupaq's litter came bustling up behind Tuya, brushing her aside. "Go, Brother," Amaru called, "Leave the guard behind."

"Inti! I want to see this through," Tupaq complained, "I want to see the water flow."

"Trust Otoronqo. Antarqui Ramram's work will be decisive. He will need us." Amaru dismounted his ride with fluid grace, Tupaq vaulted out of his, they strode away.

'He DID shoot me a little smile this time,' Tuya told herself.

Green-liveried Pachamama acolytes rushed along behind her toward the gate sentried by the monks of Ilyapa. The column seemed to go on forever, blocking her from retreating, pulling her along with them. They ignored her, though she was the only woman anywhere in the plaza.

The purple-and-black-robed militant Ilyapa monks stepped out in unison block the green monks, eyes hard, faces caved in by constant self-starvation. Their right hands were in the wool pouches at their sides; Tuya saw the glint of a bronze tumi blade.

The two ranking bishops faced off, the green-hat gentle and deferential, Simi Apaq of Ilyapa hard-eyed and haughty. Tuya knew his face and function from Qachu. “This access is restricted. Return to your assigned positions.”

“Forgive me, Villaq. We have been sent.” He displayed the khipu. Tuya edged closer, listening intently. The Ilyapa priest frowned at the knotted strings. He could not read khipu. He threw it on the flagstones.

“Sapa Inka Pachacutiq has placed his trust in us to guard these gates, and we will.”

Still no one told Tuya to leave. Something critical was about to happen.

A file of soldiers in the uniforms of Otoronqo's brigade jogged across the bridge to the scene of the impasse. With them was a disheveled official in a blue and silver unku, grave faced.

The purple monks and the soldiers faced off, shuffling. Llachaqkuna Kamay was in force here, violence would rebound on itself. No one knew how that would work. If the Pachamama priests just pushed forward, would Llachaqkuna treat them as aggressors, or let them through?

General Otoronqo Kuy forced himself between the deadlocked clerics.

“This is Water Master Unu Sunqu. He is instructed to activate the fountain system immediately. Here is our authorization. It is the command of the Prince Heir Tupaq Yupanqui.”

So that was it. Ramram’s water. Ilyapa was blocking the flow.

It was as if she was invisible. An unarmed woman in a conflict of men. She slipped between the face-off of high priests to crouch in the gateway itself, blocked by Ilyapa monks in purple cumbi cloth.

More were running from the Water Temple in double file, bearing smoking ceramic pots. Tuya recognized the stench from her time with Qachu. She turned around, slithered between the purple monks to where Otoronqo Kuy stood in command of his troops. She was blocked by a clutch of Storm God ecclesiastics in purple and gold. She pushed her head between two tall High Priests; she could see the general Otoronqo just rikras away.

"Hukwa!" she shouted, hoping to get his attention, "They are carrying hukwa!" Otoronqo turned her way, puzzled. Maybe he didn't know what hukwa was? "To kill llachakuna kamay!"

A flight of the pots arced overhead, thrown by the monks. Some bounced off bodies and rolled, spilling their contents; others hit the stone of the gate and the flagstones plaza, exploding. Acrid smoke rose like snakes heads, carrying particles of the venomous agent, covering both monks and soldiers.

She was grabbed by the hair and jerked backwards, turned violently around and choked by the neck. She found herself looking up into the pinched, glitter-eyed face of Simi Apaq, the Vice High Priest of Ilyapa, the man Qachu had warned her against. 'He is the moving force in this war,' Qachu had said, 'the master of the killer cult." His long, boney hand rose from her throat to her face, fingers digging into her cheeks, twisting her jaw. The hukwa fumes entered her, making her dizzy.

"Umu Antarqui's woman," he hissed. "He will miss you. Briefly." A half-moon blade flashed in his left hand. He wrestled her head back, baring her throat.

Rather than struggle against his strength, Tuya lifted her feet, bending her knees until her calves doubled against her thighs, putting her full weight onto Simi Apaq's hand with it's grip on her face; she dropped like a rock to the ground, leaving his fingers curled on empty air.

On her hands and knees, Tuya wormed between the legs of the monks, now in frantic struggle with the Inka warriors.

Someone grabbed her leg, pulling her backwards. With a desperate lunge, she grabbed an ankle wearing a military sandal and pulled herself free. She looked up; General Otoronqo Kuy looked down at her. She gave him a sheepish grin and wriggled in among the soldiers, now freed of the peace-enforcing *Administration of Justice*, llachaqkuna kamay, battling the armed monks.

She crawled beyond the knot of fighters, pushed herself to her knees, panting, assessing the fight.

The soldiers were outnumbered by three to one. From a side gate, a second contingent of purple monks, led by the Hatun Villaq, rushed into the caustic haze to assault the soldiers from behind. The rear squad of Otoronqo's flag company about-faced.

At a sharp hand signal from the High Priest of Ilyapa, a hundred devotees drew keen-edged tumi knives, probably poisoned Tuya guessed, and leapt forward, front and rear.

She saw the green-and-gold robed Villaq Umu of Pachamama go down, clutching his slashed throat. Two flanking soldiers dropped beside him dying. In return, K'anchay, the High Priest of Ilyapa, took a spear in the heart.

'Oh no,' Tuya thought, 'That's bad. That gives Simi Apaq command.'

Otoronqo's troops were elite veterans and their javelins flashed into the crowd of monks. Tuya pushed herself to her feet, ready to run for her life if the monks took the field.

As Inka rear guard double-timed into formation, sandwiched the Ilyapa reinforcements from behind, releasing a cloud of slingstones at close range, then deadly javelins, then closing with star-headed bronze maces. Tuya's heart lifted.

It looked like ninety soldiers still stood against more than two hundred zealots, but Otoronqo's men had the initiative. Maybe seventy Ilyapa casualties were scattered on both sides of the portal. She saw Tupaq Yupanqui and Amaru, far off, climbing the slope of Pinkuylluna, faces turned to watch their soldiers taking control of the inner gate, forming a semicircle of lances.

With shameless spite, she watched Simi Apaq calculate the odds of his own survival, hardly about to die now that the position of High Priest was finally his, slipping away toward the Water Temple, then stop, smooth his robe and rap an order to his monks, who instantly stood aside, raising their arms in concession, but still arrogant as if deigning permission to unruly children.

The soldiers formed protective lines within either side of the gateway. The priests in green filed through. Swiftly, both sides pulled the dead and wounded into the shadow of the dry double-grooved fountain carved into its writhing capstone of raw igneous rock. Workers in Pachamama green began clearing out the pots of hukwa. The violence here was over. The hukwa was dissipating in the breeze.

"Come with me." Otoronqo's aide de camp Choque Anka, still looking fifteen years old, took Tuya by the shoulder, gently but with undefiable authority. "If you go back to the crowd the Mamacunas will have you making chicha until you drop."

He left her on the first terrace at the foot of the staircase shooting up into the sacred confines of the Qoripata temple complex. Far above, she could see the flash of gold. The Sapa Inka Pachacuti would be there, watching. What had he thought of the happenings below?

She watched the Ilyapas withdraw beyond the Water Temple. Thin Water Master Unu Sunqu signaled to a clutch of chaski runners waiting outside the wall, who dispersed at top speed, toward, Tuya surmised, the water flow control points. Bronze mirrors on the mountains flashed commands.

She heard many feet rapping on the stairs behind her; Pachacuti's honor guard came double-timing down. Choque Anka loped across to meet him.

"I'm instructed to check out what's going on down here."

"What does the Unique Ruler think just happened?"

"Not much, I guess. He just said, 'Priests. Go down and see. Be polite, they're holy men.' What was all that?"

"Water. Tupaq wants it running."

"Good. World Changer is in a pissy mood. The sound of water always cheers him up."

Tuya had been suppressing a cough; now it worked free, a small explosive noise. They looked at her. She looked up. Their gaze followed hers. Water rushed down the stone channel from the mountain springs.

High up among the temples, where the Inka was, a ceremony approached its apogee, an involuntary sigh emitted from the thousands of participants arrayed as they heard, could even scent, the canals rush full of sweet spring water and the fountains gush throughout Qoripata, as the stone channels of the town filled, bringing the Pachamama in all her forms back to the streets of Pachamamatambo. The atmosphere flowed with a quickening freshness. A bank of clouds rolled in from Wayki Willka, Sacred Tears, the glacial peak to the west. For a little while, Tuya had almost forgotten that this was day that Ramram would die.

Regicide

Simi Apaq watched the honor guard descend to the esplanade. He saw that Otoronqo Kuy's troops were arrayed around the Manyaraki gate or off to open the acequia sluices. The princes were gone somewhere. Above, the Sapa Inka was unguarded. The Hatun Villaq was killed. Simi Apaq was now in charge.

He had almost two hundred acolytes below and another hundred on the terrace at the Sapa Inka's feet under his command. Many were militant monks in black and purple robes, highly trained in assassination armed with keen-edged blades. Twenty would be more than enough.

The former Villaq Umu would not have considered regicide, he would sooner put out his eyes. The still living, newly self-promoted, High Priest saw an opportunity to win this war of the Apus in one simple miraculous stroke. To kill a king.

With old Viracocha Inka, or one of his chosen sons, wearing the Borla, the minions of Pachamama would be harmless, and their flying Umu and his plotters dead.

He lifted a hand to give the command.

Tuya made her way up to the third terrace of the Qoripata where she was ordered to witness her husband fall and die as had her friend Qantuta. At her feet were ceramic braziers and painted lines of hukwa. The entire complex was planted with these because the Sapa Inka did not want his martial powers gelded by Llachaqkuna Kamay.

She heard the slapping of many sandaled feet and saw a long line of Ilyapa monks running headlong up the far staircase, out of sight of the Inka and his guard. She noted that Otoronqo's men, what there were of them, were out of range. It came to her what was about to happen. The thought was breathtaking, but she knew it would make sense to Simi Apaq. It would decide everything.

She saw the Imperial Guard at attention on the lawn. She thought she saw Qachu vanish into Inkamisana kancha, away from the fight. Where had he been?

If the hukwa had its effect, the assassins would kill the Inka. If not, they would rend only themselves.

She kicked over the smoking pot, dispersed it with her foot. She hurried to the next level, breaking every container that she could reach.

She passed her own assigned level, saw the monks ascending too rapidly, and ran frantically toward the forbidden terrace of the Sapa Inka himself.

She decided to bypass the lower levels and attack the hukwa planted on the approach to the final staircase. She arrived out of breath, just as the first of the Ilyapas appeared at the other end of the stone path, eighty rikras away, pointing and shouting. She threw three pots over the andene, smeared the lines of greasy hukwa with her heel, and started up the last staircase, peering up toward the Inka's platform.

She got to the blind bend at the top step, turned the corner, saw that the Ilyapa ceremony was still in progress on the plaza just below the imperial deck. She was blocked. She could see the Inca seated above, impassive. In despair, she looked for another approach. There, to the left.

The Ilyapas were now ascending the flight she had just left. She ran through a tall stone door into a magnificently masoned hall where nobles in sumptuous capes were lined along the inner side, tasting aromatic delicacies. She kicked over plates and bowls as she flew through, skidded on a golden server but regained her footing. She snatched aside an embroidered curtain.

She exited the matching door, coming into the light. Below, she could see the Imperial Guard returning at double-time. Far too late.

She took a corner and skidded into the Imperial Presence, between the Inka seated on his platform and the chanting, gesticulating priests. The braziers here were gold and silver and lined side by side; there must have been fifty. She snatched the first one and threw it as far over the heads of the worshippers as she could. They must not be inundated.

She heard the oncoming villaq screaming over the chanting. It sounded like "Stop her!" and then, "Kill him!" A conch shell trumpeted, close by, giving some command known only to the Ilyapas.

The Inka remained unmoved. She hurled the containers in any direction that seemed open. The tang from the silver qeros was different, she didn't know what it was but she didn't trust it. She took a deep breath, approached the Inka himself, took two vats from within a forearm's length of him, and tossed them behind her. He leaned toward her, elbow on his knee, brow furrowed.

The flagstones were smeared with spilled hukwa and hampi. The smoke was still in the air. The priests broke through, entering the patio. The villaq and the few priests behind hesitated, slowing. The counter spell was weakened, but still in effect. Llachaqkuna Kamay began to rise. Weakly.

The villaq pushed through the ceremonial priests, shouting "Take him. Kill the man!" Even now he could not speak the words

'Kill the Inka.' Purple and black monks swarmed around him, hands clawed toward Pachacutiq.

A shadow dropped from the unfinished sun temple above. There was frantic action, there were grunts, cries, curses. Then Qachu lay slain on a pile of purple and black corpses, soaked in their blood and his own.

Simi Apaq stood exposed, nostrils wide and eyes blazing, a poisoned blade high in his fist .

Tuya threw away the last of the smoking gold shells. She stepped in front of the Sapa Inka Pachacutiq Yupanqui and spread her arms wide. He seemed unconcerned.

The Ñusta Misk'i slipped onto the court, a thin, barbed lance in her hands. Simi Apaq saw her beyond the bitch wife of the Antarqui. He grinned at her. Misk'i laughed back at him, full of triumphant hatred and lethal intent.

"I will have her,' the Villaq Umu rasped, smirking into Tuya's eyes, "Over that usurper's carcass! And then you."

The ceremony in honor of Ilyapa went on as if nothing were wrong. The officiating Priest of the Storm raised his hands high in supplication to his god.

A blue web of lightning struck the peak of Pinkuylluna. Thunder stunned the ears of the town. Rain came in blinding gouts from horizon to horizon. It came so hard that Tuya was driven to her knees, and Simi Apaq covered his eyes with his cloak.

Tuya raised her eyes, wiped them clear. She saw that Simi Apaq was directly in front of the Sapa Inka with his blade, a step away, face to face with the demonic Misk'i. "Together!" he shrieked, and put his foot down hard on Tuya's neck.

The hukwa dissolved in the cleansing torrent.

The Ñusta Misk'i, a breath before the Llachaqkuna Kamay swept away her ability to hurt anyone but herself, saw both the High Priest, knife raised, and the Royal murderer of her beloved sister frozen together in a sheet of lightning. She laughed. The lust for blood was on her face. She thrust her long, delicate, deadly spearpoint into the naked throat of Simi Apaq.

The ceremony priest — now Hatun Villaq-to-be of Ilyapa — and his minions, danced as if in wild triumph, as he inwardly cursed his own traitorous deity, and blessed his luck. He had not committed. Acolytes stepped from behind to smuggle away the dead, disguising their actions as ritual.

Tuya struggled to her feet, looked up at the Sapa Inka, solid as stone, alive. She turned to Misk'i, whose face was lifted to the storm. She slipped away down the temple hill.

Inka Pachacutiq raised his gaze toward the watchtower where Ramram's last act was coming due, but the layered curtains of rain blurred the mountain. The drops were warm and packed with minuscule cells of green life. His eyes began to clear.

An Already Scheduled Death

The rain slammed into the tower. Behind Ramram to each side stood Tupaq and Amaru, tugging Ramram by a rope around his waist to keep him from falling forward too soon. Inside the tower Chaski Yuyu cradled the lichen-encrusted stone, infused with the power of Pachamama that had, as Ramram had hoped, spellbound the guards into baffled uselessness.Their plot would now bear fruit or bring death and disgrace.

The Antarqui's winged device, a construction extrapolated from the little gliding gods he had seen in the hands of the priests of Pachacamac, enhanced by refined growths from Amaru's laboratory, had been spirited into hiding in the qolqa just up the path. No one else had seen that thing fly, and Ramram had only tried it from low hills with a good western wind, and not wet.

Well, it would be only a small embarrassment for the princes, and an already scheduled death for Ramram. Though neither would be happy to explain the failure to Tuya.

CHAPTER FIFTY-ONE now

Worthless

Ollantaytambo

Dani Huallpa Quispe laughed at weakness in others. He treated the girls like servants. He ignored his mother's pleas, and his father's orders. He sold *medicina*, san pedro cactus cocktails, to the touristas, faking ancient ceremonies, screwing the pretty ones. He had climbed this mountain sure of himself. Now he grasped the pentagonal shaft of the crowbar thrust between the stone slab that had not moved in more than five centuries and the living rock of Bandolista Mountain. He wrapped his fingers around the steel with voluptuous confidence, braced his cherished trainers against the ledge beneath the frigid water, and leaned backward, prying with all his weight and strength.

Nothing moved. He shifted his grip, tried again, his fingers, shoulders, and legs straining, lips pulling away from his teeth. Nothing moved. Three more times he put all his back, his legs, his arms, his pride, his soul, into the attempt. He fell forward, pushed his face into the water, came up shuddering. He knew he had just one more try in him. If he failed, he could not return to his village or to his family.

He stood, looked at the dark cloud now lowering over the land. He re-gripped the bar, re-stanced his feet at an angle that promised to throw him off the cliff at any slip or loss of footing, and leaned into the emptiness with all his weight. "Grandfather," he cried to the sky. "Help me!"

Sentient microorganisms swarmed up from the chill waters, swallowing the rock, the bar, the boy foot to head.

The slab slid, smoothly, easily. The bar recoiled, throwing him backward to fall forever, then sprung forward, away from the great void. His hands plunged into icy water, the crowbar spinning into space behind. He stood back on the flat rock and watched pressure drive a great column of lake through its own spume far out over the precipice and down into the ancient channel carved into the mountainside, down toward the sacred fountains of his ancestors.

"Grandfather," he swore, "Tayta. Teach me. I'm ready. What you know, it's okay, I won't let it die." The sky rumbled and began to open.

The Black Lake

Katari heard the water coming fast down the Manyaraki acequia. Above, the Bandolista acequia filled, and fed the many fountains in the ruins. Canals dry for generations were flooded by the rivers Yuraqmayo and San Pablo, quebradas Phaqchapata and Pumaphaqcha. The Inka Watana canal, empty for centuries, filled and rushed to the sun-temple high on Bandolista Mountain, startling a second cousin of Camadreja-Quispe at his post. But this was not enough. There was not enough water to drown the black tide that ate its way up into the mountains.

Then there was a thundering high on Bandolista Mountain — the stampede of charging water. First it hit the canals, then overflowed onto the hills until it struck the town, flooding the plateau of the Water Temple complex with hundreds of thousands of tons of dark cold liquid. The Patacancha riverbed filled, climbing the banks, charging toward the Urubamba River. It clawed onto the streets, surging through the town. Mothers snatched their children up, automobiles pulled over, drivers honked aggressively until they saw the flood coming under their own car doors. Carried by the water were all the strains of prokaryote life vital to Pachamama.

An old woman standing near Katari lifted her puppy into her arms, laughing aloud under her battered high-top fedora. "*Yanaqocha chayapun*!" she exalted. "The black lake is back!"

"What do you mean?" Katari asked in Quechua.

“They thought we have all forgotten. Haw!” The old woman, black eyes glinting, shoulders shaking with laughter under the inevitable load an old woman carries in the Andes. “We have not all forgotten.” She pointed into the mountains with her puppy’s nose. “Not since *ñawpa pacha*, ancient times, has Yanaqocha been free. Here she comes!”

Water was everywhere. The people had listened, Katari marveled, and more incredibly, had found the power to release the blocked waters in less than an hour. The waters ran and she smiled at last. Checking her watch, which had stopped, then her cell — the battery was dead — she turned and started back up the streets to the Pinkuylluna access staircase for the last time. It was now or never. Noe and Raoul joined her from the cafe. Overhead, the sky had gone dark.

The waters came down into the town in force. Lightning struck the jagged tooth at the summit of Pinkuylluna, startling a brown-winged condor. She lifted into the black tattered sky. The rains exploded overhead. By the time Katari took the threadlike side path to the Tunupa Viracocha Corona watchtower, she could not see five meters ahead.

CHAPTER FIFTY-TWO now

Dance Cowboy Dance
Berkeley

A wind whipped up. Lily's long heavy hair heaved, then the wind caught Ephraim, kicking dust in his eye as they struggled to get him in under the hang glider, which bucked and thundered in the gale, trying to break loose. Thick dark clouds were moving in over the Pacific, black but limned with that luminous rainbow effect the bacterial being brought. And dry. The polymer wing tore free. With a groan, Ephraim went after it; Bingham stomped on a corner as it touched the ground, pinning it. Panting, they and Lily joined the rest of the nothings watching the police invading the hilltop.

A strange tableau met their eyes. The police were halted as if mesmerized as nothing girl stepped defiantly in front of them, and nothing boy inserted himself in front of her, and she in turn writhed stubbornly back between her boy and the cops. The boy fought to reverse their positions. Their feet seemed to pirouette around each other, their bodies rubbed together as they twisted for position, like snakes spiralling around an invisible Rod of Asclepius. The nearest police raised their clubs as if to strike, but hesitated, batons vibrating over the kid's heads as they vied for the sacrificial position. The armored police even backed away a step to let the drama play out, as if forbidden to strike until one or the other, boy or girl, emerged winner.

"It's like a dance," said Lily in wonder, "a weird, beautiful dance!"

"We could use a dance right now," said Ephraim. He looked at the lowering sky. "A rain dance." He did a little hop-step.

"To wash this stinking glop away," added sharp-eyed Angus, and he copied Ephraim's little caper.

"And bring back the Eye Kay, by god," interjected Bingham.

“Rain dance!” Lily called, getting other glop-sopping kids to look her way. She did a heart-stopping little side-to-side rocking dance, arms out like gull wings.

“Right. Rain dance.” Ephraim tried a couple Apache-style moves, head bent low.

'Yeah, right,' Bingham muttered, 'like I’m going to sacrifice my dignity for that.” Then, “Oh fuck, what dignity?” And he began a not-quite-satiric buck-and-wing, and yelled “Rain fucking dance!”

I look silly, thought Ephraim, picturing himself stopping after one or two more little soft-shoe moves. But he didn’t stop. Something possessed him. He felt within himself for the cadence. He dropped the funny stuff, began to stomp rhythmically, feeling a deep beat coming from his gut. No, from the earth itself. Deliberately, emphatically. His eyes closed. Something happened to time. He heard an echo to his footfalls and looked through his lashes at Bingham, who was facing him and mirroring his atavistic shuffle-stamp with animal concentration.

“Rain dance!” He heard some voice he did not recognize, a call to feet. “Rain dance!”

THUMP thump THUMP thump, he went on, and when he opened his eyes, he was facing Lily, still doing her gull wing dance, but to his beat, eyes intense on his, arms sinuous. And beside her were both of Bing’s lovers, taking their cue from her — they both minored in dance — and more guys crowding in, inserting themselves next to the girls, so Ephraim stomp-danced backwards to widen the circle.

A Zuni from New Mexico appeared in the center, doing the authentic thing, feet coming down and rising so masterfully, seeming to barely caress the earth before effortlessly lifting again, fingertips tented, chanting softly. On his other side, the only old man among the band, a professor of meteorology, was keeping perfect and tireless time, remembering 1969.

Around them formed a wider circle of dancers, some of them already peaking on mushrooms, MDMA, peyote, rosewood seed, morning glory, ketamine, lysergic acid, E.T. Thomas among them.

He wasn't dancing anymore, not Ephraim Arrowsmith. It was the earth itself, moving him, the sound of their feet was a thunder. A flash recollection of choreomania came to him, the dancing plague that had consumed medieval Europe, then just the beat again.

Nobody was ironic here, nobody was smirking. They were dancing for rain and they meant it.

And the clouds were low overhead and limned in jewel light and the first drops came down. Then the sky roared loose, vomiting deluge on the land.

The police broke out of their trance, throwing nothing girl and nothing boy to the ground, ratcheting cuffs tight on their wrists, flex cuffing their ankles together. Then they raised their eyes to the scene on the hill above, outrage flooding into their faces as if realizing that they had been duped, and they charged into the storm. Water now surged downhill between their boots, drove blindingly into their faces. Teeth bared, ravenous to beat and subdue, they stampeded into the mass of ecoterrorist snowflakes now writhing and laughing in the iridescent mud.

Ephraim, still on his feet, stood facing them, hair plastered to his forehead, warm rain sheeting his features. A sergeant of the Oakland City Police grabbed him roughly by the arm and neck, throwing him down, unholstering his service weapon, while a Berkeley SWAT team leader slammed Lily into a chokehold with his billy club, reaching behind to access handcuffs, which, suddenly slowed and uncertain in his movements, he snapped onto his own left wrist, dropping the baton, then onto his right wrist with his left. The Oakland officer, hands shaking, struggling against his own impulses, fired a round into his own leg, crumbling to the mud, grimacing in pain.

The gunshot stopped everything. The police let go of whoever they were apprehending, stared at the downed officer, at each other, at themselves. The dripping nothings, now on their feet, looked in wonder upon the Boschian spectacle of armed policemen beating and manacling themselves. Eye Kay was back.

Across the valley, NTT snipers in their Eye-Kay proofed body suits, squinted through rain-repellant scopes, waiting for a break in the rain, while their spotters kept their M151 12 by 40x fogproof weather resistant optics on their assigned targets. Ephraim, Lily, Bingham.

On Flute Mountain

Katari, Noe, and Raoul huddled in the brutal rain, finding not much shelter by the broken walls of an Inka warehouse a few meters above the faint path leading to the Tunupa Crown watchtower. The paraglider remained sheathed.

"I do believe the prokaryote aerosol is reconstituting," Noe said, voice raised over the din of the rain. She was curled into the deepest corner.

Raoul lifted his head from his sopping hoodie. "The Rainbow Cloud? Is it?"

"By the baby jesus so it is," agreed Katari, "It is bigger and brighter than when the airplanes left. I will try it."

"Even in the rain?" Raoul looked into Katari's eyes, brow furrowed.

"Can it fly in the rain?"

"I don't know. Not so well."

"This rain sounds like stampeding bison," said Noe. "Anomalous. In the US rain does not manifest that acoustic property. Wait. That's not rain!"

She saw Katari try to leap to her feet, Raoul following, then blurred figures, big ones, had Katari by the arms, a hand over her mouth. Raoul took a boxing stance, and a strike to the temple with some kind of black metal rod. He went down. Katari was dragged off, kicking. Two figures resolved out of the murk, coming Noe's way. She recognized the Briarpatch mercenary agents. She got her butt off the ground high enough to roll over the low wall onto the steep hillside. Her six-days-a-week training discipline in the mountains gave her the balance and confidence to keep her feet, using the wirey brush for support. The two mercs vaulted over the stone wall; one, the big one, immediately slipped and disappeared down the grade, "Awww fuuuck" his parting cry. The other got a tenuous purchase on the rain-slick muddy ledge, twisted around in a skillful 360, pulled himself back over the wall, then looked down at where his buddy disappeared, then into Noe's eyes. She looked back, challenging him.

"We don't have no use for you nohow," said the operative hoarsely, turned and left.

Clinging to her hillside, Noe could see Katari being wrestled down the trail, fighting all the way, hands being cobra-cuffed behind her, feet lifted off the ground every couple steps.

"What do I do?" Noe said to herself aloud, voice rasping, as she scrambled back over the wall. "Do I follow them? Do I try to rescue them? Don't be silly, Noe Zoe, they are big men, trained to fight. Oh god, is he dead?" She sees Raoul lying limp, crumpled against the wall. She lifts his big, curly-haired head, feels for the vein in his neck.

"What are you doing?" slurred from his lips.

"Oh god, you are alive. Thank heavens."

"What's happening?" He is trying to sit up, sliding his back up the wall, hand palping his temple. Noe is suddenly annoyed with the man.

"That must have been the first thing you ever said," she snarked, "and it will probably be the last."

"Oh be quiet, Science Woman, I never said I was a smart one. But I am loyal."

Loyal? Every ego clings to something, she thought. She saw the rain had tapered off. There was sun breaking through a little east of center. She saw a thick watch on his hairy wrist, raised his forearm between her hands, wiped the fogged glass with her sleeve. It was twenty to twelve.

"Here is what is happening, Raoul. They have taken Katari. We cannot expect to rescue her. She won't be able to do what she came to do, so I must try. Can you assemble your glider device and instruct me in how to use it?"

Other Points of View

Former Agent Orange lays across Split Rock, binoculars dropping from his limp fingers and bouncing down the cliff. He came here, unshaven, unshowered, credit cards maxed out, to keep watch on his ex-colleagues and to thwart them in any way he could. The rock, recognizing his intent, fills him body and mind with wave after wave of crippling inner peace and a sense of oneness so incapacitating that all he can do is spread-eagle over the stone and roll his head from side to side, moaning in ecstasy.

Flying northeast from Teniente Alejandro Velasco Astete International Airport in Cusco, the pilot of the sleek little AT502B clenches his jaw. If he gets out of this alive, he will buy his own custom plane. All he need do is take this one into that meteorologically inexplicable nebulosity he has seen on the news and release his load of unidentified fungicide, if that is what it actually is, and get out. If he doesn't, his family will be rich anyway. He is happy the sudden storm is below him.

In Berkeley, driving rains flood the streets, culverts overload, a sinkhole opens on Milvia Street swallowing a Subaru. The creeks — Cerrito, Codornices, Blackberry, Schoolhouse, Strawberry, Derby, and Temescal — fill and overflow, lifting plastic bags and Styrofoam cups from their dry banks, floating them toward the bay. Then, like a curtain rising, the rain stops. The sun shows, bringing steam from the soil, foliage, t-shirts and jeans. The air is bright and full of life.

The three NTT snipers and their spotters on Telegraph Canyon ridge locate their targets, adjust their scopes.

“What’s that?” asks Sniper One of Sniper Three, whose nose and rifle barrel moused out of a waterproof camouflage tube.

“You ain’t seen a bivvy sack before?”

“A bivouac sack is for sleeping in inclement weather,” lectures Sniper Two. “It’ll constrain your movement, limit your leg-spread in prone unsupported position, and interfere with your vision.”

“Very unprofessional,” says Sniper One. "And pointless. This protective shielding is fully waterproof, lab tested.”

“Well, guys, if I miss you can give me nuggies. But it works for me. I hate being cold and wet. I held position for eighteen hours in a blizzard in Kandahar and that was enough for me.”

“Well, see that you wait until we’ve made our shots to take yours. We don’t want you spooking the game.”

NTT headquarters, somewhere in Virginia. The once seedy place now gleams. LCD screens on matched tables, some showing maps, numbers, graphs, video reports, satellite photos of stunning resolution, spec charts of secret weapons years ahead of what the informed public is aware.

The General pushes his chair back from the long table. “So we have the numbers. The conclusive advantage. On all fronts. From the most pessimistic perspective. No bull.”

His Deputy Director concurs. “Sir, it has all been smoke and mirrors on their side. Parlor tricks. They never had a chance. I mean, look at what they think they are trying to do, and with what.”

“That’s what I told the President. Even before we had the numbers.”

CHAPTER FIFTY-THREE now

Snipers Are a Tough Audience

Noe bullies Raoul onto the spider-thin path, barely a trail, along the cliff down to Tunupa's Crown. She leads, holding one end of the sheathed paraglider, he on the other. They walk with extreme care, testing every footfall. The rain has quit, but the sun hasn't come out yet. At the bottom, they realize that there is no entrance on the path side; they will have to go around a corner to the right, bordered by a fringe of grass maybe a foot wide, beyond which is empty air forever down. Noe backs up against the rough fieldstone wall, shifting the glider's end up and down, back and forth, trying to work out an angle that won't throw one of them into the void.

"Oh for the sake of Pete," says Raoul, exasperated. "Give to me." He takes the three-meter concertina packing bag, holds it straight up, sidles past her pushing against her breasts, and, holding it over his head, steps around the scary corner and into the entrance of the roofless cube. She follows, pressed against the stones.

"Shit. Not much room," he gripes, but unpacks. Noe looks down across to the cloud, now pulsing in candy colors, just as the sun comes out.

Her knees weaken. It is more than five hundred meters, five city blocks, to the cloud, and death many meters to the valley floor. "I can't do this," she says aloud. She waits for the fearless Brazilian to say that he will.

"I do not blame you," he answers. "Neither can I. So let's go home."

"Just put it together," she sighs in a small voice.

Together, questioning and contradicting one another, turning the unfolding thing one way and another, they get it done. He holds the pillow-shaped wing up behind her.

Noe looks out across the town. Her shadow is under her. She carefully situates the chest strap of the high-performance ripstop nylon paraglider, the contoured seat to her butt. She will not be able to fully seat herself until she jumps. She maneuvers herself at an angle to avoid scraping the tower and pushing herself prematurely off the precipice.

She knows she and her vividly colored wing will be clearly visible from below and across the valley, so there is an element of stage fright. Snipers are a tough audience. But the fall, that is a much tougher one. The sky looks good; the clouds are cumulus, and warm air lifts from below, the sun is finally out, but she does not really believe she will fly. She will only fall, fall, fall, fall. And yet there is a tingle, a lifting within her. Her microbiome, her beloved prokaryote bugs, are somehow with her. It is almost time. Where is her cue? Now? Something in the air, almost a voice, and why not, the Presence is everywhere, says: Wait. Wait. Wait.

The rainbow cloud bulges, fills from the center out with a silent pink and gold explosion. A chime sounds between her ears. Now.

The Rains of Double Swirly Hill

With the police out of the equation, Ephraim decided to try the hang glider in the rain. Who knew when it would quit.

"I can't see ten meters ahead of myself," called Ephraim over the cascade rush of the rainfall, stumbling under the wing.

"I'll go ahead, warn you when you're near the edge," offered Angus.

"Okay. Thanks. Ephraim began to jog ahead, trying to keep the point of the triangle up. Angus trotted ahead, marked the danger point with a power drink can, ran back to lead Ephraim forward. The wind came from the northwest, hit the valley wall, caromed back right under the wing.

"I'm getting lift!" Ephraim exalted.

“You’ve still got thirty yards to…” called Sharp-Eyed Angus, whose head snapped back on his neck, his arms flying wide. He fell spread eagled onto the bunch grass, blood from his drilled skull diluting in the rain puddle.

On the Other Hill

“Got him,” rapped out sniper one, from his blind five hundred meters across Telegraph Canyon, lifting his rifle barrel, “right in his third eye.”

“No you didn’t,” said his spotter, flat-tone, “I told you to wait.”

“Fuck I didn’t. He was coming right at me, brown hair blue shirt, jeans. I saw my shot and I took it.”

‘You shot the wrong man. The guy you shot was leading. Your man was behind. Now you spooked him. All of them.”

God Damn You Boy

At the instant Ephraim’s quasi-doppelganger died, the sun came out. The fine failing rain seemed to prism everywhere, as if the hilltop was inside a rainbow. Ephrain hauled the wing to a halt. Bingham and Lily ran to Angus, turned him over. Bingham pushed Lily flat, lay down himself.

“Everybody down! Sniper!” he shouted. “Everybody down!” Then, to Lily, “Crawl. There’s a dip over there. Crawl.”

“Fuck crawl,” she snapped back, pushed herself up and ran to Ephraim. “Shooter, Eph. Drop that and run. God damn you boy, run!”

“I can’t,” he said low, “It’s time. You go. You can’t help.”

“God damn you my love,” she said, tears in her voice, and ran.

All over the hill the nothings took cover, many not even knowing why.

Ephraim got the wing over him again and ran for the edge of the hill.

It Is Time

It is high noon at coordinates 13°15′29″S 72°15′48″W, Ollantaytambo, Peru. E[phraim runs off the edge, falls into uncertainty, catches a warm updraft, soars over Telegraph Canyon. His chest is full of waiting for that bullet. Riding the thermal, he is wafted high over the stunted live oaks, struggling to navigate into the great blob of bioluminescence that beats like a huge heart above the valley floor. He fixes his eyes on the undulating cloud. The outer edge seems to catch fire, pulsing with waves of sliding rose and gold, heaving as if breathing. From the center comes a humming chord that electrifies his scalp and fills his head with light.

He sees black smoke chewing up from below. The black rainbow killer stuff. He forces himself to relax, knowing that, counter-intuitively, it will make steering easier. He has only done this once before and then without any particular destination. His wing tilts too far to the left, he begins to circle, corrects, then, taking a deep breath, inhales a kind of perfect oneness with his wing, the wind, and the world. “Lily,” he whispers, “live.”

He takes his shot.

The stupid shit kid gives him a second chance. Fool. Sniper One follows Ephraim’s flight through his M8541 Scout Sniper Day Scope, getting a clear, steady sight picture. He waits for the moment that his target will approach him head on; with the breeze doing what it was it wouldn’t be long. His prey was in the weird fuzzy kaleidoscope fog now, just swooping around, up and down, making tight turns and then long centrifugal glides. He takes his shot. The wing flips and drops sideways to the valley floor.

Sniper Two waits for the two dumb blondes to move away from where his slope target crouches, thinking she is safe in that dip, watching the boy and his dumbass wing. Then Lily stands, inexplicably, still as a plaster saint, hands clutched between her pretty tits. He hits her in the face, then again in her linked fingers before they could untwine. Time to pack up and boogie.

Sniper Three takes his time; what was up with the other guys? Silencers? Screw it. Not his problem. He settles into the sniper scope. The two archaeologist groupies, if there was such an idiot subculture, crawl over to flank the smug little bastard in his bush hat, each taking him by the arm. In for a surprise, girlies. He gets a perfect sight on his bearded head, strokes the trigger. The rifle butts his shoulder. Right through the throat. Adios, Professor. Now comes a rifle shot from over by the others; then another.

He Falls

In Pachamamatambo, Tawantinsuyu, a torrential rain has stopped. The unfrocked necromancer Antarqui Ramram poises in the wide south opening of the thatched tower, leaning out over the high cliff, laced into a construction looking something like dragonfly wings. His angle of lean is countered by two Princes of the Blood and General Otoronqo Kuy holding a rope around his waist.

On Pututu Mountain, across the valley and below, the Emperor Pachacutiq Yupanqui stares up at him, befuddled by warring inclinations.

The air sparkles. Ramram waits, wondering if he should just jump.

A light blooms in his belly, filling his body and head. He hears a note, high and clear, in both ears. “Now,” he says. The rope is loosed. He falls.

Fly, Wizard

The Apu Sapa Inka Pachacutiq Yupanqui watches the *rikachakuna* tower on Pinkuylluna Mountain from his tiyana. When the rains came, he had waved off the yanaconas with their canopy — they were too late anyway, it had been immediate — and had sat in the warm wet torrent gladly, no longer bored. Something strange had been going on with the ceremony, but no matter. Priests. The sound and sight of the water in the fountains, the sheets of rain, and now the moving water in the streets beyond the flooded river, has quickened him. He is alive again.

He sits knees spread, clothes steaming, looking at the tower from which the condemned man, never exactly defiant yet never truly obedient, would be ejected.

He has killed many men, in battle or by decree. His own brother, men who had fought for him and beside him, enemies he honored and would have promoted to high place had strategy allowed. Death is nothing to him. There has never been a day, not a breath, when he was not ready for his own. So, now, fly, wizard. Fly. And die.

Something out of order is happening at the aperture of the watchtower. No guards are visible flanking the gate to do the shoving. No Villaq Umu for the obsequies.

Instead, there is something polychrome shifting around up there. Something like a banner of aji red, wasp yellow, lapis blue. It emerges from behind the opening, spreads itself out on both sides, a strangely formed winglike entity, like fantastic dragonflies mating in flight. Under it, he can make out the slight frame of a man, wearing the green and gold livery of Amaru's house. Is his I-won't-fight son on that tower? No, Amaru is much taller, broader in the shoulder. Is it the Heir, Tupaq? He was supposed to be watching from the andenes below, but he was not. No, Tupaq is burlier.

No, it is the condemned man, the one-eyed, eight-fingered, recalcitrant curséd seagoing, rock-hunting Q'urpa. It is Lump, and he is spreading his arms along the winged thing, and he is balancing on the ledge, and he is...

Pachacutiq surges to his feet, spreads his arms, scattering his entourage, they unsure whether to rush to him or from him.

"Fly, Wizard, fly!"

CHAPTER FIFTY-FOUR god

What Happened, God's Eye View

The rainbow cloud hovered over Pachamamatambo, Ollantaytambo, Berkeley. A delicate foil-green hummingbird entered from Ollantaytambo, exited into Pachamamatambo, her tiny heart drumming at the richness of scents, and of so much oxygen.

The emperor Pachacutiq Inka Yupanqui and the many eyes of Pachamamatambo watched Ramram emerge from the watchtower, quadruple wings unfolding, the rear wing broader than the fore, dropping a rikra or three before gaining authority over gravity, moving with masterful control, rising, falling, canting, shifting direction, then, with intent, gliding toward the Kuychi Puyu, his hands at his chest manipulating the fine control lines, his legs stretched behind on supple bamboo struts. At the shredding edge of the cloud he backed upright for a breath, then shot into the blurring mist. As soon as he entered, the cloud expanded, filled with pink and yellow light. A multi-toned chime, a lost chord, filled the world. Far above, a brown female condor hovered on warm air.

In Berkeley, observers watched Ephraim in his blue jeans and chambray shirt run headlong off the slope of Double Swirly Hill under his green and yellow wedge of hang glider, plummet, lift on the breeze, rise and in seconds slip into the gently eddying bioluminescent fog.

In Ollantaytambo, watchers observed a lean figure pendant below the slender crescent of indigo ripstop nylon soar from Pinkuylluna Mountain in a narrow arc, into the shimmering cloud.

Onlookers in all three venues witnessed three winged figures enter the periphery, orient toward the center, approach the core.

A writhing column of oily black smoke rose from below, devouring the belly of the cloud, clawing to the heart.

From three launch points, a variant of the Israeli Harpy 2 unmanned aerial combat vehicle shot toward the nexus of the rainbow cloud, the drone itself being the warhead, a complex cocktail of chemical aerosol to dissipate the cloud and thermobaric explosive to eliminate the human components — Ephraim, Noe Zoe, Ramram, Katari, anyone too close.

A lone crop duster approached from the southwest, the pilot holding his wife and daughter in his mind's eye, they waiting in Trujillo, as he guided the plane toward the eerie candy glow of the cloud, below the Inka ruins. This is a solo mission, contingent on the failure of the others. His gloved hand closed around the release lever spilling potassium iodide to condense the cloud into fine tinted rain.

A sharpshooter in an anti-Eye Kay bodysuit sighted in from the roof of the mercado.

The black cloud clawed upward. The drones homed in. The cloud seeder drifted down. The finger stroked the trigger.

A white-gold point of light appeared in the heart of the brume, expanding, surrounding the incoming winged things, pulling them into itself, bringing them together. Six hands reached out to one another.

A silent explosion bloomed from the sunblast center of the cloud, spreading outward at blinding velocity.

The blast wave from the nexus roiled through the crowds and up the hill in all three pachas, and for an instant everyone of all loyalties and intents saw all three times and places all around them, and more, they saw the futures good and bad. And they saw each other, staring stunned at one another. Three times and places mingled in the luminous squall that enveloped the witnesses. Then that small confusion proliferated exponentially into an infinity of times, places and possibilities, passed beyond, was gone.

In Lawrence Berkeley National Laboratory, the blast passed through thirty-four physicists, their administrative personnel, graduate assistants, and custodial staff. They all saw clear and obvious the TOE, Theory of Everything, resolving all contradictions and paradoxes between General Relativity and Quantum Physics. It was so plainly evident that nobody bothered to record it. Then it was gone.

The rain shorted the generators. The LRAD sound cannons sat dead.

The Yana Turmanyay blew away in the sprinkled wind. The drones passed through and punched harmlessly into the hills. The sniper missed.

The pilot winced, waiting for the consequences of this *momento justicia*, this “instant justice,” to throw him and his plane to the ground. Nothing happened. His wife will have a husband, his daughter a father. “Nunca más,” he whispered, “Never again do I work for the government.”

That is what happened.

The Sapa Inka Pachacutiq stands, looks down to where the cloud had been. He sees the Antarqui Ramram kneeling on the flagstones below, shrugging out of his chumpi-cloth wings. His ministers, pale and silent, stand behind him.

Daniel Boone Cooper, low-level NTT agent dispatched to Ollantaytambo as a technical consultant, stands at the southeast corner of the plaza in Ollantaytambo in a faded blue raincoat torn at the shoulder and smeared round spectacles. Drops of colored precipitation glint in his hair, on his face. He is fingering the return ticket in his pocket. A man slides up beside him, wearing a navy windbreaker, cargo pants, and mirror sunglasses likewise smeared with glittering residue from the blast wave. “Did we win?” he asks from the corner of his mouth. “Did we lose? What do we do now? Any idea?”

“Yes,” says D.B.. “Be kind to someone. See what happens.”

Agent Orange wobbles back to the trail from Split Rock, sees his ex-buddies, soaking wet and crusted with something like pond scum, trudging disconsolately down.

“Hey guys,” he says.

“Hey Ron,” says Agent Guava, violating protocol. Agent Orange falls into line in front of them, leads them to the street.

“Ron Boy,” says Agent Mango, “what just happened?” Agent Orange only smiles, shakes his head. Everything seems so far away.

Sniper Three

Sniper Three wriggles out of his bivouac sack, disassembles and packs his rifle, and belly-crawls across toward his buddies. It all feels like a dream now.

A few yards away his colleagues lie silent, their fingers in their trigger guards, muzzles of their rifles in their mouths. The rain had been full of organisms bred to dissolve the anti-Eye Kay coating into harmless runoff. It had had however little effect on the man in the bivouac sack.

Ingrate

The NTT liquidator waited in the rain for Nick to come up the trail. Finding him up in the weirdness wasn't working, but they discovered that he left every few days to get supplies from one of his hick buddies. Rather than kill them both, he lurked by the marker stone for the deserter to return.

There the target came, stooped under the weight of his pack, eyes on the track, oblivious. This would be knife work.

He stood, shifted into position. He didn't get off a sound when the big cat hit him. An enormous dark cougar from nowhere slammed him down, his head impacting the boulder he had hidden behind, her teeth in his throat, severing his windpipe, then his head in her jaws, fangs in his temples. His skull cracked. She dragged him into the underbrush, took another chunk out of his neck. Stood paws apart, looking to be sure, then turned, slipped smoothly back past the marker rock.

Oblivious, Nick labored up the trail, took the turn into the Twist.

Above, the cougar watched with one eye topaz blue and one jade green. She opened her mouth wide, showing bloody teeth. After a while came a small high kwee.

We Will See

Voices hallooed from the peaks, from high up Kachiqhata hill, from the ridges, hooting from Bandolista Mountain, from Pinkuylluna, from the streets of the town, the patriarch Francisco Pizarro Comadreja-Quispe's sprawling family. Each of them standing by an open water control point.

What had happened? Who had won? Noe had seen heaven and then she had seen hell and now she stood on everyday Peruvian dirt, alive and unhurt, and maybe something had changed.

Katari staggered down onto the street by the plaza, unshackled and released. She had seen Noe leap from the tower. She laughed, and then she cried.

Francisco Pizarro Comadreja-Quispe's nephew and some of his neighbors came up on her, holding a wiry turista by the elbows, now stripped of his anti-Eye Kay body suit, prodding him with his own rifle."We can't hurt him. He can't hurt us. But the Llachaqkuna Kamay is letting us bring him to you. It must trust you. He tried to shoot you."

"It was not me, I regret to say," Katari replied. "But it was one of us." She reached into her shoulder bag, handed the boy a hundred sol bill. "Give him something to drink. Get something for yourselves. Wait to see how long this 'instant karma' lasts. Until then, he can't leave unless he intends us no harm." She exhaled, looked at the sky. Her mind seemed to rise into the blue, to belong there...

"I'm ready now" said Ephraim to Lily. The paramedics had gone down the hill, the archaeologist's body on one stretcher, sharp-eyed Angus on another. Lily nodded, pale.

“We did it. Whatever it was,” Ephraim whispered. “I don’t know what happened in there. I saw a crazy mess of times and places. I think Pachacutiq Inka — I tell you, Lily, he was scary as heck, even from a distance — saw us. I don’t know what he thought. I don’t know if we had the power to roll over the boulder and make him move. I guess we’ll see.”

“You will,” said Lily.

“Maybe you too,” He tentatively reached an arm around her. She decided to let him. “We will see.” He closed his eyes, enjoying the feel of her waist, his mind drifting…

CHAPTER FIFTY-FIVE now

After Action Report, Aat Na Rama Presides
Brasília, Brazil

“Welcome all. To the point. Eight days have elapsed since the activities in and dissolution of what were commonly referred to as the Clouds. Since, despite intensive investigation and research, apart from quotidian — easily explained — peripheral effects consequent to human involvement, no significant changes to constitutional planetary phenomena, temporal, physical, biological, or existential, have been identified.

“Of the several hundred data accumulation devices arranged to track, identify, quantify, and communicate modification or transformation of the status quo extant at the climactic interaction of forces and persons resulting in the consummation of the two critical meteorological anomalies, north and south, none have returned significant results.

“In simple terms, nothing has changed. People did things to and in the strange clouds, something happened, and they evaporated with a concussive effect, basically a gust of wind. One person was killed, an archaeologist, in what is being prosecuted as extrajudicial execution in the United States. All told, we are as we were. Nations, nature, physical law, space and time, remain intact.

"The increase in complexity and activity of microbiotic and associated organisms that preceded the event have subsided to a level significantly higher than a year ago but essentially the same as they were on the day before the clouds appeared.

“We were not wrong to take note, and action, on this issue. The preponderance of data indicated the possibility, at least, of a pervasive transformation of conditions acceptable to existing political and social institutions, to conditions unacceptable.The status quo, such as it is, survives intact and, friends, we can all go home. Questions? You, sir, speaking for the United States?"

"General Mack Jackman, NTT. The President of the United States of America demands confirmation that there will be no notable change in sovereignty or boundaries on our western border?"

"General, as we understand your question, no."

"The President of the United States of America would like to state, on record, that he told you so."

"So noted. Further questions or comments? Then, people, let us adjourn."

Unrecorded

The death of Sharp-Eyed Angus was not reported. No one knew who he was or asked about him.

Stupid Turd Boy

"I knew I was wrong." Ephraim sat on a log. "I knew I was wrong. I knew all along." He sat very still. His knees didn't jerk, his fingers didn't twist, his lips did not contort like fornicating tapeworms. His voice, like his life force, was low. "I knew it. All along. And I still sucked everybody into it. I am a toxic turd. Not the nutritious kind. It was my fault, mine alone. I know it's stupid, but I can't help feeling that I have always been alone in the world and I deserve to be."

"You have me!" Lily's eyes teared. "You had me!"

"Exactly. You should have left me there. I never would have known how sweet life can be."

"Don't you say that. Don't you dare."

"You're a dream come true. I feel like a dream come false."

"Are you trying to get into Wikiquotes? At my expense?"

“I mean, you're right. It's just self-pity. It's the best I can do." He looked up at Lily. His face felt like plastic. “I got everybody into this waste of time and life. It was all craziness. Everybody warned me. All delusion. How did I ever get you into this? Or poor Bingham. All that…masturbation...with Inkas and time travel. I think it was that...I think you...it was that…”

“It was nothing of the sort, stupid turd boy. My thing is genetic. We went to war together to save the world. So what if we lost. It’s just the world.” She took his lifeless hands in hers. “I love you, Eph. I respect you more than anyone. You always thought I had the upper hand, the high ground. I fought every minute not to show you how cheap I felt. I’m the show-off. You are the real thing. I was an empty cup, the town whore with a four-point-oh when I met you. Now I am full. Now I am real. I like being real.”

Ephraim sucked his lungs full, exhaled.

“You are going to..to...and I feel sorry for *my*self." He raised his head in a kind of wonder. "I have this voice in me I never knew was there, calling me names. It has always been there whispering at me and I never heard it. It's what makes me spaz out all the time. I'll be darned. Now I hear it.

"But you are right. We accomplished nothing except to be together trying. Bingham tried and look what happened. Noe Zoe tried. Even Katari. It seemed so real. We had good, sort of good, data impelling us. I mean, we weren’t all wrong.”

“Something did happen in that freaking mist, Ephraim. You saw it. Fuck, Ephraim, I saw it. Times, people, moving.”

“Sorry, Lil’. Hallucinations. The Crazy Cloud contained ergotamine-bearing pollen. The NTT report came out today.”

“I saw it,” Lily answered. “And the NTT is being disbanded as basically a fraud, a boondoggle based on pseudoscience.”

Ephraim laughed bitterly.

“Well, at least you are laughing. It’s good to hear. Ephraim, tell your whispery voice to go shit in his hat. Everybody feels like that sometimes. It's not the Voice of Truth. It's just something that comes and goes. All is impermanence. And the sparks fly upward." She grimaced. "Oh, I sound so bloody bombastic."

"Yeah," he laughed now simply, light coming into his eyes. "You sound like me." His iPhone played 'Colonel Bogey' in his rucksack. "Get that, will you?"

Lily fished it out, answered, "Arrowsmith and Tran, how may we impede you?" She listened, her eyebrows rising. She held the phone out.

"Eph, it's from the TSU embassy. We are being summoned. Both of us."

CHAPTER FIFTY-SIX now

Nothing Changed

Nothing had changed. The world was the world. That was that. Now Ephraim and Lily stood at the window looking out across the foil-blue bay, accepting their failure. Everything had seemed possible for a few heartbeats. They had felt themselves on the knife edge of a new history. Yet so impotent had they proven that the Powers That Be hadn't even bothered to chastise them.

In fact, Bingham Bonnaterre, recently an impoverished failure, had been quietly contacted, secretly briefed, then appointed to an elevated office and called to represent his country. There came to him a strangely cordial invitation by a rival nation, and even more unlikely, Ephraim Arrowsmith and Lily Tran were included.

"Ambassador Bonnaterre, I am Tumaqaya Curaca Molyay. Please allow me to welcome you to Chinchay Coyllur. North Star City to you. I am happy to say, I feel we have excellent news. I hope you will agree." The bronze-skinned young man in the elegantly tocapu'd chumpi-cloth unku smiled and nodded. Inkas did not shake hands. "Please accompany me, all of you, to my kancha."

They followed him from their waiting-wasi across an unroofed rock garden, into a spacious suite of rooms around what would in the United States be called the lobby but which Ephraim's studies told him would here in the Tawantinsuyu be called a "pata."

Bingham was thanking Curaca Molyay in passable Runasimi as they entered the office wasi, where four low tiyana stools awaited them around the circular biocomputer, shimmering in the smooth etched floor. Molyay sat with his back to the four large trapezoidal windows facing west, or, as the Inkas would put it, to the Kuntisuyu.

"Bingham. Lily. Ephraim. I am so proud, so grateful, to finally meet you. My ayllu has passed your names down for twenty-seven generations, awaiting this day.

"I am the direct descendant of the Antarqui Ramram and Tuya Occlo. For five hundred and thirty-eight years we have watched and waited for you to be born, to grow into your majority, to find your place in the world, and to come to this *llacta*, to be honored.

"This location was in your original Pacha, now wonderfully obsolete, called San Francisco, California. These names mean nothing to you, I know, but indulge me a short while.

"You three, in concert with a microbiologist named Noe Z. Kroeber and an archaeologist named Katari Kuntur, preserved the Tawantinsuyu from destruction by European invaders.

"You did this at the risk of your own lives, liberty, and sanity, by informing the Inka vthrough the medium of what you call The Entity and we call Pachayachachiq, of the oncoming threat, of the true nature of global geography, science, technology, economics, and politics. Thus we were able to prepare for and prevent our destruction as a people. Of the Tawantinsuyu. And, we believe, of the planetary biosphere.

"You did so on this date, in another, now defunct, historical timeline. We call it the Gone Pacha. That timeline began to wither away in your year fourteen sixty-three, when the Inka Pachacutiq instituted the plan to stop the European invasion, thus rerouting history."

"I thought the prophet Umu Antarqui did that. Convinced the Inka and saved the empire?" Ephraim asked this for them all.

"Known as Ramram. Where do you think he got the information necessary to alert us to the danger?"

"From us?" guessed Lily.

"From you. And so. You are honored beyond even our own heroes. And you will be honored among your own people, we do so hope, when you bring our offer to your government. So now."

"We saved you? We worked like heck to take this coast away from the TSU. I flew into the Crazy Cloud for that." Outraged, Ephraim thought, that's how I sound.

"We know."

"In the Battle of Silver City. And lost. Miserably. And we were in another universe on your side and won?"

"Timeline. Yes."

"Are you going to tell our people that we sold them out? " asked Ephraim. "When we were our other selves?"

"No. But as of ten days ago they know. The insiders. So:

"Ambassador Bonnaterre, on behalf of Sapa Inka Sumac Urqu, The Tawantinsuyu has accepted the petition of the United States of America for coastal access to Mamaqocha, known to you as the Inka Sea. In the Gone Pacha, the Pacific Ocean.

"Your Congress has long requested an affirmative easement, a right of way, through the Anti Urqu Mountains, your Sierra Range, to the sea. With harbor facilities and shipping rights somewhere along the coastline between our border with the Mexica Coalition and the Cowichan/Tlingit/Haida/Kwakiutl Four Peoples Federation. In exchange, your government has conditionally offered to accept influence of Llachaqkuna Kamay, what you call Cockblocker, or Instant Karma, into your borders and under your skies. Speaking formally, Ambassador, is this so?"

"Given an acceptable treaty as described, I am happy to say yes, the United States of America is agreeable."

"Then hear this. We will do more than offer Right of Way and shipping privileges. We offer you Antarqui Marka — in the Gone Pacha you called it Los Angeles — a small town to the south with a serviceable harbor. We offer you the entire Chinchay Coyllur watershed, once your San Francisco Bay Area, and we offer you all the land between the Chinchay Urqu mountain range and the Mamaqocha coast north of but not including the Hatun Mayu, your Columbia River. This was in the Gone Pacha, your State of Washington, minus the northwestern Olympic, now the Makah, Peninsula."

Bingham set aside the eerie revelations about the "Gone Pacha" — it all seemed to be based on the obscure "alternate history" novel by the madman Nicolas Nieman — to marvel at the terms of the offer. He rapidly counted eight cities coming under US control.

"Do we have complete autonomy over these territories?"

"Fortunately, no. Our population will retain residence and rights, although you may of course bring in your own mitmaqs in whatever volume you wish. Our urban population here is small. Our primary investment is in the arable land of the central valley, which we retain. But more importantly, you must agree to forgo all combustion-based energy use, as fuel for transportation, heating, manufacturing, or any other purpose, within your current borders and in the acquired territories. Likewise Llachaqkuna Kamay remains in force. In recompense, we will give you access to Kamay-based energy sources."

Bingham, Ephraim, and Lily sat stunned. "You mean," Bingham said at last, "that you will give us the key to Kamay technology?"

"There is no key. You simply have to be willing to work with it. And then it will be willing to work with you. But if you abuse it, it will fade under you like the mist. Haven't your scientists understood this for decades?"

"None have ever succeeded in finding the formula for holobiome integration. As you are aware." Bingham's voice rose and fell.

"There is an approach. We will demonstrate. You have always tried to force it into a technological context that would destroy it. Under Llachaqkuna Kamay, Kamay energy will be willing to manifest. This side of the Sierra Wall, as you call it, there will be no problem, as it is already active.

"If the United States wants full access to Kamay energy — as Nihon, The Papuan Biosphere, Korea, the Inuit Circle, Canada, Oceania, Australia, Vietnam, Bharat, Tibet, parts of China, and the Tuva Association now have, you will have to exchange your fossil-based technologies for Kamay-based surrogates. It is clean, free, renewable, and more powerful. Your people will have to accommodate the response of your commercial energy providers.

But please accept this précis of the agreement, in Khipu and Roman print, for your consideration."

"I am confident we can reach terms," Bingham said, trying to hide his excitement.

"Now, may I invite you to dinner, so I can satisfy your curiosity about our interest in you personally? Bingham? Ephraim? Lily?"

"Thou bettest," Lily replied. "You winged us here from Metropolitan Silver City to tell us you have been waiting for us to be born?"

"Yes. Please. The story is there to be told. Let's eat."

Whatever Twisted Path You Take

That night, in their tambo on the waterfront of the quiet Inka harbor town of Chinchay Coyllur, the three leafed through the documents they had been given, most published solely for them in English and in Khipu.

"California," Bingham said flatly. "No hits on the word in Findy-Pi."

"San Francisco," Lily said. "A Spanish saint."

"Italian," corrected Ephraim pedantically, "but correct, Spanish name. It says here that Spain owned this land before the US." He shook his head bemusedly. "We fought for the other side. To win this coast for the United States. That was *us*, in *this year*. Now. And now they say we fought for the Inka against the USA, and we *won*."

"So the eighteen months we spent at Mono Lake and in Pachamamatambo TSU, fighting against the Inka, was the *other* time we went to war, that time against our own selves." Lily made a weirdness face. "Wait a minute, we have a Ring here. Let's ask it. Do you know how to turn it on?"

The biocomputer circlet was sunk into the flagstone floor equidistant between the three of them. It ballooned into a shimmering dome encompassing them.

“Would you like to untangle the time-travel paradox you seem to be in?” a disembodied voice asked Ephraim in network news English.

“He sounds like my dad being satirical,” Ephraim said.

“Mine’s a she,” Lily said. “She sounds like Mrs. Gruber in Social Studies.”

“Can I have her too?” Ephraim said, “She’s hot.”

“I don’t know Mrs. Gruber,” said the Ring in a husky female voice, “but here’s our Americana Small Town Librarian persona. So, what do you say?”

“Yes,” Bingham said. “In any voice you want, how were we in the same time twice? And maybe the same place?”

“No stepping in the same river once, Ambassador Bonnaterre. It is superficially simple. The timeline — as you know, we call it a ‘Pacha,’ — in which you indirectly counseled Inka Pachacutiq no longer exists for you, and ceased to exist for the Tawantinsuyu in your year fifteen twenty-eight, when the Inka fleet intercepted Pizarro’s first expedition just north of Tumbez, changing ‘history.’

"However, your intervention is an element of the current existing reality, so to us, there is an unbroken continuity of record, although the participants gradually forgot you.

"It was remembered only as Umu Antarqui’s epic quest to convince Inka Pachacutiq of the European threat, which was finally accomplished in Pachamamatambo in fourteen sixty-three when he descended from his place of execution on his innovative biofilm-enhanced personal glider, the seed of our current air fleet, and when the Two princes brought the evidence gathered on the balsa fleet’s crossing to North Maluku for Inka Pachacutiq’s inspection. And as the evolutionary leap of the holobiome known globally as the Presence and to us as Pachayachachiq, or Pachamama. North Maluku is now in the Papuan Biosphere.

“So you are forgotten as your timeline dwindles over the decades, as those who knew you in our history died.

"The records — and our Khipucamayoq Chaski Yuyu kept meticulous, detailed narrative records — remained. They were passed on to the pertinent historians and legacies — including the lineage of Antarqui Ramram.

"There was controversy, doubt. Many thought them myth, the khipus forgeries. But the coming of the conquistadors, the existence of your 'Old World,' the establishment of a favorable trade balance between the Tawantinsuyu and, especially, Asia and Africa — Europe was less involved for over a century — these things were simple facts. The existence of the alternate timeline could be questioned, of you yourselves, even the influence of the Flying Wizard on the Sapa Inka Pachacutiq. Many credit him alone with the prescience to anticipate the newcomers.

"So, generation after generation, we waited and watched and wondered. And imagine the excitement when the father of Molyay received record of the births of you, Ambassador Bonnaterre, then of you, Lily, and you, Ephraim. In our own lands of Katari Kuntur. And others. But you, well, your births confirmed many things. And here you are. And here is the nation you created.

"Here is how that took place. Tupaq Inka's balsa fleet encountered castaways from the Chinese Admiral Zheng He, the Malian explorer Abu Bakr II, and a Venetian fleet of three caravels and a galleon, one carrying Spanish merchants and their mercenary guards, blown off course north of Java, wrecked on Ternate Island, captured by the locals, and sold to the African castaways, who traded some to the Chinese and kept others as servants. We were able to bargain with the Chinese with gold, and the Africans with textiles and geographical information. Abu Bakr never made it back to Mali, apparently. If he had, the world would have been even more interesting.

"Captives and artifacts were carried to the Sapa Inka as proof. With the information passed from you to the Antarqui, the Sapa Inka was persuaded, and all of his might was directed toward intercepting the European invasion."

"But..." Ephraim interjected.

“But, your original timeline, the one in which the Europeans destroyed the so-called ‘Native Americans,’ and controlled the ‘New World’ that timeline began to wither in fifteen twenty-eight, and memories of your own involvement with it.

"But it is in the nature of the persistence of states and entities that most of the world not directly impacted by the Difference, unfolded pretty much as in your timeline — there is a gravity to things, states tend to perpetuate — and you were born, named, grew up, met one another, and even joined in a modified version of your original quest to change history. This time at the behest of your government, influenced by their own contacts with the greatest of all non-TSU holobiome sensitives, Nicolas Nieman, to attempt to block the clueing in of Pachacutiq and thus facilitate a European invasion.”

Ephraim shifted in his seat. “The novelist Nick Nieman was on our side. And we have not been friendly to your cause, as you know.”

The Ring laughed. “You were all Lost Cause aficionados and Underdog Defenders. Completely in character in both timelines. And you never really did like abetting those federal mercenary types, did you?”

“Wait,” said Ephraim. “What happened to us all in the ‘Gone’ timeline? We won a battle to change history, so it changed. What happened to our lives then, after we won?”

Mrs. Gruber sighed. “That timeline evaporated. Consciousness diminished, with sleep, with inattention, or just blew away like dust in the wind, like bubbles in a pot. For all beings. With the last living memory it was gone. Information is existence.”

"What," Bingham challenged, "happened to all the history of the universe between the 'change' in Inka times and the 'change in our time? The Gone Pacha?"

"That history shifted over to this history, amended by the Change. Only the Gone Pacha alive at the time of the War Against Certainty faded away. The two pachas collapsed into one another."

They took this in silence. Finally Ephraim spoke.

“If this deal goes through, will the United States gain access to...you? To the ring computer system?”

“To the information technology, yes. Not to our knowledge base. A select few of you, those who have found their way to us individually, will. You included. Noe Zoe Kroeber will become the ombudsman for all of you, and Yuyaycamayoq for your nation. That means Director of Knowing Things. Saving the Inka Empire is a small part of what you, and she, have accomplished. You bootstrapped the expansion of the Presence across the planet, and defused the end of organized life on earth. Human fertility diminished by thirty percent and will remain so until the global population rests at around one billion. Llachaqkuna Kamay protects its peoples from aggression by non-participating nations.

"By the way, you understand right now that you are not communing with human beings, but with the holobiome, a synergy of global superorganisms bound together by bacteria and archaea? Including those in you? That’s me, and I am We. That we, as a shared awareness, do not see time as you do and cannot and never will be able to afford to you even a glimpse of existence as we perceive it. In fact, we do not perceive it as ‘existence.’ Please do not ask me to explain. Any questions?”

“Um,” said Lily, “Is there a laptop version of you?”

“Yes, and a cell phone and a tablet and a drinkable version."

Ephraim lifted a stealthy buttock to get off a silent fart. “How can we get one of these biophones?”

“There’s one on the inside back cover of each of your personal briefing books,” said the global hive mind. “By the way, the word in Runasimi for ‘silent fart’ is *thasa*.”

“I was going to ask. You are pretty okay, for a cryptic alien entity."

“All we want, Earthling, we the Overmind, is to love and be loved. All you want, whatever weird and twisted paths you take to getting there, is an open heart.”

Ephraim closed his eyes. Lily smiled.

“So it is all in your Briefing Packets. You have saved the world, that’s enough for tonight. Lily, your throat cancer is fully treatable here. Get some sleep.”

Later, Naked

Later, naked in bed, watching their own story on the ring in high-def holographic anime, Lily wondered, “Do you think we really did a rain dance?”

“I hope so. We were really living large in that timeline. Having a lot more fun than we did this time. If any of this is true? I mean, I bet I never had green hair.”

“And I never filled a shirt like that. But you know, I never really liked those government types anyhow; Mrs. Gruber was right. We were coerced. And I think it is true.These people do seem to really like us.”

“Did you read your personnel document? We have full citizenship, and free education. I’m going to study in Qosqo next year. Their archeology curriculum rocks. I was an archaeology dude in that Pacha too.”

“I’ll miss you. Probably. I’m doing math at Brown.”

“Me too. For sure.” They munched on baked potato crunchies.

After a while, Lily rolled over into Ephraim’s armpit. “They probably have math at Qosqo U. All that binary khipu stuff. And a better IT department."

"And no tuition." Ephraim firmed his hold on her and closed his eyes.

Bingham, one room over, lay on his back hands crossed on his chest like the sarcophagus of a Pharaoh. He dreamt that he had died in battle.

He did not dream that his grad assistant and lover the archaeologist Suzanne Cohen had stepped in front of him just as a bullet exited the muzzle of a sniper’s rifle.

In their informational folios was a list of genetic propensities eliminated by the Pachayachachiq holobiome. One of these was Amyotrophic Lateral Sclerosis.

CHAPTER FIFTY-SEVEN

What Happened, God's Eye View — Pachacutiq

The Sapa Inka Pachacutiq stands, looks down to where the cloud had been. He sees the Antarqui Ramram kneeling at the foot of the temple complex, shrugging out of his chumpi-cloth wings. His ministers, pale and silent, stand behind him.

"Prepare," he commands, still looking downward, "The *qullqi pishtacokuna*, the silver cannibals, are coming." He sees the black scum on the flagstones below. "The Villaq Umu of Ilyapa. Bring him. And the Ñusta Misk'i."

"And the condemned prisoner?" enquires the regional governor.

"Oh, him?" growls the Inka, "What of him? He flew, didn't he? I'm sure he can walk."

T-shirt Head

This is T-shirt Head. I am your writer. I was in the Twist too, when I was young, and there I became unhinged in time. Now I follow ripples in the Presence, and in these I see through the eyes of people and other beings who are drawn in. I was all over the war against certainty and when it goes, I go.

This record is written in the fading tail of the Gone Pacha. It will not vanish in a week or a month. It will take years for the last traces to dissipate into dream and then into the nothing upon which everything moves. The further you were from the event the longer it will take.

You feel it happening. Those moments when your mind drifts. When you cannot focus on the here and now. When you find yourself standing in the kitchen wondering why you are there. In deja vu, in that sense of the surreal you assume is part of the real. In those memories that may never have occurred. In what took place that is not remembered.

When you try to sink your claws into the rush of time, to hold it still, to keep it yours — that isn't foolishness, it isn't illusion, it isn't psychopathology. It is real. The time you live in is ceasing to be. Your consciousness is evaporating.

It's all right. Let it go. There is another you in a realer world, one where your eyes are sharp and your nerves are clean and colors are vivid. Where the world doesn't whisper, its voice is clear, and the song of every instant fills your heart and your heart is strong enough to hear. It is the world where the Inka won.

Oh. The cat says "MeOUCH!"

In the Twist

In the Twist, Nick Nieman woke. He ducked through the flap of his tent into a sunny morning. He stretched, yawned, stepped to the edge of the terrace to piss. There he saw tracks of the government hunters appear between patches of thick moss, deep-cut boot treads overlapping the smooth narrow tracks of the umbrella man. He smiled. The rocks were just rocks now. The distortion of the Twist was gone. It was over. He didn't know how or why, but he could go home.

As he ambled comfortably down the trail to the Elwha River, which was, strangely, right where it was supposed to be, he encountered five men in sealskin jackets hiking upward. The leader, a big man with a face like Mount Rushmore, held out his hand.

"Nicholas Nieman? On behalf of the Makah Tribal Unity, we thank you. For our being." The man spoke English with an accent unfamiliar.

Nick felt no urge to question them. There was nothing he needed to do or say. There was nothing he needed. Not food, not drink, not sex, not rest, not money, not love, not answers. Not to get there faster. He looked at the backs of the men leading him down and knew that he was not afraid of whatever was hurting them; lost wives, deep guilt, useless fear, contempt for a son, money, dead cell phone, dying brother, being so alone. He could take it all in and give what he had with no loss to himself.

His heart was light and perfectly open. A kind of love that went beyond animal feeling lifted him, rising from the misting, teeming subalpine soil. He knew what it was. When they crossed over a crest, he saw that Port Angeles wasn't there. He wasn't surprised.

Tukuri

GLOSSARY

Things to Forget:

First things first:

Umu — Necromancer, sorcerer, wizard, thaumaturge, divine

Tawantinsuyu — the Four Parts of the World — the Inka Empire

Kamay — soul; spirit; force or universal energy of the Pachamama; vital spirit present in every being

Siq'i rumi — a rock emanating lines of power, imbued with Kamay

Unku — sleeveless knee-length tunic worn by all Inka men

Kancha — walled enclosure, three to five houses set around a courtyard

Apu — Lord; used for gods, kings, mountains, larger spirits of the earth

Ari — the word "yes"

Mana — the word "no"

Alphabetical:

Acclawasi — house of the Chosen Women, dedicated to training and maintaining the Acclas, Virgins of the Sun

Acequia — water delivery system, i.e., irrigation canal or street channel to provide clean water for drinking, cooking, or cleaning

Aksu — Inka woman's dress, a length of fabric wrapped around the body and over the shoulder, pinned below the clavicle by a metal tupu

Alternative archaeologists — Graham Hancock, Robert Bauval, Frank Joseph, Michael Cremo, David Hatcher Childress; writers hoping that no one will ask them hard questions

Amauta — scholar, sage, professor, all-around wise man

Angel Eyes - the cat that killed Nick's sister. Very trusting and loving to everyone but her. There is a strangeness in this world.

Antarqui - a thaumaturge of special power, unique to his time, if one appears at all

Asnaq — demon, devil, stinking thing

Ayllu — the extended family, basic unit of Andean culture

Ayni — the cultural principle of reciprocity, sharing; practiced on the levels of community and of state

Black cougar, hybrid — melanotic *Puma concolor couguar* mix — a Craigslist ad offers ten million dollars compensation for a living specimen. Only one is known, found in the Olympic Peninsula of Washington state. Her mother hunts unseen in the Twist

Borla — red fringe worn on the forehead by the Sapa Inka denoting his status as Sole Ruler. Equivalent to a crown

Capullana - title of the Queen of the Tumbis. Names bearing great power, the queen did not share hers with the Inkas, so the Inka took her title to be her name

Ceques (pron. saykay) — a system of (invisible) lines radiating from the Qoricancha Sun temple in Qosqo marking the positions of verified *Wakame*, sacred sites.There were forty-two ceques, each with offerings and ceremonies due them

Chanka Pacha — timeline in which the Chanka were dominant at the arrival of the Spanish. Genetically immune to European diseases, they carried a virus deadly to the 'Old World' and with this pale horseman riding before them conquered Europe and West Asia. This timeline never fully consummated and was erased by Pachacutiq's victory at Hunchback Hill

Cotapampa — chiefdom west of Qosqo, eradicated by the Chanka push to the east

Ch'uspa — a shoulder bag of woven wool to carry coca leaves or small personal items

Crown of Tunupa — Qantuta's Leap; square watchtower - *rikachakuna* - on Pinkuylluna Mountain sometimes used as an arawa, i.e., a place of execution

Curaca — Chief or Head of a social or political entity. Official responsible for a designated task or type of task

Intip Churin — Children of the Sun, people of Inka blood; earplug men, the Inka upper class

Hamuq Pacha — far future, Dark Futur, term used by the Inkas for the modern era occupied by the Core and Nick Nieman

Hampi — Medicine; here a probiotic designed to replace a microbiome removed by fasting. It will impede subtle and refined thought and reaction, leaving more blunt responses active

Hanan Pacha — upper world

Hanan — upper, higher

Harakmbut — An Amazonian forest people

Hatun — big, or great.

Hatun runa — grown man, head of a household

Haw! — all-purpose exclamation or interjection. As a question, 'What? How? Eh?'

Hawa Runa, qullqi pishtacokuna - the Spanish conquistadors and other old world or oceanic peoples; stranger; foreigner

Hurin — lower

Hurin or Uku Pacha — lower world

Inka — current accepted spelling of Inca

Kamay - spirit or force at the center of every living thing, including rocks, geographical features, microbes, and people you don't like

Kay Pacha — this world

Khipu — recording device consisting of colored, twisted, knotted, strings, possibly capable of narrative as well as its accounting function

Kusi kawsay (kusi = happy, kawsay = life) - the good life, tranquil yet stimulating

Kunturpunku — the mountain annex of Pachamamatambo, the personal estate of Pachutiq's primary wife Qoya Anawarkhi, on Pututu Urqu

Macana — star-headed fighting mace of stone, bronze, or copper

Machu Qolqa - archeological park near Chinchero, scene of first contact between Ramram and Ephraim

Mita — required public service. Each hatun runa will at his majority contribute a unit of labor for the common good. The length of time will be dictated by the difficulty of the work and the distance from home; from at least one year to at most six. This will be required once in a lifetime and no more

Mocha — pulling at the eyebrow, making a kissing gesture. Sign of submission and respect

Ollantaytambo — tourist town in Peru, current name of Pachamamatambo

Pachamamatambo, Inka settlement, estate of Pachacutiq Inka Yupanqui

Papa pun — time required to boil a potato at 2500 meters above sea level; about a half an hour

Pinkuylluna (Flute) — Mountain off of which people are thrown in Pachamamatambo

Phlorp — to totally sort of get it. Ephraim's father's word, occasionally adopted within the Core

Pututu Urqu — Bandolista (Mandolin) Mountain, base of Qoripata, Pachamamatambo

Qalikantu — Runasimi name for the modern Patacancha River, Ollantaytambo

Qolqa — storehouse, for grains, root crops and other foodstuffs; textiles, weapons, etc.

Qapac Ñan — royal highway. Ñan means road

Qoricancha — the Golden Enclosure, principle temple of the Tawantinsuyu, located in Qosqo. Pantheon of the Gods, Inti being supreme

Qoripata — Ceremonial center on Pututu Orqo, now called Temple Hill, La Fortaleza

Qosqo — capital of the Tawantinsuyu, currently called Cusco

Qucha Yuyu — algae

Qullqi Pishtacos, Hawa Runa — Silver cannibals, approximately; the Spanish conquistadors and other old world or oceanic peoples; stranger; foreigner

Rikachakuna — watchtower

Rikra — Inka unit of measurement; 64 inches, 1.6256 meters, one Inka pace and half

Sapa Inka – Unique Ruler, title of any Inka emperor. In this tale there are two, Sapa Inka Viracocha, and his son, Sapa Inka Pachacutiq, born Cusi Inka Yupanqui

Schroodie — AKA Kwee; potential Quentin Tarantino film based on the struggle for possession of the sole known melanotic *Puma , concolor couguar* cub. Unspeakably violent, kickass dialogue

Tambo — state-supported lodging on the royal highway; some a single room for chaski runners, some large compounds for military, religious, or executive use

Tocapu — geometric symbols usually on fabric or ceramics, possibly logographic

Tocoyricoc — He Who Sees All, an officer of tested character and intensive training assigned to assure that every official complies with the law incorrupt. He has absolute power to punish or remove from office. There are four, one assigned to each of the four Suyus of the Tawantinsuyu

Topo — distance: 6000 paces, 4.8 miles or 7.72 kilometers

Tukuri — the end

Twist, the — Spatio/temporal dislocation situated within the Olympic National Park in Washington State. An artifact of the unconsummated Chanka Pacha

Villaq — religious official, priest, holy man

Waka — a sacred entity, usually a stone, lake, or intersection of watercourses

Wanka — a standing stone, natural or by the hand of man, with Waka properties

Wasi — house

Wawqi — brother stone, wherein Kamay is transferred from one rock to another

Willay — communication, information

Yanacona — a member of the servant class; theories exist as to how they came to be that way, but no one really knows

Yauri — a ceremonial staff, usually wooden, sometimes of precious metal

Faces to Forget

Achuqalla, a potato farmer, killed

Amaru, eldest legitimate son of Pachacutiq, removed from line of succession for lack of martial ambition

Angus, thin sharp-eyed nothing

Auqui Yupanqui, Tillca Yupanqui — generals in the Chimu war, with Topa Qapac

Agnes Bodkin, Director of the Department of Anthropology, Archaeology, Paleoanthropology, Paleontology, and Gender Studies, Beard College

Bingham, "Bing Bing" Beauchamp Bonnaterre, failing archaeologist and assistant

Professor, Beard College, member of the Core

Briarpatch Agents: 'Go Man' Mango, 'Rango' or 'Orangutang,' Orange, 'Peewee' Kiwi, 'Garcia' Cherry, 'Che' Guava, and 'Go' Fig

Certainty, the, subset of the global Holobiome, dedicated to the transportation of the planetary bio-genome to the galaxies

Chañan Curi-Coca, the warrior woman at the battle of Hunchback Hill, defending Cusco

Chaski Yuyu, Khipucamayoq assigned to Ramram by Pachacutiq, he is tasked with providing independent analyses of Ramram's work and progress

Chonta, Ramram's father, Qolqacamayoq

Choque Anka, Otoronqo Kuy's fresh-faced orderly, promoted to adjutant

Chukuri, Papa Chakra's son, undernourished and horny, killed

Chrissy, Biology Department head, Beard College

Dani Huallpa Quispe, Komadreja Quispe's effete grandson, sent to open the Yanaqocha sluice gate

Daniel Boone 'D.B.' Cooper, twenty-nine, thin, John Lennon spectacles, National Geospatial Intelligence Agency complex, Arnold, Missouri. Once sent on an unsuccessful and unknowing suicide mission to Berkeley, California. Currently on mission in Peru

Elmer "E.T." Thomas, nee Zarathustra Freeman, undercover agent of the NTT

Ephraim NMI Arrowsmith, American boy brought to Peruvian Andes by his economist father, current Pacha contact of Ramram and Tuya

Forrest Coffin, Department of Anthropology, Archaeology, Paleoanthropology, Paleontology, and Modern Dance, Beard College

Francisco Pizarro Komadreja-Quispe, full-blooded Inka, keeper of water control points from the hills, acequias,Yanaqocha. Grandfather of Dani Huallpa Quispe

Generals on the Northern Campaign: Tupaq Qapac, Awki Yupanki, and Tillka Yupanki

Inka — late horizon polity of what is now Peru. Still often spelled as Inca, but due to the evolution of orthography currently given as Inka in academic papers and other informed publications, as well as commonly in Peruvian Spanish where not keyed to tourism.

Iris Lubbock, Biology Department, Beard College

K'anchay, Hatun Villaq Umu of Ilyapa, boss of Simi Apaq, who is boss of Qachu

Kapaq Yupanki, brother of Pachacutiq, general who crossed the Yanamayu and took Cajamarca; executed by Pachacutiq

Katari Kuntur, Peruvian archaeologist and member of the Core. Excavator of Ñawpa Ñawpa archaeological site

Kwee, AKA Schrodinger — puma cub, only survivor of a litter run over by a gypsy logging crew in the Olympic National Forest. Mistaken for a house cat

Lily Tran, 4.0 student, acupuncturist, Ephraim and Bingham's GF, member of the Core

Louise Minor, DB Cooper's contact at the CDC

Mac McFarland, Department of Anthropology, Archaeology, Paleoanthropology, Paleontology and Applied Obscurantism, Beard College

Misk'i, Qantuta's younger sister, ñusta in the Pachamamatambo acclawasi, agent of Qachu assigned to ensorcel Pachacutiq

Nicolas "Nick" Nieman, video logger of It Lives in You — Temporal Displacement Technician and current Pacha contact of Qachu

Nikniman, Umu Nikniman — Inka name for Nick Nieman

Noe Zoe Kroeber, eccentric microbiologist and mycologist, exponent of the superorganism theory of bacteriology, Professor at the University of California, Berkeley, Researcher at Beard College, a member of the Core

Otoronqo Kuy, Inka officer assigned to monitor and mentor Ramram

Pachacutiq, Kusi Inka Yupanqui, World Changer, 'royal scout,' Sapa Inka Pachacutiq Inka Yupanqui, Auqui (Prince) Yupanqui, disinherited son of Sapa Inka Viracocha

Pachamama, Earth Mother, "Mother/Woman of SpaceTime," deity of the common man, Andean manifestation of the Presence

Pachayachachiq — Life Giver to the World, principal deity of the Inka theologians and intelligentsia

Papa Chakra, an old potato farmer

Presence, the — global holobiome, principally a superorganism comprised of prokaryotic organisms

Qachu, Tarpuntay sacrifice priest, Villaq of Ilyapa, Pachacutiq's first, illegitimate, son, Kay Pacha contact of Nick Nieman

Qantuta, prettiest girl in Rumipuqyu, thrown off a mountain for shirking acclawasi assignment

Question, the — subset of the global Holobiome herein called the Presence, dedicated to the preservation of planetary biosphere

Ramram (Q'urpa), Inka youth with the ability to sense Kamay, Kay Pacha contact of the Core, mate of Tuya

Rick, semi-popular boy in Thumbs Up OK High School

Rumi Uma, Headman of Rumipuqyu sector of Pachamamatambo, killed by Yana Turmañyay

Rumipuqyu, Stone Spring Village (rumi=stone;' puqyu=spring), Ramram's birthplace

Sally, Biology Department data analyst, Beard College

Simi Apaq, Hurin Villaq Umu (Lower High Priest) of Ilyapa

T-shirt Head, thin man of average height wearing various head dressings, often a t-shirt tied in back by the sleeves. Turns up at odd moments, talks to himself

Topa Qapac, Pachacutiq's bastard son, general who leads the probe to the northwest

Tupaq Inka Yupanqui, Pachacutiq's youngest legitimate son, heir to the Tawantinsuyu

Tuya, accomplished weaver, Ramram's mate, Kay Pacha contact of Lily Tran and Katari Kuntur

Uscovilcas, Chanka warlord; (Hastu Huallaca per Cieza, Asto-huaraca and Tomay-huaraca per Sarmiento)

Uca Uma, principal wife of Amaru

Uchuchukuy, potato farmer, newlywed, master birder with his sling, killed

Unu Sunqu, Yakucamayoq (Water Master) of the acequia system in the Qoripata complex

Viracocha Inka, eighth Sapa Inka (Unique Ruler), Pachacutiq's father

Waman, General under Viracocha Inka, killed in the expansion toward Chinchero

Waywash, potato farmer, one-eyed from falling on his chaquitaclla foot-plow, veteran of Hunchback Hill and the Widow's Stand

Ygritte Wurmz, ugliest girl in Thumbs Up OK High School, future Director of the Department of Anthropology, Archaeology, Paleoanthropology, Paleontology, and Bibliosmia, Beard College.

Yuquy, wife of Waywash, widowed below Hunchback Hill

Initials to Forget

BSS - Briarpatch Security Services; mercenaries

CDC - Center for Disease Control and Prevention

DIA - Defense Intelligence Agency

DCS — Defense Clandestine Service — an arm of the DIA

DGSE — Directorate-General for External Security, France's external intelligence agency

GGI - Office of the Geographer and Global Issues

IARPA - Intelligence Advanced Research Projects Activity

INR - Bureau of Intelligence and Research, oversees the GGI

MC — Ministerio de Cultura — Peruvian agency tasked with the preservation, restoration, maintenance, and exploration of archaeological sites

NGA — National Geospatial Intelligence Agency

NTT — umbrella agency responsible for monitoring the Entity, Nick Nieman, and the Core

ODNI - Office of the Director of National Intelligence

TSU - Tawantinsuyu. The TSU embassy to the USA is on TSU territory due to the reluctance of the United States to allow any manifestation of Llachakuna Kamay, Instant Karma, onto American soil. The US Embassy to the TSU resides therefor in Silver City, NV. The TSU Embassy to the US resides in Chinchay Cullyur, once known as San Francisco, CA

About the author:

Adam Seward lives in Ollantaytambo, Peru.

Made in the USA
Middletown, DE
03 November 2022

13997433R00300